Endorsements for Other Side *of the* River

With insight, compassion and beautifully evocative language, author Janice L. Dick does for the Russian Mennonites under Stalin what Dale Cramer did for the Amish of Paradise Valley. Savor and enjoy!

Janet S.

Ms Dick skillfully weaves the history of the Russian Revolution with her tale of love and loss, loyalty and commitment. This harrowing story of survival and faith...gripped me and left me wanting...to read on...I look forward to more from this author.

Marcia L.

Janice eloquently brings to life not only the characters of her novel, but also the cruelty of situation and urgency of time...The noises of revolution are loud, the consequences of decisions are harsh, and the love of family is strong.

Ruth K.

...a gentle read enriched with deep historical back-ground.

Deb E.

BOOKS BY JANICE L. DICK

STORM SERIES

Calm Before the Storm
Eye of the Storm
Out of the Storm

IN SEARCH OF FREEDOM SERIES

Other Side of the River

Other Side *of the* River

Janice L. Dick

Tansy & Thistle Press
faith, fiction, forum

OTHER SIDE *OF THE* RIVER

Second Edition

This book is a work of fiction. Although some scenes may depict actual events, they are used fictitiously, from the perspective of the author's imagination, and are not to be construed as real.

Cover design by Fred Koop Design
Formatting by Rik - Wild Seas Formatting
(http://www.WildSeasFormatting.com)

ISBN (print): 978-0-9950319-6-8
ISBN (ebook): 978-0-9950319-1-3

Published by Tansy & Thistle Press,
Box 88 Guernsey, SK. Canada S0K 1W0

To Wayne

my companion, best friend, idea-man, lifelong love

"I lift up my eyes to the mountains –
where does my help come from?
My help comes from the Lord,
the Maker of heaven and earth."

Psalm 121:1-2 NIV

Chapter One

Alexandrovka, Slavgorod Colony
Western Siberia
1926

The schoolhouse door burst open, ushering in the cold March wind and two Soviet officials, their guns directed at the group of young adults gathered for a Sunday afternoon songfest.

Luise Letkemann's fingers froze on the neck of her mother's violin, and her bow skittered off the strings as she whirled to face the intruders. From the corner of her eye she saw Daniel move across the room to her side. A frown had replaced the look of love that had lit his eyes moments ago.

Luise slipped her violin beneath a pile of coats. These men harbored no respect for person or property, and she would not let them take the only keepsake she had from her mother.

"What are you doing here?"

The sternness of Commissar Victor Magadan's voice sent a chill up Luise's spine, but it was the limping step of the second official that set her to quaking. Senior-Major Leonid Dubrowsky of the GPU—the dreaded Soviet secret police—had that affect on people.

"We have gathered here to sing," said Daniel. "Would you care to join us?"

Luise's heart skipped a beat at Daniel's insolence.

"You know there is a law against the German. You are breaking that law."

Daniel stepped forward to stand before Magadan, and Luise's breath caught in her throat.

"It is our mother tongue, the language of our hearts." He said this in fluent Russian. "When we sing, that is what comes out."

Dubrowsky elbowed his junior officer aside, his lip curled like a snarling dog as he stared at Daniel. He lacked the stature of Magadan, but the coldness of his eyes beneath their bushy brows more than made up for it. Even so, Daniel did not back down. Luise willed herself to breathe.

"Do not speak so freely to GPU," said Dubrowsky. "It is not healthy."

He turned from Daniel and limped to the food table where he helped himself to *zwieback, platz,* and barley coffee while the young people stood wide-eyed and waiting. Then, with a grunt, he heaved the table onto its side, spilling food and drink across the plank floor.

Gasps and whimpers traveled around the room like a gust of wind, but terror stole Luise's breath when she felt Dubrowsky's arm reach around her waist. She stood motionless, watching Daniel's face as he struggled to free himself from Magadan's firm grip. The GPU could do whatever they wanted. They lived beyond laws of state or conscience. Dubrowsky was a senior plenipotentiary; he made his own decisions.

Magadan looked none too pleased with the situation. It was his job to keep order in the village of Alexandrovka, but he could not overrule a senior-major.

Dubrowsky leaned so close to Luise she could feel his breath on her neck. "Another time, my little Mennonite sparrow." And then he was gone, the echo of his uneven steps matching Luise's erratic heartbeat.

The biting cold pushed in through the open door, and wrapped itself around her soul.

~

Later, while she mixed the biscuits for supper, Luise

relived the disastrous afternoon. Consumed by the memory of Dubrowsky's arm around her, she did not hear the voices outside until the door burst open. The cup of flour she held flew from her hand to the floor.

Anna Letkemann entered the house, all flutter and fuss, shooing her children before her. "Hans, take off your boots! Nela, you are shedding snow all over!"

Coughing, she slipped out of her coat and hung it on one of the pegs beside the door. "Luise! Wipe up the floor. It's wet and there you've spilled flour all over when there's none to waste. We can't have your father coming home to a dirty floor."

Luise swallowed the retort that formed on her lips, reminding herself of Tante Manya's wise counsel not to allow the burrs of her stepmother's meanness to fasten themselves to her soul.

"Supper will be ready soon, Mother, such as it is."

Luise kissed Nela and helped her with her coat, then reached out to tousle Hans' hair. In five-year old independence, he pretended not to like it, but Luise's wink roused a grin. She reached onto a shelf for a rag and wiped up the floor.

"Did you have a nice visit with Tante Manya?" She did not mention the Soviet officials at the Sunday afternoon social. That would require endless explanation.

"Nice visit? How can one have a nice visit anymore? The Soviets have taken everything of worth and then they demand more yet."

"They haven't taken everything, Mother. We still have our family."

Her stepmother's sallow eyes burned into hers. "Do not contradict me, Luise. Just because your father allows you to speak so to him does not mean you may talk back to me. Someday, girl, you will realize that not every cloud has a silver lining."

Luise turned away. Why did Mother insist on goading

her? Of course there were hardships—hunger and fear and uncertainty—but as Papa said, every day on this side of the sod is a good one.

As if her thoughts invited him home, Papa entered the house and slapped snow from his pants before removing his boots. Luise detected heaviness in his step, but as usual, he masked it with good humor.

"Good evening everyone. Luise, I hear you survived an unannounced visit from the authorities this afternoon." He smiled but his eyes conveyed concern.

Luise frowned at him. "All ended well, Papa."

"What authorities?" Mother stood as if frozen, a plate held in mid-air above the table. "I didn't hear about it. What happened?"

"Just a routine check, Mother."

Papa bunched his lips together and Luise understood his silent apology. She steeled herself for her stepmother's onslaught.

"No harm done, and we were spared again," said Papa quickly as he crossed the room to wash his hands in the basin on the countertop. "Always something for which to be thankful."

"You two and your false cheer. It's enough to—" A deep, ragged cough cut off Mother's retort and shook her slim form. She tried to finish her sentence but gave in to another fit of coughing. Luise read Papa's concern and quickly brought the bean soup and biscuits to the table.

"Nela! Hans! *Kommt essen*."

Her younger brother and sister could share her portion; she had eaten a zwieback at the schoolhouse before the officials arrived. Hans and Nela needed the food more than she did.

Daniel Martens' boots crunched through sun-glazed snow as he slipped from his horse at the gate of the Letkemann yard. He led his bay gelding into the barn.

"Move over, Samson," he told the old grey workhorse as he opened the stall and led his own horse inside. "I've brought Prince to visit."

He removed Prince's saddle and bridle and hung them over the rail, then closed the stall gate behind him. He loved his horses. He knew his father needed machinery to seed and harvest their large farm and to help the neighbors, but Daniel still preferred horsepower on four legs.

Prince leaned over the gate and Daniel patted the sleek neck of his fine mount, but this evening he was lost in his thoughts. Even the multi-hued canvas of the sunset sky had not cooled his anger. Frowning, he pushed through the barn door into the large porch connecting it to the house, and knocked at the door.

It was bad enough that the Reds poked their noses into everyone's business, bringing new rules and limitations that prevented ordinary hard-working people from succeeding. But when they threatened innocent young people gathered to enjoy each other's company, to sing in their mother tongue, those devils were crossing a clearly defined line. He would not allow Dubrowsky to touch Luise again. Next time he would not be so self-controlled. He would give them something to remember.

Daniel's anger eased when he entered the kitchen and spied Luise at the table washing up the supper dishes. She leaned over the large bowl, her dark hair wisping out of its pins, clear brown eyes wide, full lips slipping into a smile at the sight of him.

He answered her smile with his own, and nodded to Anna, who rocked in her chair, knitting needles clicking.

Abram looked up from his newspaper. "Good evening, Daniel. You look like you carry the world's worries tonight."

Daniel warmed his hands near the cookstove. "I've had more than enough of Stalin's henchmen," he said. "They think they have the right to everything we own."

"You see, Luise? Your Daniel agrees with me." Anna's

hands did not still as she spoke. "Those Reds will leave us with nothing."

Daniel turned to Luise. "You don't agree they are out to rob us of all our material belongings? I've told you how much my father and I paid in taxes this year. And what about this afternoon?" He glanced toward Anna and decided not to expand on that incident.

Luise wiped out the washing bowl, dried her hands and took the chair Daniel held for her. "I am not unaware of our situation, Daniel, but I make it a point to count my blessings from time to time so the enemy does not destroy my soul as well."

He smiled as he sat down beside her, reminded of why he loved this girl. "Listen to the preacher."

Daniel sobered and turned back to Abram. "They interrupt our gatherings, cause disturbances, destroy perfectly good food when we have little enough of it, and they spread fear. The situation will only become worse if we do nothing."

"What have you in mind?"

Sometimes Abram's easy acceptance frustrated Daniel. Luise's father was a gentle carpenter, like the One he emulated, but surely he should be anxious for the safety of his family.

Anna's knitting needles stilled. "We must emigrate," she said.

"We must what?" Luise's voice joined Daniel's.

"Emigrate. To America. Thousands have already gone; my family has all gone. If we hurry, we can go yet too. I do not wish to die at the hands of these evil men."

"We're a long way from Moscow," said Daniel. "You would have to sell everything you own, obtain passports, take medical examinations—and you're not well."

"There is nothing wrong with me but a winter cold, young man. Once spring returns to this frigid Siberian wilderness, my cough will disappear." Her cough robbed any more words she might have added. Daniel cast a glance in Luise's direction and noted the worry creasing her forehead. He knew she did not accept Anna's self-diagnosis any more than he did, but they both knew better than to contradict her.

Daniel waited for Abram to speak, as head of the home, but when he did, his words were not what he wanted to hear.

"Emigration is a possibility I am re-considering. As much as I grieve to think of leaving our home and country, I also worry about our future here, of how my children will fare. Our situation declines instead of improving, as you say, Daniel, and we have no recourse, it seems, to alter that. Perhaps Anna is correct. Perhaps we should explore the opportunity to leave this country while there is time."

"How can you say that, Papa?" Luise's words spoke Daniel's thoughts. She sat on the edge of her chair, tense as a cornered horse. "How can you talk of leaving Alexandrovka? This village is our home."

Daniel felt her eyes on him. He knew what she wanted him to say, but it was not up to him. Abram would have to make the decision for his family.

Anna spoke up. "Soon there will be nothing to leave behind if we do not act already. Then where will we be?"

"Daniel," said Abram, "what do you think?"

"I have not considered it for myself. I love the farm; we've done well, Father and I. I can make a life for myself and a family, if I am so blessed." He glanced at Luise, then looked back at Abram. "I have no wish to give up my future here. I have plans..."

"What of the increased taxes you spoke of earlier? The Communist interference? You told me of the trouble your father encountered when he purchased that new Fordson tractor." Abram's words hung in the air.

"Father assures me there are ways to settle the matter."

"We would have to go all the way to Novosibirsk for

the medicals," said Luise.

"There are trains even in this frozen wilderness, Luise," said Anna.

Daniel saw Luise's lips pull together in a thin line, and her words came out in measured tones. "I realize that, Mother, but can we afford it? We would have to take the little ones along too."

"Of course we take the little ones. They will be emigrating with us, you know."

"Now Anna," said Abram, "I'm sure Luise didn't mean we would be leaving anyone behind. She just wants to know how it will go."

"*Jah*, you always know what she thinks, eh?"

"Anna!"

Daniel felt badly that Abram had to live in a house with two women who didn't see eye to eye. His lifelong friend, Phillip Wieler, said it was up to Daniel to change that, to take Luise to his own house, one he would build with his own hands on the plot of land directly behind his parents' house. Daniel wasn't a carpenter like Luise's father, but he could learn. "Why do you wait?" were Phillip's exact words. He would ask for Luise's hand soon. He would start building that house. Meanwhile, if the rest of Luise's family planned to emigrate, he could help.

"The train ride from here to Novosibirsk is not terribly expensive. I could lend you money for travel and accommodation."

Luise glared at him, and he knew he had said something wrong. He didn't know what it was, but he felt sure he would find out shortly.

"*Nah jah*," said Abram, hands on his thighs, "we will sleep on this and talk further tomorrow."

"Yes, sir," replied Daniel. "I must find my bed too, already. Goodnight."

Luise stood with him, reached her coat down from its peg by the door and slipped it on, then stood waiting for him, her beautiful eyes icy.

Daniel looked to Abram and Anna for salvation, but they turned away to their room, and there was Luise walking out the door ahead of him. He followed her through the porch and into the barn. The smell of manure and fresh straw melded with the sound of Samson, Prince and the milk cow as they chewed hay, and the soft groan of the building as it settled itself in the Siberian night. The chickens had long since taken roost, their heads under their wings, and Daniel wished he could do the same.

When Luise turned to him in tears, he stepped back in surprise.

"Luise, why are you crying?" His sisters said Luise was an emotional sort, and if you wanted smiles from her, you must also accept tears, but he didn't know what to do with tears.

She dashed them away with her fingertips. "You really don't know? Did you not hear yourself in there?"

Daniel tried to recall his exact words. "I suggested your family pursue medical examinations so they know if they can go to America. You know Anna won't leave the matter alone until something is done."

"Daniel, you say your future is here. Then you suggest we get our physical examinations in preparation for emigration. I have been under the impression, since I was twelve, that we had a future together. Has something changed your mind?"

Daniel reached for her but she stepped back, keeping her eyes on his face. He cast about in his mind for how to go on. "Nothing has changed between us, Luise. You are part of my future. We will marry before your family leaves for America—if they go."

Luise stared at him as if he had struck her. "Let my family leave without me? Papa and the little ones and Anna, without me?" She shook her head in denial. "I cannot be separated from them. They need me."

"But how else? I cannot leave, we wish to be together, and your family wants to go. How else would you arrange it, Luise?"

She stood with her arms folded, blinking furiously, her lips trembling.

"Luise, I love you. Is that not enough?"

She stared at him, then turned on her heel and marched back to the house.

Chapter Two

"There is nothing wrong with me!"

Mother's loud protest from the examining room made Luise's skin prickle. The milder temperatures that had come with spring had not eased her stepmother's ragged cough at all, and she looked thinner every day. Even if by some miracle she passed her medical, how would she endure the rigors of travel? The four-hour train journey to Novosibirsk had about worn her out.

Luise's own medical had gone well. The woman at the desk had stamped "Healthy" on her chart and handed her a copy, as she had done for Hans and Nela. Papa had explained his blue, swollen thumbnail to be the result of a misguided hammer, and after some convincing, the examiner had agreed to pass him. But Mother's arguments helped not at all.

Luise heard her whining and Papa soothing. She heard the sharp voice of the examiner and then Mother's weeping. She knew the wailing would follow. They must get her out of this place before she created a fuss. Hans and Nela moved close to Luise, eyes wide, as Papa led Mother from the room.

"They want to separate us, that's what they want," Mother wailed. Her face was as red as the "Rejected" stamp on her medical form. "They will let you all go and I will have to stay behind to die alone."

"Hush, Anna. You know we will not leave you. Hush or you will make yourself cough again."

"It's just a cold, Abram. There's nothing wrong…" Her whining grated on Luise's nerves until she felt she would scream. The only thing that kept her from it was that she didn't want to make matters worse for Papa. Besides, her stepmother had failed the test, so they wouldn't have to leave Alexandrovka. As Papa said, they would never leave Anna behind.

Tomorrow they would catch the train home and Daniel would be there to greet them. They would settle back into routine. They would adjust to the Soviet limitations. Somehow they would survive. Her relief gave her the strength to tuck the children into bed at the small inn where they stayed, while Papa looked after Mother. Tomorrow they would leave this dirty, noisy city and threats of emigration and separation.

❧

"We must leave this place now, while we can."

Mother's hoarse whisper pulled Luise from slumber. The attic room she shared with Nela and Hans was shrouded in the blackness of a summer night. She propped herself on one elbow, careful not to startle Nela beside her, and listened to her parents' muted discussion in their room below. Luise tensed as she awaited her father's answer.

"But Anna, we cannot emigrate. Remember the results of the tests."

"I will not soon forget them. But now we must make other plans before they come for us. They will come, you know. They always do. We must move east."

"East? We are already deep into Siberia."

"We are not far enough away from *them*, Abram. They will come for us if we stay here. Lena Sawatsky says there are people going."

Luise shuddered at her stepmother's raspy reply.

"Shh, Anna, don't wake the children."

"Do not shush me, Abram. I left Orenburg, moved here with never a complaint—"

Luise imagined her father's brows lifting. How often had Mother bemoaned her situation, wishing to be somewhere else, anywhere else, than where they were?

"—and now I am the one asking to move, but you will not even discuss it."

"Anna, we will talk about this in the morning. Right now we need to sleep."

Mother's voice continued to rise and fall, soothed by Papa's calming counterpoint. Luise lay down again beside Nela. The little girl's soft whiffles created a background of tranquility, but Luise's heart raced as if she'd run all the way to Chernovka and back. Mother was bent on leaving Alexandrovka behind, one way or another, and after hearing the news Daniel had brought with him that very evening, she couldn't really blame her: two more Slavgorod preachers and one of the wealthier farmers arrested and taken who-knew-where. Just when she had tamed the monster of fear, Luise felt it creep close again, threatening her faith, and it wore the face of Senior-Major Leonid Dubrowsky. The smothering black night gave way to pale pink before she slept.

Luise eased herself down the rungs of the attic ladder next morning, hoping to avoid the inevitable unpleasant after-effects of Mother's nighttime angst, but before she could step foot on the floor, the voice assaulted her.

"Luise! There you are." Mother coughed into her handkerchief and stuffed it into her apron pocket. "There is no time for laziness. We have much to do."

The words buzzed like droning bees in Luise's mind. "Yes, Mother."

Before Luise could escape, Mother had recited a long list of tasks for her to accomplish. Later, on her way back from the well for water, Luise detoured past the corral behind the barn. She stood for a few minutes and watched her father pitch hay to old Samson and the cow, and scatter seed for the chickens.

Luise loved the earthy smell of the large animals, the liquid brown of their gentle eyes like molasses in summer sun. She endured the annoying chickens only because she enjoyed the eggs they provided.

Old Samson nickered as she approached him, and nuzzled her arm in greeting.

"You have already fetched the water?" Her father walked over to where she stood.

"Yes. I stopped to enjoy a moment of peace before returning to the house."

"Luise, Mother is upset this morning. She…"

"I heard you and Mother talking last night, Papa."

He leaned on his pitchfork and nodded his head, then smiled. "Well Lise, you don't have to worry about our discussion. Everything will be fine."

"Papa, I'm seventeen."

Blowing out his breath, he opened the gate for Luise, leaned the long-handled fork against the fence and motioned for her to take a seat on a square of salt-lick while he sat on another. Removing his hat, he smoothed his hair back with one hand and firmed the hat back into place with the other, then leaned forward with his elbows on his knees. His familiar action etched itself on Luise's brain as one of the few things that had not changed lately.

"Very well, we shall talk."

Luise leaned forward also and held her breath for a lifetime before her father finally spoke. Everything familiar had begun to fall out of place, and she dreaded his words, even as she awaited them.

"You are well aware of the thousands of Mennonites from the colonies in South Russia who are leaving the country for America, Mother's family included. Now that she knows we cannot follow them, she is even more fearful of our future here."

"Yes Papa, but what good would it do for us to go east? Everywhere there are food shortages. Moving to another location would not change that."

"Perhaps, but Stalin's men have become more involved in our daily lives here. It is becoming increasingly difficult to live as we are accustomed."

"Daniel says somehow we must adjust so we can live in relative cooperation with them."

Her father pursed his lips. "Our people in South Russia have had it much worse than we have. We suffer hunger, but for them, the civil war and the ensuing famine tore them apart and they are still reeling from it. So many deaths and arrests and disappearances. They cannot take any more so they flee."

"As Mother wishes to do."

He sighed again. "Jah. As Mother wishes to do. She hears what has happened in Molotschna and the Old Colony and is sure it will happen here also. She only wants to be safe."

He remained silent for a time, then caught Luise's eye and said, "Commissar Magadan stopped by the barn yesterday."

She stiffened. "What did he want?"

Papa grimaced and scuffed the dirt with his boot. "More taxes."

"But we cannot pay what we do not have."

"I must find a way to get it."

"But how?"

"Collect outstanding payments for my furniture sales or borrow it from others in the colony, I suppose. That's the only way I know. I don't think the officials are concerned with how I get it, just that I do. I suppose they want to line their own coffers now that harvest is soon upon us. I'm not sure how to cooperate with them anymore."

"Did Magadan threaten you?"

"I think it was more of a forewarning. He's not a bad sort, really, just doing his job. He said I had a week to get the money."

Luise snorted. "How very kind and thoughtful he is. Why do they pick on you, Papa? You do not harvest fields of grain; you only build furniture and fences."

He sat with his arms on his knees, as if staring an answer from the ground beneath his boots. "I preach the word of God."

"Only occasionally."

"Doesn't matter to them. Too much religion or too much money, these seem to be the worst infractions these days. Now I must practice what I preach, eh? I am trusting God to help me get the money for taxes."

"And if He doesn't?"

Papa did not speak because they both knew the answer. Last fall Jakob Derksen had failed to deliver the required quota of grain. He now served a five-year sentence someplace in northern Siberia. The only thing his family knew was that he was still alive.

Apprehension tightened Luise's throat. "Is relocating really the only option? If you go, I am forced to make a very difficult decision."

Her father looked away and Luise realized anew that there would be no simple solution, no matter how much she wished for it. The decision she'd hoped to avoid had not gone away.

She heard Mother's shrill call from the house and stood quickly. "I came here for answers and now I have only more questions."

Her father rose to his feet and retrieved the fork from its corner. "Trust in the Lord, Lise, and He will work things out for the best. Can you do that?"

She sighed. "I will try, Papa."

"Good. I depend upon you to keep a level head."

She nodded, the responsibility squaring her shoulders. Nela rounded the corner of the barn at full speed and skidded to a halt at the gate, staring at them between the corral boards. "Lise, Mama is calling for you. You better hurry or she'll paddle you."

Luise forced a smile. "I'm coming, Nela. Go tell Mama I'm coming."

"Mama, she's coming."

Her repeated shouts echoed in Luise's ears as she turned to glance once more at her father. He stood watching her, worry lining his face, meekness in his very bearing. Well, he could be meek if he wanted, but she had a battle to fight within herself.

ঔ

As much as Luise hated to think of her family leaving Alexandrovka, she recognized the communist cloud blotting out the sun of freedom in their daily lives like a biblical plague of locusts. Papa had applied to Novosibirsk for passports to move his family east. But what of his eldest daughter?

While walking to the village pasture to bring the cow home for milking, Luise gazed at the vastness of her surroundings, kilometer upon kilometer of rolling land and birch trees. Yet even as far east as Slavgorod, Stalin would not tolerate autonomy from his subjects. It made her shudder to imagine such power, and she wondered when things would settle down. Daniel said they would and she wanted to agree with him, but she was not convinced.

The breeze teased Luise's hair against her face in a soft caress and the sun's rays warmed her. She knew this land was not stunningly beautiful like the fertile far-off steppes of Ukraine where her parents had been born. Sometimes in the evenings Papa would tell stories of his boyhood, of orchards boasting heavy-laden cherry and peach and apple trees, of fields of waving wheat, of long summers and mild winters. He remembered playing wild games of gypsies and police with the other boys in the village, and how everyone knew everyone else's business. He remembered peace and prosperity—and freedom.

Luise sometimes wished she had been born there too, but if that had been the case, she might well be dead now, for she had also heard, mostly through her stepmother, of the horrors of the revolution and the resulting civil war, of famine and plague and the dreaded *Machnovitz* bandits that dealt in human cruelty of which she would not allow herself to think.

And so she was content, or had been until now, with her life in the subtle beauty of the perseverant grasses of the Siberian steppe, the muted colors of short-stemmed flowers, the eternal impressions of the undulating landscape, like a quilt shaken out and left to fall onto the bed. Even in her limited experience, spring had always followed winter.

Papa had said, "If we starve, we starve, but I would rather die in freedom than live in oppression." She hoped they would be able to do more than that, to thrive rather than just survive.

For that she fervently hoped and prayed, until two muted gunshots shredded her prayer.

She lunged for the cover of the nearest out-buildings, forgetting about the cow and milking time. Ducking behind Penners' machine shed, she tried to discern from where the bullets had come. It was not the first time the Reds had used guns to intimidate residents of the Slavgorod villages. For the most part, they were not aimed to kill, but one never knew these days.

She hoped Anna had the forethought to hide the little ones. Hans was quick to react to perceived danger, and would no doubt slip into some cubbyhole and wait until that danger had passed, thinking it all a great adventure. But Nela could scream like a wounded sparrow hawk when vexed or frightened, and the enemy fed on fear.

Luise crept along the side of the shed and peered around the front. No one moved on the dusty main street. Curtains had been hastily closed. For once, everyone minded his own business.

She ran low from Penners' to Martens' place, wishing Daniel were home but knowing he would be out in the fields cutting the early wheat. That's where most of the men would be, not expecting soldiers in the streets in broad daylight. But then she thought of the horrors of the bandit raids on the villages in South Russia less than ten years ago, the stories Mother and others had told, and she knew the time of day had no bearing on the degree of violence.

Luise moved into the shadow of Tante Manya's little house and slipped in the back door, hoping she wouldn't frighten the woman to death. She was old, Tante Manya, had been old as long as Luise could remember. Papa said she had been old when he was a boy, but when his own mother passed away, her sister Manya had become a second mother to him, and he loved her fiercely and forever. To Luise, she was the most beautiful woman in the world. The kerchief tied beneath her chin cradled a toothless smile between weathered-apple cheeks, and framed frost-blue eyes that sparkled with wit and warmth.

"Tante Manya!" she called softly. "Are you here?"

She heard a rustle and a creak, followed by shuffling footsteps and the dull thud of a cane on the wood floor.

"Who calls?"

"It's Luise. I'm here in the back porch." She tried to still her shaking hands and pounding heart.

Manya's hooded eyes searched the dimness until they lit upon Luise, and then she smiled and held out her free hand. "What are you doing here, child? Why are you sneaking around my back door? Are you running from the law?"

Luise snickered in spite of herself. "Aren't we all?" Then she sobered. "Did you hear the shots?"

"Jah, I heard them. I thought someone was hunting rabbits maybe. You know how we do when something happens, just sit still until it goes away."

"I was on my way to the pasture to fetch Dolly when I heard the shots. I thought there was trouble. I suppose I should go home and find out. There doesn't seem to be anything further happening. You're probably right, that it was just someone hunting."

"Jah, you go. Use the back door at home too, Lise, just to make sure. When all is well you can send Hans to get the cow." Manya patted Luise's cheek and nodded reassuringly as she left the house.

Luise watched Willy Derksen walk from his family's general store to their house next door. He glanced back over his shoulder twice. She heard a mother somewhere raise her voice in warning to a child. Determined, Luise moved silently through backyards where she had played as a child, wending her way home by the most covert route. She inched open the back door of her house and peered inside. All was still, so she slipped through the door and gently closed it behind her, moving soundlessly. The bedroom door was closed but she thought she heard movement within, possibly the little ones wearying of silence.

Luise decided the gunshots had come from somewhere else, but when she stepped into the front room, her gaze passed over the door and she was robbed of that small comfort. Two holes adorned the otherwise smooth surface of the wooden door, about head height. She whirled around to see her stepmother dozing in the rocker, Papa's rabbit gun resting across her lap.

Chapter Three

Luise crept forward and seized the gun from her stepmother in one swift movement. The woman awoke and leapt at her, snatching unsuccessfully for the gun.

"Mother, stop. It's me, Luise."

"You can't have us. Leave us alone."

After her initial burst of energy, her stepmother weakened and collapsed in a paroxysm of coughing. Luise opened the chamber of the gun and removed the bullets, her hands trembling. Snapping it closed, she placed it in a corner of the porch under Papa's winter coat and slipped the bullets into one of his pockets. She would ask him to take it away when he came home from helping the men in the fields.

Luise returned to the sitting room and eased Mother into her rocking chair. She looked totally spent.

"What were you doing, Mother? Why were you sitting in your chair with a loaded gun and why are there bullet holes in the door? You could have killed someone."

Mother turned glazed eyes on Luise. "They were coming to take Abram. I could not let them have Abram because then where would I be? The children and I would be alone. I had to shoot them."

Luise felt her skin prickle. She rose and gingerly opened the front door, half expecting to see a body lying on the front stoop. To her great relief, there was none, but her relief lasted only a moment. If no one was there, then who or what was Mother imagining? What was happening to this woman? She was not old enough to suffer the mental maladies of the aged; she still had young children to care for.

Luise stared across the room at the woman she called Mother. She dozed again, her thin face sagging in exhaustion from her real or imagined trauma.

Luise sought solace in her attic bedroom, bending beneath the rafters that only rose high enough for her to stand straight at the peak. In spite of the distance between herself and her stepmother, Luise thought the woman had proved to be a good mother to the two children born to her and Papa. But something had happened to her after Nela was born, something subtle enough to deny for a long while. It happened sometimes, Tante Manya said, that women became emotionally fragile after the birth of a child, but Mother's condition gradually worsened instead of improving. And then there was the coughing.

Luise sensed her father's denial of his wife's condition, but after today's incident, she knew the time for discussion had come, for the sake of the children as well as the rest of the family, and by the looks of the front door, the neighbors as well. Once people knew what had happened in the Letkemann home this day, there would be questions to answer. She would have liked to find her father and prepare him for what was to come, but she couldn't leave Mother alone with the little ones, not now.

Perhaps leaving this village for a place farther east would be a good idea after all, but what would that mean for her and Daniel? How could she leave Mother in charge of Hans and Nela when she couldn't be trusted? The passports would be arriving soon to expedite their departure, and Papa had ordered one for her as well. She had not planned to use it, but how could she not? Circumstances were unfolding in a most disastrous manner. Instinctively, she reached for her violin, tightened up the bow and slid it over the strings, softly, her fingers finding their way through the chords.

"Luise, what happened to your door? Looks like

someone shot through it."

Daniel brushed his hand across the surface of the door when Luise met him outside. Instead of responding, she changed the subject and suggested they walk down the field road and enjoy the autumn evening.

He was content with that. Fine fall evenings were few here in the north, and each one was special. With harvest nearly completed, he could till the fields and still have time to visit with his friends, Phillip Wieler and Jasch Fast, but especially with Luise.

He had been thinking seriously of confirming his future with this girl who had captured his heart so many years ago. Phillip had joked that if Daniel didn't soon claim her, he would. Daniel had known Luise almost all her life, and had watched her grow and mature in quiet confidence.

Perhaps today they would wander farther into the trees and he would ask her to be his wife. His mouth went dry and he thought his tongue would not obey him when the time came to ask, but he could not imagine life without her. He was relieved that Anna had failed her medicals. Now they wouldn't be crossing the ocean, leaving Luise behind.

Luise walked silently beside him, not slipping her hand into his, although he gave her opportunity. Well, he would sweet talk her and she would gladly accept his offer. He led her into the woods even though she hesitated

When they were out of sight of the path, he took her shoulders, looked into her eyes and said, "Luise, we have shared most of our lives together and we love each other. I've been thinking that—"

"Daniel, please don't ask me."

Words failed him completely as he stared into her eyes, uncomprehending.

"I know what you're going to ask, and I dare not let you ask it."

The capacity for speech returned to him in a rush. "What do you mean? You don't want me to ask you to be my wife? We have both been waiting for the time to be right, and I don't want to postpone it any longer, Luise. You know I love you and—is it Phillip?"

"Phillip? What are you talking about?"

He knew then from her eyes that Phillip had no part in this, but it was small comfort.

Tears filled her dark eyes and spilled down her cheeks. She pressed her fingertips to Daniel's lips where they burned like hot tea. "I can't expect you to understand, Daniel, but my family is moving away from here, from the place where your future lies, and I must go with them. They…there are things that have happened…I must help with the children and I can't leave Papa to face this alone."

Daniel grabbed her hand away and held it tightly. "What things? What does he have to face? What do you mean you are leaving? Anna failed her medicals." His body shook in spite of his concentrated effort to still it, and beads of sweat formed on his upper lip.

She tried to pull her hand free but he held fast, afraid that if he let go, she would flee and be gone from him forever.

"Please, Daniel, can we sit?"

They settled against the trunk of a birch tree, the evening sun filtering through the brightly colored leaves onto the dying grass at their feet. His hand still firmly clasped hers, and he waited in fear for the reason behind her unreasonable behavior. When she spoke, she didn't look directly at him. He let her talk, let her spill out her heart and prayed Jesus would help him to understand.

"Daniel, you asked what the holes in the door were from. I'll tell you, but please don't speak of it to anyone else. I'd rather postpone that revelation." She took a deep breath, picked a blade of grass and fingered it as she spoke.

"Mother shot through the door."

"Mother, as in Anna? Why on earth?"

"That is the crux of the problem, Daniel. She has been

acting strangely for a long time, ever since Nela was born really, but we deny it because we don't know what to do about it. Tante Manya says it happens to women sometimes after childbirth. I think part of the reason she has gotten worse is due to her general ill health and her fear of the Soviets. It's a combination of physical and mental failing.

"But Daniel, when she starts shooting through doors, we must face reality. People will never see her the same way again, in fact, I'm sure they would prefer not to see her at all. There is something seriously wrong with her. Which brings me to my decision." She blinked furiously but a tear still escaped from each eye.

"I cannot in all good conscience stay behind when they go east. I need to help care for the little ones. They are not safe with her. I need to be there for Papa as her condition worsens. If I stay here with you, I am deserting my family. I…I cannot do that."

Daniel, his heart thundering in his ears, reached out and turned her face toward his. "You are saying you love your family more than you love me. I thought we had an understanding all these years. I have never wanted anyone but you, Lise. You are not responsible for your father's marriage or family."

Tears continued to fall unchecked from her dark eyes and the sight stung him.

"Am I not? Truthfully, Daniel, you are as loyal to your family as I am to mine. You refuse to leave, either to emigrate across the ocean or to go farther east, because your father expects you to carry on the farm. Now which of us must give in?"

Daniel jumped to his feet and paced in the spot of sunlight. "You cannot expect me to leave my father alone with the farm, and Johannes not of an age to help enough, and with the challenges this present government places upon us."

"No, I cannot. I would like to, but I cannot ask that of

you. Which is why I must release you from any and all promises, spoken or understood, that we have made to one another. Daniel, I will never forget all you mean to me, and I will never find anyone who would make a better husband, but I must go with my family. I'm truly sorry, but it's the only road for me to take."

She choked out the last words as she jumped up and fled back to the road and toward the village, leaving him dumbfounded, in alternating spasms of pain and disbelief. His plans and dreams had been suddenly snatched from him like a rug from under his feet and he had landed gasping on his back.

"Benjamin Janz has resigned from the VBHH and has emigrated," Papa was saying to the neighbor, Bernhard Loewen, when Luise returned to her yard. She had spent the past hour in tear-stained prayer and still didn't feel like facing anyone, so she stopped in the shade of a crabapple tree to listen, needing to collect herself.

"He no longer represents us 'Citizens of Dutch Extraction' here in Russia," said Loewen, worrying a blade of grass between his teeth.

"It's called the Soviet Union now," corrected Papa, "and I'm glad for Janz' sake that he emigrated while he had the chance or he would surely disappear like so many thousands of others. He is like Moses, that man. Without his wise and patient negotiations not many Mennonites would have made it out of the country."

"Jah, you are right. I just wish I were one of those thousands who owed him my life—from the other side of the Atlantic."

They shared a sad chuckle, then Loewen said, "Did you hear the news about the Romanovs?"

"Tsar Nicholas was murdered and the rest of them exiled out of the country. We have known that for years."

"That is what we have been led to believe. It is true that

Nicholas was murdered," Loewen stabbed his finger at Papa, "but so was his entire family. Shot at close range and buried in some hole somewhere. I heard it at the general store. People have read it in the newspapers."

"His whole family? I understand why they would kill Alexis because he was the heir apparent, but why the girls?"

Luise heard the catch in her father's voice. She saw Loewen rub a gnarled hand over his face and shake his head. "I don't know, Abram, I don't know. The world is coming undone and we are here to witness it. Guilt and innocence have no bearing on what happens to people. This is a difficult time."

Luise trembled as she moved silently toward the house. She had seen pictures of the royal family, four daughters of varied age and beauty with long, thick hair and large, serious eyes. Ordinary sisters at first glance, but decidedly regal. And Alexis, the ailing heir to the throne. She shuddered as she thought of the last moments of this family, comforted only that they had died together. Could that be a comfort? And if the Reds did these things to royalty, what exemption could she claim, she and her people?

When she entered the kitchen where Mother and Nela sat calmly cutting crabapples, Luise brushed her sister's thick curls from her eyes and kissed her. "Hello, dumpling," she said.

"Your father wishes to talk to you, I don't know what about," said Mother when Luise tried to take over her job with the crabapples. "Strange you didn't see him when you came in."

"He was busy talking with Mr. Loewen. I didn't want to interrupt."

"Well, go find him. We will have supper as soon as these crabs are in the pot for applesauce."

Mother seemed so normal this day. Luise wondered if she were imagining things, but then she saw the bullet holes in the door as she went out, reminding her of her stepmother's splintered reality.

When Papa finished his conversation with his neighbor, Luise approached him.

"Ah, Lise, I've been looking for you. Come walk to the well with me."

"I'll fetch the water, Papa." She tried to catch hold of the handle of the bucket but he transferred it to his other hand.

"This is not about water," he said. "It's about your life."

She glanced at him and kept walking. He would speak when he was ready. He pulled a pail of water from the well and poured it into his bucket. Then he set it down and leaned against the well.

"Daniel has asked you to marry him, has he not?"

Of course he would know; Daniel would have first asked his permission. Still, her father's uncharacteristic personal questioning surprised her and she hesitated. "Not really."

He tilted his head at her. "Come now, either he asked you or he didn't. I am sure you remember either way."

Luise stared at the ground and tucked an errant strand of hair behind her ear. "He tried. I wouldn't let him ask." The memory of his stricken face haunted her.

"Why not?"

Luise raised her eyes to her father's. "Because we are leaving and he is not."

"Lise, as you mentioned recently, you are seventeen, old enough to live your own life. You need to reconsider your response to Daniel's question without reference to my situation."

"But Papa, I must go east with you. Mother cannot manage the little ones alone. She needs me, even if…"

A strong silence separated them until Papa spoke.

"Even if what?"

Luise's voice was small as she answered. "Even if she does not care for me."

Papa's lips thinned and he watched a hawk riding an air

current in the clear blue dome above them. He didn't look at Luise when he spoke. "I betrayed your trust when I married Anna. I refused to see her jealousy of you, and you have had to live with the consequences of my decision. Now I must accept those consequences for myself. You have given up enough."

"I cannot do it. The little ones are not safe with her."

"I have spoken to Tante Manya. She is willing to accompany us when we leave to go east. The authorities will easily issue a permit for her."

Luise's eyes widened. "She would go with you?" Tears spilled down her cheeks before she had a chance to check them and she quickly turned away. Her mind whirled with the prospect of living without her father and the little ones. How could she also bid farewell to Tante Manya? The woman was more of a mother to her than anyone since her own mother, of whom she held more vague impressions than actual memories.

"When are you planning to leave?" Her words were a whisper. She crossed her arms to still her shaking.

"Maybe before winter yet, or possibly in spring, as soon as it warms up enough. We have decided to go to the Amur Region, on the border of China." He chuckled and to Luise it sounded forced. "As far east as we can go and still remain in the Soviet Union. Apparently one can see the Blue Mountains of China across the Amur River on a clear day."

She turned back and the sadness in her father's eyes choked her. "Oh Papa, that is so far away. Why must life be always full of pain? How can I live without all of you? I cannot."

Gently, he lifted her chin to look into her eyes. "But can you live without Daniel?"

Luise heaved a shuddering sigh and shook her head. "I had decided I must, but it hurt him deeply when I told him, and my own heart is in despair."

As Papa drew the water, he said, "We must go for

supper or Anna will wonder where we are."

Luise wiped her tears with the handkerchief her father handed her. She linked her arm in his and held fast to it. This man had shown her a love that helped her understand her heavenly Father's love, and for that she would be eternally grateful.

But what should she do about Daniel? How could she make such a decision? Her head ached and she had no appetite for the simple supper Mother had prepared, sure she wouldn't be able to choke down anything with the lump of sadness blocking her throat.

Papa glanced over his shoulder as they neared their house.

"What is it, Papa?"

He hesitated and shook his head. She scanned the street, but saw nothing either. Perhaps that was what Mother had shot at that day, a nebulous shadow seen in the periphery of the mind's eye, a shadow that one day became a reality in her mind. They climbed the steps and pushed open the wounded door.

Chapter Four

Since Luise's refusal to entertain his proposal, Daniel had kept busy from first birdsong to wolf's howl, helping his father with the harvest. He had welcomed the distraction, but every night after washing his dirt-clogged face, neck and arms, he would think of Luise and grieve.

His body had hardened with the work of cutting and binding, stacking and threshing, until his shirts fit snug across his already broad shoulders. He'd always thought farming would be his life, but as he toiled, he began to realize that without Luise, the things that had meant the most to him seemed gray and purposeless. He toyed with the idea of other occupations, but not many were open to a young man in a Mennonite village in Siberia.

The idea of teaching interested him, but the Stalinist regime had greatly narrowed the scope of creativity in that field, and any mention of religious beliefs led to harsh and sometimes fatal results. Besides, he could imagine his father's disgust should he turn from "the soil that feeds us" to such a lowly pursuit as teaching. That was for those, said his father, not man enough to tame the land and coax a living from it.

Daniel thought of his father, Peter Martens, confidently forging his way through life, ruddy of face and corpulent of form, always on the edge of bursting a blood vessel. He had succeeded materially through hard work, excellent managerial skills and fierce competitiveness, and he expected his son to do the same.

Daniel knew he possessed similar gifts in diligence and competitiveness. Luise had gently told him more than once that he could use more tact. But Daniel had also learned much from the example of Luise's father, Abram. He greatly admired the quiet carpenter of Alexandrovka.

These thoughts threaded through Daniel's mind as his feet found their own way to the Letkemann home. He would confront Luise again and hope she had changed her mind.

He could not discuss these matters with his own father, to whom the land and the farm were his life and purpose. To him, nothing else mattered; if not Luise, then some other woman would tend his kitchen and produce sons to farm the land after him. Somehow the intensity of his father's obsession with the land had lately dimmed Daniel's own vision in that regard, but nothing his father or anyone else said could eclipse his love for Luise. He must persevere because he could not accept the thought of life without her smile, her understanding. She owned his heart and he felt like an empty husk without her.

As Daniel approached Luise's home, he wondered what his welcome might be. Anna usually ignored him or called him a shiftless boy, a pronouncement that never failed to irk him. He pretended to laugh it off, but he knew he did not fool Luise. Her dark eyes shimmered with shame at Anna's thoughtless remarks, causing Daniel's heart to beat faster.

He loved Luise as he loved himself. She must see that. He must change her mind about leaving with her family. After all, there were no alternatives. After five years of assuming she was his, he could not let go of the dream. Perhaps time would work its wonders. And prayer. Yes, he would pray and even fast if that's what it took.

If Daniel had been nervous before about asking Luise to marry him, he was much more so now. If she refused him again, he did not know how he would gather up his shredded pride, but Abram had convinced him to try. She will agree this time, he had said, as if he knew. Daniel wished he could conjure up the confidence he saw in Abram.

He willed himself to march to Luise's front door, to knock, to wait as footsteps approached from within. When the door opened, it was Abram who met him. Luise had gone out, he said, but there was a cup of coffee for him if he would come in and sit awhile. Daniel accepted, glad that Anna busied herself putting Hans and Nela to bed. He could not have endured her meanness this evening.

❧

Luise smelled *vereneche* frying as soon as she pushed open the door of Tante Manya's cottage. The comforting aroma invited her through the parlor and into the kitchen where her great-aunt stood over the sizzling pan.

"Here I am," said Luise as she approached the woman.

"So I see," said Tante Manya, looking up from her frying pan. "Supper is ready, so set the table."

Luise kissed Tante Manya's withered cheek and set the dishes on the table. After her aunt asked the blessing, Luise sprinkled her browned-in-butter cottage cheese dumplings with salt and doused them in cream gravy, then swooned over the flavor. As long as they had cows there would be cheese, butter and cream. With harvest finished, they also had a supply of flour. It would dwindle quickly, but for the present, she would enjoy this fine fare.

"Tell me your heart, my girl."

Luise smiled at Tante Manya's directness. "You waste no time in getting to the matter at hand."

"I haven't time to waste," Tante Manya mumbled as she gummed her vereneche. "I have lived seventy summers, and according to the Psalmist, that is all I can reasonably expect. So talk. When the Lord calls, I will not stop to say goodbye."

"Don't go yet, Tante Manya. I need your help. I need advice on a personal matter."

"I think I hear the trumpet."

Luise's laugh filled the little kitchen and kindled more spark in the old woman's eyes. "All right then. Daniel has asked me to marry him, or at least he tried, but I have not agreed to his interrupted proposal."

"You have other suitors lined up at your door?" Tante Manya shook her head and fork-cut another vereneche. "She's seventeen years and tempting time."

"You don't understand—"

Tante Manya stopped chewing and stared into Luise's eyes, then returned to her meal.

Luise placed her fork on her plate. "That is untrue. I know you understand because you have been through much in your long life—"

"Which is swiftly coming to an end, my little chatterbox." Tante Manya punctuated her statement with a jab of her fork in Luise's direction.

"I don't know if I can marry Daniel, because if I do, I forfeit moving east with Papa and the little ones."

"You neglected to mention Anna. Jah, I see your dilemma."

"All would be solved if Daniel would agree to come with us."

"Ah. Your young man should give up his life and plans for you. That seems reasonable."

"But Tante Manya, how else can this be solved? My family needs me."

"And his does not? Did your father not tell you I agreed to go with them? I cannot take your place, but I can be of some help to Anna and look out for Hans and Nela."

"Yes, he told me, and that makes one more separation to consider. How could I ever do without you?"

"You should practice. I do not intend to live forever on this earth."

"But do I love Daniel enough to give up all connection with my family?"

"You're asking me? I think you already know the answer."

Luise stared at this woman she loved so completely. Nothing rattled her serenity. Nothing shook her faith. Never to see her again in this world would be a tremendous sadness. But Daniel…

"Why do you love this young man?"

"I cannot remember a time when I did not love him." Luise picked up the dishes and carried them to the washing bowl. "He has always been there for me to depend upon. He is strong, in mind and body. He is kind and just and fair, although somewhat outspoken at times, but he is also full of fun, and his ideas, oh Tante Manya, sometimes I wonder where he gets these wild ideas. He is respectful, my Daniel, even to Mother who belittles him constantly. And he is handsome. Such broad shoulders and strong hands. I feel he could protect me and love me forever. Without him, I would be but half a person."

She looked at her aunt in surprise. Perhaps she really did love him enough to make this sacrifice.

"Now tell me what you do not like about him."

Luise frowned and toyed with the dipper hanging on the edge of the water pail. "What I do not like?" She hesitated. "Is it a good idea to think on negative things, Tante?"

"Better now than later. Give voice to what you are hiding from yourself."

Luise sat down again and smoothed her dress over her knees. "I, well, please don't think me selfish, but I do not appreciate the fact that I am the only one who must make sacrifices in order for us to be together. He believes his work and life's plan to be more important than mine."

Tante Manya said nothing.

"I know it is the place of a woman to follow her man, that she must leave her father and mother, but I do not like it, even if it has always been so and will always be."

"You predict the future now? I would not be quite so bold. Is this, then, the only fault you find in your young man? If so, he is as worthy a mate as you could hope to find."

Luise laughed in response to the words but also the comical expression on her aunt's face. "You make life seem much less severe, Tante Manya. Yet you have suffered and have known separation and distress too."

"Ach jah." Tante Manya's receded lips twitched at the remembering. "First my father, then my husband, then you and Abram for a time. Jah, I have had my share of sorrows. But I have decided long ago that it is more beneficial for everyone to be thankful for what I have than to lament what I do not have. If I had a chance to live my life again, would I choose differently?" She shrugged. "Probably not, eh?"

Luise watched Tante Manya, imagined the memories crowding her mind, joys and sorrows mixing together like sunshine and rain, both inevitable, both necessary.

"Do not hide from sorrow, my child. When it comes—and it will—embrace it and believe the rainbow will come after. That is the promise of our Lord, and He never fails."

"Never, Tante?"

"Only in our limited understanding. We see our path in the light we have. He sees the whole road right to the end. Step out and trust in Him, child, not looking back, not revisiting your decisions nor chiding yourself overmuch."

Faith shone from her eyes and warmed Luise's heart, building on the foundation already laid by her father and others. So be it. Amen. She stood to go.

"You have made a decision." Tante Manya's words were a statement rather than a question.

Luise nodded. "To go forward, that is my decision. To trust. To throw off fear and embrace life." She bent for a kiss and Tante Manya's hand cupped her cheek.

Luise realized that the God who had sustained this dear woman would also sustain her. Now she only needed to live by what she believed. Her steps quickened as she approached her house.

Chapter Five

Daniel started as Luise charged through the door. She looked flushed, excited or distressed, he couldn't tell which. She closed the door and stood staring at him, her hands behind her. He stopped speaking in the middle of his sentence to Abram.

"Daniel," she said.

He tried unsuccessfully to read her eyes. Shrugging off all rehearsed speech, he rose and said, "Come for a walk?"

She looked at her father, who merely shrugged a shoulder. She nodded and allowed Daniel to open the door for her. They walked in silence through the evening calm, a choir of crickets accompanying them from the wild ryegrass along the path. A full, red moon had begun its ascent into the cloudless sky, gradually losing its hue as it rose. Like my life, thought Daniel, if I do not accomplish my present mission.

Daniel's heart beat unsteadily as he tossed about ideas of how to initiate the subject of his concern, and the longer he waited, the more difficult it became. At the end of himself, he glanced at Luise and she smiled. Taking his hand, she led him to a large rock off the road under a canopy of birch trees, with a view of the harvested fields under the silvering moon.

She sat on the rock.

Daniel fell to his knees before her. "Luise, I've been living in a desert since you refused me. My soul is parched and I cannot imagine —"

Her smile broadened and he stopped speaking.

"Oh Daniel, you're waxing poetic. It's so unlike you."

She giggled and brushed his cheek with her fingertips. "Just ask me."

"Just ask you?"

She nodded and he wondered if he would ever understand her ways. Heart in his throat, he said, "Luise, I love you. Please, will you be my wife?"

She bit her lip and nodded. "Yes, Daniel, I will because I love you too."

He pulled her into an embrace, and his desert became an oasis there in the dusky Siberian evening.

He had to know. "What made you change your mind? Was it your father?"

He sat on the rock now and pulled her onto his lap. She leaned into his shoulder, and he felt her head shake.

"No. In my heart I could never live without you. My mind just needed to catch up."

They sat absorbing the sweetness of the moment, and then Luise asked Daniel a question that would haunt him into the future.

"Daniel, can you love me enough to make up for what I will lose when my family leaves?"

Luise thought of her wedding as she scattered grain for the chickens, as she milked the cow, as she washed dishes and scrubbed clothing on the washboard. Plans formed in her mind even as Phillip, Jasch and other friends helped Daniel construct walls and rafters for their new house, set back in the trees behind his parents' home. In two weeks Luise would be *Frau* Daniel Martens. The thought both frightened and excited her.

In spite of her determination to remain positive, the gravity of her situation presented itself at unexpected times. Soon after the wedding, her family, including Tante Manya, would board the train that would jostle them east to Blagoveshchensk. And she would remain behind. With Daniel. Pain and joy danced together inside her.

Anna, in a moment of introspection, told Luise how it had felt when her own family left for Canada. "I had not seen them in years, but I knew where they were, and we would write letters. Now I don't even know what it's like where they are. I know I shall never see them again in this life." Her words offered small comfort.

Abram kept busy in his woodshop, and Luise knew he fought his own despair. She would catch him looking at her, wistfulness in his hazel eyes. But there was something else, something she could not read. It felt as is he had disengaged himself from all of them. He still watched out for Anna, cared for his children, worked hard in his shop building furniture for the people of Alexandrovka and area. But the joy of life seemed to have deserted him and he walked determinedly through the days, often glancing over his shoulder.

"What bothers you, Papa?" Luise leaned against the doorpost, observing him at work.

Abram looked at her, then back at the wooden chest he was sanding.

"What do you mean?"

"Papa, anyone can see you are worried. It might help to share it with someone."

"Like you?"

Luise frowned at her father's evasiveness. He grimaced and set aside the sanding block, turning to sit on the box. He rubbed his hands together and brushed sawdust from his trousers. Luise moved closer and waited.

He met her eyes, a smile slanting across his face. "You are very demanding in your quiet way."

"I worry about you, Papa, among all my other worries. If something concerns you, I need to know. Perhaps I can help."

"Hmm. Well then I suppose I must tell you. It is the same problem that has faced me before: my preaching. The Atheism Society has been in contact with me and warned me not to preach the good news of Jesus Christ." He paused and searched her eyes. "We both know I cannot do that."

"But Papa, surely there are others who could take your place for a while, until the authorities forget about it."

"We are all in the same predicament, and if we all stop preaching Jesus, who shall encourage the brethren? Where will our children hear the word of God?"

"And what will happen to your family if you continue?"

He hesitated before answering. "I don't know. But I do know I must follow God's call in my life. He has promised to look after everything else. 'Seek ye first the kingdom.' You know the scripture."

Luise spoke into the silence of the woodshop. "It seems you and I are called to make sacrifices. May God help us."

Abram put a hand on her arm. "I believe He will," he said, a soft smile creasing his face.

Luise kissed his cheek and left the shop.

Daniel tensed at the sound of trotting hooves. He set down his hammer and nails on the floor of his house and wiped perspiration from his brow with his sleeve. Had GPU officials decided to visit the Slavgorod Colony again? Not many others still owned horses that could run. Most of the ones left were too old, tired and weak from lack of feed and long days in the fields. Daniel had somehow managed to keep Prince from being requisitioned, but he knew the GPU would take him if they saw him.

Daniel's tension eased as he spied the horse trader pulling up on the reins of his gray Don gelding. The man definitely kept the best for himself. Three smart ponies trailed behind, pulling uncertainly on their leads. Daniel grinned and approached the trader.

"Marcowiscz, you thief. Where did you steal these fine beasts?"

Two chestnuts and a bay pranced and tugged at their tethers while Marcowiscz' own horse stood proud and still.

Marcowiscz tied them all to a stout fence rail and dismounted with the ease of a young man, although his graying hair and moustache revealed his age to be closer to Daniel's father than to Daniel.

The men met with a firm handshake and a few slaps on the back.

"I will not answer such accusations," Marcowiscz said in German, drawing his eyebrows together in a fierce frown.

Daniel grinned, and Marcowiscz's frown turned again into a handsome smile. "Shall we turn them loose in the corral for a while? I fancy the tall chestnut. Definitely Don. Fine head, muscular chest. Looks like he could run for days."

Marcowiscz slapped Daniel on the back again and laughed aloud. "No doubt his ancestors once belonged to the Cossacks, but he is not for you. These are for GPU.

"Say, what kind of chicken coop do you build here? You are expecting to be evicted from your parents' home?"

"This is my house," said Daniel proudly. It was obvious Marcowiscz did not wish to talk about GPU and neither did Daniel. It was more comfortable sometimes to pretend you were still your own boss. "I am to marry Luise Letkemann in two weeks. I hope to have it ready enough to move into by then."

"Married! You look for trouble—as if you have not already enough."

Daniel showed him the house, mostly closed in from the weather, awaiting doors and windows and a packet of shingles for the roof. Excitement bubbled up inside him as he displayed his workmanship.

"You want to buy a nice little filly for your sweetheart? I expect she does not possess as good a horse as your Prince."

Marcowiscz lowered his voice and glanced around them. "You should watch that horse of yours. Dubrowsky has his eye on it."

"What? He has his pick of horses. What does he want

with mine?"

"He knows good horseflesh. But you did not hear this from me. Now, think you your mother might have some fruit *perishky* for a weary traveler?"

Laughing, Daniel led the way to his parents' home and invited Marcowiscz inside. "Mother!" he called. "We have a guest." Dubrowsky indeed. He had better leave Prince alone or he'd be sorry.

Greidl Martens bustled into the front room, wiping her hands on her apron, and smiled wide. "Josiah Marcowiscz, welcome to our humble home. Come both of you to the kitchen and we will have coffee. I am just pulling out from the oven some perishky."

Marcowiscz raised his eyebrows and nodded in Daniel's direction. "My timing is excellent, as always."

Abram arrived late for supper, answering Luise's prayer for his safety. She noticed that Anna too had been casting frequent glances out the windows, watching for her husband. She seemed particularly anxious this week, spoiling the festive mood of the upcoming wedding. Luise wondered what it meant.

"Next Sunday you will be Frau Daniel Martens," said Hans at suppertime.

"Will you still be my sister?" asked Nela, her eyes threatening tears.

"Of course," said Luise. "I will always be your sister."

"Even when you are far away from us?" Hans demanded the truth.

"Always and forever, Hans. And perhaps, Lord willing, we will see each other again."

Nela stopped chewing and Hans laid down his fork. Luise steadied herself for the tears.

Instead, Anna responded. "You will see each other."

Everyone at the table stared at her as she continued to sip the thin soup. Sensing their stares, she looked up. "What is the matter with all of you? I know things."

The silence was punctuated by the scraping of her spoon on the bottom of the bowl. "I suppose the soup pot is empty."

That evening after Luise had climbed the attic ladder and eased into bed beside Nela, she thought again about Anna's prediction that she would not be forever separated from her family. Her heart swelled as she watched the quick rise and fall of Nela's chest as she slept, her dark curls splayed out across the starched pillowcase as if arranged by an artist. Her mouth was a cherub's kiss, her hands tucked up under her chin.

Luise settled onto her back, arms behind her head, thinking that whatever lay ahead, she would no longer take her rest at Nela's side. She prayed that all things would work out according to God's plan, then sat bolt upright at a sudden pounding on the door downstairs. Miraculously, Nela slept on. Luise pulled a shawl around her shoulders and eased open the trapdoor at the top of the attic ladder. She could see a corner of the entry door and her father's torso as he lifted the latch, tucking his shirt into his pants as he did so. Two activists stood there demanding that he accompany them to the local *volost* headquarters, the administration office for Alexandrovka and area.

"May I ask the reason for this untimely request?" Abram asked. Luise marveled at her father's composure. She could not still her trembling limbs nor slow her heartbeats.

"We do not give reasons; we follow orders," said the first man.

"Whose orders?"

"Look, Letkemann, come now or we drag you. You want the family to see that?"

It irked Luise that people her father had lived alongside of for years would suddenly become the enemy. She moved to catch a glimpse of the other side of the room. Anna peered out from the bedroom, eyes wide with fear. Please stay where you are, Mother. If Anna involved herself, this event would degenerate into a debacle.

"May I not report to the office in the morning?"

"You will come now."

Sighing, Abram pulled his coat off the hook beside the door and smoothed his hair before firming his hat into place. With a lingering look back, he preceded the men outside.

The door shut with a thud that threatened to stop Luise's heart. A voice at her ear nearly sent her hurtling downstairs without aid of the ladder. Hans knelt beside her in his nightshirt.

Hand on her heart, Luise whispered, "Oh Hans, you nearly frightened me to death."

"I'm sorry, Lise. I heard the men. Why did they take Papa?" Anna's wails drowned out his next words, but his trembling voice revealed fear too deep for a child of five years.

"I don't know. Listen Hans. I have to go down and take care of Mother. Please watch over Nela. If Papa isn't back by morning, I will go and find out what is happening."

"All right." Without further words he went to sit on Nela's bed, hands over his ears to shut out his mother's wails, and Luise scrambled down the ladder to Anna's side. The long night stretched before her, hours upon hours to contemplate her recent prayer that all things would work out according to the plan of God. Was this His plan, then?

Chapter Six

Daniel heard the knock on his door before the sun was up. He recognized the small voice of Hans and hurried to see what had happened.

"They took Papa away. Lise aksed me to get you." The boy's wide eyes tugged at Daniel's heart.

"Who took your papa?"

"The men. The fishuls. Will you come?"

"Of course." Daniel already had his boots tied. He grabbed his coat and ran after Hans. Anna's words came back to him now, "We must leave before they come for us. They will come for us." How did she know? She would be impossible to placate this time and Luise would need his presence.

He thought about his and Luise's upcoming wedding and stumbled. This would change everything. Please, Lord, he begged inwardly, please don't take Luise from me.

Luise ran to Daniel in great relief as soon as he arrived and accepted his embrace like the lifeline it was. "I need to go to the volost office to find out about Papa," she said, her thoughts jostling wildly in her mind. "Maybe I can bring him home."

Daniel took her by the shoulders. "Let *me* go. I don't want you going there alone. You know Dubrowsky's attitude toward you."

"His attitude toward you is certainly no better. Maybe he won't be there; he has other villages to terrorize. Magadan is not as harsh." She could not allow herself to think too much of what might happen; she only knew she must help her father. She would have run from the house that instant but Daniel restrained her.

"Luise, give me five minutes and I will bring Tante Manya over to sit with Anna and the children. Then we can go together. Strength in numbers, you know."

Luise hesitated, then nodded. "But hurry or I may have to start out on my own. Mother is settled at present, but I'm sure she won't remain that way for long."

"Luise. Wait for me."

She nodded again and began to pace as he ran out the door. He returned shortly with Manya in tow. The old woman collapsed breathless into the rocker and waved them away. "Go. Help Abram. I will pray."

Daniel grabbed Luise's hand and together they ran down the streets in the direction of the volost office, not caring about the stares that surely followed them from windows, doorways and yards.

"They probably think we're eloping," said Daniel, wishing it were true. He slowed to allow Luise to catch her breath. "Why did you not call me as soon as it happened? I would have come immediately."

"I know, but there was nothing anyone could do then. They were determined to take him and I couldn't leave Anna and the little ones. I prayed, Daniel. Papa was not alone this night."

She wished she felt as confident as her words implied. As they neared the volost headquarters and its improvised jail, her heart beat faster and her spine tingled as if the building itself were evil. She told herself that people had been arrested and released again after a night or a few days. She tried not to think about the other situations, the men who had disappeared into the night, never to be seen or heard of again. But that couldn't be her papa. He was in God's hands. Sometimes the righteous must suffer with the ungodly, Tante Manya had said. Please don't let it be Papa.

"I will speak," Daniel told her. He took a deep breath and knocked on the door. Luise gripped his arm as they waited. The door opened suddenly, sending them both back a step, and there stood Leonid Dubrowsky. Why was he here again? As Senior-Major, he only came through from time to time to check on the officials in charge of the individual villages. Luise's heart dropped at the sight of him and she sent up a prayer for help. She was inexpressibly thankful that Daniel had insisted on accompanying her.

Daniel stepped forward and addressed Dubrowsky. "We have come to inquire about Abram Letkemann. He was taken from his home last night."

Dubrowsky sneered at Daniel. "What business is it of yours? Is your little bird worried?" He moved to shut the door but Luise held it open.

"Please, sir," she said, disregarding Daniel's frown. "I need to know why my father was arrested and how the situation can be rectified."

Dubrowsky limped to a desk, sat down, propped his feet up and stared as Daniel and Luise moved to the other side of the desk. "What is the name of the criminal?"

"Ab—he is not a criminal. My father's name is Abram Letkemann."

"Letkemann. No such man here," he said without glancing at his papers.

Luise felt Daniel beside her, sensed his indignation and dreaded his words. "There are not many people in this village and I'm sure with all the records you possess, you even know the color of his eyes."

His words terrified Luise.

"You think so? Let me see..." He shoved some files around on his desk, sending a stack of paper to the floor. "Now how will I find his records?"

"Sir," said Luise, "Abram is the carpenter who lives on the west side of the village."

Dubrowsky's eyes moved from Daniel to Luise. "I have

many villages to oversee. This man no doubt makes much money selling furniture so he is a *kulak*. All kulaks are to be arrested."

"He is not a kulak. We are not wealthy nor do we own land," interrupted Luise. "We have been existing on bread and soup for months now."

"You live in a sturdy house with thick walls. He is a kulak."

Sobs rose in Luise's throat, restrained only by Daniel's hand on her arm. "We ask that you check your records. Surely it is not against the law to know what you have done with her father."

"Do not make me angry, boy, or your little sparrow will be asking after *you*."

Luise shuddered. They were at the mercy of this cold fish.

Just then, a local activist entered the office, muttering to himself. "Good to be rid of that batch of religious prattlers."

"I will ask this one if he knows the criminal." Dubrowsky smirked as he swiveled his chair. "Vladimir Josepivich, was one prisoner named—"

"Abram Letkemann," said Luise and Daniel together.

"Letkemann? Yes, for sure. Religious fanatic."

Luise's mouth felt dry. "Where is he?"

"By now he should be at least an hour away from us."

"Where are they being taken?" asked Daniel, defeat coloring his words.

The man shrugged. "Not my business."

"But why?" Luise stood before the activist.

"Get out now," said Dubrowsky, pushing himself to his feet.

Daniel did not respond to Luise's tug on his arm. "I will take Luise home, but I will be back. I will know why and where you have taken Abram."

Luise tried again to draw Daniel back, but Dubrowsky, moving with more speed than either of them expected, grabbed him by his collar and twisted. "Get out, dog. Your time will come. Out before I shoot you."

He released his hold on Daniel's collar and shoved him toward the door, then stepped between Daniel and Luise. "Maybe I keep your little bird, eh?" He touched her cheek as she stood frozen to the floor. "What do you think, sparrow?"

Luise turned and fled.

❧

"We must begin packing," said Anna the next day, and marched directly into her bedroom to retrieve a carpetbag and a wooden crate.

"Where are we going?" Luise watched her and wondered if the woman realized what had happened to her husband. She shuddered, recalling the touch of Dubrowsky's hand on her face, of that same hand twisting Daniel's collar around his neck until his face turned purple. She had no strength for Anna's strange behavior this day. Everything had changed—again—and they had taken Papa.

Anna glared at her. "We are going to Blagoveshchensk, where else? As we planned."

"For heaven's sake, Mother, the officials took Papa. We cannot go without him."

Anna's expression softened and she spoke to Luise as if to a child. "Luise, we must do our part. As soon as Abram returns we must be ready to leave."

Her pronouncement sent chills along Luise's arms. Manya, who sat in the rocker with Nela on her lap, glanced from Luise to Anna. Then she said, "Anna, the winter snows will soon be here. We must wait now until spring. There is a group of families planning to leave in March. Abram will expect us to wait until then."

"Do you think so?"

"Of course. Besides, the other families will not be prepared to go until then, and we certainly cannot travel all that way alone. I don't even know the way, do you?"

"Well, no, but I know it is east. We would travel east by

rail."

"We will go east, but we will wait until spring, Anna."

Anna studied Manya's face, then nodded. "Very well. We will leave in spring."

Luise felt enormous relief at Anna's capitulation, but it proved to be short-lived.

Anna's pacing was worse than her packing. For the next two days she walked from window to window, then paused at the door and fingered the bullet holes. Then back to the windows on every side.

Luise felt as if the door to her own heart had been opened and left to bang in the wind. Before her father had been taken, she had been preparing for her wedding. Now everything had stalled. Tante Manya had come to stay, and her presence helped, but the tension and uncertainty in the house eroded Luise's strength.

She knew Daniel tried to support them, but the aura of grief made it difficult for someone who liked to be doing, and she suspected his pride still suffered much from his humiliating encounter with Dubrowsky, with her there to witness it.

"Those bullet holes will need patching before winter," he said when he dropped by. "I will fetch something to fix them."

Luise appreciated his contributions to their lives more than she could say, but her emotions were so raw she had little heart left for her fiancé. Her plans and dreams were unraveling like a ball of yarn spilled from Anna's basket.

It had been several days since Anna had spoken of Abram's return, so when she did, it took Luise by surprise. Anna stood looking out the south window facing Main Street.

"He should be here soon," she said.

"To whom are you referring, Mother?" asked Luise after listening to several repetitions of the same statement.

"Your father, whom do you think?"

"But Mother, he has been sent away. It is unlikely he will be back very soon." She did not include the words *if at all.*

"If you had faith the size of a mustard seed," said Anna, focusing directly on Luise, "you could believe."

Luise matched her stepmother's stare. "Let's pray for Papa then."

They gathered in a circle on their knees: Luise, Daniel, Anna, Hans and Nela, and Tante Manya. That is where Abram found them some minutes later when he stumbled into his house, cold, hungry and obviously exhausted.

"Abram!" Anna rose with difficulty and hurried over to where her husband stood, weary but smiling all over his face. She collapsed into his arms and he buried his face in her neck.

He opened his arms to the rest of his family, all of them clamoring for a piece of him and for answers. "They let me go," he said. "No reason. I didn't wait around to ask why."

Joy filled the house, and Luise decided she could contentedly remain with Daniel knowing that her father was safely returned to his family. They held another much more joyful prayer meeting then. Daniel offered to accompany Tante Manya to her house on his way home, and Luise let him go, with a promise whispered in his ear. She watched his face light up, and read the hope and anticipation in his eyes. Soon, she would be his wife. Soon.

⁂

Daniel's steps lightened as he walked home from Manya's house. Abram's return had been so sudden, so unexpected, that they had not had the opportunity to discuss reinstating wedding plans, but Luise's whispered promise had given him renewed hope.

He entered his parents' home excited to tell his family that Abram Letkemann had returned, but the faces that met his were dulled by some news he had yet to learn.

His mother forced a smile and rose to put on the kettle.

His father stopped his pacing long enough to bluster about interference and coercion, while Daniel's sisters and young brother, Johannes, looked up from their now-abandoned game of *knipsbraat*.

"What has happened now?" asked Daniel. "I have such news and I come home to long faces all around. What is bothering everyone?"

His mother eased to his side and led him to a chair. "Perhaps you should give us your news first, son. I'm sure we could all use it."

Daniel did not sit, but paced as his father had been doing. "I bring very good news indeed. Abram Letkemann has returned. For some unknown reason he was allowed to come back to his family."

"That is truly wonderful," said his mother, a smile creeping into her frightened eyes. For it was fear Daniel saw in their green depths. "Isn't it, Peter?"

"Jah, very good for the family," added his father. He opened his mouth to say something further, but one of the girls interrupted.

"So you could have gotten married after all, if—"

"Hush, Maria," said her mother.

"If what? What is now preventing me from marrying Luise?" He looked from one to the other, waiting for someone to tell him what had transpired in his absence.

"Peter…"

"Jah, Greidl, I will tell him." Daniel's father motioned him to the chair. "Now sit."

Daniel sat.

"The volost committee was here earlier. They meet once each month, making decisions for the colony which we have always made for ourselves, which we should still be making for the good of our village, of our colony."

"Yes, Father, I know these things. What did they say that threatens to change my life? Am I to be arrested for something now? Perhaps for working too hard?" He tried to remain calm, but he felt again Leonid Dubrowsky's fist at his throat, and the memory restricted his breathing.

"No, son. But they decided, in their infinite wisdom, to send a group of *volunteers* north to the forests for the winter to gather wood for the colony, members of various villages, chosen no doubt for their physical strength and youth."

Daniel's breath left his lungs with a hiss like cold water spilled on the stove. "And they have chosen me." It was a statement, not a question. "When do I leave?"

"Tomorrow morning."

He sat unmoving, as his gut clenched with anger and his head pounded with questions. "How long will I be gone?" He kept his voice flat.

"They did not say, exactly."

"Approximately then." He glared at his father as if the whole affair were his fault. "All winter?" His mother put a hanky to her mouth and busied herself with the kettle again.

"And if I refuse?"

"You will be jailed and most likely taken away."

He banged his fist on the table, clattering the teacups. "To end up *volunteering* somewhere else with no end in sight." He pushed himself to his feet. "I shall go pack." He spit the words out through clenched teeth. "I will have to tell Luise tomorrow on my way to the station. Let her enjoy her happiness until then."

He wondered about appealing his volunteer position, one of myriad questions swirling desperately in his mind, but knew it would be fruitless. How he dreaded telling Luise. How many postponements could she endure? Was this a sign from the Lord that they should not marry? No, he would not accept that. It was a scheme of the devil, in the form of the local volost leaders, and most likely at the specific suggestion of Senior-Major Leonid Dubrowsky of the GPU.

He heard the low buzz of the family in conversation on the other side of his bedroom door. Leaning his head against the smooth varnished wood, he closed his eyes and appealed to a higher power than the volost. After all, God had answered their prayers for Abram. He had been on his way home before they had even prayed. But something told Daniel the answer this time would not be the one he sought.

Chapter Seven

"Daniel, no! Not again. We are to become husband and wife in a few day's time. You cannot leave now."

"Luise, it is not my choice, but if I do not go, our marriage will be postponed indefinitely. At least this way we can look forward to spring."

She kicked at the pack he had dropped beside him on the step and his heart lurched. "It's a game they play with us, Daniel," she hissed. "We are simply pawns to them."

He had no argument with her there, but neither had he any answers.

"Daniel," she said, holding the lapels of his jacket with both hands, "you must promise me you will take care, dress warmly. Come back to me..." Her voice broke and Daniel pulled her into his embrace.

He held her as long as he dared, knowing that if he did not reach the station in time, his future would be even more radically altered. "We have no choice, my love, but I promise we will be married the day I return home." He tweaked her nose. "So you must be prepared for your bridegroom. Will you be ready?"

Sniffing and swiping tears, she nodded and forced a smile. "My lamp will be lit. Only do not step in the way of danger while you are gone. Be careful with the axes and saws. Remember me here, waiting, whenever you feel the need to act heroically."

Daniel held her chin in his hand and bent to kiss her. He admired her pluck, her courage. Or perhaps it was resignation she portrayed. The colonists seemed to own less autonomy with each new day. Some functioned quietly from inside the shell in which they had taken refuge, others tried to pretend they were masters of their own fate. Opportunists sprouted from various dark corners, even in the villages themselves. Of this Daniel also warned her. She would not have his protection this long winter.

He squared his shoulders and fell into step with several other young men walking to the station. He turned once to wave, then set his mind forward to the work that would separate him from his Luise, until the warmth of spring melted winter's menace and allowed him back home where he belonged. Perhaps if they worked very hard, the return date would be sooner than later.

Daniel had been gone only a week when Luise overheard her parents' conversation from her attic room. She had set out to Tante Manya's but returned for the new hanky she had embroidered for her aunt. The voices floated up from the bedroom below hers.

"I can be packed by tomorrow, Abram. If we hurry, we can get to Blagoveshchensk before winter."

"We need to wait until spring, Anna, we have discussed this. It is too late to go now. Besides, we cannot leave Luise alone here without Daniel, and he will not be back until spring, most likely."

"Ah yes, your Luise always takes the upper hand, doesn't she?"

"Anna! Be reasonable. Think of how she would feel."

"I know how she feels." Anna's words reminded Luise that her stepmother had indeed sacrificed things in her own life, even though her tactlessness cut like a knife.

"Yes, you do, my dear. And now we must keep our Luise in mind. We will be ready to go in spring, as soon as Daniel returns and they can be married."

Luise heard this conversation repeated in various forms at regular intervals during the long winter.

❧

When the spring sun of March 1927 slanted through windows now clear of frost and ice, warming the floor and cheering the inhabitants of the house, Luise began to watch as Anna had done previous to Abram's return last fall. She wished Anna would offer another of her predictions. She had heard frequent discussion and planning throughout the winter from Anna about the move to the Mennonite villages near the Amur River, and once wheels replaced sleigh-runners on the wagons of Alexandrovka, Luise knew the time would come to bid her family farewell.

Would Daniel return before her family left? Would they have opportunity to celebrate a proper wedding? She needed her father for that occasion, and Tante Manya, of course. Prayers and pleas were her lullabies in the cool nights in her attic bed beside Nela. Her trousseau had been ready since early fall and her heart had remained committed to her upcoming marriage. All she needed was her groom.

"We must begin packing in earnest. We will be leaving on the 24th of this month. Willy Derksen said so when I was at the store this morning." Anna chattered on about their departure as the family sat at supper.

"Are you sure you still wish to go, Mother?" asked Luise.

"What do you mean by asking such a question? Of course we are going. I am most anxious to leave these evil Bolsheviks behind."

Abram poured some of his barley coffee into his saucer and drew it in with a practiced slurp. "We will still be living in Soviet Russia, my dear."

"Yes, but they won't bother us so much out there. I've heard word that the government doesn't really care about those so far east."

"They opened the land for settlement for a purpose, so do not expect to be completely out from under their shadow."

"Abram, you seem intent on dampening our spirits today. We are all excited to be leaving here." She glanced around the table. "Oh well, there is Luise. I suppose you will miss her."

Overwrought with longing for Daniel, the pain of Anna's words sent Luise from the table, her tears already flowing.

She heard Anna's words behind her, "She is certainly flighty today."

And Abram's soft answer, "Anna, she has chosen to remain behind with Daniel, but he is not here. Imagine how that would feel."

"Nela, lean over. I don't want to wash that dress again."

In her attic room, Luise covered her face with her pillow and sobbed. Had the Lord not heard her prayers? Did He not care? What was His will for her, for her and Daniel?

After supper, as Luise and her father walked along the main street of the village, he said, "I'm sorry for Mother's outburst at supper, Luise." They picked their way along the street now muddy with spring thaw. "She is unaware of her harshness."

"I don't believe that anymore, Papa, and I'm not sure you do either."

A silence on her father's part reinforced her belief that Anna's barbs scarred him as much as they did her. "She is preoccupied with putting as much distance as possible between herself and the powers that rule us."

"Yes, I know. I believe her personal belongings have been packed since before Christmas, and she keeps putting things we need into boxes. Tante Manya and I are forever digging them out again."

"She's not herself lately, Lise."

"Lately?" She stopped walking. "This is not something new that has just come upon her, Papa. Surely you know that."

He stared at her, then continued to walk, head bowed,

shoulders sagging.

"Papa?" She put her hand on his shoulder and he stopped. "Papa, there is something happening to Mother, and it's getting worse instead of better."

"What am I supposed to do about it, Luise? She is my wife and I love her. I made a promise for life."

Luise recognized the pain in her father's eyes. They turned their steps toward home. "I'm sorry, Papa," she whispered, "but ignoring it will not help."

When Abram pushed open the gate and stepped back to allow her to go ahead of him, she demurred. "I'll be along soon," she said.

Her feet led her to the familiar little house halfway down Main Street, to the wizened woman who always seemed able to dispense the wisdom and courage for life.

"Tante Manya?"

Daniel harnessed the horses with ease and anticipation. This day he and his fellow workers would begin the journey back home to their various villages in the Slavgorod Colony, to the life they had left behind several months before.

In spite of the hard work and meager diet, his body had hardened to muscle with not a spare inch of superfluous flesh remaining. He imagined Luise's expression when she saw him ride into Alexandrovka next week.

The scene assailed him again, the one that had invaded many dreams both day and night: he would return only to find Luise and her family gone. She would have reconsidered her decision in his absence and chosen to accompany her family to the Amur.

He shook off the negative thoughts. How could he imagine these things of the young woman who had been his closest friend and confidant for so many years already? He fastened the last straps around the horses' necks and shook out the driving reins. "All right, Rock and Jenny. Let's go home."

The animals snorted and shook their heads, adjusting once again to the weight behind them, only this time the wagon carried men and bedrolls as well as cords of wood. Spring sun cheered hearts as it warmed bodies.

Home had never seemed so desirous. Several of the men were set to leave with their families for the east as soon as they returned, providing there were no delays on the way back. Daniel knew his fellow workers were as anxious to see their families as he was to see his.

He felt a tightening in his chest when he thought of Tobias Tiezen, trapped beneath a felled tree, eyes large as the weight crushed his lungs. They had not been able to free him from his burden soon enough, had buried him as deeply as the frozen earth would allow, had written to his young wife and son, had hoped the letter reached its destination. What if it had been him?

Daniel treasured the few letters he had received from his parents and from Luise, guessing that many communiqués had been lost between the colony and the northern forests where he had been working. But he hoped to speak to his Luise in person in just a few days.

He slapped the long reins on the horses' rumps and urged them onto the road home. The countryside passed much too slowly for his liking, but the horses could move no faster with their loads. He must be patient, trusting that Luise still waited for him. So much could have happened since his departure more than four months ago.

At least the days were long, and the men glad to move as daylight allowed. Soon, Luise, soon.

ঌ

Luise heard the familiar thump of a cane from the dim parlor and then the creak of the rocking chair.

"Tante? It's me, Luise. I'll come there."

"Jah, good. Come."

Luise entered the parlor as Manya eased herself back into her padded rocker.

"Tante Manya," Luise burst out, "does Papa not realize the state Mother is in?"

"What do you mean? Is she overwrought?"

"Not overwrought, at least not today. Just tactless, hurtful. Papa says she doesn't mean to be so, but sometimes I think she does. And he excuses her for it."

Luise noticed sadness in Manya's eyes and a sag to her face. Her sparse hair wisped in frayed strands from beneath the ever-present kerchief like thin clouds in a tired gray sky. She looked older than usual and the realization sobered Luise.

Manya had enough to think about without Luise's problems too. Her life's belongings sat in a few boxes and sacks around the perimeter of the room, awaiting relocation to yet another frontier. At her age, she should be rewarded with a stable home, a family to look after her, a rest. Instead, she was giving that up in order to take Luise's place with the family.

"What did she say this time, Lise?" Love lines wrinkled into place on Manya's face, easing the apparent weariness, and her toothless mouth pulled into a smile.

Luise moved from her chair to the floor beside Manya's chair and rested her head on the old woman's lap. Tension eased as Manya's hand caressed her hair.

"She's so abrupt. Does she care nothing for me after twelve years, after all the help I have given her with the little ones?"

Manya continued to stroke Luise's hair. "Anna was never one to mince words, Lise. A warm person she has never been, and now her mind has lost any tact she may have possessed."

"I've noticed."

Luise felt Tante Manya's breathy laugh. "Listen to me, child. Suppose Anna had lost an arm in an accident and was unable to care for Hans and Nela without help. How would you have responded?"

"You are a wise woman, Tante Manya."

"You have not answered me."

Luise raised her head. "If Mother had lost an arm, I would have helped her with the children just as I have done. As it is, she is crippled in mind, not in body. And so I have done what I needed to do. The difficulty for me, Tante, is the complete lack of gratitude, or even acknowledgement of my contribution."

"Is that why you help? To be praised?"

She was unrelenting, this woman. "No, but—"

Luise laid her head back down on Manya's lap and thought about it. Did she really act from love or from the need to be praised?

"I am a selfish girl," she said, as much to herself as to Manya.

This time she heard Manya chuckle. "Lise, we all want people to appreciate us. That is natural. The test comes when reality veers from expectation, which it often does. Look at me."

Luise shifted her position and knelt before her aunt. "I have obviously failed the test of humility and grace."

"Be quiet now and listen." Sharp humor sparkled from the old woman's eyes. "These tests are given to us over and over in our lives. The good Lord knows our frame. He remembers that we are but dust. And so He allows us to try again. There will be many opportunities in your life to learn humility and grace, Lise. When once you become aware of a specific failing, you have come halfway to a solution."

Luise gently cradled Manya's arthritic hands. "Jesus must become very weary of our failings."

"Nah, child, that is unscriptural. Our Lord is longsuffering. Stop thinking of yourself, of your trials and tests. Think of the Lord. Love Him and serve Him. Listen to His voice and obey. That is all He asks."

The Kroeger clock chimed the hour and Luise stood. "It's late. I must get home. Thank you for listening and for your wise advice. I will persevere."

"Liebe Vater," prayed Manya from her seat in the rocker, still holding Luise's hands, "Thou knowest we often fail Thee and we beg forgiveness. I ask that Thou wouldst fill Thy child with Thy strength to love Anna, who is not easy to love, and I ask that Thy joy would fill Luise, that she would serve Anna as if she were serving Thee. We ask these things in Christ's name and for His sake. Amen."

"Amen," echoed Luise. She kissed Tante Manya, hugged her narrow shoulders and whispered a goodnight.

The next morning, Hans awoke when Luise did, and hovered near her all morning. "You must come east with us, Lise," he insisted. "You're family."

Luise's heart cramped at the temptation to flee with her family to the east, but the thought of Daniel coming home and finding her gone forced her to think reasonably. She had made her decision, and she would not turn from that. Alexandrovka would remain her home as long as it was Daniel's. But there were forty-one other families leaving the colony on March 24, and the Letkemanns needed to leave with them if at all possible.

"You need to pack your things," Anna said as she marched toward her bedroom, coughing as she went. "You do not want to be left behind."

"I am not going with you," Luise reminded her patiently. "I am staying behind to marry Daniel."

"You are coming and you must pack. Now off with you."

Frowning, Luise climbed the ladder to her attic room, if only to separate herself from Anna. She had, in fact, packed her few belongings to move into the house Daniel had begun last fall. When he had been called away, Abram had worked on the house. It still required some finishing touches, but once the Letkemanns had moved, Daniel and Luise could stay in this house until the other was completed. But she would not be living in the attic anymore.

What would it be like to be married, to belong so completely to another person? Perhaps Daniel had changed his mind over the long winter months. Perhaps he would encourage her to go east with her family. She shook off the thought, chastening herself for her silliness. Of course Daniel loved her. What in the vast northern forest would have changed that? Still, she could hardly maintain a calm demeanor until they had spoken their vows and made their commitment public. Soon, Daniel, soon…

She added a prayer that it would happen before her family left, and then set off down Main Street to visit Daniel's family. The men of the village, the ones who had decided to leave the colony with the Blagoveshchensk group, busily mended harnesses and reinforced wagons. They would only need the horse-drawn wagons for the short drive south to the Slavgorod station. At that time these would either be sold or loaded onto the train to be taken ahead to the eastern colonies. Now was the best time for any fixing to be done.

When Luise neared the home of her friend Valentina and her husband, she could not resist a quick stop. Here was someone else who would not be traveling east, someone with whom she could visit when her family had gone. Valentina welcomed her with a warm hug.

"Oh, I'm so glad you're not going off to that unknown land across the river from China," said Valentina. "It's so far away and I'd never see you again."

Luise steeled herself to her friend's lack of tact. "I can't help but be torn, you know. How will I live without my family?"

Valentina's eyes widened and she covered her mouth. "I'm sorry. I didn't think."

Luise shook her head and smiled. "You never do, but I love you anyway. I'm just glad you'll be here with me."

"Is the wedding all planned? Come, sit down.

Everyone's bringing zwieback and platz, and I believe Father made extra cheeses last fall. It will be a lovely wedding."

"We are a close community," said Luise, sitting on a straightback chair and leaning her elbows on the kitchen table. "It will be strange when forty-one families leave."

"We'll soon fill the void, I'm sure. Listen," and Valentina leaned closer to Luise, "I was going to wait to tell you, but I can't. You're here now. I'm...we're..."

Luise shrieked. "You and Wilhelm are going to have a baby! I knew it. I'm so happy for you."

They hugged and giggled and planned until Luise remembered her mission. "I need to go visit Daniel's family. It's been too long."

"Soon you'll be living so close you'll be able to smell her perishky baking."

"Don't remind me. That will take some getting used to. Come visit when you can."

Luise approached the Martens place with her head full of Valentina's news. She'd love to have a baby too, but so far she hadn't even been able to snag a husband. She had been to call on Daniel's family several times over the course of the winter, but today she needed to know if he had sent word about his arrival home. She had written him the date of the Blagoveshchensk departure. If only he would return in time.

Luise's steps slowed when she came within sight of the Martens house. It stood taller and wider than other houses in the village, added onto in various stages as God had blessed the family with good crops and grain sales and children. No matter how often she had been here, the house always seemed imposing to Luise's humble standards. The house Daniel had built for her was more conservative, for which she was thankful. After all, a house only became a home because of the people within its walls, so it mattered not whether those walls were high and long or low and modest.

She turned in at the high gate and followed the cleanly swept walk to the door. Knocking, she stepped back and waited, wishing Daniel himself would answer and welcome her in. But it would not happen that way today. She heard what she guessed were Greidl's footsteps and then the door opened to her.

"Ah, Luise. How nice. Come in."

"*Guten tag*, Frau Martens, I have come to ask if you have heard anything from Daniel."

"Jah, so I thought." The woman smiled and Luise relaxed. "You have waited long for my son."

Luise took a chair in the large parlor, careful not to rub mud on the rug beneath her feet. The delicate tassels that hung from the tablecloth danced as Greidl Martens brushed against them. Luise smoothed the antimacassars on the arms of her chair and straightened her shoulders, waiting for Frau Martens to speak.

"We have had no word from Daniel for several weeks, Luise," she finally said, and Luise felt scrutinized.

"The post has not been dependable for quite a while already, so I'm not surprised, but I thought perhaps a letter might have gotten through to you.

"And then I thought," she continued, "that I might feel closer to Daniel if I spent some time in the presence of his family."

The comment seemed to please Frau Martens and she rose to bring coffee and freshly baked plum perishky. As Luise bit into the flaky pastry, the sweetness of the sugared plums filled her with satisfaction. Everything would work out. She caught a glimpse through the parlor window of the house Daniel had built for her. She hoped she and Greidl would suit one another with the passage of time.

"I am grateful you are not tearing my son away from his home and family and livelihood." Greidl refilled Luise's coffee cup and sat down opposite her again. "He loves the farm, you know."

"I have always known that, Frau Martens," said Luise. "I have never presumed to lure him away."

"Well, I never meant it that way."

"It doesn't matter. Soon he will be home to help his father."

Greidl reached into a basket beside her chair and adjusted her knitting needles. Idle hands are the devil's workshop, Anna always said. It seemed Greidl subscribed to the same adage.

"Do you knit, Luise?"

"Yes, but I prefer embroidery. Tante Manya taught me."

"Not Anna?"

Luise watched the woman's face, but her eyes concentrated on her handwork, even though she could have done it blind by now. Was she digging for inside information on Luise's relationship with her stepmother? Daniel had often said his mother loved gossip, and his words put Luise on her guard.

"Mother has been busy enough with Hans and Nela these last years, and Tante Manya was more than willing to step in to help wherever she could."

"Does Manya help often?"

"She never intrudes, if that's what you mean."

"Oh, I meant no such thing, Luise."

"Well, thank you very much for the perishky and coffee. They were delicious. Now I must get back to help Mother with supper."

"Too bad you cannot stay a bit longer. My girls will be home from school shortly and would like to see you."

"Perhaps another time, but thank you for the invitation."

Before they could make their way to the door, Daniel's father burst through in a foul temper. "Those Bolshevik fools are going too far. They threaten and warn and talk nonsense no sane person—oh, Luise. Forgive my outburst; I didn't know you were here."

Luise's tight smile took the place of words. She moved toward the door but Peter stopped her. "Perhaps it would not be out of line for you to hear what happened. After all, Daniel will be your husband when he returns home, and he will eventually take over this farm."

"If you think it best, sir, but I don't need to know your private affairs."

"You should know, the officials have threatened to arrest me for owning a new Fordson tractor. Can you imagine? What business is it of theirs if I own a machine I have bought with money I earned fair and square? The people in the surrounding villages depend on me to help them but they cannot afford to buy shares in a tractor. What else should a community-minded man do, eh?"

"Ach, Peter!" exclaimed Frau Martens. "What now?"

"What must you do to avoid arrest?" asked Luise.

"I must sell the tractor and then repurchase it together with at least five other farmers, to whom I will most likely have to lend the money. Such insanity. I do not intend to give in to their demands."

"But Peter, you will be arrested." Greidl wrung her hands but her husband paid her no mind.

"Well, Luise, what would do you think Daniel would say to this?" Peter Martens stared at her from beneath heavy brows, and waited for an answer, while his face became more ruddy with each second that passed.

"Perhaps he'll be home soon enough that you can ask him yourself. I must be going now."

She slipped out while Greidl again tried to coax Peter to sit down. The man would kill himself with work and worry if he did not take heed, Luise thought. She wished she had been able to garner at least some information about Daniel, but it had not been available or forthcoming. Sighing, she trekked back through the town, past homes where families prepared for supper, perhaps also waiting for a son or a brother or a father to return from the forests.

Most of the foot and buggy traffic had already passed for the day, but one buggy still approached, so Luise kept to the side of the street to avoid being splattered with mud. Intent on getting home, she did not notice the driver haul on the reins, but she did hear him holler "whoa," and the sound of that voice stopped her as surely as if her shoes had become mired in the mud. She turned as one in a trance and watched the driver vault over the edge of the wagon and run toward her.

Chapter Eight

With a strangled cry, Luise leapt into Daniel's arms and he whirled her around, kissing her and repeating her name as if he had not said it for months. Luise wished the moment would go on forever, but eventually he stood her back on the ground and stared into her eyes. "Oh, Luise, you are here. Waiting still."

She laughed at his serious expression. "Of course, Daniel. I promised I would wait. My lamp is burning and you have returned." She felt the joy and contentment of being held by the man she loved better than anyone else on earth. This moment would be a jewel she would hide in the secret place of her heart forever, taking it out often to cherish and remind her of their wonderful love.

They talked of little things and big things, of how they had missed each other, of the wedding that could now become reality. Their sentences hung in the air unfinished as they lost themselves in each other's eyes. And then Luise told him to go home.

"Your mother misses you and your father is absolutely apoplectic with anger at the village officials. They need to see you and be encouraged by you. So go now, my love."

"But I must see you again today. I will come after supper. Oh Luise, I don't want to let you out of my sight; you're so beautiful."

"Ach, you're silly. Come over later; I'll be there."

Smiling wide, her heart bursting, she laughed as he jumped back onto the wagon and snapped the reins, watching her until she shook her head and turned to walk home.

Daniel was home. Her Daniel. And he was in time to claim her for his own before her family left for Blagoveshchensk. Praise be to the Lord. He had answered her prayer at the eleventh hour. Now there was indeed much to do.

❧

Luise could scarcely stay seated at supper, never mind eat anything. Her eyes kept drifting to the door, waiting for Daniel to knock and walk in. She saw her father try to hide a smile, but Anna seemed oblivious to Luise's eagerness.

"When is Daniel coming?" asked Hans. "I want to show him my train set that Papa made for me for Christmas."

"Me too," said Nela.

"You don't have a train set."

"I can show him yours."

"No, I'm showing him."

Luise deflected the storm. "Nela, I'm sure Daniel will want to see the new clothes Mother sewed for your dolly. He will be here soon."

"I thought we were rid of that boy." Anna coughed into her hanky and helped herself to another piece of bread.

Luise felt the joy being squeezed out of her. Her father spoke to chasten Anna, but her words lingered in the air. Not that they were news to Luise. Anna had never pretended to appreciate Daniel, but her tactless words hurt.

"You may as well accept Daniel, Mother, because he is about to become your son-in-law. I do not appreciate your cruel comments."

"I wanna see Daniel." Nela's bottom lip pushed out and her brows lowered.

"You will, my dear," said Luise, glaring at her stepmother. "Now eat the rest of your soup before he comes."

The words were no sooner out of her mouth than a knock jerked Luise to her feet. She stopped, took a deep breath, and opened the door. Daniel stood looking at her, hidden from the rest, motioning outside with his head, a smile tilting his mouth.

Luise grinned and shook her head, opening the door wider. Rolling his eyes, he entered, looping his arm about her shoulders in a gesture that spoke to Luise of security and love and promises kept.

Abram rose and embraced Daniel. "Good to have you home, son. You look like the work has not hurt you."

Daniel greeted Anna while Hans raced up the attic ladder to fetch his train set. Nela hurtled toward Daniel, leaving him no choice but to sit. He hugged her and tweaked her nose before answering Abram.

"The food ration was a bit meager, but the muscles have hardened. It was very beautiful where we were, but isolated. Besides the weekly mail and supplies, we never saw anyone outside of our group...except one day a group of Russian-speaking Yakuts came through our camp. They stayed with us a few days, shared their meat and ate some of our preserved food. It was a fair exchange, but I believe we came out ahead because they told us their stories. They are survivors in that cold north land."

"What did they tell you?" asked Hans when he had returned with his train cars and set them up on the table for Daniel's appraisal.

Daniel admired the cars and pushed them back and forth on the tabletop. "Well, they told of hunting grouse and ptarmigan and goral, even bear sometimes. They live completely off the land, using every bit of the animals they kill for clothing and shelters and packs."

"Were there women with them?" Luise wanted to know.

"Not with this group. They were hunting for the winter and keeping up with the reindeer. By now they will have returned to their homes to raise a few small plots of corn and barley and root vegetables. But mostly they live off the game they kill."

"They are away for long periods of time just like you were."

"And they return in spring, as I did."

Luise suddenly realized she was staring at him and everyone was silent. Embarrassed, she cleared off the table and poured hot water from the pot on the stove into the basin, adding chips of lye soap.

Abram whispered something to Anna and she frowned and moved toward Luise. "I will do the dishes tonight. Your father says you are free to go walk with Daniel, and I suppose you had better use the time you have together."

Luise winced at Anna's twisted favor and wondered what she had meant by her last comment. Daniel coaxed the children off his lap and promised to come see them every day now that he was home. Luise remembered with a start that those days would be few and busy, and she began to steel herself for the ultimate separation. Her prayers followed her as she walked out the door hand-in-hand with her betrothed. At least she would always have his hand to hold.

Daniel pulled Luise's arm through his as they walked past the edge of the village and onto the dirt road that led to the village tree lot. Her chatter delighted him, especially after months of listening to the rude and sometimes crude talk of the other volunteered woodsmen.

"Daniel, I want to get married."

"You do? To whom?"

She slapped him on the arm. "I haven't decided yet. Do you have any suggestions?"

"I'll think on it, but it seems rather sudden."

He caught her eye and his smile faded. They stepped into the skeletal shelter of bare birches and held a silent conference by mutual consent. Her kisses spoke to him of a love that matched his own, of a desire to make a life together.

"When can we get married?" Luise's whisper tickled his ear and sent tingles through his body.

"Tomorrow."

"Why not today?"

He chuckled into her hair and breathed in the smell of her.

"Tomorrow you shall be my wife."

After a time, she pulled away and sought his eyes. "And where shall we begin our wedded life, my dear? In my attic room with Nela and Hans or in your bedroom at your parents' house with Johannes?"

"Not to worry. In a few days we shall be able to live in our new home, but the first few days we must make do until the house it ready. Leave it to me; I will arrange it. I will see you back to your attic room and I shall retire to my bedroom at my parents' house for one more night. And then you will be mine."

Daniel could hardly imagine this dream coming true. "I have loved you ever since I first saw you, Luise." He traced the line of her jaw with his finger. "You have grown more beautiful every year, every day. I am so blessed to have you. I promise to do everything in my power to love and protect you, and to provide for you the necessities of life. I cannot promise I will always be able to give you everything you want, but I will always love you."

"I know you will, and I trust you. Tomorrow cannot come soon enough. I shall not sleep a wink."

"Perhaps you should try," said Daniel. "You may not sleep tomorrow either."

Luise ducked her head and Daniel knew she blushed. He pulled her toward the path and they started back to her house.

He thought of how much she had to give up to marry him. "Luise, I'm sorry we cannot celebrate *Polterabend* tonight. I wish we could sit at the front of the schoolroom and be showered with gifts and well wishes by our friends and neighbors."

"Best not to wish for things we cannot have. My dream of becoming your wife is all I require."

He smiled at her acceptance of the situation. "Good night then, my love," he said. "When shall I see you?"

"I will need you to help me decorate the church in the morning, Daniel. I want pine boughs and greenery and a wreath of green in my hair."

"I will beseech the trees to send out their new leaves for you." The love in her eyes sent his heart spiraling upward. "Until tomorrow, then."

He backed away from her, almost tripping at the gate, not wanting to let her out of his sight. She tipped her head back and laughed softly into the evening breeze. Tomorrow he would take her with him. They would be one. Tomorrow.

Luise floated down the church aisle on Daniel's arm like one in a dream. Her white dress fit her perfectly, and a circlet of new leaves crowned her hair. She had no idea where Daniel had found the leaves at this time of year, but he had.

She had thought this day would never arrive. That morning when Daniel had helped her secure the pine boughs, decorate their chairs and drape the communion table with a cloth Tante Manya had made, she had wished the minister would just come and pronounce them husband and wife instead of waiting for the gawking eyes of the villagers.

But now as she caught sight of friends and family, and especially of Abram's proud face in the front pew, she was glad they had waited. She even glimpsed Daniel's friend, the horse trader Marcowiscz, watching from the back of the building. The scent of pine made her think of Christmas. A few more hours had not significantly shortened her life with Daniel. From now on they would be together.

They took their seats on two chairs set at the front of the

room and Luise tried unsuccessfully to still her shaking hands. The second preacher finished his sermon and moved into the marriage vows. In spite of her dreamlike state, Luise managed to answer in the right places, and Daniel's bass voice did the same, sending shivers through her.

"I now pronounce you husband and wife," said Minister Peters. "Whom God hath joined together, let no man separate."

Luise wanted to shout, but she reined in her emotions and walked sedately from the church on Daniel's arm. After all, she was now a married woman and must act as such.

The program that followed the ceremony seemed to go on forever, filled with singing, more sermons, recitations and best wishes, but Luise determined to enjoy and remember it as another of her treasures. She knew the plates of zwieback at *Faspa* had meant sacrifice for the women who had little enough cream and butter and sugar, but chose to share it with her and Daniel for this celebration. Someone had even found some sugar cubes for the bridal couple's *Prips*. The barley coffee hadn't tasted so sweet in a long while.

"Where have you decided to take your new bride?" asked Luise as Daniel led her out of the church.

"You shall see, my dear. It is not far."

He helped her into his buggy and Prince pranced ahead.

"Now close your eyes until we get there."

Luise did as he directed, but soon realized he was doubling back to confuse her.

"We should be out of town by now, Daniel. Wherever are you taking me?"

"Don't peek. We have arrived."

He lifted her down and carried her inside a building, then invited her to open her eyes. Manya's cottage. She laughed as he explained how the old woman had joyfully offered the use of her house and asked him to move her things to the Letkemann's home in anticipation of the journey east.

As they entered Manya's little bedroom, Luise noted the care the old woman had taken to make them feel special, perhaps remembering her own wedding night a lifetime ago. A brightly colored quilt covered a freshly made bed, a flask of water and two cups perched on a box beside the bed, and a rag rug adorned the recently scrubbed floorboards.

Daniel cleared his throat and held out his arms for her, and suddenly Luise froze. As much as she had longed to be Daniel's wife, to share his life and his bed, she had not anticipated the confusion she felt at this moment. All her life she had kept herself pure, her actions, her words, her thoughts, and now she felt as if she were giving in to what she had always held distant. As if it were a sin.

"Luise?" Daniel tilted his head, questions in his eyes.

She licked her lips and swallowed, then pushed the prudish thoughts from her mind and walked into his arms. Her voice muffled in his chest, she whispered, "How can I convince myself this is acceptable to God?"

He stood unmoving for a few moments, then gently led her to the bed and sat on it with her beside him. He began to speak and it was a moment before she realized he did not speak to her.

"We are so thankful for this day, for this joining of our lives and our families. But it's all so new, Lord, and we ask for Thy love to cover us, for Thy blessing to descend upon us. Give Luise—my wife—peace for both the present and the future. We thank Thee in Jesus' name..."

"Amen," they said together.

Luise forgot about the house and her surroundings then, her eyes only for Daniel, but when she awoke to the morning sun streaming across the bed, and her head on Daniel's bare shoulder, she leaped from the bed in alarm. Daniel jerked up as well, blinking sleep from his eyes.

"Luise? What is it?" He rubbed his hands over his face. "Have I turned into an ogre during the night?" His eyes traveled the length of her.

Luise felt her face flush hot, and slipped back under the covers. "I forgot."

"What did you forget?" His voice held a teasing tone now that caught her heart and flipped it over. "That when you get married you have to take the groom home?"

She ducked her head into his shoulder and mumbled, "I forgot it was right."

"What's that?" He found her face and kissed her passionately.

Daniel held her face between his hands. "Luise, who do you think invented marriage? God smiles on our joy. It is His design for us." He held her to him and she relaxed into his embrace.

It would take her some time, she decided, to think of their relationship as normal. To exult in years of dreams coming true. It was indeed a strange and wonderful reality. A prayer for peace slipped from her soul to the Father, and she returned Daniel's embrace. In the centre of this love, she could withstand anything.

At that moment a desperate pounding on the door sent Daniel scurrying for his clothes. Luise did the same, wondering who would bother newlyweds so early the morning after their wedding.

Chapter Nine

Seeing his brother Johannes through the window, Daniel hesitated in answering, but something about the boy's attitude convinced him the message was urgent.

Daniel opened the door and his little brother rushed inside and clung to him, burying his gutteral sobs in his elder brother's shirt.

"What is it, Jo—"

"It's Papa." The boy's cry was muffled. "He fell down dead."

Daniel felt the earth shift beneath his feet and he pulled Johannes away from him. "Dead? How could he be…"

"He was very angry, and then…he fell down and jerked and didn't get up. Mama couldn't wake him."

In a fog of disbelief, Daniel reached for his jacket and, pulling Luise along by the hand, started running toward his home.

"When did this happen, Johannes?" gasped Luise.

"Just now. He fell. Mama screamed, told me to get help."

"Why was Father angry?" asked Daniel as they neared the house.

"The officials," panted Johannes. "They came for the Fordson tractor. Said he must bring it before dark tonight to the volost office."

Daniel heard wailing as they ran through the garden gate. He pushed through the door, followed by Luise and Johannes. His mother sat in her chair in the parlor, rocking back and forth, her apron cast up over her face, her hands holding it there as if to hide from the reality of what had happened.

Peter Martens' body lay stretched out on the divan, his daughters hovering around, their faces streaked with tears. Luise went to comfort Greidl, and Daniel stood staring at his father.

"So he is dead." Daniel could not fathom his father falling prey so suddenly, due to a fit of anger. He had always been one whose ire could be swiftly aroused, but Daniel had never thought it would snatch him so suddenly from this life.

Luise pulled up a chair beside Greidl and managed to draw a few words from her, bringing her back to the present. Daniel was glad Luise had come with him. A woman in grief needed another woman, the comforting sounds women made that men did not understand.

Daniel watched his sisters, his mother and his brother as if from afar. His wedding, waking up with Luise in his arms, his dreams for a life with her, all seemed to desensitize him to the reality of his father lying dead. He stared dumbly, numbly, until a roar formed inside, rising in volume until he thought his head would burst. He smacked his fist into his palm and marched out the back door into the yard, to the nearly completed house he had built for Luise.

He stepped through the doorway and walked through the house, his boots loud on the bare floors. What now? He needed—wanted to give his time to his wife, but his family depended on him as the eldest child to take up where his father had stopped. Picking up a hammer, he hurled it against the wall, where it made a dent and fell heavily to the floor. Why had his father left him with such a burden so soon after he and Luise had married?

Daniel returned to the house. His hand shook as he opened the back door, and he heard his mother sobbing. Luise should not shoulder this burden. He set aside his anger and took charge. What happened next was up to him.

"Mother, I will go fetch the doctor and we will see to

Father. Girls, call a few of the neighbor ladies to come help out. Johannes, go find Minister Peters and ask him to come to the house." He wanted to ask Luise to go with him, to hold his hand and give him strength, but he knew he must find his own strength. She would need all of hers.

"Shall I go, Daniel?" asked Luise. "You could stay with your mother."

"No, I will go if you don't mind staying." Her sad smile answered his plea for strength as she walked with him to the door. She kissed him before he left the house.

When Luise returned to the parlor, she saw Greidl's chair empty and heard the sobs again. Her mother-in-law knelt beside the divan on which her husband lay and embraced his still form. Luise stepped back through the doorway to give the woman privacy. She would get little of it once word spread of Peter's death.

If her Daniel had died, she would want time alone with him too. She supposed that in the days to come, she would be spending more time here than she had earlier thought, although the girls, Hannah and Maria, were physically able to take care of the house and their mother. Well, it would give her an added responsibility to make up for the emptiness of her family's leaving. *All things work together for good to them that love God and are called according to His purpose.*

After stopping at Dr. Schmidt's house beside the school building, Daniel walked back along Main Street, past the flour mill and the volost office. He remembered when his father and Luise's father had both sat on the volost committee for Alexandrovka and area, making informed and reasonable decisions about the life and future of the villages. Perhaps if they were still allowed their say, his father would not be dead.

The door of the volost office opened as Daniel passed by and Leonid Dubrowsky stepped out into his path.

"Speak of the devil!" he said. "Where is your father? He has disobeyed orders. Tell him to come immediately."

Daniel stiffened. "He is not available to you."

"Not available? He does not choose. Perhaps I will lock you up too."

If it had not been for Daniel's grief he would have taken delight at the irony of this little interchange. Instead, he said, "You will find him at home, but he will not speak to you, nor will he give you what you want."

"You cur." The snarl fit the name he called Daniel. "He will speak. He will hand over the tractor or we take him too. It is very cold where he will go after."

"He doesn't care about the tractor anymore, and he will not go with you. There is nothing more you can do to him."

Light began to dawn in Dubrowsky's eyes. "What do you say?"

"He's dead, Dubrowsky. You killed him with your ridiculous demands. Why could you not leave him alone? His entrepreneurial spirit helped many people in the colony and would have made it prosperous but this regime would not allow it."

Dubrowsky took a limping step to stand directly in front of Daniel. "Do not speak so bold. Perhaps you will take his punishment, eh?"

"Punishment for what? For being a good farmer?" Daniel could not think past his anger. "For working hard and using his brain to develop agriculture in this area? Is that why he was to be punished?"

Dubrowsky narrowed his eyes and stared at Daniel. "You tempt me, boy."

"I am not a boy. I am a man, a married man."

"A married man, you say? Ah. You have taken my little Mennonite sparrow. And I was not even invited."

Daniel tried to change the direction of Dubrowsky's

thoughts. "I have a mind and ideas that could help you and your cause, but instead, you try to ruin me and others like me with preposterous laws that stifle any independent spark. It is independence and individual motivation that foster success, not repression."

"Just like your father. Too bad for you."

"You have had my family in your sights from the beginning. What have we done to deserve this unfortunate attention?"

"It is what you represent, you dirty kulak. Like your father. Like your murdering brothers in Ukraine."

"Ukraine? I have never even been there." Daniel searched his mind for a clue to understand Dubrowsky's rant. He knew of the *Selbstschutz*, the Self Defence Corp instituted by young Mennonite men during the awful days of the revolution in South Russia, but he did not know the details. Had Dubrowsky been there?

"You say you are pacifist, but you are not. You are a hypocrite like the others and you will pay."

The words sounded like a death knell in Daniel's ears, and his gut clenched. Luise had warned him to rein in his tongue with the Bolsheviks. She had told him one day it would bring trouble. That thought reminded Daniel that he needed to get back to Luise and his family.

"Forgive me, I have let my temper rule my words. I should not have spoken thus."

"But you did speak thus, and now I take you for questioning the teachings of the state. I will silence father and son on one day." He moved toward Daniel and grabbed him by the arm.

Daniel tried to wrench from his grasp but Dubrowsky held him firmly, and Daniel knew better than to fight. "I need to see to my father's affairs, to his funeral. I need to look after my mother."

Dubrowsky marched toward headquarters with Daniel in tow, the officer's limp not slowing his progress. Sweat ran down Daniel's body in spite of the coolness of the spring air, and he began to understand, with rising fear, that he had become the stand-in for someone who had offended Dubrowsky in another time and another place. Ukrainian brothers? Self-defense corp? What did he know of those?

"You should better think before you talk."

Dubrowsky's voice had taken on a cold, metallic tone that Daniel could almost taste. He tried to swallow but his mouth had gone dry. His mind raced as he contemplated the situation he had created for himself. Think first, speak later, his mother had said, though he didn't remember her clinging to that adage any more than he did. And his father always spoke what was on his mind. When he considered the Martens family from a Bolshevik viewpoint, he realized why they had been oft threatened. Now the Reds would have their vengeance. But there must be some way out. After all, he had only celebrated his wedding yesterday. Surely they wouldn't...he refused to think further. He would be back home with Luise in a few hours.

"Where is Daniel?" Luise had been thinking the words, but it was her sister-in-law Maria who voiced them.

The doctor had come and gone, the neighbors had arrived and were preparing the body for the funeral—they needed to have the service before the families left for the east—Minister Peters had stopped by to pray with the family and offer condolences, but Daniel had not returned.

"Shall I go find him?" Johannes seemed eager for an excuse to escape the heaviness that cloaked the Martens house.

"Yes, try," said Luise, "but be discreet. We do not wish the whole village to come yet. There will be time for that tomorrow."

She watched Johannes dart out the door and wished she too could leave, but the women needed someone to stabilize them. She would not leave until Daniel returned and took charge. Where could he be? She felt confusion at all that had happened in the last twenty-four hours. As much as she dreaded bidding her family farewell, she longed to return to some kind of normal routine, to a certain sense of security in knowing what each day would bring.

Half an hour later, Johannes burst through the door, eyes wide, breathing hard. "They've got him."

Luise ran forward to calm him. "Take a breath, Johannes. Who has whom?"

"The Reds!" His voice rose in pitch and volume. "They have arrested Daniel."

Luise held Johannes' arm and stared at him. Behind her she heard Hannah and Maria begin to wail. No, this could not be real. Not now. Surely those men still had the decency to respect a death in the family. And why would they take Daniel?

"With what is he charged?" she demanded of Johannes.

Tears forced themselves from his eyes as he answered her. "I don't know. They would not let me talk to him. He is at the volost office. I came back as fast as I could to tell you."

Luise pulled on her coat as she spoke to Daniel's sisters. "I am going to get my father. Take care of things here until I get back." Then she turned to Johannes. "Do not give up hope. Perhaps we can reverse this decision and bring Daniel back with us tonight yet. Help your sisters here, will you?"

He nodded dumbly and squared his shoulders, swiping unbidden tears from his cheeks. Luise hurried out into the evening with prayers for her husband ascending to heaven like flocks of desperate doves.

Daniel's defenses were down. Opening his heart and soul to Luise had so consumed him these last hours that he had all but forgotten the state of political affairs in Alexandrovka. He had put everything out of his mind except Luise. His Luise. Staring at her blanched face now from his room at the back of the volost office, he felt a sharp pain in his chest. She stood at the office door, eyes darting from him to Dubrowsky. Abram waited helpless behind her.

"What is the nature of your request?"

"I wish to see my husband."

"We tell you when to come."

Dubrowsky slammed the door in her face, and the sound reverberated in Daniel's ears like a shot fired from a gun. What now? Would they let him go home if he cooperated, or would they send him away without a farewell?

Dubrowsky limped over to where Daniel stood and stared at him through the opening in the door. "Fine little woman you have, Martens. Pray nothing happens to her." He turned and walked back to his desk.

Beads of sweat formed along Daniel's hairline. "What more do you want from me? You already told me you plan to take the tractor, and all the remaining grain in storage. My father is already dead. What can I offer for my freedom, for my wife's safety?"

Dubrowsky did not even turn to look at him. "Do not look for a conscience; I have none."

"But surely there is no reason to keep me here."

"Shut up your nagging. You are worse than a wife." He cast a cheerless laugh back to Daniel. "Think what I save you from."

His laugh chilled Daniel to the core, freezing his hope into a block of ice. Never before had he felt so much anguish with so little idea of what to do about it. He was a man of action; it drove him crazy to sit waiting for something completely beyond his control. Last winter in the forest he had hard work to keep him occupied. If things did not improve, he would probably have similar work to do again, only without promise of return.

He prayed as intensely as he knew Luise must be praying. He knew of angels that had opened prison doors because of prayer. Perhaps it would happen again. He held his head in his hands and beat upon heaven's gates throughout the long night.

⁂

The morning light had no sooner filtered through the dirty windows of the volost office than Daniel heard a knock on the door. Earlier that morning, Dubrowsky had gone, replaced by Commissar Victor Magadan, who had been with him at the schoolroom fiasco. Daniel watched through the small open window in the door of his room as Magadan rose to answer the knock. Abram stood framed by the doorway, his arm about Luise's shoulders.

"We beg permission to visit the prisoner."

Magadan stood staring, then said, "Dubrowsky will be back soon, then you must leave." His gaze lingered on Luise, and Daniel's ire rose, but he did not speak. He would not jeopardize this opportunity, since his prison doors had not flown open during the night, not even in his dreary dreams.

Luise ran to Daniel and reached for him through the opening.

"Give me a moment, woman, and I will open the cage."

Daniel could not believe Magadan would consider allowing Luise into his room. Perhaps God was working in unexpected ways. Daniel would take whatever small crumbs of blessing fell around him.

As soon as the door was unlocked and opened, Luise slipped through and into Daniel's arms. He held her to himself as if she were the missing part of him.

"Luise! Thank God I can hold you once again." He whispered the words into her hair, all rational thoughts suspended.

He brushed away her tears with his thumb. "Do not cry. This is a good sign, is it not? That they let you in?"

"Oh Daniel. This is like the candy the witch gave to Hansel and Gretel. It is sweet and alluring but will lead only to sorrow."

"Did Anna tell you that?" He whispered the words for

her ears only and she whispered back.

"Not her exact words, but sometimes she knows things. What if you are taken away? How will I ever survive? We've only just begun our journey together. One night, Daniel. One night."

He held her face in his hands, ever so gently, and looked deeply into her eyes. The pain and fear he saw there hit him like a blow beneath the ribs, but he swallowed and said, "I am yours always, Luise. What we have promised will never be altered or forgotten. I love you. Now listen to me: You must help me by being strong."

Her gaze flitted from one eye to the other and Daniel watched determination replace the fear. "First I am to be strong for Papa, now for you. Who will be strong for me?"

Daniel signaled for Abram to approach and the three of them knelt on the cold stone floor to pour out their hearts in prayer.

"Get up!" Magadan's voice scattered their prayers. "Dubrowsky is coming. Go now."

Abram lifted Luise to her feet and clasped his son-in-law in a wordless embrace. Luise gave him one more longing hug and Abram pulled her gently away.

"I will come again later," she said, walking backward to keep his face in sight.

Daniel watched her go and felt his heart die within him. When would this nightmare end? The sun had risen and still it persisted.

Chapter Ten

Luise wept as she gathered her nightdress and personal items from Tante Manya's cottage and stuffed them into a pillowcase. She had no alternative but to return to her father's house now that Daniel had been apprehended. As she walked through the door of her parents' home, her small bundle of clothes under her arm, Luise heard Anna's cough and the words that followed it.

"I told you to pack for the trip, Luise. There is Peter Martens' funeral this afternoon and we leave two days from now. You must be ready to come with us."

Luise turned to Abram, but he shrugged and looked away.

Tante Manya rocked in Anna's chair, knitting something green, no doubt unraveled from an old sweater. "Welcome back, child," she said. "It has been hard for you."

Luise knelt beside Tante Manya's chair and felt the familiar roughness of the old woman's hand on her cheek. "I think I am beginning to understand some of the suffering you must have gone through in your life."

"Life is not easy, but it is a proving ground for us poor sinners, a winnowing in the wind. The chaff flies away but the true seed remains. You are true seed, Luise. Now, I believe Anna has baked more zwieback that need to be roasted and packed away for our journey."

Rising from the floor, Luise climbed a few rungs to the attic and tossed her bundle up. Until Daniel comes home, she thought.

She attended the hastily planned funeral for Daniel's father later that afternoon, sat with his family at the front of the church, endured stares and whispers, soaked up the sorrow-filled love from Valentina's hug, then escaped to spend the rest of the day helping Hans and Nela pack their few belongings. She roasted zwieback in a slow oven and cooled them on the table before packing them into sacks to take on the train to Blagoveshchensk. The activities proved a good diversion, but thoughts of Daniel imprisoned in the volost office and her family's imminent departure never left her mind.

Daniel could not believe the circumstance in which he now found himself. He had not been allowed to attend his own father's funeral before they shipped him out. Not even a goodbye to his wife or his family. Only a fleeting glimpse of Johannes hiding behind Friesen's shed next door to the volost office.

The rickety wagon in which Daniel rode threatened to break apart, much like his heart, at every bump in the rutted road heading north from Alexandrovka. He had no delusions that everything would work itself out, but he had certainly not expected to be sent away so soon. In fact, he had retained hope that he would be allowed to return home to care for his grieving family. Why had Dubrowsky sent him off so quickly? And why had Mr. Thiessen and the Enns brothers from Ebenfeld also been arrested? There were more men he didn't even know.

He supposed their crimes must be similar to his: owning more than one's neighbors. Everything was to be shared equally in this new regime, but he knew as well as anyone that some people were always more equal than others in a communist state. It was the way of greed and power and would be so until Christ ruled on this earth.

Slumped over with helplessness, Daniel imagined Luise's ashen face when Johannes told her of his exile. He moaned aloud and felt a hand on his shoulder. He saw the face of Klaas Enns through a blur of unshed tears.

"Do not give up hope," the man said in a barely audible whisper. "All is not lost."

Enns dropped his hand and his gaze when Dubrowsky pulled up beside the wagon. "No talk from the prisoners," he growled. "Save your strength for survival."

Daniel's eyes widened as he looked up at Dubrowsky.

"That's my horse," he rasped, but even as the words left his lips he knew he had no recourse but to accept this added blow. The man was out to break him, bone by bone. He must resist the urge to give in. He had too much to lose.

Prince nickered at the sight of him and tossed his head, but Dubrowsky yanked the reins and turned him away. Daniel felt the pain as if the bit were in his own mouth.

As Luise prepared to set out for another visit with Daniel after Peter Martens' funeral, a knock sounded on the door. She answered, since Abram was busy in his shop, packing up whatever was not bolted down. Johannes poked his head in, his hair sticking straight out like fresh straw from beneath his *peltzmetz*. Luise read dismay and fear in his large blue eyes, feelings all too familiar to her.

"They've sent Daniel north."

"What do you mean? Have they sentenced him? He didn't have a trial." She pulled her shawl from a peg and pushed outside past Johannes, knowing her reasoning did not matter to the GPU. "How do you know this?"

"I saw it. They brought a wagon and loaded up Daniel with some men from other villages and said he would be going very far away and I was lucky to be as young as I was or I'd have to go too, 'cuz I'm the son of a dirty kulak."

They ran down the main street side by side, Luise with one hand holding up her skirts, the other pulling the shawl together at the front, her eyes focused straight ahead to where she had last seen Daniel. She had held him and he had promised to love her forever. Neither of them had heretofore considered how long forever might be. Together it would pass in a twinkling, but apart it would stretch on endlessly.

Luise pounded on the volost office door and threw it open. Inside, Victor Magadan leaned over the desktop, filling in charts. He jerked perceptibly when the pair entered, a frown replacing the intensity on his face.

"What is the meaning of this intrusion?" he demanded.

She sent up a prayer of thanks that she would not have to confront Dubrowsky. "I'm sorry to interrupt you," she said, "but I have just received word the Daniel Martens is to be transferred to another place. I wish to see him before he goes."

"You are too late; he is gone. Now you must leave. I have work to do."

Luise could not give up so easily. "Where are they taking him and for how long?"

"North," he said, meeting her eyes, and for a moment she sensed a snippet of compassion. The realization gave her courage to continue.

"They must have a destination. They wouldn't just drive and then dump him off somewhere."

He shrugged and aimed his words at Johannes. "It has been done. What Dubrowsky does with them is up to him."

Luise's panic rose. "Dubrowsky went with them?"

"I should have consulted you first?"

His bantering tone unleashed a stream of words from her lips that she would have thought might come from Daniel. "My husband and his family helped their neighbors. Someone had to take charge. All you and your government have done is discourage progress, driving the economy into the ground. At least they—"

Magadan's chair fell backward as he pushed to his feet. Several books cascaded from a dusty shelf to the floor, and Luise's speech ended with the thud. The official moved around the desk while Luise and Johannes backed toward the door. He was even taller than she remembered. "You, young woman, are in danger of offending me and my government. Women can also be exiled, you know, and you would not be sent to the same place as your man, so I suggest you go back home and stay there."

His eyes now were black as coal and unreadable. Shaking with fear and fury, Luise and Johannes fled. Some distance away, they stopped of one accord and leaned against the side of an outbuilding. "Why could they not tell me where and for how long? Would that be breaking the law?"

Johannes patted her arm uncertainly. "I'm sorry Luise. I will try to find out."

"How can you do that? If we go back—"

"They do not always see me. I'm just a child playing with a stick. I will listen and see what I can find out."

She reached out and touched the brim of his hat. "You are a dear brother, Johannes. Just promise me you will be careful."

"I promise. I will see you home and then come back." The maturity and courage in his blue eyes so similar to Daniel's eyes tore at Luise's heart. He was too young to endure this evil. She felt she had aged decades over the last day.

She trudged like an old woman toward her father's house, or what would be his house for two more days. Johannes walked by her side like a military attaché, matching his steps to hers, glancing at her from time to time, helping her up the stairs. She hugged him before entering the house and he ran back in the direction from which they had come.

Later, when the dilapidated wagons stopped to rest the horses, Daniel sought out Klaas Enns again. "Why are you here?"

"Same as you, I expect. I work hard, help others, and make a little money along the way. God has blessed me."

Daniel nodded. "Right now I wish we had not been so blessed. My father died yesterday so they took me instead. But he would not have lasted. He always spoke his mind and they were watching him. Besides, he had a bad heart, got too excited about things." Daniel's heart quaked within him as he spoke of his father's death. Had it really happened? Had it been just yesterday?

"I knew your father. A good man, but too outspoken. Seems to me if we want to survive we have to learn to say less than we think."

Daniel glanced about and saw Dubrowsky facing away from them, talking to the wagoneer.

"Where do you think they're taking us?"

"Don't know the answer to that question. Sometimes they let you go, sometimes they keep you, depends on their whim."

They paced the area, working the numbness from their legs and backsides, and Daniel asked, "Did you leave a family behind?"

Enns glanced up through lowered bushy brows. "My wife, Tena, and five children. We had just purchased the property of one of the families leaving for the east. I don't know what they will do." He stared at the ground, then blinked and asked, "You?"

Daniel blew out his breath. "I got married two days ago, and now my mother is also alone with my two sisters and younger brother."

Enns stared at him, pity etched on his features.

Daniel glanced at Dubrowsky, frustration squeezing his resolve to remain calm. "And he stole my horse." Perhaps he could slip into the birches and disappear, retrieve Prince and ride away. But they would know his destination and bring him back here again. No, next time they would just shoot him. When he looked up Dubrowsky watched him, gun at the ready, and Daniel realized he would have to plan carefully to carry out an escape.

If only he could talk to Luise, tell her to go east with her family. Then she wouldn't be alone and maybe by some chance or divine intervention, he could meet her there. But right now, intervention of any kind seemed highly unlikely.

⁂

"I think that when we go to to Blagoveshchensk, you should come with us."

"I must be here when Daniel returns. I will not leave." Luise turned from her father where he sat at his workbench, planer in hand. "I'm going to help Mother pack."

Abram stood and moved between her and the door. "Hear me out, Luise."

Frowning, she nodded and sat on a stool. Her father paced the room as he spoke.

"Forty-one other families are preparing to leave day after tomorrow. I have been listening around the village, and I've overheard some of the activists talking. You are suspect because you are my daughter—I have been arrested for speaking God's Word, remember—and because you are the wife, however new, of a confirmed kulak. I do not think I could bear it if you disappeared, or if they…hurt you in any way.

"And to leave you here alone to wait for Daniel would be unthinkable. The times have become more difficult and this is no longer a safe place. Come to the Amur Region with the rest of us and settle there. Everyone here will know where you have gone if Daniel comes back— "

"*When* Daniel comes back. He will come back, Papa."

"So we hope and pray. Lise, if I were Daniel, I would want you to go. He would never expect you to remain here alone. The Martens family has decided to go east as well. The women have nothing left here and no one to do the work if they did. The boy is too young for that level of responsibility."

"I worry about what is happening to Daniel, what they are doing to him, how hard he will have to work. And then to return and find me gone…what if…"

"We must trust the Lord to care for us and bring us together again, if it is His will."

Luise felt bereft as she thought of Daniel and of her impending decision. How could she trust that she and Daniel would be together again? How could she leave Alexandrovka without him? All her hopes and dreams had been situated right here, but as much as she hated to acknowledge it, her father was right. Daniel would want her to go.

Luise entered the house and climbed the ladder to the attic. She reached into the corner behind her meager wardrobe and pulled out her mother's violin. Sitting on the bed, she began to play music that mirrored her mood, hymns mingled with sad folksongs and wordless melodies.

"Luise!" Anna's harsh voice cut through the fragile peace that enveloped her. "Luise, put that instrument away. I've told you I do not wish to hear you play. It grates on my nerves."

"You grate on my nerves," muttered Luise. She knew it was not the music that offended Anna but the fact that the violin had belonged to Abram's first wife, Sarah, Luise's own mother. While the music soothed her, it seemed to torment Anna.

Luise replaced the violin behind her clothes. She would gather strength from these few moments of music and save her desire to play for a time when Anna was not within earshot, but that would not happen soon if Luise went with them to the east. The music called to her. As long as Abram was present, Anna dared not deny her that outlet, but when he was not, the rules changed.

She expected Anna to demand that she leave the violin behind, but Luise was adamant. She would not abandon the last memento of her dear mother, no matter what the repercussions.

The horse trader, Josiah Marcowiscz, watched the procession from the top of the hill overlooking Alexandrovka. Wagon after wagon of household goods, packed and stacked and tied with heavy ropes. Children running alongside or leaning out the back. The family cow tied on behind. A lifetime crammed into a wagon or two.

He saw a young woman in one of the wagons, Daniel's woman he thought, sitting beside an old babushka. The younger one turned her whole body around to look back until the hill blocked his view of her.

The entire exodus seemed to him a forced exile. He raised his chin as he watched. His was a gypsy life; he did not need a home. But these were people of the land, industrious folk who thrived on organization and cooperation, who lived in community and looked after one another. The Stalinist system was intent on robbing them of their independence, and Marcowiscz didn't believe they could function without it. Perhaps that was the intention.

His anger flared within him at the thought of Daniel Martens exiled to the northern forests. If only he had handled his tongue as well as he handled horses. How many times had Marcowiscz warned Daniel to keep his opinions to himself?

Marcowiscz would voice his opinions to no man; he was a survivor. But his heart went out to these people. His own people, the Jews, also suffered, as did Catholics, Lutherans, Ukrainians, Russians. It mattered not to the GPU. Their mandate of coercion and enforcement held no respect for race, creed or age. In fact, it held no respect for anything but power.

His horse shook its head, jingling the bridle. Marcowiscz reined it around and rode back into the village. He would complete his dealings here and move on to the bazaars in Omsk, where he would purchase a couple of Altai horses for his journey through the north country. They came at a good price this time of year. He would put this injustice out of his mind and concentrate on his horses. And yet the plight of Russia's people marked itself on his mind.

As Luise looked back at the village of Alexandrovka disappearing over the hill, memories of her life in the village tugged at her: running to Tante Manya's house, bringing the cows home from pasture, playing her violin at singings and weddings, walking hand-in-hand with Daniel down one of the field roads, their wedding, their night in Tante Manya's cottage.

Household goods and foodstuffs filled the space all around her and Tante Manya, things they would need on the journey and at their destination. Everyone left behind memories; some sweet, others bitter. In the wagon behind them her father had packed his wordworking tools, pails and forks for feeding the animals. Their milk cow was tethered on behind, hips swaying as she followed.

Luise felt cheated. She remembered her night with Daniel, she longed for him with every fiber of her being. Oh God, why did you give me a taste of heaven, only to leave me empty and alone. Quiet tears slipped down her cheeks and she turned her face away from her family.

Her father had sold everything that was not packed in the wagons. Luise owned nothing of her own except her mother's violin. She had nothing with which to set up a household. They had received some gifts of furniture for their wedding, but she could not take them with her. In any case, she wouldn't need to set up house until Daniel returned. He would return. He must. Otherwise how would she survive? With one last look behind her, she abandoned herself to the sorrow of leaving the place she had called home.

"You will survive."

Luise glanced at Tante Manya without responding, and

then leaned into the train car to retrieve a sack of zwieback and a block of cheese for supper.

They had repacked all their belongings, including the wagons, animals, implements and household goods, into train cars at Slavgorod station and continued north to Tatarskaia. From here they would join the Trans-Siberian Railroad for the rest of the journey to Blagoveshchensk, but at the present time, Luise must serve some sort of supper.

The firm ground felt good beneath her feet, a respite from the restless rocking of the train, and she blessed Lena Sawatsky for inviting Anna to sit with her and visit while Abram spoke with the men.

"I'm not sure I want to survive," she said at last. "I have an ache in my chest that makes it difficult to breathe."

Tante Manya smiled. "God seems to believe you capable of a great deal, my child."

"I wish He did not trust me so."

"Hah. You will not disappoint Him."

"You have more faith in me than I do in myself, Tante Manya. If I think further than this day, desperation threatens." She found a knife and set about slicing the cheese.

"Nah, Lise, we do not give in to desperation. We persevere, as God's children are meant to do. Besides, God has blessed us by allowing Abram to come back to us."

"Of course I am thankful every day that Papa was allowed to return to us, but the days are so long without Daniel, without knowing where he is or what is happening to him, or if we shall ever see each other again." She stopped slicing and fixed her eyes on the old woman. "It's not likely, is it?"

The old woman shrugged. "Who can say? We must live one day at a time. You can no more deal with the troubles of your whole life at once than you can make all the meals for the entire journey this day."

Luise resumed her work. "I dislike uncertainty, and

here we are in a strange place with no home to speak of. I ask for God's strength, but I don't receive it. I must push through on my own, it seems."

Tante Manya leaned back against the side of the rough plank wall of the station and winced. "God does not give us more than we can bear. Our part is not to question but to obey."

Luise lay awake for a long time that night in the crowded rail car, watching the stars twinkle through the open door, listening to the drone of mosquitoes in the night, thinking about what Manya had said. Did God really know how much was enough for her? What lessons were she and Daniel supposed to learn through this tearing of their hearts? She knew in her head that she would not likely see him again, but her heart still held out hope, still believed against all the odds. She hugged herself and trembled with grief.

Daniel lay awake watching the stars twinkle, listening to the mosquitoes buzz in the darkness. With no roof over his head, he could imagine he was on a hunting expedition with his friends, Phillip and Jasch, except for the guards patrolling the campsite. The stars reminded him of God, distant and unreachable, and he turned onto his side. He wanted to curse and holler, but he could not even do that without punishment.

He missed Luise with a pain like a severed limb. What was she doing tonight? Was she lying alone in Manya's house or had Abram persuaded her to accompany them east? He had faith that Abram had prevailed. Without that belief, his pain would be even more acute. No father would leave his daughter alone in danger of arrest or worse.

He, Daniel, should be taking care of his new wife, should be lying beside her now, loving her as he had promised to do a few short days ago. Instead, he traveled ever farther north, on a wagon path paralleling the railway.

Tomorrow they would reach Novosibirsk. Perhaps he could slip away in the city. The idea gave him something to think on while he waited for sleep to interrupt his circular thoughts.

Chapter Eleven

Daniel had been to Novosibirsk many times, only then he had possessed the freedom to move about as he pleased. Now he sat on a wagon, shackled to a dozen other enemies of the state, praying that God would intervene and set him free.

On the short journey thus far, his eyes and ears had been wide to the opportunity for escape, but as long as the thick rope linked their steel wristcuffs together, that would be nearly impossible. Yet he would not give up. Luise could not come to him, so he must go to her. He must escape.

However, it was Daniel's own words that robbed him of the opportunity. He recognized the shortness of his temper, but when Dubrowsky consistently mistreated Klaas Enns, Daniel could not stand by without reacting. His own father had been buried only two days past, and Daniel's grief translated to the man currently under the whip.

"Only cowards pick on those who cannot defend themselves." Daniel's words, spoken aloud and in the hearing of the entire group including the other guards, surprised even him. But the deed was done, the sentence pending. Oh yes, he was his father's son.

Dubrowsky pushed Enns into a puddle in the alley where they had stopped. The rest of the men staggered and some fell as the rope connecting them tightened. Then he limped up to Daniel, his whip smacking the palm of his gloved hand. "Smart-mouthed cur," he said. "I will teach you to question me."

When Dubrowsky brought the whip up to strike, Daniel inhaled and prepared for the lashing. The first swipe caught him across one cheek, but he refused to cry out. Dubrowsky struck him savagely several more times and would have continued, but at that moment, two finely clad women stepped past the alley, all eyes and exclamations, and the senior-major dropped his arm. But the deed had been done and Daniel's resolve deepened. He would live, he would escape, and he would make this man pay when he did.

A soft voice in his heart hinted at love and forgiveness, *for they know not what they do,* but each time rawhide met flesh, more hatred rose inside him, and he pushed the soft voice back. They had killed his father, robbed him of his livelihood and his wife, and taken his freedom. But he would defeat them, however long that might take. If God would not help him, he would help himself.

As he stared back at Dubrowsky through swelling eyes, he knew the man understood. Daniel had been and still was an enemy of the state in Dubrowsky's eyes, as well as the object of his personal vengeance, but now the vendetta had become mutual and they both knew it.

"I watch you," said Dubrowsky, dropping his arm to his side in obvious exhaustion, and Daniel felt hatred like a flash of lightning between them.

The train rocked relentlessly and Luise tried to find a more comfortable position on the hard seat. Outside the dirty window, the kilometers flew by at an alarming rate. She rubbed the glass with a hanky and stared out as the train rumbled through another deep mountain gorge, high walls of stone rising majestically on both sides of the track. She wondered what kind of people existed in those mountains, isolated by such wild beauty. Life was full of contrast, life and death always in a tug-of-war, vulnerable strength, fragile beauty.

The train pulled out of the gorge into brilliant sunshine, then dipped into another valley. Luise stared at her own reflection in the window of the train and imagined the excitement of this journey with Daniel's face beside hers, but if he were with her, they would have remained in Alexandrovka. Here she was, chugging into the unknown without her husband. Was this truly God's plan?

Her reflection frowned at her and she looked away. She eased Nela's drooping head onto her lap and brushed her curls out of her eyes. Across the aisle, Hans knelt on the seat, eyes glued to the changing scenery outside his window. Life would always be an adventure for him, no matter what obstacles presented themselves. She whispered a prayer for both children and determined to make their unsettled condition as pleasant as possible. She would learn to grieve in private.

Luise glanced out her window again and gasped, overwhelmed by the scene before her. Lake Baikal. The conductor had talked of it this morning, describing it as one of the largest bodies of fresh water on earth, and definitely the deepest. Those were the statistics.

The reality was a gigantic basin of aquamarine sea fading to the green of an emerald, reflecting mountains and sky, sparkling in sunlight so bright it was almost blinding, its rim stretching to the farthest horizon. The railroad followed the southern shore, with the rugged Chamar-Daban Mountains overlooking it like huge folds pushed up from the earth.

The train engines chuffed clouds of black smoke as they strained around the curved rails. The other cars followed behind, looking like the toy train Abram had carved for Hans last Christmas.

Around the next corner a tunnel blocked Luise's view. She wondered how the engineers had managed to blast a path through tons of rock. How many lives had been lost so she could ride through? Nothing we do is lost, she thought. She allowed her head to fall against the back of the seat. There would be much to do when they arrived at their destination. It would be best to indulge in a little rest while she could.

⁂

The rest of the journey north from Novosibirsk had dulled in Daniel's memory, as had the days since his arrival at the destination. It had not been an actual camp they had stopped at that cool spring day, but a drop-off point several days past the last village through which they had passed.

"Must be the end of the world," said Klaas Enns when Dubrowsky moved out of earshot.

"Might as well be," lisped Daniel through swollen lips.

He felt Enns's stare but refused to look him in the eye.

"Even the end of the world is not beyond the Lord's sight, young man. 'I will be with you, even to the ends of the earth,' so says the Lord in Scripture."

Daniel met his eyes then, one corner of his mouth lifting in a sneer. "With all due respect, if that is true, then He must enjoy watching us squirm and suffer."

"Nah, son, He is not that kind of God."

"What kind is He then? Good, gracious, loving, kind, how do those characteristics fit with what you see?" Daniel lifted his manacled hands, revealing thick scars forming around his wrists. "This life is difficult enough without a God like that."

Enns pinched his lips together and looked away. Daniel felt badly for contradicting the man, after all, they had formed a bond of sorts on the journey northward, but he could no longer see God's hand in his life. It all seemed out of control.

"You have experienced too many blows in quick succession," said Enns. "Do not pronounce judgment on your faith so soon."

"You are correct that I have experienced too much. Every time something good comes to me, it is taken away. I cannot make anything good out of this, I'm afraid. If this is the best God can do, I would rather go it alone."

"I pity you, then. At least I have spiritual comfort in the

midst of this chaos."

Daniel wondered how this humble man retained his strong faith, and wished he could do the same. He turned away as Dubrowsky approached.

"I untie you now," said the GPU official, "but do not attempt escape. You would be dead in three strides."

He looked hard at each man as he unlocked the shackles, and Daniel, for one, believed him. He stifled a gasp as Dubrowsky roughly removed his metal cuffs. Daniel's wrists began to bleed again, the pain throbbing, but he refused to give the brute the satisfaction of revealing the extent of his suffering. If they were allowed any water at all, he must use some to cleanse his sores so they would not fester.

He wondered why he cared, but the truth stared at him every time he closed his eyes. Luise. Her face etched itself on the inside of his eyelids. He had not given up hope of being reunited with her. He would never give up hope, no matter how slim the chance. And so he must fight against infection and illness…and despair.

Dubrowsky's voice interrupted his thoughts. "You will clear the trees from here to that rise. Cut them into boards and use them for shelters. You will build the guards' hut first."

Dubrowsky reached under a tarpaulin in the front of the wagon and pulled out several axes and rusty saws. These he threw on the ground in front of the men and turned away.

One of the men, Jonas Thiessen, ventured a comment. "We would work better if we had sustenance."

Dubrowsky turned back and sneered at them. "Here you earn your food."

He lifted a knapsack from the wagon, found a place to sit beneath a pine tree, and pulled out bread and cheese for himself.

The one who does no work is the one who eats, thought Daniel. He took a breath and opened his mouth, but closed it again, even without the warning look from Klaas Enns. Defeated, he exhaled and reached for an axe. He was hungry, but he was strong. He would endure and he would one day emerge from this place.

ɣ

The wagon ride from Blagoveshchensk, where they had spent more than a month in a large immigration facility, to the village of Shumanovka, seemed long to Luise, even though it took only a few hours. The sun warmed the dry spring air, and little dust devils spun about on the fields bordering the road.

Old Samson clip-clopped his best, but it had been a while since he had pulled a wagon, especially one so heavy. The train ride must have been an unwelcome adventure for him, thought Luise, but he had rested in Balgoveshchensk. Luise jumped out to walk beside him, her limbs aching for exercise and her mind for distraction.

Every kilometer added to the great distance between her and Daniel. She had come east willingly, due to lack of an alternative. She felt completely helpless to change anything regarding her situation. Trust, trust, trust, she repeated in time with Samson's hoofbeats, and began to hum a hymn.

Her father had chosen to relocate to the nearest Mennonite colony, Shumanovka, in the village of the same name. He had also considered the villages of New York and Orlovka, but had decided on Shumanovka in the end, partly because Jakob Siemens said it was a good place to go. Luise respected Jakob Siemens because Papa did, but also because of his organizational skills and calm demeanor. Perhaps the man could keep the Soviet influence from overwhelming them as it had in Alexandrovka.

Luise had heard Siemens speak to their group in Blagoveshchensk, telling them of the government's offer of free land along the Amur. It was good land, said Siemens, rich and potentially productive. The Soviet paid transportation for families and livestock, plus four hundred rubles per family to help them start up. Nothing to sneeze at, he'd said.

If one let go of the past and ventured out to the eastern land, it seemed he would profit by it. Luise certainly hoped so. She needed purpose.

As Samson strained to pull the wagon up a low hill, Luise urged him on. They reached the top and she caught her breath. There in a wide valley lay a village that reminded her very much of Alexandrovka. The main street ran straight through the village, and some homes had already been built on both sides of the street, facing each other, with barns attached behind and fields beyond that—the old but efficient settlement plan conceived by Johann Cornies back in the early 1800s in South Russia. Luise doubted if cherry and pear trees would grow here near the banks of the Amur River with its long, cold winters and short, hot summers, but birch and aspen obviously thrived. And plums would grow, the small tart kind that made tasty perishky.

The orderliness of the village before her gave Luise courage and a sense of belonging, of a wider scope than just her own life. They were a family, these people who had traveled from Slavgorod. They would survive or perish together.

The wagons moved more quickly down the other side of the hill into the village of Shumanovka. Besides the houses that already stood along the straight street, there were also dwellings of dirt, dug into the ground to insulate them from the wind and cold. Temporary dwellings.

Even more temporary would be the Letkemanns' billet with another family until Papa could dig out a dirt hut and then build a house. Luise knew he would need time to build the house and would want it done well. She did not mind living in a dirt hut until then, but the prospect of being billeted with strangers, even fellow Mennonites, caused her some apprehension.

Aaron and Njuta Peters opened their home to the Letkemann family group of six, not entirely from a charitable heart, if Luise understood Njuta correctly. The Peters already had six children of their own, so she could understand their reluctance at bringing in six more people. However, everyone sacrificed for the brethren.

In exchange for lodging, Luise baked bread for the fourteen people crowded into the modest house. She also helped with the general housework and meal preparation. If only Daniel were here, the two of them would live together joyfully in a dirt hut or even a tent. If only. She had thought Anna difficult to live with, but Njuta Peters proved to be another test of her endurance.

"She acts like the queen bee of the hive," Luise told Tante Manya one day in a rare moment of privacy.

"And so she is," replied the old woman. "We would do well to remember that."

"But she treats us as if we were her servants."

"Would you rather live out under the stars?"

"Sometimes."

Tante Manya chuckled, her sagging cheeks jiggling. "Jah, so would I, but my old bones would not endure it."

Luise continued kneading the bread dough. She worried about Tante Manya.

"The journey was too difficult for you." Luise directed the words over her shoulder.

Tante Manya laughed. "Life itself is too difficult, but we cannot resign." Luise saw her grimace as she rubbed her hands together. "Look how crooked they are. I used to have lovely hands. I was young once, you know."

"Tell me about it."

"My, it was so long ago I hardly remember. When I was born, Alexander II ruled Russia. He emancipated the serfs, bless his heart. Left them to starve in freedom. Some radical group tried to assassinate him a few years later, but he was a tough old soldier. They tried again fifteen years after that and succeeded, and Alexander III came into power.

"There was a famine in the country then. I remember it. Those with large families had a difficult time keeping their children fed."

She shook her head and resumed her story.

"Then the Tsar was murdered and Nicholas II became Tsar of all the Russias, heaven help us all."

"Why do you say that?"

"Oh child, he was a decent man, faithful to his loving wife, which is more than can be said for any of his forebears, but he had no idea how to rule a country. He was a socialite, an aristocrat, not a leader. Gradually, he gave in to his wife's nagging and she ran the show—with the advice of that snake, Rasputin. And then the Bolsheviks got Nicholas."

"And his whole family. I heard Neighbor Loewen tell Papa. The government lied to us for years about that."

"Don't put too much stock in what the government says." Tante Manya lowered her voice.

"You don't have to tell me that. I was there when they took Papa..." her voice caught in her throat. She choked out the rest. "...and now they have my Daniel. I don't know if he's dead or alive."

Luise rested her head against the wall for a few moments, and then continued to knead the bread dough. "Please tell me more of your story. It helps pass the time."

"Jah, child. I know how it feels to lose a loved one. I was only ten when my father died of heart failure. He was so young. I remember how he used to stand near the stove and rub his arms because they pained him, and then one night he was gone, just like that." She tried to snap her crooked fingers, but they made no sound. "Mama went to fetch him a drink of water and when she came back to the bed, he was dead."

"I'm sorry, Tante Manya."

The old woman nodded. "Well, there we were, my

mother and I. My elder brothers and sister had married and left home and the two of us were alone. My eldest brother insisted we come to live with him, which we did for a while, but we needed our own house, so we moved into a tiny place on the edge of the village. We missed Papa, but we forged a strong partnership and carried on, Mama sewing and cleaning for people, and me working hard on my schoolwork and helping others with theirs. I loved school. Arithmetic, composition, music, French and Latin, I loved them all and excelled.

"I did my best for Mama's sake and she was proud of me. Then one day a man and his sister came to visit. I assumed it was an ordinary, friendly visit, but he had come to court my mother. I had no idea, and when I realized what was happening, I reacted badly. Mama was lonely and the man was kind, and they were married in spite of my opposition.

"By that time I was of age to marry, so to show my mother that I didn't need her anymore—which was far from true—I married a man who had been frequenting our young people's group at church. He was from a neighboring village and had for some reason taken a fancy to me."

Tante Manya handed her the greased bread pans and Luise formed the loaves and dropped them in, pushing out the air bubbles.

"Tell me about him."

"Ach, it was all so long ago. Another lifetime."

During spring seeding, almost as a sign of welcome, the trees in the village blossomed white like fairy princesses dressed for their weddings. Luise rejoiced in the beauty of it, thanking God for His creativity, even here at the edge of the world. Then two weeks later, the princesses shed their dresses in a summer snow that both charmed and saddened Luise. Withered blossoms littered the ground beneath the trees with the remains of glory. Luise thought of the wedding dress she had sewn with such excitement. It lay packed in the trunk in her small bed-corner and there it would remain.

Instead of digging a dirt hut, Abram set up a large tent-like structure for his family, and then began work on the house. He set up the framework, assisted by men of the village, and then began setting stone upon stone, using mortar he mixed from the mud near the river.

As soon as he had laid down the stone floor, the Letkemanns moved in. Luise breathed a sigh of relief. If not for her wounded heart, she could have more fully enjoyed their new home. Even the Soviet official assigned to the Shumanovka Colony, Yevgeny Rashidov, seemed less threatening than the GPU presence back in Slavgorod. She watched him ride down the streets of the village, nodding to those he met. He looked so young in his Soviet uniform. But she knew better than to trust first impressions.

Besides, Luise was far too busy to mope. She would count her blessings as she worked, she would think of Daniel in private, and she would pray.

Chapter Twelve

"What is with you?"

Tante Manya's words forced Luise to face the facts. She was getting sick. She had tried to bake the bread early in the mornings, before the heat of the summer days descended, and before other chores claimed her attention. The new house was roomy, but not as cool as the open tent.

Apparently, dry heat was normal this time of year, not this unusual humidity that made Luise feel as if she would melt into a puddle. She couldn't seem to crawl out of bed as early as she had planned the evening before. Then, this morning, she felt the first real symptoms of illness. The smell of the softening yeast made her stomach swirl, and then dizziness came upon her in a wave.

"I'm not sure, Tante Manya. I think I must be coming down with something. Or perhaps it's just the heat. I feel I need to sit down or I shall fall." And she sank unceremoniously to the floor and leaned her head back against the wall, thankful that Anna had gone over to visit with Hertha next door.

"Lower your head, child," said Tante Manya. "Keep it down and breathe deeply."

Tante Manya pushed out of her rocking chair and shuffled over to where Luise sat. The old woman's hand on her brow felt comforting and gradually the lightheadedness lessened, but her stomach had not settled. Realizing what was to come, Luise crawled quickly to the back door and lost her breakfast in the flowerbed.

Tante Manya came with a hanky and a cup of water. "Here, drink."

Luise drank and leaned her head against the doorjamb.

"Can you walk now to your room?"

She blinked and nodded. Carefully, not trusting her balance, she rose and leaned on Tante Manya until she reached the safety of her bed.

"Lie down until the feeling passes. I will see to the bread."

"But that's my job. Your hands…"

"These hands have made more bread than you've ever seen. Rest now."

Luise felt her eyes close, and she dozed. When she awoke later, she felt better and ventured into the kitchen. Tante Manya sat near the counter where six loaves tented the tea towels covering them.

"Feeling better, child?"

Luise grimaced and nodded. "Thank you for forming the loaves. They are rising nicely."

"Jah, almost ready for the oven. The stove is hot, as we shall soon all be."

"I can't think what came over me. I feel fine now, but I don't wish for you to catch it."

"I guarantee I will not."

"But how do you know? It could be a type of influenza." Luise wondered where she could go to stop from spreading the disease. Why did God keep sending her trials?

"I do not believe it is the influenza."

"How do you know? I've never felt this way before."

Her great-aunt raised her eyebrows under the halo of her ever-present kerchief. "I should hope not."

Luise narrowed her eyes and tried to read Tante Manya's thoughts. "What do you mean? What could—"

Her hands flew to her mouth and her eyes widened. "Oh no! It can't be. Not after only one night." Her eyes pleaded with Tante Manya's. "Can it?" Her voice squeaked.

"The facts of life are what they are," said the old woman. "Apparently you are made to be a mother."

Tante Manya's voice calmed her. "Don't worry, child, we can keep your secret a while yet if you like, until you come to terms with it."

Instinctively, Luise's hands went to her belly. Her fears leaked from her eyes and ran down her face, even as a smile pulled up the sides of her mouth. A baby. Hers and Daniel's. A witness of their love.

Her tentative smile crumpled into sobs. "But my baby will not have a father. What if Daniel is not released as Papa was? What if he doesn't return in time? What if he doesn't return at all? How ever shall I care for a child, raise him on my own?"

"Luise," Tante Manya's voice brought her to her senses. "Look around you. Are you alone?"

"No." She wiped her eyes and blew her nose.

"Nor will you be alone as you walk this path. God has given you a gift. If Daniel returns, you can present this child to him. If he does not, you will have part of him to cherish."

Nodding, Luise tried to catch her breath. "I just can't believe I'm carrying a baby, or that I hadn't worked it out on my own."

"You have had many thoughts to fill your mind lately, Lise. As you said, you have never felt this way before."

With nervous energy, Luise uncovered the loaves of bread and put them into the oven two by two. "Except for a few precious hours, I feel as though I was never married. It was so short, almost a dream. I never guessed so much change would result from those few short hours.

"Tante Manya, what would I do if you weren't here?" She closed the oven door and reached her arms around the shrunken woman. "You are a mother to me."

Kissing the old woman's cheek, she helped her back to her rocking chair. Her hand went again to her belly, and she felt a smile tug at her lips. How surprised Daniel would be to see her expecting his child. She prayed anew for his return and that it would be soon.

৯৵

By the time full summer reached the northern Siberian taiga, life had taken on a routine of sorts for Daniel and the other men exiled with him. Up with the dawn, they worked until full sun, all the while fighting black flies and fish flies and mosquitoes that Daniel swore rivaled the size of small birds. Only then did they receive their allotment of food. After a brief rest, the men were forced to push back the line of coniferous trees until darkness rescued them. Then again, they were awarded bread, sometimes beans or rice, and something resembling coffee.

"Moldy bread again," said Daniel, eating hungrily after a morning of hard labor.

"At least it's bread," said Klaas Enns. "The wild berries are good but they do not fill the corners of my shrinking stomach."

"Better than green salt soup," said Daniel quietly, "but the fish was excellent, eh?"

A grin tipped his mouth. Dubrowsky had detected the small fire Daniel had built to roast a few fresh fish caught in the nearby stream and had beaten him severely, but it had been worth it at the time. What Daniel had not counted on were continued beatings, delivered almost daily. He had suffered the punishment bravely, but it hardened his heart as well as his hide, leaving scars both inside and out.

"Never tasted such good fish."

The men shared an uncomfortable chuckle that faded the instant Dubrowsky and another official appeared. The new man, Felix Kubolov, was younger than his superior. He had arrived at the camp that morning. Daniel wondered what was up. Was Dubrowsky leaving? He could only hope. Perhaps the beatings would end.

Daniel's pulse quickened with the possibility of a change. He could disappear and find Luise. He could leave this place behind. He planned his escape as he felled more trees.

Kubolov took over the running of the camp the next day. The prisoners momentarily stopped their labor to watch Dubrowsky ride south out of camp on a sorry-looking horse with a limp almost as pronounced as his rider's.

Once Dubrowsky had gone, Kubolov relaxed and didn't seem to care if the prisoners did the same. Daniel watched the official, observed his habits, his patterns. The man didn't even seem to know who the prisoners were. Time had come for escape.

Chapter Thirteen

August followed July with unseasonably humid weather in the Amur Region. The clouds dropped frequent rains on the land. Combined with the heat, the humidity transformed the world of Shumanovka into a sauna. As her baby grew within her, Luise felt ever more oppressed by the heat. While the late-seeded crops flourished, the residents of Shumanovka and area languished.

"This land is new and rich," said Abram. Only the whites of his eyes and his teeth showed through what he called the clean dirt of the fields.

"You are becoming a farmer," said Luise, a smile tilting her mouth. "Just like Daniel. It was all he ever wanted to be." Her smile slipped from her face and she turned to her chores.

Busyness, it seemed, was her best diversion these days. Not that she had a choice, with the garden flourishing like the fields, and meals to make, clothes to sew, socks to mend, the cow to milk. She had no idle time even to play her beloved violin, but then Anna could not abide her playing it anyway.

Luise moved outside to the bench in the shade of the house and set about cutting the ends from the bushel of green beans she had picked earlier. Tante Manya joined her. The old woman's hair lay damp against her temples where it had eased from beneath her kerchief, and Luise wished she could do something to make her more comfortable.

"Evening will bring relief," said Luise. "At least we have that comfort." They sat companionably snipping beans as the sun moved westward.

"I'm sorry to leave you before we're done," said Luise later, "but I must fetch Dolly from the pasture so I can milk her before supper."

"You go," said Tante Manya. "I can sit here and snip beans, and then start the supper."

"Thank you, Tante Manya. You are a great help to me."

"Jah, I know," she said, squinting up at Luise. "Without me you would get nothing done."

Luise pushed herself to a standing position and stretched, her hands on her lower back. "I'm glad I can still move around. It will only become more difficult in the next weeks."

She passed through the gate and out onto the road in the direction of the community pasture where the cattle grazed during the day. Just like in Alexandrovka. A good system. If Hans had not been helping Abram out in the fields, he would have been sent for the cow, but Luise did not mind the walk. It gave her time to think, away from the rest of her work and the annoyance of Anna's constant nagging.

Dolly waited for Luise to take her by the halter, and then followed the trail she walked twice each day. Luise heard the sound of hoofbeats from behind them before she rounded the bend in the road, and pulled the cow to the side. Who would be riding so fast in this heat? Most people knew better.

But the rider who appeared suddenly from around the bend was not most people. He was a GPU official in uniform, his whip smacking the horse that already foamed at the mouth. When he caught sight of Luise and Dolly, he yanked on the reins, but the horse fought him, throwing its head and snorting. Luise tried to move out of the way, but her condition hindered her, and Dolly refused to move, her eyes wide with fear.

"Get out of the way, woman," the official shouted, still battling his horse, but the animal was too spooked to obey and Luise could not move fast enough. She closed her eyes and raised her hands instinctively. The next moment she was thrown to the ground beneath Dolly's stamping feet. She rolled into a ball to protect herself, her mind racing. My baby. I must protect my baby.

"Stupid cow!" The GPU official cursed. "Get off the road, woman. You almost caused an accident!"

He struck his lathered horse and galloped away.

⁂

"What in heaven's name is the cow doing tied to the gatepost?" said Anna when she returned from a visit to Hertha's before supper. "Manya, what goes on here?"

"Anna, cease your harping. Luise is hurt."

Luise heard the voices, but she didn't care. The tea Tante Manya had made soothed her into a blissful state. She drifted into a restless sleep, but awoke in the night with severe abdominal cramps. Not wanting to disturb the sweetly sleeping Nela beside her, she rose quietly and moved to the rocking chair in the parlor, but she could not find comfort there. Visions of dark panting horses galloped toward her whenever she closed her eyes.

The pains grew sharper and deeper until Luise had to cover her moans with a pillow. In between pains, she lay against the back of the chair, completely exhausted. Why had the GPU official been in such a hurry and why was he here in Shumanovka? Were Stalin's men closing in on them already, so soon after they had settled into a good, quiet life here on the Amur?

Just as the morning sun showed signs of rising in the eastern sky, Luise felt her whole body contract. Sweat poured from her and she cried out. Her father, on the verge of rising for the day, came to see what the noise was about. He stared at her, then ran to Tante Manya's room and roused her from sleep. Together they helped Luise to her bed and moved Nela to Tante Manya's room.

"I'll be back shortly," said Abram in clipped tones.

Luise tossed in pain.

Abram returned within a half hour, ushering before him an elfin woman with spectacles half as large as her face.

"I've brought a midwife—Frau Klein."

"Frau Klein! She's nothing but a witch doctor." Luise raised her head at Anna's rasping voice and saw her stepmother hovering in the doorway.

With a longsuffering smile for Anna, Frau Klein approached Luise and set about her ministrations. But it was too late for the midwife or anyone to save the baby. By the time the sun had fully risen, Luise lay spent on her bed, the lifeless body of a tiny girl beside her, a girl with Daniel's broad brow and Luise's turned-up nose and the faintest tinge of hair on her head. Luise squeezed her eyes shut to ward off reality.

"Gone back to Jesus without ever seeing the light of one morning," the midwife sighed. "So it goes."

Luise heard a "tsk, tsk" from Tante Manya and imagined her shaking her head, wringing her arthritic hands. She heard the ticking of the Kroeger clock, marking off the time until—until what? The return of a husband who was most likely dead? The arrival of a baby who had gone back to Jesus?

Luise turned onto her side and stared at the wall. Her hopes and dreams had all been stolen from her. Her soul felt as dry as her eyes.

Later, Tante Manya brought soup, but Luise could not swallow it. The midwife took the tiny form, wrapped her in a soft blanket offered by a subdued Anna, and laid her in a box Abram brought in from his shop behind the house.

Luise felt a hand on her shoulder and heard Tante Manya's voice. "Would you like to see her once more before we take her away?"

Her words brought fresh pain into Luise's confusion. "Where are you taking her?"

"Luise, she's dead. We must bury her now."

The words brought Luise back to the present. Her baby had died. One minute she had been curled up safely inside her womb, the next she was dead in a box. Pushing past nausea, Luise pushed herself to a sitting position on the bed. Tante Manya set the little box beside her and shuffled out of the room.

Luise glanced at the box, as small as a bread pan, and reached out to touch the shining wood. It felt smooth and soothing to her fingers, but when she gently lifted the lid, a cry tore her throat. Sweetness lay in the box, wrapped in yellow, tiny eyes closed, little ears hugging her head, nose calling for a kiss, little hands at her chest.

All the pain Luise had held inside burst out in heart-wrenching sobs. Tante Manya hurried in, mumbling, "I thought it would help."

"Well," Luise heard the midwife say as she entered the bedroom, "so it goes." She carried the little casket out of the room.

Tante Manya sat with Luise, stroking her hair, her face, rocking her and whispering prayers and comforts that entered Luise's soul through her heart more than through her ears. When the storm had abated, Luise insisted on attending the burial. Her father set chairs for her and Tante Manya beside a small, deep hole dug under the new crabapple tree. Luise was faintly aware of Nela and Hans, subdued, standing on either side of their mother.

Abram himself spoke words of comfort and offered Scripture at the burial, and Luise's tears shook loose again. Her arms ached to hold her little girl. In the privacy of her heart, she named her Sarah, after her mother, and prayed that Jesus would allow the Sarahs to look after each other until Luise was able to join them.

The morning Daniel planned to leave the camp, he emerged from his crude hut to find Kubolov standing nearby with a rifle in his hands.

"Have you seen this?" Kubolov asked, lifting the gun to the light and admiring it.

"Only issued to officers." He pumped the bolt that allowed the magazine to feed another cartridge into the breech, and sighted an eagle in the distance. "They say the Tokarev semi-automatic will replace this one, but it won't. The Mosin-Nagant is reliable and accurate. I could drop a man at the treeline there and he'd never know he'd been hit."

His finger tightened on the trigger and the eagle screamed and dropped down through the trees. Kubolov flashed a grin Daniel's direction and snapped the breech open to eject the spent cartridge. It fell at Daniel's feet.

He felt sweat bead along his upper lip even in the cool morning air. He couldn't draw in a full breath. The smell of the gun riveted him to the spot. He had underestimated his enemy. Kubolov was nobody's fool; he just didn't exert unnecessary energy. And perhaps a cold-blooded official was as dangerous as one driven by senseless anger. Daniel did not wish to die. He must live for Luise's sake.

"Luise!"

Luise almost dropped the mixing bowl onto the floor. "I'm sorry, I didn't hear what you said."

Tante Manya sighed and shook her head. "You must come back to the land of the living."

"Why?" Luise dried the bowl and placed it on the shelf, waiting for Tante Manya's pity, but it did not come.

"Listen to me, girl. As long as God allows you to draw breath on this earth, you have reason to be here. The best cure for a broken heart is honest work."

Tante Manya pointed to the back door. "Hertha sent over a chicken for supper. I've plucked many a bird in my life, but my old hands won't do it anymore. And when you're done, there's a letter for you from Valentina. Some of the men went today to Blagoveshchensk for the mail."

Disregarding the chicken squawking in the yard, Luise pounced upon the letter and tore it open.

> *"Dear Luise,*
>
> *I hope your journey went well and that you are settled in your new home. I wish we had come too. The officials watch our every move and we live in constant anxiety that our actions will warrant arrest or punishment. I must send this letter along before someone finds it and reads my words. I'm sorry to report that we have heard nothing yet about Daniel or the others who were taken with him. I wish I had better news for you. It's been a long, hot summer.*
>
> *I have been feeling quite tired and shall be glad when our baby joins us. I'm already at least a week past my time…"*

Luise set the letter aside. There was no news of Daniel, but the letter was most likely written quite some time ago. She was sorry for Valentina's fatigue, but she had a husband and probably a child by now. She should be thankful.

Luise set a large pot on the stove and filled it with water. While it heated, she asked her father to behead the chicken, and then to carry the pot of scalding water behind the shed. He poured it into a stout barrel and Luise thanked him, willing to do the rest of the job herself. She hefted the headless bird from the box where Abram had left it, and dipped it repeatedly into the scalding water until her arms and sides ached. She tried a feather here and there until they began to pull out easily. Then, seating herself on the overturned box, she briskly plucked the feathers from the chicken, pretending it was a GPU official.

When she finished, she carried the bird back to the house, eviscerated it and scrubbed it thoroughly. Exhaustion threatened, even though she tried to ignore it. Just as she pushed the roasting pan into the oven, she heard a sharp rap at the door and Hertha stuck her head inside.

"Luise, hello. It's me, Hertha. I see you're having that chicken for supper. Listen, there's news. Those two young friends of Daniel have come."

"Which friends?"

"The Wieler fellow and Teacher Fast's nephew."

"Phillip and Jasch? Here, in Shumanovka?"

Luise removed her apron and smoothed her hair. "Where are they staying? Maybe they have heard something from Daniel."

"Well, I wouldn't hold my breath," said Hertha, and hurried off across the yard to her house.

"Thank you for the chicken," called Luise to Hertha's retreating form. Hertha raised a hand in response, not bothering to look back. Luise's heart beat faster as she left the house and headed up the street. It seemed where Phillip and Jasch appeared, Daniel should not be far away. Out of breath, she found them at the home of Phillip's aunt and uncle, looking tired from their journey.

"Have you heard from Daniel?" she asked as soon as they had greeted each other and accepted the cups of tea Phillip's aunt handed them.

"We haven't seen Daniel since you have," said Phillip, his eyes full of pity, "not since he was taken away by the GPU."

Jasch nodded to confirm this statement while Luise's heart shriveled within her, leaving an empty space. She set the teacup on the table with shaking hands and turned imploring eyes on Phillip. "Nothing?"

"I'm sorry." He smiled sadly to relieve the tension but it did not have the desired effect on Luise.

"The GPU are not a forgiving lot, nor is Siberia. We can only hope and pray for the best," added Jasch.

"Such comforting words," said Luise, standing to go. "Daniel is not dead."

"I wish I could tell you what you want to hear," said

Phillip, rising to see her to the door, "but if he is alive, he'll be in no shape to make the journey here to the eastern edge of the country. And once cold weather descends, well, no one survives northern Siberia in the winter without shelter."

Luise felt a great weariness descend upon her, but she raised her chin. "I won't give up on him, Phillip. He has always been resourceful. He promised me ..." Her voice trailed off. She turned and hurried out the door, damp hair clinging to her face, breath coming in short gasps.

"Luise, may I see you home?" Phillip followed her out. Her heart felt numb, but her mind refused to believe her Daniel was dead. There was absolutely no proof, after all, only probability, and she would not accept that.

"I'm fine," she lied, and kept walking until she arrived at her house.

The humidity inside choked her but she needed to get out of the street, to be alone, away from prying eyes, from neighbor Hertha's questions and her own doubts and fears. The reality of Daniel's possible or even probable death was that she was a widow. *That's the Widow Martens. Married for one day when he was taken. Imagine.* The words tumbled about in her mind in Hertha's gossipy voice until her head ached.

She felt ready to explode, and yet there was Anna, staring at her as if she were an intruder.

"What now, girl?" Anna barked into her handkerchief and sat up on the edge of her cot, her eyes hollow. "You seem to attract trouble as the sparks fly upward."

Luise hated to share her heart with Anna, but she needed to talk to someone.

"Two of Daniel's friends from Alexandrovka arrived today. They have no news of Daniel. They think he's dead, but I don't believe it, Mother." She steeled herself to the insensitivity she knew would come, but Anna's words shocked her.

"Well, for once we agree on something."

Luise spun toward her stepmother. "What do you

mean?"

Anna leveled her gaze at Luise. "I know things. Now fetch me a cup of water. You leave me to fend for myself all the time. The children become disruptive while you go gallivanting, and Manya can't do anything helpful with those hands of hers."

The contradictions jangled her nerves; the inconsistencies made her want to scream. She needed to think, to ask herself and God if she could believe this woman's words that Daniel was alive. She fetched a cup of water for Anna from the drinking pail, checked the chicken in the oven and quietly slipped out the back door, heading for the creek. The cool shade of the aspen felt good as she settled herself at its trunk and listened to the water's quiet gurgle.

Why Lord? Why have you taken everyone from me? My mother, my husband, my daughter? Am I being punished or are you trying to teach me something? My heart is so heavy I don't care to learn anymore. I just want to go to sleep and wake up in heaven. The tears she had been repressing welled up and overflowed, and she grieved alone.

The voice she heard next sounded concerned but not quite angelic.

Chapter Fourteen

"Luise."

She heard her name called as if from across a wide river. The roaring in her mind ebbed and her eyes blinked open. She had fallen asleep on the creek bank, under the shade of the trembling aspen. Her face felt puffy from crying and she knew her eyes were likely red-rimmed and swollen. She sat up and looked into the face of Daniel's friend, Phillip Wieler.

A worry line creased his forehead and concern showed in his grey eyes.

"Luise? Are you all right?"

She wiped her face with her palms and tried to compose herself, but the effort only released more tears and she shook her head.

Placing his fishing tackle under the tree, Phillip lowered himself to the ground and sat beside her, hands clasped around his knees, leaving a respectable distance between them. He focused his attention across the creek.

"Missing Daniel?"

What could she say? Of course she was missing Daniel. It was all too painful to talk about, especially with a young man. So she nodded. Phillip had not asked if she was also missing her baby girl. Most people refrained from mentioning her, as if little Sarah had never existed. It was a personal matter, not one to be bantered about.

"Thank you for your concern. I really should get back home."

"Let me walk with you." He offered her his hand.

She stared at it and pushed herself to her feet. "I don't want to take you from your fishing. I'll be fine." She swayed as she said it and he reached out to steady her. How she hated it when her body refused to obey.

"I'll walk you home. I can come back here later."

He carried on an amiable monologue all the way back to the village, his hand on her arm, and Luise pulled herself together. Her body ached both emotionally and physically. Maybe Daniel would come back to her after all. How sad he would be to hear about his daughter. He would have nothing to remember her by, no picture in his mind of her sweet face and perfect little body, so still and pale.

Luise thanked Phillip for seeing her home and went directly to her room. Nela was in school, so Luise lay on the bed and stared at the wall. Thoughts muddled around in her head, casting about here and there for reason and logic, but there was none to be found. Darkness hovered on the periphery of her spirit, threatening bleakness and despair.

Gradually, in place of the loneliness and ache of loss, she began to feel again the pull of pent-up anger toward the GPU in general and Leonid Dubrowsky in particular. That enemy had stolen her husband and precipitated her miscarriage. Anger was easier to carry than the heart-wrenching grief.

Luise ignored the tapping at her door, hoping whoever it was would go away. Instead, the door opened and Tante Manya entered, closing the door behind her.

"Nah, child, what are you cooking up in here?"

"Nothing but what's been thrown at me."

"No, I think you are stewing something that won't be good for anyone."

Luise sighed and kept her eyes closed. "Tante Manya, I don't wish to talk of it now."

"Of course you don't. Move over so I can sit down. I am too old to stand here while you feel sorry for yourself."

Scowling, Luise moved over and sat up so Tante Manya could sit beside her.

"Have I ever told you about my husband?"

Reluctantly, Luise shook her head. "I know you weren't married long before he died, and that his name was Rudy." She closed her eyes and leaned her head back against the wall, inviting bitterness to remain.

"He was an older man, my Rudy, at least twenty-five, and I not quite seventeen. He was handsome and intelligent and he adored me, and I was young and loved being adored. I pushed my mother and stepfather into allowing me to marry Rudy, partly, I will admit now, because I disapproved of their marriage and wanted to hurt them as I had been hurt by their decision to marry.

"Rudy and I moved to his village and set up house. It was a dream life at first, being mistress of my own home, of my time. But Rudy worked as an administrator in the village, and often traveled. I missed him and hated being alone. Then one day on his way home from Halbstadt, his horse bolted, tore the buggy harness and upset the buggy. Rudy was thrown into the ditch and died there. Broken neck, they said."

Luise opened her eyes and watched Tante Manya stare at nothing in particular. After a few moments and a heavy sigh she took up her story again.

"I didn't believe he was dead until I saw him, and even then I refused to accept the fact. We had only been married six months, you see. I stayed in my house alone for days, hiding behind a locked door, not eating, not caring for myself. Then my stepfather came, took the door off its hinges, and walked in. He lifted me from my couch of mourning and carried me back to my mother's house. They looked after me, allowing me to come to an understanding of my circumstances and to heal."

Luise's eyes homed in on Tante Manya's, waiting for more.

"My parents were my rock during that time. They led me to Jesus. Over and over again they reminded me that He cared and that He had a plan for my life. Eventually I realized they were right, and that's when I began to return to the land of the living."

"Did...did you ever wish to marry again or...to have children?"

Tante Manya's face folded into a smile and she shook her head. "I never wanted anyone but Rudy and he was gone. I looked after my parents as they aged and then, when my older sister died, I took her son, Abram, into our home and raised him."

"Papa." Luise smiled. "He said he had a happy childhood."

She watched the dear old woman's face soften with the memories.

"Abram was like sunshine after rain. Whenever he entered a house, he brought joy. Not that he never got into trouble. My goodness, that boy attracted trouble like sugar attracts flies. He had an active mind and a resourceful one when it came to explaining himself out of a corner." Tante Manya laughed like a young girl when she said it. "But he was so sincere and lovable it was difficult to remain angry with him for long. 'I suppose I deserve discipline again,' he'd say, a sorrowful look in those hazel eyes that changed from one moment to the next.

"My parents adored him. He lived with us until they died, and then he met your mother, Sarah. Abram and Sarah. We laughed about that, until they followed the biblical script and moved to a country they had never seen, up to Orenburg in the Urals."

"Why did they leave?"

Before Tante Manya could answer, they heard the back door open and little feet run through the house.

"Nela and Hans are home from school," said Luise. "I didn't realize so much time had gone by." She rubbed her hands over her face. Every muscle in her body ached. Even breathing had become a chore. "Thank you for the story, Tante Manya. I'll think about it."

"I hope so. It may seem like the end of the world, but I assure you it is not. Acceptance and obedience are the tools to get you through this, child. We do not see the whole picture but God does. So trust Him already.

"Nela! Hans! We are in the bedroom. Come tell us about your day."

❧

Luise stopped in the street and turned at the sound of someone calling her name. Hans stood with her. She saw Phillip Wieler and Jasch Fast hurrying to catch up with them and sighed. Every time she saw these young men, she expected to see Daniel with them. Jasch was a small man like his uncle, Schoolmaster Fast, but slower of speech, and without the nasty streak. Phillip stood at least a head taller and always took the lead.

"Hello Jasch, Phillip," she said. "You look better than when you arrived here."

Hans began to hop from one foot to the other beside her, excitement on his face.

"My aunt has been feeding me as if I need to catch up on all the meals I missed on our journey," said Phillip. "Jasch here isn't quite so lucky."

"I get enough."

"Well, you could use more. Come to my place for supper and you will be satisfied for once. That uncle of yours is a skinflint."

Half a year ago, Luise would have enjoyed friendly banter with other young people, but she felt as if she had aged many years since that time. She was a married woman—perhaps a widow—and she had lost a child. She wondered what the boys wanted and felt an urge to escape to the safe routine of her family's home. Before she could do so, Phillip continued.

"I hope you're feeling better, Luise."

She resented his reference to finding her at the creek. Some things needed to remain private.

"I am better, thank you, Phillip."

"We're having a singing at my uncle's place later tonight," he said, looking at her with something in his eyes she could not discern. "We're hoping you might join us."

Luise's eye twitched. A singing? When had young people last gathered to sing? It hadn't been allowed anymore in Alexandrovka, after the fiasco at the schoolhouse. And she supposed she hadn't paid attention to what the young people did here in Shumanovka. She missed Valentina and the excitement of carefree youth.

"Oh, I don't know that I can. I have to look after my mother and the children, and I haven't felt much like singing lately."

"We could use your violin to help us along," suggested Jasch, standing up straighter beside Phillip. "There aren't many of those around and our pitch isn't very good." He smirked exactly like his uncle.

"I'm sorry," she said. "I can't—"

"Can't or won't?" Phillip stood looking down at her, a few blond curls dancing on his broad forehead, his eyes grey as a winter sky. Luise couldn't remember ever really looking at him, but here he stood in front of her, demanding to know her reasons. It was none of his business.

Hans spoke before Luise could. "She plays real nice, but Mama won't let her play, 'cept when Papa's around."

"So you're needing a place to use your musical ability?"

"Phillip, don't push me. I love to play, but my heart is too heavy for music these days."

"Perhaps your heart needs lifting. Music has a way of doing that."

"You should go, sister. You could make everybody happy."

Phillip smiled at the help from Hans, but Luise felt a deep pain. She forced a smile but shook her head and turned away before the tears came.

Phillip's voice followed her, kind but probing. "You're

going to have to face the music eventually," he said.

Luise wanted to whirl around and tell him he had no idea what he was saying and that she resented his pun. Instead, she blinked away tears and hurried in the direction of home, while Hans skipped along at her side, oblivious to her tumbling thoughts.

Daniel, where are you? I cannot go on with my life until…until when? Her steps slowed. Until she knew for sure that he was dead? What if she never found out? But what if she let herself begin to forget him and then he returned? No, her heart was his for as long as *she* lived, because she didn't know how long he lived. If that meant forever, well then, so be it.

As she entered the house, Anna greeted her with a command. "You need to go to the sing-song tonight at the Wielers'. All the young people are going to be there and it would do you good to attend."

Luise stared at her stepmother and then at Tante Manya in her rocking chair. The older woman glanced up at her and then concentrated on her knitting.

Hans bounded in behind Luise. "Phillip aksed her to come but she said no."

"Well, Luise, how about it?" Anna stood to her feet and put her thin hands on her hips.

Heat rising in her cheeks and feeling cornered, Luise cried out, "Will everyone let me be? I'm a married woman, possibly a widow, and I do not require the company of other young people to emphasize the differences between us."

"You should have married someone who would provide for you." Anna's words stabbed at Luise.

"I married Daniel because I love him." she said, her voice rising. "He didn't choose to leave me. He has been gone for half a year and you all expect me to forget him. Tante Manya, have you forgotten Rudy? Mother, have you forgotten how you felt when Papa was taken from us? Did people expect you to forget and carry on as if you had lost nothing? I have loved Daniel for as long as I can remember, and I shall not give up on him now."

Anna coughed into her hanky and sat down on the edge of her cot. "You can't expect your father to take care of you forever."

Luise felt the knife twist. "I don't expect him to. I take care of you, the children, the house. Is it never enough?"

"Luise, that is enough shouting." Abram entered the back door with a scowl on his face. "Our home is not a place for loud and angry words."

"I'm sorry, Papa, but everyone thinks I need to forget Daniel and continue on with my life, and I can't do that."

Abram looked at each face and then back at Luise. "I realize you're grieving, but please don't take it out on the others. Some can't help what they say."

Luise pinched her lips together and marched into the kitchen where she began peeling potatoes as if her life depended upon it.

Chapter Fifteen

In spite of the hurt Luise felt at what she considered her family's lack of understanding, she began to consider their words. Even though she prayed daily for Daniel and thought of him often through the shortening days, her thoughts were not as painful as they had been. Was she forgetting him? Forgetting the difficulty he might be in? She didn't believe so, but she simply could not exist in constant grief, or in anger. Where there was no going back, one must point one's feet forward. It was not easy, but it was necessary.

In this gradual acceptance, Luise discovered life in Shumanovka to be almost pleasant, to see Mother breathe easier in sunshine and fresh air, to watch Hans and Nela play out in the yard or in the street with the other children in the evenings, these things brought a quiet peace.

It often seemed to Luise that most people had forgotten about Daniel in their own need to settle into this place, but Luise knew his family had not forgotten, and she felt guilty for neglecting them. To lose two family members almost at once would be devastating.

She decided she would pay them a visit. She would go to the village of New York to see Daniel's family today, before the ground froze and the snow gathered in dunes like sand blowing across the desert.

"Where did the name New York come from, Papa?" asked Luise. "It sounds like the great American city."

He chuckled. "A bit of nostalgia, I imagine. There was a village named New York in the Ignatyevo Colony in Ukraine. Apparently, the wife of Count Ignatieff, from whom the land was bought, was an American. She requested that they name the village after the city in her home country."

"I see. And being a people who carry our names with us, we called another village New York in this region."

The next morning at breakfast, Abram said, "I heard Phillip Wieler wanted to drive up to New York one of these days. Perhaps he would take you along."

"Provided they have a reliable chaperone," added Anna.

Luise cocked her head at her mother. "It's not like we're courting, Mother. I'm going to visit my in-laws."

"If I were younger, I would go along," said Tante Manya. She sat thinking a few moments, then caught Luise's eye. "It's not such a great distance, just over the hill, really. If I can travel for so many days on the train and then by wagon to get here, I can certainly withstand less than an hour by horse and buggy." She looked out the window. "The air is not cold. It will do me good."

Luise grinned.

"You cannot go, Manya. I need you. I woke up feeling poorly today." Anna coughed into her hanky and sighed loudly. "And the children are so loud sometimes, it just echoes in this big house."

Luise's grin faded as quickly as it had come. She blew out her breath and rose to clean up the breakfast. Abram stopped her with a hand on her arm. "Tante Manya isn't the only one seeking a change," he said. "I'd like to speak with a builder in New York, ask him about a few things for the house, perhaps pick up more materials for my shop. I'll find out if Phillip will take us along, eh?"

Her happiness restored, Luise hurried to clean up the breakfast. Even though she had never felt close to Greidl Martens, Luise knew they shared much more now than they had earlier. She liked Hannah and Maria all right, and she and Johannes had formed a bond during those horrible days of Peter's death and Daniel's arrest.

Luise wondered, as she removed her apron and smoothed her dress, if she would ever be able to recall her wedding day with joy, or if it would always be overshadowed by visions of death and fear and stolen promises. She shook off the dismal mood that threatened to drape itself around her heart. She would enjoy this day and, God willing, be an encouragement to Daniel's family. In some way, seeing them would bring her closer to her husband.

Abram sat in the front seat of the buggy beside Phillip while Luise sat in the second seat, bundled in her winter coat and scarf. The breeze had a sting to it that warned of the winter to come, but the air felt clean and pure and she breathed it deeply into her lungs. She would gladly have jumped on a horse and ridden to New York, but old Samson would have taken all day to get her there.

Phillip had seemed distinctly disappointed when Abram asked to ride with them. Luise's face pulled into a frown. What was the young man thinking?

She had attended a couple of singings at the Wielers' and the Harders', and even enjoyed playing her violin and singing with the rest, but at the end of it, she always felt out of place. She tipped her head back to watch the winter clouds. Life could be a lonely ordeal. When there were people around, one didn't always want them because they didn't understand, but sometimes being alone was equally unbearable. She had visited with Martha Lepp a few times, the girl who worked at the mercantile, but felt no kinship there.

Phillip had twisted in his seat and spoken to her but she had no idea what he had said.

"I'm sorry. I'm afraid I was wool-gathering."

He grinned. "I just wondered if you were cold. My aunt sent another blanket along. It's there behind you if you need it."

"Thank you, I'm quite comfortable."

He nodded and turned his eyes back to the road.

When they arrived in New York, Phillip stopped at Kornelius Martens' place where Greidl and her family lived, and helped Luise down from her seat in the buggy. "I'll help your father collect his things and then stop for a bit at my cousin's. Then I'll be back in, say, two or three hours, just so's we get home before dark. The days are a lot shorter now than they were a month ago when I came here."

"You were here last month?" Luise pulled her hand from his and shook out her skirt. "I didn't know. I should have visited Daniel's mother long ago. Now the days of traveling are more limited."

"Oh, we might have opportunity to come here again before winter settles in. I'll let you know if I go." His grey eyes grinned at her and the ever-present curls on his forehead bobbed. "My cousin and I like to get together often."

She smiled and nodded, then approached the house and knocked on the door. A woman she had never met answered and stared at her blankly. "Yes? May I help you?"

Luise introduced herself. "I've come to visit my in-laws."

The woman inclined her head in understanding and opened the door wider to admit her guest. From the kitchen, Luise heard a gasp and a shout.

"It's Luise!"

Before she could remove her coat, Hannah came running and threw her arms around her sister-in-law. In a moment, Maria did the same. Johannes, almost as tall by now as Luise, stood shyly to the side, but as soon as the girls had released Luise, she reached her arm around his shoulders and squeezed, sharing a long look with him. Greidl stood from her rocking chair in the parlor and came to greet Luise warmly.

"Mother Martens, it's good to see you. I've thought of

you often and decided to come see for myself how you were doing."

"Good of you to come, Luise. Let's sit in the parlor. Girls, take her wraps."

"I'll go prepare some tea," said the woman who had met her at the door.

"My sister-in-law, Katie," said Daniel's mother.

They settled themselves in the parlor, and Johannes disappeared. Luise felt sorry he did not stay. She joined the women to talk of settling into a new community, of the summer heat, of harvest and the coming winter. Luise wondered what people would talk about if not for the changeable weather.

"We heard of your misfortune," said Hannah.

"Hannah, that is not our business," said Greidl.

Luise bowed her head to collect her emotions, so suddenly spun out for all to see, then raised her eyes to Greidl's. "But it is your business. The baby I lost was your flesh and blood through Daniel." She stood and wandered to the window so she didn't have to see the pity in their eyes.

"She was beautiful. A perfect little girl with Daniel's face."

"Too perfect to draw breath on this earth. I too have experienced this."

Surprise caught Luise and she turned back to Greidl. "I'm sorry. I didn't know."

"Not many did; it isn't something we speak of. I gave birth to a son after Maria and before Johannes. Thankfully, the good Lord sent us another son to take the name."

"Speaking of Johannes, where is he?" Hannah said.

"I'm here." He came from the shop and stood before Luise, hands behind his back.

"My brother was making something for you before he got arrested," he said. From behind his back he brought out a set of carved candlesticks in varied shades of wood, each about twenty centimeters tall. He held them out to Luise, and with trembling hands she accepted them.

"I finished them."

She didn't trust her voice. She studied the candlesticks and blinked at the tears that threatened.

Daniel had held these in his own hands. He had worked on them for hours, thinking of her and how she would love them. She had nothing of his, not even a shirt or a jacket to wrap around herself. Her fingers stroked the smoothness of the wood. She turned one upside down and saw, carved into the base, the initials LLM. Luise Letkemann Martens.

Greidl's sister bustled in with a tray of tea and loaf cake and Luise used the distraction to thank Johannes and gather her emotions.

Hannah and Maria sniffled and Greidl blew her nose. "Well, now we've all had our cry, let's remember Daniel with smiles." They shared memories and Luise's heart expanded to hold them all. There was so much of her husband she hadn't known, so much of how he interacted with his family. It was obvious his sisters adored him and his brother emulated him. Also clear from Greidl's reminiscences was the fact that Peter felt pride in his eldest son and looked forward to working with him as two men together. Sadly, their partnership had been cut short.

When Phillip returned to fetch her, Luise stepped back to speak to Greidl alone. "I have not given up hope, Mother Martens. I still believe Daniel is alive and that he will find us. That is my prayer."

"Yes, mine too." Greidl dabbed her eyes again. "But only God knows. Such a sad life."

"But you have your children to sustain. Don't let them forget their father or Daniel."

"You're right. And we have a place to stay and people who care for us. But I miss them, you know." She bent her head and wept.

"Don't lose faith, Mother Martens. Daniel may yet return to us."

"I hope so, Luise. I'm sorry to cry so much when you've come to visit."

"I understand. We have something in common which can't be shared with the others."

This time Greidl reached out and encircled her daughter-in-law with her arms. "God bless you, child. Stay warm on the way home."

"Where's Papa?" Luise allowed Phillip to help her into the front seat of the buggy. She carried the candlesticks wrapped in a towel.

"He was visiting with Loewen when I stopped by the lumber yard. Said he'd be ready as soon as I had collected you."

Phillip slapped the reins against the horse's rump and the wagon bounced off toward the west end of Main Street. "Did you have a nice visit?" he asked.

"Very nice, thank you."

"I suppose you had a lot to talk about."

"Yes. How was your visit with your cousin?"

"Fine. We played games and talked and ate fresh zwieback with raspberry jam."

"Sounds tasty."

Luise absentmindedly watched people walking down the street, all with important things to do. "Do you miss home?"

"Alexandrovka?" Phillip pulled on the reins and rounded the corner at the lumberyard. "I miss my parents and the familiar things of home and the village, but I'm glad to be away from there. The Soviet officials were getting too interested in us. Rashidov isn't a bad character so far, for a Soviet official. I just hope he leaves us alone. We always do best that way."

Yes, we always do best on our own. "There's my father."

Phillip pulled the buggy to a stop and leaped to the ground to help Abram load supplies. While they were thus engaged, Luise climbed back to the second seat and tucked the candlesticks beside her. When the men approached the buggy with a load of supplies, disappointment washed briefly across Phillip's features.

The ride home passed more quickly than the first stretch, especially since the clouds looked like they might shake down more snow. When Phillip dropped her and Abram at their house back in Shumanovka, he said he would let them know when he next went to New York, but it was to Luise that he directed his words. When he urged the horse on toward his own house, Abram narrowed his eyes at Luise.

"Is there something between you and Phillip, my dear?"

Luise's heart constricted. "Not on my part, that is certain, and hopefully not on his either. I am a married woman."

Chapter Sixteen

Luise stood atop the windswept hill overlooking the village, watching Hans and Nela struggle up the snowy hillside with their sled in tow. Curls of smoke rose lazily from many chimneys through the crisp air, and she thought how comfortable they were here. Such an idyllic setting with the Amur River nearby and the Chinese mountains in the distance against a slate blue sky. She imagined Daniel flying down the hill with the children.

"Nela," she said when they reached her. "Let's make snow angels."

She let herself drop backwards into the snow and flapped her arms and legs, then stood carefully so as not to mar the snow around her. Nela watched, then flopped down and made her own snow angel.

Luise tossed some snow into Hans' face. He threw some back, and ran off to form snowballs. "I'm glad you didn't stay in Alexandrovka," he called to Luise as he worked. "It wouldn't be nearly so much fun if you weren't here."

Luise considered all she would have missed if she had stayed behind. Life was uncertain, a fragile flower that bloomed for a day and then withered without leaving a trace, as the Psalmist wrote. Life was difficult enough without dismissing the God who watched over them all. At least He knew the end from the beginning. How could she not trust Him?

How did God expect people to trust Him when He abandoned them, cut off His mercy in their times of greatest need? Daniel contemplated his sorry life as he swung his axe at the trunk of another conifer, the blow sending shards of pain along his arms to his icy hands.

The problem was, how could he free himself from this exile? Always observant, he had still not seen opportunity for an escape attempt. Besides, winter had come. Where could he go and how long could he survive? Any child would be able to follow his tracks in the snow, unless a blizzard covered them, but in that case, he would not survive much longer than his tracks.

Later, as he carefully cradled a cup of lukewarm soup in his frozen fingers, he cursed the day he had first laid eyes on Senior-Major Dubrowsky. Why had the man come to Alexandrovka in the first place?

Commissar Magadan had managed quite well without Dubrowsky's interference. It was as if fate had matched them and then stepped aside to watch the outcome. Well, the villain was winning this round, and Daniel didn't know how many more rounds he could go.

He vowed that if he ever had the opportunity to flee the camp, he would find Luise and take her as far from Russia as the east is from the west. And he would not look back.

"Several of our young men have ventured across the Amur to China," said Abram one winter night once Hans and Nela had been bundled into their beds.

"Who went and why would they go now in winter?" Anna wanted to know.

Luise held her embroidery needle in midair.

"I heard it was George and Franz Hiebert from here and another fellow from Konstantinovka, don't know his name."

For some reason Luise had expected her father to say it had been Phillip and Jasch who had crossed into China, and she realized she was glad he had not. "Are they returning?"

"Oh, I think so, for now. They said they were scouting out markets for our wheat over there. I think they're looking for opportunity to work there and eventually go across to

America. They're young and unattached and probably feeling adventurous."

Luise frowned. Nearly twenty thousand Mennonites had left South Russia in the last few years. Were they now starting a pilgrimage from the eastern borders of the land? Would she be one of those left behind? She hoped against hope that she would hear one way or the other about Daniel before she was expected to make such a decision. "Are they—we—free to come and go?"

"It seems so at this point, but if more people follow that path, I imagine something will be done to discourage such things. The government granted us privileges in order to settle here and work the land, and I'm sure they won't look kindly on a mass exodus as happened in Ukraine."

Tante Manya had been listening without comment, her gnarled hands knitting another pair of mittens from an old sweater. "How far can we run, eh? Will there always be another place to go when we feel restricted?"

"Who knows?" answered Abram. "Right now I'm comfortable to live here in the house I built, and help the men on the fields and build things for other people. What more could we ask? We have sufficient food—much more than we had in Alexandrovka—a comfortable home, a community as we are accustomed, and we are relatively free of interference."

Luise kept her eyes on her work, her thoughts veering to the day she had been run over by the GPU official and his horse. They were still here, Stalin's men. They knew what went on here in the east, of that she had no doubt.

Even so, Luise knew she must be grateful for what she had, even while praying always for her one outstanding desire. With these thoughts a peace settled on her heart and she smiled across the room at her father. His responsive smile added a trimming of joy to her heart.

"Soon it will be Christmas," she said. "What are we going to do to make the holy days special?"

On Christmas Day the family found gifts at their plates on the table, for each one a few cookies and nuts, and—joy of joys—an orange. The sweet, sticky juice dribbled down Hans and Nela's chins as they ate the fruit. Anna set hers aside, saying she would eat it later. Luise worried about her stepmother's lack of appetite. She was so thin she hardly cast a shadow, and her cough worsened with the cold winds of winter.

Luise wore her best smile, even though her heart yearned for her fondest wish. Hans was excited about the little carved trees and buildings to add to his train yard. Nela squealed with joy at a doll with a carved wooden head and two dresses. Sewing the small ensemble had been a welcome distraction for Luise the past few weeks.

The new house stood firm against the winter winds, the stove blazed with warmth, and the woodpile reached high along the leeward side of the barn. Snow blew in from the fields into drifts that wrapped the house in an insulating blanket, rising to the bottom of the windows. Ice formed on the glass, printed with intricate frost patterns and scraped in places to allow a view of the outside.

On days when the temperature mellowed, Luise took the children out to the hill to slide and play. Anna thought the idea ridiculous, as if she had forgotten the need for children to shout and run and wear themselves out. She had become more and more concerned with her own limitations, and perhaps she thought that if the cold hurt her lungs and increased her coughing, it would do the same to her children.

"Children need exercise and fresh air, Anna," said Abram. "Remember when you were a child?"

She rolled her eyes. "Oh Abram, I was never that young."

Luise wondered how it felt for her father to watch his spouse lose her grasp on reality, and decided it might be worse than losing her to death. At least Luise could remember Daniel as he had always been, strong, alive, opinionated, kind.

"How do you endure the changes in Mother?" she asked Abram one day while Anna slept in her bedroom and Tante Manya snoozed in the rocking chair.

Abram kept carving at the piece of wood he held in his hands. He did not answer for so long she wondered if he had heard her. Finally, after blowing sawdust off the wood, he said, "There are some things we cannot change. To fight against these things reduces our strength. We gain nothing by it." He turned his eyes on her then. "I mourn for her often inside, Lise, just as I'm sure you mourn for Daniel more than anyone will ever know."

Luise bowed her head as Abram continued. "One of the greatest keys to living this life is to accept the things we cannot change." He turned back to his carving. "There are enough battles to fight in this life without fighting against God."

"But how do you know when to fight and when to let go? Sometimes fighting is all that keeps us alive." Luise snipped the end of her embroidery thread.

Abram chuckled. "How do we know? Through experience. By mistakes. Wasted energy and years. Clinging to the Word of God for answers and beating on heaven's door."

Acceptance and obedience; an invincible team. Luise laid aside her handwork and stood from her chair. "I'll go check on Mother."

"I was passing by so I thought I'd stop to see if you'd like to attend the singing at Friesens' tonight." Phillip stood on the doorstep, slapping his hat against his leg.

Life would have been simpler if Phillip Wieler had not arrived from Alexandrovka last fall with Jasch Fast following behind him. Phillip had been thoughtful, polite, patient, and insightful, but he had also shown perseverance in his pursuit of Luise's friendship.

Luise stood undecided, not wanting to go but needing to escape the sameness of the winter evenings. With a brief smile she said, "I'll fetch my coat and hat. You'd best come in and shut the door."

Luise saw Anna's head come up from her knitting, saw her eyes lock onto Phillip's and then flicker to hers. Luise steeled herself for what her stepmother might say.

"Good evening, young man. I see you've come for our daughter."

Our daughter. That was a rare phrase from Anna's mouth.

"Yes, Ma'am. There's a singing—"

"See you come straight home when it's over."

"Yes, Ma'am."

Anna resumed her work as if Phillip wasn't there and Luise pushed him out the door with one hand, her violin case in the other.

Her heart began to thaw with respect to some of the young women as they visited together, but she sorely missed Valentina's exuberance and the confidences they'd shared. Frieda Klassen sought her out as Luise tuned her violin to match the pitch of the guitars, and sang as Luise played the songs so long absent from her life. When someone suggested *Gott Wird Behuten Dich,* she closed her eyes to keep back the tears. Yes, God would take care of her, of them all. She knew this. She must also show she believed it by her actions.

Martha Lepp stayed at Phillip's elbow throughout the evening, but avoided speaking to Luise. On the way home, Martha waltzed along beside Phillip, but he paid little attention to her. He led the way to Lepp's house to see her home, and the girl seemed none too happy that Luise walked with them.

As Phillip and Luise continued on toward her house, he

said, "Have you ever gone swimming in a pond in the summer, and when you leave the water there are leeches on you?"

Luise bit her lip. "Phillip, that's unkind."

"All right, how about this: have you ever been to a picnic in summer and a particular fly buzzes incessantly around your head and you just want to smack it?"

Luise couldn't help the laugh that escaped her lips. "She's young—"

"And desperate. Spare me the excuses."

They walked in silence for a bit while Luise mulled over his words. "Are you desperate, Phillip?"

"What?" He stopped walking and his breath puffed out in white clouds. "Please tell me I'm not like Martha."

"You're not like Martha, but as much as I appreciate your companionship and protection, I already have a husband, Phillip. And he's your best friend, I might add."

His head bent to his chest as they walked on in silence. "I have overstepped the bounds of propriety," he said. "Forgive me. I only wish to look after you in Daniel's absence."

She put her mittened hand on his arm. "Yes, Phillip, but you must be willing to accept my situation for what it is or there can be no friendship."

When he had seen her home, her thoughts continued in the direction Phillip had led them. She had her memories of Daniel and they would suffice. Would they not? Sometimes she thought it would have been easier never to have married him than to know such a commitment and then have it torn away from her.

She stopped herself at that thought. No, she would not trade her friendship and marriage to Daniel in spite of the pain that had resulted. She decided not to hover over her losses; it would only make her bitter. Instead, she would face the new year with renewed purpose: to follow God and His plan for her. He would show her the way, one step at a time.

She must persevere. Like Job.

The first step God showed Luise came as a complete surprise.

Chapter Seventeen

Early in March, while the snow still lay in drifts across the settlement, Luise received a summons by way of Hans.

"Lise, you're s'pose to—"

He stopped speaking when he saw his mother lying on her cot in the parlor. Luise noticed his hesitation.

"I know, Hans." She smiled, getting up from her chair. "I promised to help you with your schoolwork."

He blinked at her, glanced at his mother, and fetched his speller from his room. They settled at the kitchen table and bent over the book.

"What is your message, little brother?"

He grinned, then sat straight with an air of importance. "You are to go see Frau Klein."

Luise's smile turned upside down. Her association with the woman exhumed memories buried in sorrow, but she waited for him to finish.

"She says come to her house tomorrow right after breakfast, and I am supposed to bring you. She wants your company until suppertime."

Luise raised her eyebrows at Hans. "When did you meet her?"

Anna's voice interrupted from the parlor. "Hans, come practice your spelling words with me. I still know how to spell." A fit of coughing followed, and a groan.

"Coming, Mama," he said. Then to Luise, "Her wagon was stopped by the schoolhouse. She called me over."

"Thank you, Hans. You're a good messenger."

"Hans, are you coming?"

Luise handed the book to Hans and winked as he left

the room. She thought he was too young to have to deal with a mother who wasn't quite right, but then she had been dealing with Anna since she was his age. Perhaps that fact strengthened the bond between her and Hans. Nela seemed to thrive on the love and attention of so many adults in her life.

"What a ridiculous idea," said Anna the next morning as Luise prepared to go with Hans to Frau Klein's. "We need you here, girl. How do you expect me to carry on without your help?"

Luise glanced over at Tante Manya and saw her toothless mouth pucker in even further than normal.

"Well, Anna, we get old and we no longer can do much but exist, eh? We should perhaps be more thankful for Luise from day to day. When she goes away, we realize how much we need her."

Luise grinned and pulled her coat from the peg behind the door. Hans walked with her past the schoolhouse one block, and there sat Frau Klein, bundled in her sleigh, her stocky Siberian horse stamping its feet and shaking the harness. Daniel would know what kind of horse it was, but to Luise, it was just small and hairy. Small woman, small horse, small sleigh. Luise felt like a giant as she climbed into the sleigh and pulled a sheepskin over her knees.

"Thank you," called Frau Klein to Hans, and tossed him a tiny paper sack of sweets. "To school with you now. I will drop your sister off home by supper."

Luise waved at Hans and he ran off.

"He is a good boy, that one." Frau Klein clucked to the horse and slapped the reins on his rump.

"Yes, he is," agreed Luise. "Perceptive for his age."

"As are you."

Luise eyed her companion, whose spectacles fogged up as she hunched into her sheepskin coat and hat. She looked like a child playing at being a queen. Knowing that Tante Manya trusted this woman helped her to do the same.

"Frau Klein, I'd like to thank you for helping me out when...when my baby came. I don't know that I've ever told you that, or even seen you since."

The little woman held the lines in one hand and patted Luise's arm with the other. "So it goes. I come at the hour of crisis; people do not always remember to offer thanks."

"But you gave of your time..."

"I always get by. Some people are generous, your father being one of them, Frau Martens. All is settled between us."

Embarrassed, Luise turned to study the path ahead. "Where are we going, Frau Klein?"

"Konstantinovka. 'Tis not far."

"May I ask why?"

"Because that is where they built it."

"No, I mean—"

Frau Klein cackled. "Perhaps you are not so perceptive as I thought."

Luise grinned back. "I'll learn."

"Yes, you will. Quickly, I think." She urged the horse into a trot as they left the protection of the village and turned onto the main road heading south. The runners of many sleds had packed the snow down to a smooth, hard surface.

"I believe you possess what my patient needs."

Luise turned to stare. What did this diminutive woman know of her? What had she and Tante Manya talked about during their visits?

"The Russian women from Konstantinovka, they call me when they need a midwife. I know them; they trust me. I was there two month past, delivered a young woman of her first child. Fine son, healthy mother, but they have called me back. Seems Tatiana, the young mother, cannot cope. She has no energy and cares for no one, barely rousing herself to nurse her child."

Luise listened, but again her memories stirred. "What's wrong with her? It seems to me a woman with a husband

and a healthy baby should be supremely grateful."

"Exactly so. But sometimes childbirth affects a woman's emotions so she can't see what she has—like Anna. Sometimes she can't hear what we say, so we have to show her the truth."

"Ah. Enter Luise, who has suffered and survived."

The little woman's voice sharpened. "Is your suffering for naught or are you willing to help someone else heal through your experiences?"

The sled bumped along the ruts in the road, jolting Luise' body even as thoughts bounced around in her brain. Was she willing to make herself vulnerable for a stranger, for a Russian?

❧

"She is Tatiana Bakunin," said Frau Klein. She reined in the horse at a dilapidated *izba* on a rutted street in Konstantinovka and the two women climbed out onto the frozen slush.

Taking in the lack of fence or lane or gate, Luise wondered what she would find inside, and her first impression was one of dimness. The ragged, dirty curtains were drawn shut. Dirty dishes littered the table and counter and Luise decided not to remove her boots when she noted the dirt floor.

"I will call you," said Frau Klein. She was about the same height as Hans, and her figure, when she had removed her heavy coat, had a strange shape, her stomach crowding up to her chest, her shoulders unnaturally stooped. The little woman bustled into a side room and left Luise alone in the kitchen.

While Frau Klein tended to Tatiana, Luise busied herself tidying the tiny house. She pulled aside the filthy curtains to let in some light, but when she saw how dirty the windows were, she was tempted to close them again. Instead, she heated water and washed the panes until the sun smiled through, then put the curtains to soak in hot water.

"Luise, what a difference that makes. Do the bedroom windows too." Frau Klein beamed at her from the doorway to the bedroom. "And when we get home, you can clean my house!" She cackled and beckoned to Luise.

"Would you take a moment to help me settle Tatiana? I have washed and changed her and need you to help straighten the bedding."

She turned back to the bedroom, still talking. "Such as it is."

Luise followed the woman into a small, stuffy bedroom. On the bed lay a pale young woman no older than Luise, but the emptiness of her eyes made her look much older. Pity flowed from Luise until it struck her that it could well be her, lying listless and wan if she had let herself succumb to self-pity and despair. No, she did not want to be that woman. What would Daniel say if he came home to that?

She smiled as Frau Klein introduced them. When they had straightened the thin sheet and helped Tatiana settle, Luise sat with her while Frau Klein occupied herself in the kitchen concocting her remedies and the tea she prescribed for all ailments.

"What can I do for you?" asked Luise. She fluffed the pillow so Tatiana could sit up, and brought Baby Vojtec to her to nurse. The feel of the little baby in her arms made Luise ache for the one she had lost.

Tatiana shrugged.

Luise tried again. "Your baby is beautiful."

Tatiana looked mildly surprised. "Yes, I suppose he is."

"How old is he?"

"I don't know. Two month perhaps. I've lost track of time."

Determined to keep the young woman talking, Luise asked more questions. "What was the birth like? Was it difficult?"

Tatiana turned hard eyes on Luise, the first spark of spirit she had so far portrayed. "Have you ever given birth?

It was hellish." Her emerald eyes bored into Luise's.

Luise blinked back tears but returned Tatiana's stare. "My experience was hellish too, because my baby was only five months along. It died, of course."

Tatiana's gaze faltered and she smoothed her hand across Vojtec's downy scalp.

"Was…was it a boy or a girl?"

"A girl."

"Why did you lose her?"

Luise tried to compose her emotions, but her voice trembled. "I was run over by a mounted GPU official."

Tatiana covered her mouth and closed her eyes. After a silence she whispered, "What did your husband do?"

"He…I…" Luise fetched her rag and water and began vigorously cleaning the windowpanes. "He was exiled before I came here, a year ago. We had been married the day before and then…he was taken."

"Taken where? Why? Is he alive?"

"I don't know where they took him. North, I suppose. His father was under duress for buying a new tractor on his own and died suddenly of heart failure the morning after our wedding. When the officials pushed Daniel about his father's tractor, he spoke his mind and they didn't appreciate it. He has always been rather outspoken. I don't know if he's still alive. I feel I would know if he had died."

Tatiana seemed shaken by Luise's revelation. Frau Klein stood soberly in the doorway.

"Is it time to go already?" asked Tatiana. She turned to Luise. "Will you return?"

Is this what you want of me, Lord? To serve this woman? "I'll consider it."

Frau Klein smiled and chattered about the sun going down and the drive back to Shumanovka and the coming of spring. Luise bid Tatiana farewell and followed Frau Klein outside to the waiting sleigh.

"It hurts to care," she said as the horse pulled them

home.

"So it does, but it is a good hurt. It reminds us we are alive."

Luise looked at Frau Klein's profile, but her face, buried in furs as it was, gave nothing away.

"Is Tatiana's husband a farmer?"

"No. He is GPU."

Chapter Eighteen

One can survive with minimal food, water, and even air, but never without hope.

After one year, only half the prisoners in the northern camp still survived. Daniel stood in the clearing and surveyed the scar he and his fellow exiles had created in the midst of otherwise unspoiled taiga. An uneven row of crude hovels stood questionable sentry at the bottom of the hill.

The third hut belonged to Daniel and six others, the place they called home, the place where cold followed, where hunger remained, where lice bred and thrived in the seams of every piece of clothing and in every blanket, where hope was indeed a scarce commodity, but still evidenced itself in subtle ways.

Day followed day in monotonous sequence, and Daniel struggled to maintain clarity and purpose. Why plan when there was no chance of escape, when so many had already succumbed to cold, hunger, disease and depression? Could he hold to hope even now?

A mild spring breeze brushed across his face, bringing with it memories of Luise's touch and her soulful eyes, but he viewed these memories as if looking through dirty glass. The facts were locked in his mind, but his heart was dying daily. He had needed all his energy to survive, and now he wondered why he had tried so hard. He would die here like all the rest. And yet the men seemed to lean on him for leadership.

Daniel recalled the hardy clan of Yakut who had brought meat and hides for shoes and clothing, in exchange for lumber. Kubolov didn't seem to care if the horse people helped them. He knew no one would escape in winter. So those exiles not oppressed by sickness survived. If he'd still believed in a God of mercy, Daniel might have considered the Yakut presence a miracle. Instead, he grudgingly called it luck.

The guards occasionally threw the men old bread and other scraps, and the prisoners fell on the food like the wild dogs that skulked around the edges of the clearing. Keeping in mind what he had learned from the Yakut who had visited the Mennonite lumbering camp the winter before his arrest, Daniel encouraged the men to find added sustenance in the forest to keep their stomachs from shriveling. Trout populated the streams, and the guards no longer minded if the men found supplementary food, as long as they shared it with their supervisors. Wild ptarmigan berries would flourish again in the summer months, tasteless but nourishing.

Just as Daniel was about to turn to his work, he noticed a mounted horseman entering the confines of the exile camp. His heart thudded as the rider dismounted and limped toward Kubolov, who stood watching Daniel. Was Dubrowsky back temporarily, or for good? Daniel didn't know, but the man's presence charged the atmosphere with dread. Every man seemed to draw within himself.

Daniel wondered if his beatings would resume now that his nemesis had returned. Dubrowsky stared at him with fresh hatred revived over the course of a comfortable winter in Moscow, or wherever he had gone. When no words were forthcoming, Daniel turned and walked away, picking up his axe as he passed his hut. The heft of it felt good in his calloused hands. He fingered the blade and felt its sharpness, images of revenge filling his mind.

He straightened his shoulders. While some of the men had grown gaunt and ill, Daniel recommitted himself to survival. He would not forget Luise and his promise to return to her. Neither would he forget his promise to himself that Dubrowsky would pay for his cruelty. He let himself believe that those two goals were not mutually exclusive.

Daniel realized that one of the reasons he still lived was that Dubrowsky preferred to watch him suffer as long as possible. Klaas Enns still fought the good fight, for which Daniel was glad, but his brother had fallen prey to a stomach virus and passed on in agony, his earthly suffering at an end.

During the day, Daniel worked with the goal of building himself up physically and keeping his mind sharp, but the short nights nearly defeated him. Luise walked through his dreams, her eyes wide at his arrest, her voice pleading for his release. These memories caused him distress, but what undid him completely in the lonely hours of darkness was the memory of her hands and her body and her whispers of love in the sweetness of Manya's cottage. The whippings administered by Dubrowsky had been easier to bear.

Spring days lengthened and the men worked longer hours. In spite of the coolness of the nights, there was a hint of change in the air, a change that Daniel also felt within himself.

❧

With the emergence of spring and her probable return to Tatiana's, Luise concentrated on spring cleaning. In league with her female neighbors, she scrubbed every corner of the house and porch, stopping only at the barn door.

"Lise," said Abram as he met her on his way in from the barn, "Hans will help me with cleaning in here, as usual. And I beg you not to set foot in my shop. I promise to tidy and sweep it myself."

Luise grinned. "What's the matter, Papa? Don't you trust me?"

"For cleanliness, yes. For interference in my workplace, no."

Luise returned to the house, rags and pail in hand, to

find her great-aunt stirring a large pot of soup on the cookstove. Relief flooded her as she realized how tired she was.

"Thank you, Tante Manya. I was about to add the vegetables to the stock so the soup would be ready for supper, but I wanted to finish washing the porch first."

Manya looked up at her through the aromatic steam. "You have enough to do. I must stand from my chair now and then so I don't become one with it."

Luise put away the pail, hung the rags to dry and washed her hands in the bowl on the table. "Once the cow freshens, I'll be back to milking too, but Nela can help me feed the calf this year.

"Nela! Go gather the eggs now, please."

Luise took up the broom, swept the kitchen and tossed the dirt and crumbs out the back door. It suddenly struck her that with all her household busyness and the added spring cleaning, she had forgotten about Daniel. She stood still, the broom before her like a dance partner. How could I forget you? She asked herself the question over and over. How had she become so involved in physical activity that she had let her heart forget?

Leaning the broom into the corner behind the kitchen door, she stepped outside into the cool spring air and stood there until she shivered. It would be worse for Daniel, she knew. Spring would come more slowly in the far north. She prayed for him, that he would not suffer excessive cold, that he would have shoes to protect his feet, that he would have sufficient food, and that he would not place her on the back burner of his mind as she had temporarily done to him.

Feeling somewhat mollified by her penance, Luise slipped back into the kitchen to resume her work, but this time thoughts of Daniel claimed her mind.

Daniel had consistently refused to allow Dubrowsky the pleasure of seeing his pain, hiding it deep within, not even acknowledging it to himself. He watched Dubrowsky as well, watched for his weaknesses, his overlove of drink when it was available, his laziness, the flaccidity of his body when he returned to the camp in the spring. The man had grown weaker, the revolver he carried beneath his coat his only assurance of power as he limped about or slouched in a chair. Why did the man waste his time in this forsaken place?

Dubrowsky had ordered the men to go down to the river to catch a mess of fish for supper, as even the guards' rations had seriously dwindled. Dubrowsky himself had chosen to stay behind in the clearing, picking at his fingernails with his pocketknife. Daniel intended to cross the stream and disappear into the woods, giving himself a day's head start and a chance to cover some territory toward the south while the weather held.

While the other men bobbed their fishing lines in the stream, Daniel slipped back to the camp for a blanket and a fishing line. When he saw Dubrowsky seated on a camp chair in the sun smoking, primitive instinct kicked in, born of the hatred that fed his determination. Daniel crept from the shadow of one of the huts, his thoughts clear and cold. He slunk up behind Dubrowsky as quietly as a blue fox on a ptarmigan, wrapping the ends of his fishing line around his hands as he moved. He stretched the line taut. The man would not suffer long, but at least he would not inflict further suffering on others as he had done to Daniel and his mates.

Surely he was doing the world a favor by ridding it of this fiend. How many Bible stories dramatized God's people dispatching evil men because God said their time had come?

So now you are on a mission for God? Thoughts of David refusing to kill King Saul, who hunted him, flitted through Daniel's head, but he pushed them away. He raised his arms and brought the wire down around the Dubrowsky's neck. The man jerked, his cigarette falling to the ground. His eyes bulged, and he swiped at the garroting wire that robbed his breath and cut into his neck.

Before Daniel could pull the wire tight, he felt a blow to the back of his head and lurched forward on top of Dubrowsky. In a daze, Daniel felt arms drag him, and then the pain of well-placed kicks until his consciousness fled. As blackness engulfed him, he thought perhaps this was a punishment from the God he had ignored in his resolve to secure vengeance on his own. If so, he deserved it, but he'd broken his promise to Luise, because now he knew he would die.

Luise knocked at the door of Frau Klein's little house, but the place remained silent as death. Had the woman gone out to visit patients in other villages? Luise wished to speak to her today, before her resolve weakened.

She had decided to return to Konstantinovka to help Tatiana. She would go next week and stay long enough to be of help, perhaps a few weeks. Whether her husband was GPU or not, Tatiana needed someone to help her through this valley and onto the road that led to full recovery. The winter must have been long for her. Luise didn't have a child of her own to nurture, but she could help another woman learn to nurture hers.

Giving up, Luise turned back up the path to the road. Just then she heard a shout and the clatter of an approaching horse and sleigh. She could not see the driver, almost hidden in a coat several times too large, but she recognized the horse.

"Are you looking for me?" shouted Frau Klein as soon as the horse stopped.

"Yes," said Luise. "I want to speak to you about returning to Konstantinovka."

"Well good. You could probably find your way. They haven't moved it."

Luise laughed. "I wanted to discuss Tatiana's care with

you since I think I will stay with her for a while."

"Come sit in the sleigh, then. This day is too beautiful to go inside that dingy house."

All Daniel felt was pain, radiating from his back down to his feet, and he couldn't open his eyes. The beasts must have had their fun with him after he lost consciousness. He deserved it this time, but his decision to kill Dubrowsky had cost him his opportunity for escape. You must temper your temper. He heard his mother's words even now.

He forced his eyes open a crack—only the left one obeyed—and saw darkness. Panic set in and he twitched uncontrollably. They had blinded him. He couldn't see as much as...wait. There. A crack of light above him, a slit of relief from outside this place. He lay back in relief at the realization that he could see, that he was alive.

Where there is life, there is hope. Luise's words. Luise. From a world away her hands caressed his broken body as her words comforted his soul. He floated into a place of nothingness, as if he were swimming in a pool of dark water. He didn't worry about keeping his head up; it didn't seem as if he needed to breathe. He would just give in to Luise's ministrations.

Sudden brightness pierced his eyes and he groaned. "Luise?" He winced and his lips cracked. A cruel laugh and another sharp kick brought him out of his dream of solace and back to reality. Then blackness and silence again. He realized that although he wasn't dead yet, he soon would be, and he did not want to die. Not only was he unprepared to meet his Maker, but he had promised Luise he would return.

He heard a faint scritching like that of a mouse and listened, tension gripping his body. A hand reached behind his head and he tried to scuttle away, but a voice soft and low whispered, "Do not fear. Drink this." Cool liquid dribbled onto his face, into his mouth, over his parched lips. His tongue felt large in his mouth, but the water soothed it ever so slightly.

He could see nothing of the one whose presence he sensed, nor could he respond, and then the person left as quietly as he had come. Was it Klaas Enns? But how would he gain entrance to "the hole?" Perhaps it was an angel. Or just his imagination. He gingerly reached the one arm that moved and felt his face. Wet, as was his collar. Someone had been here. Someone cared. He could not give up hope. Not yet.

❧

Even though Luise had decided to return to help Tatiana in Konstantinovka, the fact that her husband was GPU preyed upon her mind and formed a knot in her stomach.

"What is the husband like, Frau Klein?"

"He is stern, but I believe he is a fair man."

"How can a GPU officer be a fair man? Is not evil a prerequisite?"

Frau Klein lifted her chin and glared into Luise's eyes. "Good thing you are not a medical doctor, or even a midwife like me. We practitioners cannot refuse our services because of personal prejudice."

"Personal prejudice! The Soviets have taken my father, my husband, my home, and my child. How can I serve a man who works for them?"

Frau Klein's eyes were magnified through her spectacles. "Vasili Bakunin did not take your husband. He did not kill your baby. Bakunin is a man who does his best to survive within the system."

While walking home, Luise prayed that God would give her a sign if He really wanted her to return to Konstantinovka and Tatiana. She did not have to wait longer than a few hours before Phillip knocked on her door.

"Luise, I am going to Konstantinovka this afternoon. Would you like a ride there?"

"Do you have a cousin there as well as in New York?"

He grinned. "I'm making a delivery for my uncle, but I could maybe find a cousin if I searched."

Luise cast about for an excuse and looked to her father for help, but the idea of going with Phillip seemed to make sense. She had finished her cleaning and had begun planting the garden seeds in little pots of dirt to start them off. Tante Manya could finish that and the seedlings would still be ready for seeding later in May.

She hastily folded a few clothes and her personal items into a satchel and stood ready at the door when Phillip returned with his sleigh. By next week he would have to replace the runners with wheels as the snow gradually melted and the black earth and grass showed through. She reminded herself to maintain her distance from this man so he wouldn't imagine things that didn't exist.

Luise's reserve lasted only until they passed the last buildings of Shumanovka and headed south along the still-snowy road to Konstantinovka. Phillip, with his usual candor, told her all about his long winter, cooped up with his female cousins until he thought he might tear out his hair with all their talk of pillow embroidery and dress patterns and gossip. He had Luise laughing before Shumanovka disappeared behind the low hill.

She tried to maintain a sense of decorum, but Phillip did not seem to care for decorum. He was easy to visit with, and before long, her tension eased and she found herself telling him of Hans and Nela in the snow and about some of Anna's less complimentary comments.

"It's been a pleasant trip. Thank you for taking me." Luise reached for her satchel. Phillip sat staring at the house.

"I know," she said. "It doesn't look very inviting, but those within need my help."

Phillip jumped from the sleigh and assisted Luise to the ground. "How long are you staying?"

"Several weeks, maybe a month. Why?"

He frowned. "How well do you know these people?"

Luise had not told Phillip or anyone else of Tatiana's husband's identity. "I know and trust Tatiana, and Frau Klein assures me that the husband is a decent man."

Her words did not seem to satisfy Phillip. "You are a brave woman," he said, "and I hope also a discerning one."

"Phillip, I'll be fine. Don't worry about me."

He straightened his shoulders, climbed back into his sleigh and nodded to her, but his smile seemed strained.

Luise, however, felt energized by the cool, fresh air and the prospect of putting hope and order into the life of Tatiana and her family. She waved her thanks to Phillip and walked toward Tatiana's door. Phillip slapped the reins on the horse's rump and drove off.

Chapter Nineteen

The unmarked passage of time gnawed at Daniel's slim thread of hope. For days and probably weeks, he'd lain alone in "the hole," drifting in and out of consciousness. Voices came and went, sometimes with kicks and whacks, sometimes with a thin gruel to keep him alive. It was Klaus Enns who fed him; somehow he'd received permission to do so. The prison remained dark, but for a few rays of weak light when Enns entered. At least it was a kind voice that murmured to him as he spooned life-sustaining soup into his mouth. Why did they bother to keep him alive? If this present suffering of his gave them pleasure, they were devils indeed.

His thinking had become muddled. Every part of him hurt. He wondered how many bones had been broken and how they would heal, should he survive. Would he walk again?

Then came the day when he heard several voices at once outside his prison.

"Get him out."

Daniel tried to place the voice.

"Where shall I take him?" The gentle voice of Enns.

"To his hut, where else?" Was that Kubolov? Had Dubrowsky gone?

Enns knelt at Daniel's side. "I'm going to take you out of this place. I'll try not to hurt you, but I don't know what to be careful of."

"Take me...out..." Daniel couldn't form more words, but he wanted out of this place before he lost his mind.

"Easy now. Don't panic. You're not very heavy, I think I

can lift you."

Daniel sucked in his breath at the pain that seared through him as Enns moved him bit by bit toward the opening of this den of death. Enns apologized but kept moving him. When he brought Daniel out into bright sunlight, Daniel screwed his eyes shut and covered them with his good hand. The light he had so missed hurt like fire.

Daniel felt himself lifted up, and then lapsed into darkness as Enns stumbled over rough ground toward the hut. As he drifted, Daniel drew in fresh air. It seemed to seep all the way to his toes.

❧

"When will your husband return home, Tatiana?" As Luise washed the walls of the little bedroom, her spring cleaning fervor still driving her, she tried to think of ways to engage her patient in conversation. The woman seemed to have lapsed into deeper depression since Luise's last visit. She imagined her Russian friend suffering the same fate as Anna, gradually regaining some strength physically, but never emotionally.

Tatiana turned her head toward Luise. "What did you ask?"

"I wondered when your husband would come home. He's been gone a long time."

The woman sighed. "He is sent away on business for long stretches of time. I'm not sure when he will return."

"Your mother thought it might be soon."

"Well then, you know more than I do. Why must you wash everything so thoroughly? It only gets dirty again."

"A clean house is a happy one," said Luise.

Tatiana turned her face away and closed her eyes. Luise ignored her and continued washing. She had already set the kitchen and parlor to rights, much to the amazement of Tatiana's mother, Mrs. Gromyko, who stopped by regularly.

Luise wondered when Vasili Bakunin would return. Her hand stilled as fear settled over her, but she shook it off and finished her job. Soon little Vojtec would wake and the washing would have to wait for tomorrow.

After Luise had taken Vojtec to his mother to be nursed, she set about cooking a substantial supper. There were provisions enough in the shed out back—hams, bacon, roasts—as well as an abundance of potatoes, carrots and onions in the root cellar. The stew she had created smelled rich and hearty as it bubbled in its juices. She reached for plates to fill and carry into the bedroom, since Tatiana claimed she could not sit at table.

Suddenly the door opened and a tall, moustached man entered, a rifle in his hand.

Luise froze, the plates gripped in trembling fingers. So this was Vasili Bakunin, the man Frau Klein defined as fair.

"Who are you?" he barked. "What are you doing in my house?"

Vasili walked around her to the bedroom and peeked inside. His conversation with Tatiana was clipped and harsh. He turned once more to Luise and then frowned as he stared about him. "What have you done to my home, woman? Who gave you the right to interfere with my family? Get out."

He turned from her, unloaded the gun he still held, and hung it over the door while she watched.

"What are you staring at? I told you to leave."

From the corner of her eyes, Luise saw Tatiana watching from the bedroom, her face as animated as it had been so far. Luise took a deep breath, squared her shoulders and glared at Bakunin. "If I go, I take the stew with me."

He glared back at her. "I'd like to see you carry that pot very far."

Turning her back on him, she began to ladle the stew into smaller pots with lids, and then placed them one by one into a wooden crate. Hefting the crate, she marched toward him and around him, avoiding his eyes. "Please open the door."

At his silence, she glanced at him. A bemused expression had replaced the anger. "On second thought, you will leave after we eat. I am about to starve."

"So I shall feed you and then be turned out into the street?"

"From where have you come?"

"Shumanovka. Frau Klein sent me."

At the mention of Frau Klein's name, Bakunin's face changed. He blew out his breath and muttered something unintelligible.

"Pardon me, sir?"

He stared at her through lowered brows. "Serve the supper. I am hungry."

Luise carried the crate of stew back to the table and set it out. "There is plenty, but I will eat mine with Tatiana in her room." The husband said not another word, and she feared she might have stepped across a line. If so, she would face the consequences, but she was not about to be cowed by this man, even though he was GPU.

When Luise had helped Tatiana with her supper and brought Vojtec to her to nurse, she cleaned up the dishes. Vasili brought a harness into the house and threw it onto the kitchen table to mend. She bit her tongue when she saw the grease and dirt that left its mark. He glanced at her once or twice but she maintained her distance and retired as soon as possible to the lean-to off the kitchen. She wasn't about to set off for home in the night, on foot, alone.

Luise slumped down onto the low cot and stared at the darkness through the tiny window. At least she had a window. She thought about the difference between this house and those in the Mennonite colonies with which she was familiar. She had known some of the Russian girls in Slavgorod, the ones who came to the village to work for the Mennonite women, but she had not visited a Russian home. A sense of hopelessness prevailed in the Bakunin house and she didn't know how to dispel it.

She huddled on the cot, the rough blanket wrapped around her to ward off the chill and the oppression that had come home with Vasili Bakunin.

"If it were any colder outside, I'd freeze to death in here."

She sniffed and rubbed her eyes. "But then despair would win," she whispered. "I can't let that happen. God sent me here for a reason and I intend to fulfill it." Luise turned down the lampwick, snuggled under the covers and made a plan to win the battle, and to win over Vasili Bakunin in the process, with the Lord's help.

❧

"Good morning, Tatiana," Luise said the next morning as she bustled into the bedroom and opened the curtains. Vasili had apparently gone out before anyone else had awakened, taking his mended harness with him and leaving the dirt and grease behind.

Tatiana groaned and covered her face. "Please," she mumbled. "Close the curtains."

"What, and miss the brilliant sunshine? Let's invite it in to melt our winter doldrums. Now, sit up and I'll bring you breakfast." She propped the pillow behind Tatiana, who appeared too surprised to argue. "There now, I'll be right back."

Luise surprised even herself as she set to the task with determination. She hummed while she encouraged Tatiana to eat some of the warm porridge sprinkled with dried berries.

"This is a special occasion," said Luise. "You are going to get well. Won't it be wonderful to rise from this bed and see to your baby yourself, to cook and clean for your husband and be the wife he remembers?"

"I cannot eat any more," said Tatiana. "I feel faint when I sit up so long."

"I will settle you back for a nap as soon as you've nursed Vojtec, but we will sit for lunch again and soon you'll become used to it as you grow stronger."

Tatiana gave her a long look, but Luise only smiled as she tucked her in again and pulled the curtains closed. "Drink this wonderful tonic Frau Klein sent for you. I'll bring little Vojtec in now. You are the only one who can bring the contentment he requires."

Vasili had returned while his wife ate breakfast. Luise felt his eyes on her as she straightened his wife's hair and washed her face with a damp cloth. Luise braced herself for the encounter she knew would come.

She closed the bedroom door behind her and faced Vasili in the kitchen. Her voice low, she said, "It looks like a decent day outside. I will pack my things once I finish cleaning up the breakfast, and start on my way home."

"Where is your horse?"

"At home. I was brought here by a friend."

Vasili frowned at her. "So you are stuck here with us."

"I said I'd—"

"I heard what you said," he snapped, then quieted with a glance at the bedroom door. "You may remain as long as you stay out of my way. Understood?"

Luise tried to read his eyes, but she could not. She supposed the GPU were trained to mask their feelings and Vasili had learned well. "Yes, but I must ask you to keep your harnesses outside. They create a—"

Vasili leaned forward, his eyes hard. "This is my house and you will stay out of my way. Understood?"

"Understood." Luise took a big breath to slow her racing pulse. She had no choice but to cooperate with him. It was, after all, his home.

"You will be disappointed if you think you can bring her around so easily," said Vasili, indicating the bedroom with a jerk of his head. "Her mother has tried for two months to get her to develop an attachment to that baby."

Luise bit her lip. "With all due respect, Commissar Bakunin, I have met Tatiana's mother, and she does not strike me as having the capacity to bring cheer to any home."

Vasili's face remained passive, but Luise thought she detected a slight twinkle in his eye. "And you can do better?"

"I have had some experiences that help me understand her. Frau Klein thought I would be able to help."

Vasili grunted. "Just keep that baby quiet."

Luise narrowed her eyes. How had such a young man become so cold and cynical? Did he have no fatherly instincts, no pride in his son?

"His name is Vojtec."

Vasili tilted his head at her statement. Once again, Luise felt fear rise in her, but she refused to give in to it.

"He is not a nameless child, sir. He is your son. He will grow to be like you."

"Then I pity him." His voice sounded as full of despair as that of his wife in the next room.

"As you say."

"Kubolov seems to be in control here again," said Klaas Enns when he returned to the hut where Daniel lay. "But I've seen Dubrowsky here too. Maybe he's still recovering from your attempt on his life."

Daniel winced as he shifted on the narrow cot. "Why doesn't he just kill me?"

Enns looked at him.

"Kubolov allowed me to take extra food for you, but I doubt that will continue. How is your leg?"

"Still broken, I would guess. Takes a long time for a broken bone to mend."

Enns brought the cup of thin soup to Daniel and handed him a slice of dry bread. "Perhaps we can fashion a splint for you, so you can walk."

"That's fine, Klaas, but how do I swing an axe with one arm? I can't move the other one."

Enns grimaced and walked toward the door. "I'll do all I can for you, but I don't think they'll let you lie around much longer." He turned back to Daniel. "I will keep praying for a way out for you."

"If it makes you feel better."

With a swiftness that surprised Daniel, Enns returned to his bedside and crooked a finger in his face. "Listen, Martens. There is nothing else for you to rely on anymore. Only God can help you. Do not spit in His face."

"I didn't spit in His face."

"That's what you do every time you deny Him. Believe it or not, He loves you."

Daniel felt his face grow hot. "He certainly has strange ways of showing it."

Enns blew out his breath in obvious exasperation, and Daniel felt badly for confronting him, but his doubts were bigger than his faith. So far, prayer hadn't helped at all. Yet, he still clung to a fragment of the faith of his fathers.

"Maybe your prayers will have more effect than mine."

Enns left and Daniel drank the sour soup and lay back to heal and think. Had God spared him for a reason? Deep down, he knew God and believed in Him, but he didn't trust Him. Or perhaps it was himself he did not trust.

⁂

When Phillip came to call on Luise two weeks later at the Bakunin house in Konstantinovka, she thought him very forward indeed, until he gave the reason for his visit.

"Anna has become weaker, Luise, and Manya is playing out. They need you to come home."

Luise's heart longed to see her family, but she had only begun to break through the barrier between herself and Tatiana.

"Is Anna very bad off?"

"I don't know, but I said I'd come for you."

Luise narrowed her eyes at him. Was this his idea? She sighed as she realized he would not stoop to lies and deceit to bring her back to Shumanovka. "Could you give me a little time to say goodbye to Tatiana and Vojtec?"

"Of course. There is time enough to get back home before dark."

Luise spent the hot summer days back home in Shumanovka, but in the fall, after the garden had been harvested, she asked her father for permission to go back to Konstantinovka again.

"For how long this time?" he asked.

"Not long. Perhaps two weeks. I miss the little fellow and Tatiana, and I think there is still hope she will get better."

"Very well. Anna seems to have settled, and I can help Manya since the harvest is done."

"He's going to put me out of my misery any day now," said Daniel as Klaas Enns helped him sip the tepid soup. Daniel saw concern in Klaas' eyes when he touched him. He too must feel the fever that weakened him.

"I haven't seen Dubrowsky for a couple of days. Maybe he's forgotten about you."

Daniel sputtered and choked. When he had regained his breath he said, "No, he will not forget about me. I wish he would. He will see me die yet. I haven't been able to contribute to the work here and he won't continue feeding me. Besides, I'd never survive the winter."

Enns' lower lip trembled and Daniel felt fresh pain in his chest.

"Thank you for caring for me. My mother would thank you. Too bad I couldn't live to tell her."

Enns rubbed his eyes with his thumb and forefinger. "You've been like a brother." His voice cracked and he looked away. "But I can't save you."

"I know."

"Don't lose faith, whatever happens."

Daniel pulled his lips into a weak smile and sank back

onto the cot. "Pray for me." His breathing became labored and he lost consciousness.

Dizziness woke Daniel. The incessant pain of constant motion kept the darkness on the edges of his mind. He couldn't move his arms and his head pounded. Forcing his eyes open a slit, he saw the ground moving below him and clenched his teeth to keep from retching. He had apparently been tied hand and foot and slung across the back of a horse. They were taking him somewhere. But where would they take him in this endless wasteland? Searing pain seized him and fogged his mind.

He heard a grunt as hands pulled at him, and then jolted with a thud of unreasonable pain. He had fallen from the horse and landed with his face in the dirt. He tried to turn his head but his neck locked. Spitting, he cleared his mouth to breathe, and a shadow covered him.

"May you rot with the leaves, you murderer."

The voice belonged to Dubrowsky, and the hate it carried felt like a suffocating hand on his soul.

"If you were to live, you would no doubt be maimed, as I am. But you will not live, so I've had enough of you."

With a kick to Daniel's side, Dubrowsky limped away. "Shoot him. He's not worth my bullet."

A low autumn sun warmed Daniel's body. He heard creaking saddles and the soft thump of horses' hooves in sandy soil, every sound and sense vivid. A shot punctured the still air and ripped into Daniel's side, making him gasp, but the pain he already endured so overwhelmed him that this last attack meant only one thing: death would come sooner.

The horses kicked up sand that settled on Daniel's body. Struggling to breathe, he lay twisted as he had fallen, with no strength to move, and listened to the departing sounds of life. He remembered working in the fields on days such as this, throwing off his shirt and letting his body bronze in the sun. He recalled the months of felling trees and cutting them for the village of Alexandrovka. Not his choice, but good, honest work. He thought of working alongside his father, threshing the crops of his neighbors, helping them bring in the harvest. It had been a good life until that spring, the spring of his arrest and exile.

Thoughts of that spring brought thoughts of Luise. He recalled her as a child, her solemn expression as she led the cows home from pasture as if it were the most important mission in the world, then her laughter bubbling forth when he marched beside her like an army general leading his troops. He remembered watching her blossom from a girl into a young woman, recalled the day he had told her of his love, of his intentions. She had been walking near the stream with her friend, Valentina, when he had met them. Luise had been shy at first, Valentina had giggled and run off with thinly veiled excuses, and they were alone.

"I know you're young," he said, "but I want you to know you are the only girl for me. Someday I'm going to marry you."

Shaking her shyness, she raised her eyes to his. "Is that so? Well then I think you'd better start courting me."

She turned with a saucy smile and walked away. He hurried to catch up.

"Luise, I have chosen you."

She stopped and turned back. "Yes," she said, "but have I chosen you?"

Her words then in the quiet beauty of the summer sunshine had taught him that he must work for what he wanted, that he could not take things for granted or make people do his bidding without their will. That was not his way. So he had pursued her, and soon everyone accepted that it was to be.

And then she was his, that night in Manya's cottage. His whole body groaned at the memory. He considered what his quick temper and spontaneous actions had cost them both and knew the price had been too high. Now his time had come to die and he had lost everything.

"Forgive me before I die, Father God. Forgive me...." His voice rasped as he forced it through swollen lips. Clouds blotted out the sunlight. He felt the chill of coming winter as flakes of wet snow settled on him. They felt to his tortured body like gentle touches of an angel. His mind sharpened and he finished his prayer: "Look after Luise."

His amen dissolved into darkness as the first snow swathed his broken body.

"Little chickens, little chickens,
What are you doing on our yard?
You are picking all the flowers,
And throwing them into the dust.
Mama will scold you,
Papa will spank you.
Little chickens, little chickens,
How will you feel then?"

Luise sang one of the German songs she had learned in childhood as she bounced Vojtec on one arm and gave the borscht a stir with the other. Then she lifted the baby up in her arms and grinned at him. "You are a darling little man, aren't you?" He squirmed, reaching out his chubby arms, his eyes locked on something over Luise's shoulder.

She turned her head to see Vasili standing in the doorway, glaring at her. Self-consciously, she lowered the baby and brought out the plates for supper. Was he angry about her use of German? Or was he just angry because that was his nature? Luise seldom saw Vasili go to the bedroom to speak with Tatiana, although she assumed he slept there at night, since there was no other place for him to sleep.

Even so, she felt Tatiana had begun to thaw, to show an interest in daily life and in her child. Meanwhile, Luise had come to love the "little man." When she laid him on the bed to change his diapers, he would focus on her eyes as if trying to read her mind. Then he would laugh and kick so she could scarcely accomplish the task.

"He has a bright mind, this son of yours," commented Luise. "He is growing so fast."

Vasili sat waiting for his bowl of borscht and a slice of fresh bread, and merely grunted at Luise's words. Time, thought Luise. Time and prayer heal all—most—wounds. Surely it was not God's will for a father to ignore his son, nor was it normal for a young woman to lie abed day and night, avoiding responsibility for her family.

"She is coming again today," said Vasili, between slurps of soup.

Luise waited for him to clarify his statement. He rarely initiated conversation.

"The mother-in-law."

He said the words as if they were a curse, and possibly to him, they were. To Luise they were a test of endurance.

Mrs. Gromyko nodded her way into the house shortly afterward, her face drawn with worry, and began to speak even before she had closed the door behind her. Vasili sopped up the last of his soup with the bread without looking up.

"My own dear mother, God rest her soul, died when I was a child of five. Papa tried several arrangements, girls who came to look after us. But they couldn't abide his gruffness, due of course to his broken heart, and soon left. We became used to a parade of young women who looked after our physical needs but not our emotional ones."

Vasili pushed back his chair, nodded at his mother-in-law, and left the house. Mrs. Gromyko followed him with her eyes but kept talking.

"Now my poor Tatiana languishes alone in her room, and no one can help her."

She began to weep, and Luise put a hand on her shoulder. At that moment, Vasili poked his head back in the door.

"Frau Martens, you have a caller." He stood waiting for her to come outside.

Luise's spirits brightened at the announcement. "Please excuse me." She rose to go to the door, but held back for a moment, unsure of how to respectfully contradict the woman.

"Mrs. Gromyko, your daughter is gradually coming out of the darkness and we need to help her, not hold her back."

"I would never stand in the way, but it's been so hard for her, poor thing. She almost died, you know, giving birth to that child."

"I realize the birth was difficult, but her body is healing. We must help her mind heal also."

"And that poor little baby."

Luise sighed and walked toward the door while Vasili marched toward his mother-in-law at the table. Luise heard his low-spoken words. "Mother, the child has a name. It is Vojtec, and he is a fine, growing boy. Any grandmother would be proud."

"But what his coming did to my daughter."

"Vojtec is not at fault for that. You must take him now while I talk with Tatiana."

Vasili took little Vojtec from the bassinet where he sat playing with his toes and gave him to his grandmother. She looked at him fearfully, and Luise, watching the entire episode, realized the woman had not accepted her position or her grandson. She prayed that Vojtec would work his magic on her heart.

Luise looked quickly away, so as not to be caught eavesdropping. Or had Vasili meant for her to overhear? Perhaps he was not as cynical as she had thought. Something in him must have drawn Tatiana to him when they met.

Luise pulled the curtain aside and peeked out. There, leaning against the buggy, stood Phillip Wieler.

"*Ach, Himmel,*" she said. "What am I to do with him?"

Chapter Twenty

"**Phillip, what brings** you to Konstantinovka?"

"I know people here and I'm scouting for horses."

"Who do you know here?"

Phillip met her eyes. "I know you."

Luise squirmed. "Of course you do, but I don't think you would come all the way from Shumanovka to see me."

Phillip shook his head slightly as a smile played about his lips. "You think not? Perhaps you have not been paying attention."

Luise blew out her breath in frustration. "Phillip, we have been over all this. I am a married woman. I'm not looking for a man. My heart belongs to Daniel Martens and will always belong to him, whether he is dead or alive. I choose to believe the latter."

"Luise, would you take a drive with me? I would have you back shortly."

The thought of fresh air and conversation in German tempted her. The sun shone strong, melting the snow and ice, and chickadees and sparrows filled the air with song.

"Very well."

"Please don't sound so excited about it." He helped her into the buggy and snapped the reins gently.

She ignored his retort and said nothing, frustrated that she was even riding with this man. How could she make him understand she was not interested in pursuing a relationship? He had more perseverance than an ant at a picnic. Perhaps he did remind her a bit of Martha Lepp.

"Luise." His voice interrupted her thoughts. "There is something I need to tell you. Someone has to tell you, and since I feel the need to look after you…"

He hesitated and she waited, with no inclination to make things easier for him.

"Luise," he said again. "I don't know how to say this, but you must know that if Daniel were alive, he would have come back by now. Logic suggests that his absence means he has not survived."

Luise reached for the reins and pulled on them. "You are cruel to say such a thing. You have no more information than I do."

"Actually, I do."

Luise shaded her eyes against the sun. "What do you mean? What do you know?"

She saw pity in his eyes, and his arm reached out to her, but she leaned as far from him as she dared, without falling out of the buggy.

"Just say what you have to say, Phillip."

He grimaced and pulled his arm back to his side. "First of all, instinct and common sense suggest that Daniel did not survive. No one survives Soviet exile."

Luise's eyes burned and her insides recoiled at his words. "They have and they do. Not all who go north die a horrible death."

Phillip held up a hand to silence her. "Yes, well I suppose that's so, but if they don't escape early on, they never do. They either die later of hard labor or exposure, or they accept their lot and settle into the area where they've been exiled."

Luise wanted to slap his face. "You are Daniel's best friend; you know him well. Do you really believe him capable of staying up north, knowing we pray for his return? Do you really think he has forgotten us all? Well, whatever you think, I do not believe it. I won't forget him. I will remain faithful to my marriage vows, and you can leave me be."

She climbed from the buggy and trudged back through

the slush and mud in the direction of the Bakunin house, muttering through angry tears, swiping her face with her hand. How dare he? Did he think the presumption of Daniel's death would make her want him? What nerve!

She heard the buggy turn and Phillip cluck his tongue to the horse as it pulled up beside her.

"Luise, wait. There is more."

Her chest heaved as she glared up at him through a mist of tears. "What more could there be? Can you not see that my heart is already breaking?"

Phillip looked away from her and she thought she saw tears in his eyes as well. She told herself she didn't care. He had hurt her.

Phillip climbed down from the buggy, seemingly oblivious to the mud, and stood before her. Fixing his eyes on her face once again, he said the words that completed her devastation.

"Luise, my…my mother sent a letter. I just received it yesterday."

He had her full attention now. There was something stronger than conjecture in his tone. She took a big breath and held it, as if it might be her last.

"She said Leonid Dubrowsky came back through Alexandrovka to update the records in the village office." He watched her face. "He made it perfectly clear that Daniel Martens was dead. He died, Luise."

She shook her head in disbelief. "No!" She choked on the word, her lungs crushed by an invisible hand.

"He…he was executed. Shot." His voice failed him and he had to clear his throat. "That's what the official said."

She watched him swallow and pinch the bridge of his nose.

"Dubrowsky killed him?"

"I don't know, Luise, I imagine he might have, or at least have witnessed it."

She grabbed the edge of the buggy. "Did they bury

him?"

"I don't know. It was a letter, Luise. Words on a page. I only read what Mother wrote." He shook his head and let out his breath forcefully. "I'm sorry, Luise, but I thought you needed to know since you were his wife."

Luise couldn't remember taking another breath. She felt numb, like her fingers and toes when they almost froze in winter. Her voice sank to a murmur. "And you were his best friend. Why did you come here, Phillip? You and Jasch?"

He took her arm and led her to a pile of wood and stumps near the Bakunin yard and motioned for her to sit. She had no strength to resist.

"We were being questioned because the three of us always spent time together. We decided to get out of there before we ended up like Dan—" He coughed and apologized. "We left because we were afraid of being arrested."

She nodded and hugged her arms around herself. "Thank you for telling me this, Phillip. I'm sure it hurts you too."

"Of course it does, Luise. We have all suffered at the hands of this insane regime." He sighed. "I'm sorry you have to hear this while you are away from your family."

She shrugged. "What could they do about it?"

"Surely your father would comfort you, and Manya. She loves you."

He seemed about to say more, but Luise had heard enough. She stood and turned to him as he also stood.

"Thank you for the information. You will not wish to come by this house again because the head of the home is GPU. Goodbye, Phillip."

She could not feel her feet as she moved toward the house. A wave of sorrow carried her and she only muttered an apology when she bumped into Mrs. Gromyko coming out of the house. Luise stumbled through the kitchen and sought refuge in her lean-to room. She closed the door and dropped to the floor beside her bed, pent-up tears from months and years of grief spilling from her eyes.

Luise lay on her cot thinking about all Phillip had said. Surely she would have felt something if Daniel had died, some sudden grief. There was a good chance Phillip's news was true, but there was also the slim chance it was not. Until she received official confirmation, Luise determined to maintain her belief that Daniel remained alive.

Then she remembered Phillip's exact words. "He was executed—shot." Could she believe against all hope that he would return to her, even from the brink of the grave? Perhaps that wicked Dubrowsky was tricking them into believing the worst for some reason.

She wept again, trying to let go of the ache and refresh herself for Tatiana. The woman did not need to see tears and sorrow; she had enough of her own troubles.

When Luise entered the bedroom later, she felt Tatiana's eyes on her. Luise forced a smile and chattered about the beautiful sunshine and the sparrows singing and what she would cook for supper, but Tatiana said nothing.

Luise brought little Vojtec to his mother to nurse, and as Tatiana leaned back into the pillow, she motioned her to sit in the chair beside the bed where they could see one another.

"What is it you need, Tatiana?" Luise wondered what she had missed.

Tatiana shook her head. "It is not what I need but what you need. What happened with that young man?"

Luise broke eye contact and began folding the few diapers the woman had. "Nothing with which to concern yourself, Tatiana."

"Luise, you have been pouring your energy into my life, listening to my incessant whining, and I appreciate your efforts. Whether you believe it or not, those efforts are helping."

"That's wonderful, Tatiana. I want you to be whole

again."

"And I shall be. I don't understand why you came though. We did not know each other, yet you came here to help me."

Luise shrugged. "The first time I came to please Frau Klein. She is a difficult woman to refuse."

Tatiana smiled and nodded.

"I didn't know why I should come, but something told me it was important and that God wanted me here. Now, well, now I have grown to care about you and little Vojtec."

Luise picked up the baby from the bed where he played with his fingers, and held him to her chest.

"I think my great-aunt had something to do with the initial invitation. She shares a friendship with Frau Klein. I...I think they wanted to kill two birds with one stone, so to speak."

Tatiana tilted her head to one side, her eyes questioning.

"I believe they thought we could help each other." Luise smiled at Tatiana. "I think perhaps they were correct."

Tatiana leaned toward Luise. "So would you tell me what has happened between you and your visitor and let me help?"

Luise's joy faded and she sat back against the chair.

"He came to tell me my husband is dead."

"What?" Tatiana sat forward, the indignation flaring in her eyes. "How does he know this?"

Luise let go of all her good intentions and allowed her sorrows to spill out to Tatiana. "His mother wrote to him that the GPU official who arrested Daniel had returned to our village of Alexandrovka, and had announced that Daniel was dead, that he had been executed. Shot. That's what Phillip's mother wrote to him. He thought I should know."

Tatiana's eyes held compassion. "Is it the truth then?"

"I don't know. I don't feel it in my heart, you know. I feel like I should still be hoping. I don't mean to resist the truth, but sometimes things are not as they seem. I still think of my Daniel as alive, and hope he will return to me. Is that crazy?"

"Of course not, Luise. Anyone would do the same. Listen to your heart, pray to your God, ask Him to make it clear for you."

"But what if the news is true? I know Phillip wants to court me, but I don't want him."

"Has he been pushy about it?" asked Tatiana, her brows lowering. "I will alert my husband and he will watch for him."

"No! Your husband is GPU. The less we have to do with them, the better for us."

"Don't worry, then. I won't tell Vasili. But your people are not the only ones who live in fear of the Soviet system." She glanced toward the door of her bedroom. "We shall not speak of that again."

"I'm sure that Phillip means well," continued Luise. "He's polite and cheerful, kind and protective. But I'm not looking for a man. I am a married woman. My husband has been gone a year and a half, and it has been heart-wrenching for me, wondering where he is and how he fares. But I will not forsake my marriage vows or my heart. What is Phillip thinking by pursuing me?"

Tatiana nodded and waited for her to continue.

"Daniel and I have known each other all our lives. He waited for me to grow up, to realize I couldn't live without him. Our love will last the rest of our lives, and if his life has already been cut short, our love will still live within my heart. I cannot bond with another."

She laid the sleeping Vojtec back on the bed beside his mother and covered him.

Nodding again, Tatiana reached out and took Luise's hand. "I cannot imagine what you have gone through. Here I am in my own home with a husband who provides for me, I have a healthy baby, and I waste my hours in selfishness while you, having lost everything dear to you, reach out to help me. I am ashamed."

"No, Tatiana. There is nothing to be ashamed about. There are illnesses of the body and illnesses of the mind and spirit. We tend to dismiss the latter when it is as real as the former. I gladly serve you these days. It gives me joy and a diversion from the sorrow in my heart. To see you progressing is a greater reward than I could have imagined."

"I have an idea." Tatiana kissed her son, tied her nightgown at the neck, and leaned conspiratorially toward Luise. "I want to surprise Vasili. He has been so patient with me even though he cannot understand my malady."

Luise felt joy well up inside her. "How do you want to surprise him and what can I do?"

"I would like to eat at the table all together this evening."

"That's a wonderful idea, Tatiana. You can be seated when he returns home for supper."

"Or I could enter just as you are seated."

Luise narrowed her eyes. "Tatiana, you have not been out of your bed for weeks except to use the chamber pot. How would you manage to walk to the table alone?"

Tatiana grinned, her excitement lighting the eyes that had been dull for so long. She pushed the blanket aside, careful for her baby beside her, and dangled her legs over the side of the bed.

"Tatiana?" Seeing her intent, Luise fetched Tatiana's house shoes from under the bed.

"I've been practicing the last week. I believe I can do it." Slowly, she rose and waited for her balance to return, and then she walked across the room and back to the bed. "And I'm not even tired."

Luise clapped her hands. "Well, I believe you are on the mend. You'll make your husband very happy. Hope is what keeps us going, and hope has returned to this house. Praise the Lord for His goodness."

Tatiana took Luise's face in her hands and looked into

her eyes. "Let this hope be in you as well, Luise. Never lose hope that your husband will return."

"Thank you for believing with me."

A small smile played upon Luise's lips as she stepped into the sparsely stocked general store at the centre of Shumanovka. It was good to be back home, even though she missed Tatiana. Her new friend's change of attitude filled her with joy and a sense of accomplishment, and Frau Klein was much gladdened by the news.

Luise remembered Vasili's surprise at supper that evening. He loved his wife, of that she was convinced, even though he schooled his features against emotion. A young man like him would have dreamed dreams, fallen in love, hoped for a future. Now, with the Soviets in charge, his personal dreams would have been pushed aside. Yet he still had his wife. He needed hope, and that evening when Tatiana had emerged from her room to join him at the supper table, Luise had seen hope return to his eyes. He was not a bad man, Luise supposed, for a GPU official.

Luise moved to the mercantile's fabric shelf and ran her fingers along the few bolts of cloth, feeling their textures, considering the weight and drape. A medium weight green calico sprinkled with delicate yellow flowers caught her attention, the best of the limited selection. She moved to pull the bolt from the row, but a sharp voice stopped her.

"Please do not handle the fabric unless you intend to buy it. You'll soil it."

Luise turned in surprise to see Martha Lepp marching up the aisle toward her, a scowl on her face. It surprised Luise to be thus chastised by a peer.

"I'm sorry," she said, "but how am I to examine the cloth to see if it suits me if I am unable to touch it?"

Martha reached out and pulled the bolt of fabric from Luise's hands. "If everyone wipes their hands on it, no one will want to buy it. If you want some, I shall measure it and cut a piece for you."

Luise's eyes narrowed as she tried to discern what she had done to raise Martha's ire. She was certain it had nothing to do with green and yellow calico.

Just then the shop door opened and Phillip walked in with Jasch trotting at his heels. The only time Luise ever saw Phillip without Jasch was when he pursued her. Phillip saw her immediately and moved in her direction. She sent up a prayer for strength.

"Luise. How good to see you. How are you today?" He stood almost in front of Martha and simply nodded in her general direction.

"I'm well, Phillip. Martha and I were just in the middle of a sale, if you will excuse us."

"Oh, of course." He stepped back and nodded again at Martha. "Jasch and I stopped by to pick up the plough shares my father ordered, but I'll wait until you two are finished."

"No need," Martha said. "She doesn't know what she wants so I'll help you first. Come right this way."

As Luise watched her talking with Phillip, she realized why Martha was upset with her. The young woman chatted and laughed and batted her eyelashes, leading Phillip by the arm to the most distant corner of the store.

"Oh, good heavens!" muttered Luise. "Please take him off my hands. I certainly don't want him."

She turned to find Jasch Fast smirking at her. He looked just like his uncle, Schoolmaster Fast, with that disgusting sneer on his face. Flustered, she left the store without her fabric, too irritated to think straight. She would come back later.

As she hurried down the street, she heard Phillip calling after her, but she did not stop. Running feet matched the beat of her pulse as he caught up with her.

"Luise! For heaven's sake, slow down. Didn't you hear me calling you?"

She looked away from Phillip's bright eyes. "What do you want, Phillip?"

His puzzled frown made her feel guilty. "I wanted to apologize for taking the salesclerk away from you. I had no intention of doing so; it was rude of me." He smiled as if to emphasize his words.

She couldn't believe he had no idea what Martha had done. "You boys are so innocent. You did not steal her away; she stole you away. I don't think she wanted me to buy the fabric."

"Why not? Surely they want to sell their goods."

"I really must get back home. I've been away so long and I've missed my family."

He still looked puzzled as she bid him good afternoon and walked briskly back to her home—her father's home. Anna had reminded her just this morning that she needed a husband who would provide her with a home of her own.

And now this altercation with Martha, which she had done nothing to warrant. If the girl wanted Phillip, she was welcome to him. It wasn't Luise's fault that Phillip didn't notice Martha.

But it seemed that whether or not it was her fault, she would have to deal with it. As she ran up the steps of the house, she heard her stepmother's complaining voice, and was doubly glad that Tante Manya also lived there. It helped to have someone who understood.

"He's not coming back, you know."

Martha's words the next day, whispered from behind her, sent chills down Luise's spine. She turned to stare at the clerk, her grip tightening on the bolt of green and yellow fabric.

"Why are you angry with me?" she asked, understanding why Phillip did not wish to become involved with this young woman.

"Oh, I'm not angry. I almost feel sorry for you, losing

your husband like that, but seeing you throw yourself at Phillip Wieler robs me of compassion. I mean, you could wait a while longer before seeking out another husband."

Luise was glad the bolt of fabric separated them; she wanted to slap Martha.

"I wouldn't even bother to answer your false assumptions, but I know you won't leave it alone until I do. I'm not seeking the attention of Phillip Wieler. He continues to put himself in my path, but I'm not interested. I'm a married woman."

"Then you should act as such."

Luise realized there was no reasoning with the woman. She sighed and handed her the fabric. "Cut me three meters, please."

Martha glared at her, lips white with fury, eyes blazing. "You have no shame." She grabbed the bolt of cloth and whisked it away to the counter to cut it. Luise followed closely to make sure she did it properly.

Making a little snip at the three-meter mark, Martha grabbed the fabric and ripped, as if the action could further injure her customer. She snipped the last end and rolled the fabric into a wad, then roughly wrapped it in brown paper and string. Pushing it towards Luise, she demanded immediate payment and folded her arms to wait for it.

As calmly as her shaking hands would allow, Luise counted out the rubles and placed them on the counter. Picking up her package, she said, "You can have Phillip. In fact, I would be most grateful if you'd take him off my hands. I'm sure he'll notice a pretty girl like you."

Martha's mouth opened and shut, but she had no retort to Luise's compliment.

As Luise walked home with the bundle in her arms, she decided that suffering her stepmother's insults had hardened her heart to a certain extent. She had learned to process the words in light of the speaker. She would do the same with Martha. She would also suggest to Phillip that there were indeed other fish in the stream, fish eager to be caught.

"That young man has come to call again," said Anna when Luise returned to the house with her purchase. Anna coughed until she doubled over on her cot.

"Which man?" Luise reached for a cup, but Tante Manya rose painfully from her rocking chair to fill it from the pail on the counter and bring it to Anna.

"It was Phillip again," she said quietly to Luise. "I told him to go home and leave you be, but he only smiled and said he would come back later."

"Himmel!" said Luise. "Why does he not take my no to mean no. That Martha Lepp from the store would love to win his affection, but with her prickly personality, I doubt she ever will. Perhaps I need to be more prickly myself and he would leave me be."

"You can no more be prickly than a fish can breathe air," said Tante Manya with a chuckle.

Anna drank the water, then settled her gaze on Luise. "You should accept that young man. He would do right by you, build you a house and take you in. You can't expect Abram to care for everyone."

Luise squeezed her eyes shut and breathed deeply.

"Mother," she said, kneeling down in front of Anna, "I am married to Daniel Martens. He is not here because he has been taken away by the GPU, but he is still my husband. Perhaps he is dead even now, but I have loved him as long as I can remember, and it's a hard habit to break. I'll not marry anyone else. Please do not keep pushing me."

Anna reached out and tucked a strand of hair behind Luise's ear. "You're not bad looking, you know. You may even grow up to be pretty someday."

Luise rocked back on her heels and stared at her stepmother, then snorted. Tante Manya, shook her head and her mouth caved into a smile.

"May as well laugh as cry, eh?"

"Who is crying?" Anna wanted to know, but she didn't give either of them a chance to respond before a coughing spell again bent her double. "I need to lie down," she gasped between coughs. "Please be quiet now and keep the children outside until supper."

She pulled her legs up onto the cot and lay back against her pile of pillows while Luise covered her with her crocheted day blanket and stroked her hair from her forehead. Whatever you do for the least of these—the words came to Luise's mind—you do unto Me.

❧

"Ernest and Peter Rogalski have crossed the Amur River into China," said Frieda Klassen when she met Luise on the street one day in late September. She looked over her shoulder before continuing. "Their families are packed and ready to go when their men return for them."

Luise had heard rumors but had not paid them much mind. "Do the authorities know?"

Frieda laughed. "Of course not, Luise. The Rogalskis said they were going to look for markets for our wheat, but it's an *escape*." She said the word as if it were the biggest secret ever to cross her lips. "You don't tell the enemy about an escape."

Luise rolled her eyes. "What I mean is, how can the guards not know? They seem to stay abreast of most everything here in Shumanovka as well as in the other villages."

"Well they don't know about this—yet." Frieda seemed personally insulted by Luise's questions. "What are you going to do to help support your family, since you are without a husband?"

Luise knew Frieda meant no harm, she had not been blessed with an excess of sensitivity, but the question begged an answer. Luise refused to reveal the pain Frieda's words caused. "I will manage, with God's help," she said, and crossed the street to the school building.

In fact, a plan had been forming in her mind since Anna's recent tactless words. She marched resolutely up the steps of the schoolhouse and rapped firmly at the door.

After a short silence, a voice from within bid her enter. She let herself into the small but adequate building to approach the desk at the other end of the room.

"May I help you?" The schoolmaster had watched her approach and, she felt sure, analyzed both her person and her purpose.

She looked into the small, hard eyes behind the round spectacles and felt sorry for the children under his tutelage. He seemed completely devoid of imagination or creativity, but then, that was purely speculation on her part. She chided herself inwardly and spoke.

"Mr. Fast, I am here to ask if you would have need of an assistant at the school. I'm sure I could manage it, and I had heard you might need to take time off to help with harvest again. I'm thinking you would be more qualified than I for that task."

She forced a smile but he answered with a scowl.

"First you come here from who knows where," he stood and walked around the desk to stand beside it, slapping his palm with a ruler, "then you invite yourself into the home of perfect strangers, and now you seek to push me out of my job, my livelihood. That takes a lot of gall, woman."

Luise would have been humble enough to accept his accusations as at least near the truth, but when he called her *woman* to her face when she had a name and he knew it, she felt the ire rise in her.

"I'm sorry for not introducing myself. I thought most everyone knew everyone else in this village, but I was apparently mistaken. My name is Frau Luise Martens. I have come here from Alexandrovka in the Slavgorod Colony. The reason I am here is to offer my assistance in order to fairly earn some money with which to help support my family."

He continued to stare at her, and then the scowl gave

way to a small, crooked smile. "I'm sure that is your objective here."

Luise, to her own credit, did not stamp her foot. "Yes, it is." She clasped her hands behind her back.

"Well, you will have to earn honest money somewhere else, because I will not be going anywhere, especially to the fields. I am not a farmer." His words dripped with disdain. "I studied in the university in Germany, you know."

Luise did not know whether to be sorry for the man or discouraged for her lack of success.

She bowed slightly, thanked Mr. Fast, and walked away. At the door, Fast's voice stopped her. As if reading her mind, he said, "And do not go asking the school board for permission to teach. They have no authority in the matter. It is completely up to the Soviet representatives, and I do not believe they would favor a poor, uneducated woman in this position."

Luise did not bother to answer, but marched back home and burst into tears. No matter how hard she tried to keep them in check, her emotions rested at the surface these days. The children were playing outside, but Anna lay on her cot and Tante Manya sat on a low stool peeling potatoes.

"What happened now?" Tante Manya kept peeling as she spoke.

Luise wiped her eyes with her sleeve. "I asked the schoolmaster if I could help teach his classes for pay when he goes to the fields to help with harvest. He was rude and heartless and told me to go away."

"Selfish swine," said Anna. "The Fasts are all alike, even back in Molotschna."

"Anna," said Tante Manya, "such talk is not becoming of you."

"Becoming or not, it is true. But why do you want to teach? You are busy caring for me."

"Yes, Mother, but I wanted to help provide for the family."

"The cellar is full of food. I put it down there myself."

Luise shared a knowing look with Tante Manya. "Yes, Mother, but the supply has dwindled. We need more."

"Tell Abram. He will get it. That's what the man of the house does, girl."

Luise ignored her comment. To her aunt she said, "I don't know what to do next."

Tante Manya dropped the last of the potatoes into the pot and Luise set it on the stove. "Don't worry; the crops look good this year. There will be enough food once they are harvested. We have only to follow God's plan."

God's plan came in the form of a bountiful harvest. Schoolmaster Fast was moved bodily out to the fields, for every able hand was needed to bring in the crop. Luise took his place with some trepidation, but fell easily to the task of teaching the eager children gathered each day.

Chapter Twenty-one

Even as the village buzzed with harvest intensity, a discernable disquiet crept into conversations and attitudes. No matter how much the farmers brought in from the fields, the Soviet demanded more. It seemed to Luise like a dangling carrot, this fine harvest, the proceeds of which would never be realized in the coffers or storage bins of the village folk. But no amount of conversation or dissatisfaction made a bit of difference to the officials who came to collect.

Hearing a commotion in the street outside the schoolhouse one day after classes, Luise stepped out to observe.

"How can you demand twenty-five *pud* of wheat when I harvested only twenty? I cannot pay that and if I did, what would we eat through the winter?" Aaron Peters harped on while the village official, Rashidov, and another officer Luise had not seen before, stood with their hands on their hips, waiting for him to draw breath.

"Shut up, you dirty kulak," said the new man. "You have been squirreling away funds for years, pretending you are in need." The official stepped dangerously close to Peters, but the ruddy-faced fellow did not change his course of complaint. Luise noticed Rashidov dart a worried glance at his fellow officer, saw him say something, but the new man told him to shut up.

"I have long since used up any reserve that I had laid aside for a crop failure," said Peters, "and now when the crops flourish, you do not allow me to benefit or even at least to survive from my hard work. This is totally unreasonable."

Quick as a striking serpent, the new officer backhanded the unsuspecting deacon across the face, sending him to the dirt howling, while his wife Njuta stifled a wail with her hands to her mouth, her eyes large and fearful. Conversation ceased in the crowd that had gathered. Opinions faded away with their originators and soon only Peters and the two officials remained.

"Go your way," said Rashidov. "We will expect your wheat by tomorrow."

Peters found his feet and hurried away, his hand on his face.

"Any more rebels waiting to be straightened out?" The new man glanced around and his eyes fell on Luise. She slipped quickly into the school building, but not before she heard Rashidov's response.

"We have done enough, Ivan Petrovich. There is no need to create so much animosity."

"Indeed? And why not?"

Luise wasted no time, but gathered up her things and left the schoolhouse by the back door. Shivering in spite of the pleasant day, she hastened home. Reality struck her yet again—if the GPU demanded more from the farmers than what they had harvested, what would they ask of her family and how would they pay it? And who was this new man?

Tante Manya welcomed her at the door when she returned for supper. "Come in, child. We have fresh bread for supper and cabbage borscht."

"It's a feast, sister," said Nela, twirling with her arms spread.

"Where...how...?" Luise stared at the table, at the meal prepared there. "Are we celebrating something?"

"Yes," said her aunt. "We are celebrating good news."

"Papa has a new job." Hans grinned, standing with his hands on his hips, waiting for Luise's response. "We will have plenty of food now."

"A new job? Tante Manya, whatever does he mean?"

"Sit, Lise, and we will eat. I hear Abram whistling down the street and he will tell you himself."

Abram entered the kitchen like a king entering his throne room. Luise rose when he came in, questions bubbling out of her, but he just smiled, took his place at the table and bowed to ask the blessing. When he lifted his head, he first asked after Anna.

"She has gone to see Hertha. She had a better day today and we thought she needed a change." Tante Manya turned the handle of the soup ladle in his direction.

Luise could no longer contain herself. "Papa, what happened? Hans said you had a new job."

Abram smiled as he ladled borscht into his bowl. "I have been hired as bookkeeper for the volost office." He lowered his voice as if the stone walls had ears, but his smile did not fade. "I would have thought that with the new man, Ivan Petrovich Mironenko, they would have sufficient heads and hands to keep their books in order, but apparently they have so much information to process they need another."

Hans snorted and Nela laughed because everyone else did.

"There's so much paperwork to be done for the Soviet they cannot keep up with it. Since I am—or I was—a minister, they assume I'm literate, so I have been informed, not asked mind you, that I will be working at the volost office from now on."

"For pay?" Luise asked.

"Of course, for pay. We at the volost office do not work for nothing."

"For shame, Abram," interrupted Tante Manya. "You begin to sound like one of them."

"Yes, Papa," said Hans. "You sound like a Bolshevik."

Abrams smile disappeared and Hans' face fell. "I'm sorry, Papa. I shouldn't have said that."

The lines around Abram's mouth softened as he looked across the small table at his young son and his voice lowered even more. "I will never be a Bolshevik, my son. But you must never speak so to anyone at any time. Do you understand?"

❧

The night after her father received news of his new job, Luise tossed and turned on her bed, longing for morning. At least then she would have the distraction of the children at school. Her poor sleep had been riddled with dreams of dark places and frightening monsters and Daniel. Shouts and groans and fear and Daniel. Between nightmares, she had prayed for him, begging God to take care of him and not to leave him alone.

At first light, she slipped out of bed, dressed herself and took the trail from the village to the trees to find solace. When the weather turned, she would no longer be able to escape the confines of the house, so she would make the most of it now.

Her mind wandered from prayer to conjecture as she walked the worn path. What did the future hold for her, for her neighbors? The GPU had been a thorn in the flesh of the villagers in Slavgorod Colony, but here on the border of China, they had been relatively unintrusive. Luise did not fear Rashidov, but the new officer, the one Papa called Ivan Petrovich Mironenko, reminded her of Dubrowsky. Power bred cruelty, as she had witnessed on the village street. If the oppression heightened, where could they go from here? How could they escape the advances of the enemy that enslaved them?

A sense of despair crept over her. Before she realized it, she had nearly stumbled into the path of two horses, ridden by Rashidov and Mironenko. Gasping, she backed off the road and waited for them to pass, training her eyes on the ground at her feet. Her surprise changed to apprehension as the horses stopped and Mironenko dismounted.

"Well, if it isn't a little lost Mennonite girl. Can I help you find your way? I could entertain you well."

Luise's heart pounded and her mind whirled. No one knew where she was. No one would hear her scream, and even if they did, what could they do to help? Her eyes flitted to Rashidov but he looked away.

"I need to get to the schoolhouse," she said. "The children will be waiting soon."

"There's plenty of time, eh? Such a beautiful day." He stood so near now she could smell his breath, and she turned her face away, but he took her chin and forced her to look at him. "Come now, no one will ever know."

She shook her head fearfully, glancing over his shoulder at Rashidov, whose horse had begun to prance.

"Please let me be." Luise directed her plea to Rashidov and he reined his horse around.

"Ivan Petrovich, the officials from New York village will be arriving at any time. We need to get along."

Mironenko snarled, his wolf teeth yellow, sending Luise back several more steps until she tripped into a low spot. "That's right, kneel before Ivan, girl. Do not forget who is in charge here. I could have you anytime. Right now I'm busy, but I will be watching you."

He climbed back onto his horse and stared down at her for a long moment before turning his horse in the direction of the village. Rashidov followed his superior, face taut, fists white-knuckled on the reins.

Luise shook like a lone birch tree in a high wind as she stumbled back to Shumanovka and into the house.

"Where on earth have you been?" Anna whined. "My breakfast is still not made and I am hungry today."

"It is almost ready," said Tante Manya from beside the stove. She looked into Luise's eyes, and seemed to read her terror. Abram had already gone to work at the volost office, and Luise was glad. She didn't want him to know of her fear, of the threats, especially since he had to work with the perpetrator. She took a deep breath and forced the whole incident from her mind, but not before vowing to be more careful in the future.

Tante Manya hovered near, and Luise leaned over to whisper, "I am unharmed, only shaken."

The old woman's hand rested briefly on her shoulder and she wondered if her aunt's prayers had saved her that morning. Later, at the schoolhouse, Luise's tension would not ease. She expected at any moment for *Ivan the Terrible,* as she had now dubbed him, to burst through the schoolhouse door. The thought of him caused goosebumps to rise on her arms.

She jumped at the sound of a pencil dropped to the floor, and forced herself to take stock. She was in charge here and she must not infect the children with her fears. Had she not asked God to watch over her? Nothing escaped His notice or His control. Enough of this cowering; she must be an example to the children.

Unbidden, her thoughts turned again to Daniel. What would he think of her fear? With a shudder, she was glad he didn't know. He would seek to protect her at any cost. She pushed the thought away, realizing that nothing could get him into more trouble than he already faced.

A thick, raspy voice tickled the edges of his darkness.

A higher, clearer voice answered, but he could understand neither.

Sensations of warmth nagged at his consciousness. Voices. Rising and falling cadences. Pain. His body convulsed and he lapsed again into the realm of the silent dark…

Smells seeped beyond the borders of the darkness and tugged at his mind. Pain assaulted him. Fuzzy memories and vague impressions shimmered like fog in his brain, and for the first time, he wanted to emerge from his quiet cocoon. He willed his mind to focus and gradually became aware of his existence.

Pain seemed his closest companion in this transitional

place, and so he clung to it, to distill his thoughts into reasonable form.

The clear voice spoke briefly, nearby, as if watching him.

Rustling. Subtle air currents. Awareness.

Slight, pleasant pressure on his forehead, both cool and comforting. More words. The smell of food and an arresting rumble within him.

He concentrated, tried to awaken, to open his eyes, to move his hands. Nothing worked. Perhaps more sleep…a sharp clap made him jerk and his eyelids fluttered, allowing muted light into his soul. He must awaken. He could sleep later.

Raspy words, more encouragement.

He struggled against invisible cords that bound him. Gradually, like a flame licking the edge of paper, sensation returned to his feet, his legs, tingled through his torso, arms and head. He groaned and thrashed at the new pain accosting him. As it subsided, his hands felt soft fur beneath him, and his eyes blinked open, wincing at the light. Above him, two weathered brown faces stared down with eyes black as soot. A man and a woman. He blinked back at them, at their leather and fur clothing, at their sleek bound hair. When he looked up beyond the faces, he saw thatch. A hut. He lay on a fur mat. In a sod and thatch hut. Somewhere.

He listened to their speech, but it escaped his understanding. He inhaled deeply, feeling life return. His head pounded when he turned his eyes too far, so he focused on the black eyes of his saviors, who continued to chatter and laugh.

The man spoke, as if in explanation, but the words meant nothing. He tried to shake his head, but the slightest movement brought sharp pain. He squeezed his eyes shut and gritted his teeth.

When the pain relinquished some of its intensity, he looked up and opened his mouth to speak, but his parched lips refused to form words. The woman murmured something and left, returning momentarily with a cool, wet cloth, with which she dabbed his lips. He blinked in thanks.

He tried his voice again. "Where am I?"

They giggled as if he had told a joke. He was alone in a foreign world with the people who had saved him from—from what? He tried to remember what had come before the dark silence, but he could not. In fact, he could not remember who he was. He hoped that would come as his mind awakened. He sipped the soup they fed him—the smell that had caused his stomach to growl—and fell into a relieved sleep, leaving his questions in the room as he faded from it.

Chapter Twenty-two

Luise dreaded the coming winter, her second without Daniel, if she didn't count his winter in the lumber camp. The skies were often gray, the sun reluctant to emerge through the dome of cloud, and the mood remained somber in the villages. Men contemplated their dismal portions of an abundant harvest. What would they feed their families? How would they survive? Many of them now worked at building traps to catch wildlife during the winter. The women gathered berries and dried them for winter use, along with everything their gardens had produced. With her hopes for Daniel's return crushed, Luise felt crushed as well. It would be a very long winter.

"Rogalskis and Siemens have gone." Hertha Claassen had trotted over from next door to tell Luise and Tante Manya the latest, as they prepared supper. "Left last night after dark. Rented a boat to take them down the Amur. Long way, but they should be safe by now."

Luise wondered how these people Hertha spoke of managed to escape without the knowledge of the officials. What did they do once they arrived in China? She wondered if she would go if Daniel were here and suggested it. On the other hand, why didn't they all go, those who were getting fed up with the fear and control tactics employed by the GPU, if it was that simple? Or was it? Only if you didn't mind the threat of being shot in the back of the head, she supposed.

She had been teaching at the village elementary school ever since Schoolmaster Fast had been manhandled out to the fields in his best suit and shoes, and she had received several visits already from the two men in charge of Shumanovka, Yevgeny Rashidov and Ivan Mironenko. Although Luise dreaded the distracting visits, she was relieved that the two officials came together. Mironenko alone would have frightened her, with his lustful leers and inappropriate comments, but Rashidov seemed able to bring things into perspective, inconspicuously keeping Mironenko in check. Luise attempted to maintain a sense of decorum and routine during these interruptions, but she knew some of the older children saw through her thin veneer of calm.

Luise chopped a carrot and spoke one of her questions aloud. "Why don't we all go to China if it's that easy?"

Tante Manya smoothed her apron over her knees. "Some of us are hoping things will turn around, that we won't have to leave again. Others are afraid to even think of going."

"Seems to me, anyone who made the journey you made to get this far would have the courage to continue," said Hertha.

"I suppose it's much easier to settle in and make do," said Luise. "We were hoping to stay here and make it our home." Somewhere Daniel could find me. "We came here, built a house, planted a crop, started to feel content. But it's all changing. It seems to have all been for naught, as Stalin's men tighten the cords every day."

"Next they will want to know what we ate for breakfast," said Tante Manya. "All the information they have collected must fill half of Moscow by now."

Hertha snorted. "More like serfs than citizens, I'd say. Stalin is reversing the emancipations made by Alexander II."

"Thing is," added Luise, lapsing into Hertha's fragmented speech, "it's not just the body he is enslaving but the mind. Every time Rashidov and Mironenko intrude on our classes at the school, they come with new rules. We cannot speak German, we cannot teach religion, we cannot teach anything relating to our traditional way of life. Even science is monitored to make sure nothing biblical is offered to the children."

"Have to keep teaching those things at home then."

"We must be careful about that too. The officials and the local activists are becoming more intrusive about what goes on at home. Some of the parents have been warned about teaching the Bible at home."

"Don't tell them. We weren't born yesterday."

"Yes, Hertha, but the children are not so discerning. They divulge information about what happens at home and the officials move on that information. It doesn't necessarily have to be true."

Hertha stared at her, fear in her eyes. "What is going to become of us here, Luise? How can we cooperate with these restrictions?"

Tante Manya had been sitting quietly, but now she said, "My mother used to say there's more than one way to skin a cat. We will find a way to deal with this growing crisis, but not by running scared. Action must be planned. But right now, with the Rogalski and Siemens families gone, we need to bide our time."

"You do not give up hope?" Hertha spoke but Luise also awaited the answer.

"We never give up hope, Hertha. God knows our situation. He will intervene in His time, if that is His will."

Luise wished again for Daniel. What if she were faced with the decision to leave Russia without him? What would she do? How could she leave Daniel behind? Or was he already dead, as everyone seemed to believe? *Oh God, help me to trust You.*

Luise rinsed the freshly churned butter in cold well water and watched Tante Manya knitting near the cookstove. The room smelled of yeast and milk and home, just as she had dreamed her own house with Daniel would smell. She would have made a good wife. Phillip would ask her if he thought he had a chance of her acceptance.

Tante Manya glanced up at her. "What's on your mind now, although I'm afraid to ask by the looks of you."

Luise smiled. "You're a mind reader."

"No, I am a student of life. You are thinking deep thoughts. You may as well spit them out, since I'll have to listen to them sometime anyway."

Luise hid her smile and pulled a kitchen chair beside her great aunt's rocker. Anna lay in blessed sleep nearby on her day cot, a welcome reprieve from the constant hacking that rattled her bones.

"Was it difficult to remain alone?" Luise didn't know how to begin.

"Keep talking until you start making sense."

Luise tightened her lips. "Did you ever feel, after you lost your husband, that you wanted to love someone else?"

"Ahh. You are letting go."

"I'm not forgetting him. I will always love him, but what do I do if I never know for sure if he's dead? I mean, I could keep pining for him forever, or I could move forward in my life and make a difference."

"You need a man in order to make a difference?"

"I have always wanted a home of my own. Children. Doesn't every girl want these things?"

"Many do, yes. Some are blessed to enjoy them; others are not. Is it family you wish for or a man to hold you?"

Luise felt her cheeks warm at her aunt's words and looked out the window where snowflakes fell softly from a gray sky. "I don't know. Sometimes I want so much to be loved, to be exclusively special to one other person. That's what Daniel and I were to each other. Can that ever be reborn with someone else?"

Tante Manya rocked in the chair, her feet tipping her back and forth, her hands stilled at their knitting. Her toothless mouth puckered inward, and she stared straight ahead, while Luise waited for her wisdom.

Finally, the old woman sighed and looked toward Luise. "What can I tell you, my child? My life is not a blueprint for you to follow. We each must find our own way. Have you prayed about this?"

"Of course, daily. But I hear no answers."

"Then you must carry on in the direction you are going until you receive an answer. Even God cannot steer a buggy that's standing still."

Luise rose from her chair and put it back beside the kitchen table. "I need to send Nela to collect the eggs and then I will make supper. That much of my life is clear."

Tante Manya chuckled. "That's my girl. One foot in front of the other. That's how we get through these times."

"But how shall I deal with Phillip?"

"I've lived my life; I cannot live yours. God will give the answer when it is time."

Luise grimaced. So simple yet so difficult. With a huge sigh, she threw flour and water into a bowl and reached for the eggs. Maybe *kjielkje* would make her feel better. As long as they turned out as individual noodles and not one wad of dough.

Netmetsiki. That was what they called him. It was a strange handle, but since his hosts couldn't seem to pronounce the name Daniel, it would have to do. Bit by bit, his damaged mind began to clear, but it hurt to think too much. Sleep became his salvation from pain, but sleep brought dreams of Luise. Helpless as he was in his recuperative state, he despaired of ever seeing her again.

As the dark-skinned woman cared for him, he realized his injuries had been near fatal. A large, ugly wound in his side had begun to heal, but he still moved carefully, doing no more than sitting up on his mat of furs. His shoulder pained him, and his head continued to feel twice its normal size. Debilitating headaches often left him hunched in a silent ball. Yet time, and the constant gentle care and rich broth began to strengthen him.

As he was able, Daniel sat for prolonged periods, and then one day ventured outside, with the help of his male host and a stout stick to support his injured leg. If his rescuers had not splinted it at the first, it would not have healed as straight as it had. The sparsely wooded terrain outside the hut lay blanketed by a thick layer of snow that reflected the winter sun so brilliantly he had to shield his eyes. A few moments and he sagged in the arms of his caregiver, his wounded side stabbing him like a sabre. He had no strength to leave this place, nor did the northern cold allow for such plans. He sighed heavily with the realization.

There seemed to be no understanding of time here in the hut, and since Daniel could do nothing to alter that, he let go of time restraints as well. When the sun slipped behind the trees, they ate their evening meal of rabbit or deer or fish, and lay down on their mats until the sky lightened again. They ate two such meals each day, and in between the man left, always taking his bow and arrows, his axe and his fishing gear. While he was gone, his wife beaded intricate designs on clothing and footwear, or worked to prepare food for the next meal.

As Daniel was able, he performed menial chores, and sometimes as he did them, a flash of memory would hit him, accompanied by sharp emotion. When the man brought home a line of fish and the woman was otherwise occupied, Daniel reached for them and began to scale and fillet and de-bone. The couple stopped to watch him, and he saw in his mind a picture of a group of men fishing, cleaning the fish, bringing them back to the huts in the clearing of a camp. The memory brought fear and anger, and as soon as he had completed his chore, he settled himself on his mat and turned his face away from the other two, trying to calm himself.

He had remembered Luise as soon as his mind began to work again. He longed to return to her, but he still had no idea where he was or how he had come here.

The people who had taken him in—Ostic and Blen, he heard them call each other— showed more patience and acceptance of him than he could have expected. They must know that since they had rescued him at the outset of winter, they would be stuck with him for the duration of the season. Once the worst onslaught of winter had receded, he would have to move on. Until then, he intended to keep his eyes and ears open to learn how these people survived in this land. Once begun, his would be a long, lonely journey.

The more Daniel searched his memories, the more the headaches diminished him to a huddled form on his sleeping mat. Then Blen would nudge him and hold out a mug of tea she had made from the bark of the white willows along the banks of the stream. He drank it out of respect for her, and it seemed to dull the headaches, even though it tasted bitter on the back of his tongue.

From time to time, others of the tribe entered the crude hut and sat to talk in thick, stubby syllables and smoke pipes carved from antlers, filled with heady smelling stuff. The women chatted in subdued tones and giggled with their hands covering their mouths.

One day, Ostic and Blen sat talking, casting glances at him, referring, it seemed to his neck. Daniel knew his neck had been twisted; he could not turn it far in either direction, but what could be done about that? Old Mr. Friesen, the Bone Setter in Alexandrovka, might have been able to stretch it out and wrench it back into place, but what did these people know? With a swift twist of an ankle, Friesen could fix a sprain. With a careful manipulation of the neck, he could relieve headaches. Daniel tried to convey his interest, but Blen giggled and brewed him another cup of tea.

One brilliantly sunny day in mid-winter, a shriveled old woman entered the hut, conferred with Blen, and approached Daniel. He stared at her nervously, wondering what she intended. Reaching into a skin bag, she pulled out a bead necklace, which she placed around his neck. She opened a pot of ointment. He gagged at the vile smell and backed away but she gave a sharp command and he stilled, eyes flashing to where Blen stood.

She approached and made signs to her neck, then to his neck, and he stilled. Did the woman intend to use charms and spells on him, or did she have a natural knack like Bonesetter Friesen? He decided he didn't have much to lose. The headaches had not improved.

He lay down and tried to relax as the old woman smeared the vile paste on his neck. She massaged it into his skin, exploring his neck with nimble fingers. She probed more deeply, almost uncomfortably, and exerted pressure on his head, pulling under his chin. With a sudden swift movement, she pulled and twisted his head. He felt a crack followed by a flood of heat coursing through his skull.

Breathing heavily with surprise and shock, he closed his eyes and waited. The woman massaged gently a while longer, then rose and gathered her things, murmuring softly to Blen. With astonishment, Daniel followed her with his eyes, turning his head as she looked back from the door, her smile covered by a brown hand. He sat up gingerly and tried his neck. He could move it without pain although he felt weakness there. It must have been severely dislocated. His shoulder too felt better than it had. He was lucky to have retained movement of his limbs, even though his leg had healed slightly out of place, causing him to limp.

Daniel wanted to share his appreciation with Ostic and Blen. He wanted to help with something, to ask where he was, but whenever he tried to speak, they shook their heads and smiled, their dark eyes all but disappearing under hooded lids.

They were not old, in spite of their weathered skin, but that was all Daniel could ascertain. No children lived with them, although a few dropped by from time to time with their elders to sit and visit and stare at him. The people subsisted mostly on dried fish and reindeer meat and a staple of crushed, dried berries. Ostic supplemented this diet with regular offerings from hunting and trapping: squirrel, marmot, hare, ptarmigan, partridge and grouse.

At first, Daniel was unable to do more on his own than step out of the hut to relieve himself, but after his leg healed and his strength began to build, he tramped about outdoors as often as the weather allowed. His headaches were now a thing of the past, thanks to the old woman, and he felt a new freedom from that pain. He needed to build himself up for his eventual journey. He hated staying inside the small, claustrophobic hut, because he had nothing to do and Blen simply ignored him.

He watched her grinding berries one day and signed that he wanted to help. She giggled into her fur collar, and continued her work. Later, when Ostic returned with two hares, she rattled off a story of some kind, pointing at Daniel with her head and giggling. Ostic snapped a reply, which quieted her chatter as she trimmed the rabbits for supper. She kept glancing at him and shaking her head, still muttering.

The next day when Ostic had gone, Blen prepared to pound berries again. She kept glancing at him, still shaking her head, then asked him something.

How was he to answer?

Again, she asked him a question and pounded berries for a few moments.

"You want me to do that?" He moved forward and reached his hands toward the bowl and pestle.

She nodded her head, all smiles, and handed him the pestle. Making room for him, she handed him the bowl and indicated more berries in a skin bag on the floor. He pounded while she giggled, but after some time she went about other tasks.

Daniel wondered why he had wanted to do this. His arms ached and his neck tired. But, he supposed, it was better than dying of boredom. As the dark days of winter wore on, he learned more household tasks. He took advantage of the short daylight hours to walk about outside. Snowshoes enabled him to tramp farther from the hut, and to build his leg muscles at the same time, and the fresh air healed him inside as he inhaled it, like new life entering his body.

Eventually, he gained enough strength to join Ostic on his traplines, learning and imitating. Ostic pulled a fish up through a hole in the ice, flopped it down in front of Daniel and said, "Kul."

"Kul."

Ostic nodded and handed him the pole and line. He pointed at the ice hole and said, "Kul."

So began Daniel's language instruction. The tongue of these people was nasal and difficult to pronounce, but he began to hear certain words and repeated them at what he thought were appropriate moments. Sometimes they praised him, sometimes they laughed, sometimes they covered their mouths in what could only be shock, but he kept trying.

He remembered learning to read in his first weeks of school. He could see the schoolroom, he could hear the voice of the teacher, he could see the faces of his friends, and the memories filled him with nostalgia. He wanted to return, not just to Alexandrovka, but to simpler times, to the time when his and Luise's love was new.

How much time had passed since he'd seen her? Did she still wait for him? Or did she think he was dead? Worry niggled inside him, a constant reminder of his helplessness.

One night Ostic and his fellow hunters did not return, and Blen listened long for them before serving a small meal for her and Daniel. Eventually, she settled onto her pallet and turned away to sleep, the lamp extinguished. Daniel felt uncomfortable in the small space with this woman. What if Ostic never came back? He supposed Blen would move in with another family. He would certainly have to leave.

The following days seemed to last forever, even with long snowshoe runs and checking the traplines. On the fifth day, Daniel had managed to snag a marmot and a couple of Siberian vampire hares. When he neared the hut, he saw new tracks, a deep set of ruts carved through the snow. A travois of sorts leaned against the hut, and off in the trees, Ostic and some of the other men raised large pieces of meat into the thickest branches with a series of ropes.

A huge bearskin lay draped over a log beside the hut. Deadly sharp teeth gleamed in the late day sun, set in an eternal growl in the enormous head. Claws like daggers now hung innocuously from the ends of great limp paws.

Ostic approached, victory and pride lighting his face, and gave Daniel the word for bear. He repeated it, but there seemed to be more to this prize than if he had brought home fish or fowl.

That evening the entire community gathered in one of the larger huts in the center of the settlement to share the bounty, and Ostic motioned Daniel to join them. After everyone had eaten as much as he wanted, several of the men brought out instruments that resembled five-stringed zithers. The strumming of the *naras-yukh* brought to Daniel's mind Luise's violin, and a sudden homesickness overwhelmed him. He stepped out into the numbing cold and stood staring at the millions of stars in the clear, distant dome above him. Why have You brought me here? When will You finish toying with me? He felt like a pawn in a celestial game of chess, as Luise had suggested the day he left for forestry duty.

Daniel returned to the celebration in time to witness what could only be a religious ceremony. An intricate carving of a bear, fully as big as one of the dogs that roamed the settlement, stood in the middle of the floor, and the hunters danced around it, chanting as they did so. One of them, an old man Daniel had met only once, led the dance.

He wore an elaborately beaded headband, and his caribou skin jacket bore beaded likenesses of bear, reindeer, horses and ravens.

Feeling like an interloper, Daniel slipped out of the lodge and trudged through the knee-deep snow back to Ostic and Blen's hut. I've had enough of this. As much as I appreciate the care of these people, I just want to go home, to be in the presence of my own people. I want to be a husband to Luise. I want to be a leader in my own community.

In the days following the celebration, constant work pushed Daniel's inner turmoil aside. These people used every part of the bear from fur and skin to tendons and claws. What he did not anticipate was how much of that work would be assigned to him. He learned to make soft skinned boots, complete with beadwork on the toe and a fur cuff at the top. They were the most comfortable boots he had ever worn. As the winter days gradually lengthened, he felt keenly the need to be on his way home. To Luise. The worry reminded him that he did not know where he was…or where she was.

Chapter Twenty-three

Daniel had become so accustomed to his new name, Netmetsiki, that he rarely thought of himself as Daniel. At least until the day when from the vantage point of a nearby hill, he watched the fur trader duck under the dripping icicles on the edges of Ostic's hut and enter the door.

From that distance, the visitor appeared to be a man of the south, dressed in cloth instead of leather. He had tethered two short, hairy horses in the trees near the hut, where they pawed through the snow for last year's grass.

As Daniel approached the hut, he heard the visitor conversing with Ostic and Blen in their language, and something inside him stirred. By now he understood a few words and phrases, and he wondered if this man spoke Russian as well.

He let himself into the hut. The three inside—Blen, Ostic and the trader—sat cross-legged around the firepit like old friends, talking in rapid syllables. At his entrance, they stared up at him.

When Daniel's eyes became accustomed to the dimness of the hut, his glance passed over Ostic and Blen to rest on the visitor, and the sight of the man jolted him.

The trader leaped to his feet with a cry of greeting and embraced him. "Martens! You look like a Siberian John the Baptist! What in the name of all that's sacred are you doing here?"

The words, spoken in German, fell like music on Daniel's ears, but all he could do was stare and stammer.

"What's the matter with you, Martens? Are you having a seizure? I am Josiah Marcowiscz, horse trader—"

Daniel gulped a deep breath and found his voice. "I know who you are, Josiah, I just can't believe you're here." He started to laugh, joy welling up from the pit of his stomach and trickling from his eyes. "My father and I bought and sold many horses through you. Mostly you were a fair man, but sometimes you cheated us."

"What? I cheat no one. I trade value for value." He shrugged, and then a wide grin lifted his thick moustache. "If my idea of value differs from yours, that is your lookout."

They both laughed and embraced again, slapping each other on the back. Then Daniel stepped back and stared. He closed his eyes and shook his head to clear it.

Marcowiscz gestured for them to sit, but Daniel could hardly remain seated. "When were you last in Slavgorod? What can you tell me of my family?"

"Where to begin? Your father had died, just before you left—"

"He died and I blamed them and they took me instead." Daniel leapt to his feet and paced the small space like a cornered Siberian tiger. "That's what happened. I committed no crime."

"Easy, Daniel," said Marcowiscz, using the same tone he often used to calm a nervous horse. "Not much is required to make one an enemy of the state these days. It is good we have this conversation here in the seclusion of the north and not in the city. You must be extremely careful what you say about the regime."

"I will think about that later. Tell me more."

Marcowiscz stroked his moustache and looked into Daniel's eyes. "I saw those families leave Alexandrovka in March of '27, shortly after you were taken."

"Was Luise among them?"

Marcowiscz shrugged. "I think so, but how would I know for sure? I watched from the top of the hill, far enough away so they didn't notice me. I couldn't recognize faces. I left as soon as I had completed my business in the village."

Daniel swiped his sleeve across his face. "I must find Luise."

ஒ

Luise awoke in the night and sat up in her bed. She heard Nela's soft breathing beside her. The house was quiet. What had awakened her?

She lay back on her pillow and stared into the darkness. Her heart pounded and her mind was alert.

"Jesus, please make your presence felt by Daniel this night, if he still lives. Give him peace and bring him back to me...if it is Your will. And grant me peace too."

With that, she drifted into a sleep filled with sweet dreams and memories.

ஒ

After Blen served a meal, the three men sat around the fire inside the hut, with Blen sitting off to the side. Daniel entreated Marcowiscz to interpret for him.

"Last I remember I was thrown out into the bush some distance from the exile camp and left to die. These people saved my life, and I have been unable to thank them."

Marcowiscz translated Daniel's words for Ostic and Blen, who nodded and smiled and chattered.

"They say you were nearly dead when they found you, beaten and bruised, with a bullet in your side. You remained unconscious for many days after they brought you here. They say it is their way, they would not leave someone to die, even if he was a burden and knew nothing of their way of life."

"They speak directly," Daniel said ruefully.

"They call you Netmetsiki. Do you know what that means?"

"Do I want to know?"

Marcowiscz shrugged. "It means strange man, outsider, in the Khanty tongue."

"Khanty? These people are Khanty? Josiah, where are we?"

"Where...man, you are a piece of work. We are roughly six hundred kilometers from Tomsk."

"North?"

"Of course north, you are north of everything here. I imagine your exile camp was the relatively new one near Nizhnevartovsk. Martens, were you the only one they mistreated like that?"

"What do you mean? They are beasts without conscience. They tried to work us to death or starve us, whichever came first. Many died."

"But why were you treated so inhumanely?"

Daniel stared into the fire, his mind reeling with memory, and then met Josiah's eyes. "It was Dubrowsky. He made sure I suffered the most. He hated me from the beginning."

"Why?"

"I stood up to him on the journey north, intervened for a fellow prisoner."

"And?"

And? There was something else, something that had evaded his memories until now, but it suddenly became as clear as if it had happened that very day. "I tried to kill him." Daniel's voice was a whisper.

"You tried to kill Dubrowsky?"

Daniel nodded. "Tell them." He jerked his chin toward Ostic and Blen. "They deserve to know what kind of man they have harbored."

After a slight hesitation, Marcowiscz began to speak, inclining his head toward Daniel. Ostic and Blen listened, nodded and replied.

Daniel looked to Marcowiscz for clarification. The trader cleared his throat. "They say you are a decent and good man and they are not sorry they took you in."

"You didn't tell them the truth."

"I told them enough."

Daniel lay awake long into the night while Marcowiscz snored nearby. He drifted into a dream in which he saw Luise. She reached for him, her dark eyes intense. She seemed to be pleading with him, but when she opened her mouth to speak, Daniel started awake. He dozed again. Flashes of Luise's face and dark eyes teased him through the night and he awoke before dawn, distracted and frustrated. He pulled on his boots and trekked out onto the taiga, almost running to escape the haunting dreams.

Sleep eluded Luise. Every time she closed her eyes, Daniel's face appeared before her. He wore the same shocked expression he had worn the last time she had seen him, at the improvised jail in Alexandrovka, and it tore her heart.

She rose from her bed and slipped quietly into the kitchen to pace. She missed Daniel as much as she ever had, and his appearance in her dreams made him seem real again, not like some imagined memory. Whether he was dead or alive, she needed some sort of connection with him.

Luise stopped her pacing and stood still in the middle of the kitchen floor. A connection. She lit the lamp and fetched paper and ink. When she had seated herself at the table, she took a deep breath and began to write…

My dearest Daniel,

It has been two years since I saw your face in the jail in Alexandrovka. I remember it as if it were yesterday, your desperate embrace as Magadan forced me to leave. And then Johannes told me you had been taken away without a goodbye.

I have been living like half a person since that time, but thanks to God's strength and Tante

Manya's wit and encouragement, it has become somewhat more bearable of late. Then you come to me in my dreams and I am faced with the realization that if you are still alive, you are no doubt enduring terrible trials. I pray that you have sufficient food and clothing, and that you are physically well.

Besides these things, I hope and pray that you are trusting God in the midst of your struggles. Only Jesus can give you the strength and courage to face the desperate situation that has come upon you.

It is well past midnight and I must return to bed, or I will not be able to stay awake in the schoolroom tomorrow. Yes, I am teaching school again so Schoolmaster Fast can help the farmers with their seeding. He is not impressed by this state of affairs, nor with me, but that is of little consequence to me. I don't trust that man. Poor Jasch must live with him.

I will also mention the trouble I'm having with one of my students. Ironically, he is the brother of one of my friends, Frieda Klassen. Gerhardt is fourteen and feels too old to sit with the other children in the classroom, so he graces us with rudeness and belligerence. I believe he is a bright young man, but I can't get through to him, and sometimes he makes me so angry I could shout. But I don't. I must keep praying for patience and ideas to win him over.

I will write again tomorrow and tell you what has transpired since you left us. May God grant you peace, wherever you are.

Goodnight, my darling husband,

Your Luise

Luise blew the ink dry as she returned to her bedroom,

then slipped the page beneath the mattress. Finally, sleep claimed her.

ڪ

Josiah Marcowiscz had just finished a morning meal when Daniel returned from his early morning trek. Josiah's pack sat ready beside him, along with a large bundle of skins and pelts. He felt anxious to be on his way, but Daniel's plight ate at him.

Daniel sat down beside him in the dim hut. "I must find Luise."

"Then you had better be on your way. You cannot traverse the taiga after spring thaw or you may be swallowed by a bog or attacked by a bear, and only the ravens would know what happened to you."

"But I don't know where to go. Did Luise go to the Amur with her family or did she stay in Alexandrovka? How am I to know?"

Josiah grimaced. "The only way you can know is to go back to Alexandrovka."

Daniel nodded, staring into the glowing coals. "Yes."

"Martens. Come with me. I'm going as far south as Tomsk. We could journey together and then you could carry on to Alexandrovka while I head west."

Josiah waited for Daniel to process his invitation.

"Yes, your idea is good. I will come."

"I have two Altai horses with me. The kilometers will pass much more swiftly on horseback than on foot, and I have traveled this route many times. Pack your things and we will be on our way."

Josiah felt his spirits lift at the prospect of company on the long trek back to civilization. He had an almost fatherly urge to help Daniel. The young man had been crushed beyond what most people could survive, but he was determined.

"I will await you outside."

Daniel emerged from the hut a short time later with a

skin bag filled with supplies that Blen had no doubt pushed on him. It would have to be enough to see him through a journey of thousands of kilometers.

Josiah interpreted for Ostic. "He says he wishes you safe journey and sufficient food."

Blen had joined them, and added her own wishes. "She hopes you find your woman and your hut."

"Tell them I will never forget what they have done. In years to come, I will tell my wife and my children of my experiences here."

When Marcowiscz had translated Daniel's words, he said to him in German, "Let's get going, man. It's a long way home."

They mounted the ponies and started off through the snow, letting the horses pick their way across the meadow and up the hill. At the top they stopped to look back. Ostic and Blen stood together, watching. Daniel raised a hand in farewell and turned to join Josiah in whatever lay before them.

Chapter Twenty-four

"You seem considerably happier of late, Luise."

Tante Manya sat on the bench outside the kitchen soaking up spring sunshine while Luise bent over the newly pulled rows in the garden plot.

Her aunt's comment sent conflicting emotions through Luise. She frowned on the beans as she dropped them into the soil. On one hand, she felt lighter knowing she had released Daniel into the Lord's hands, yet she still felt guilt at her own cheerfulness.

"Heavens above," exclaimed Tante Manya, "she takes my observation to be a reprimand."

"What?" Luise looked up from the beans toward the wiry old woman on the bench. "Oh, I'm sorry, Tante Manya. It's just that even while I find peace in the knowledge that God is looking after Daniel, I still feel as though it is my faith that sustains him."

"You believe God is helpless without you? That's an arrogant thought."

Frustration seeped through Luise's façade of calm. "But what then is prayer? Does it not make some difference that I pray? If not, I have spent many hours uselessly."

"God is not a celestial conjurer upon whom we call when we want something, like a genie in a lamp. The purpose of prayer is not to get what we want, Luise, but to lay hold of God Himself. He seeks always to reveal Himself to us. Once we begin to see Him as He is, we can relinquish our tight hold on our will and trust Him for His. Do you understand?"

"Sometimes I don't understand anything, Tante. I feel as

if I'm living in two worlds, one where Daniel is dead and I must carry on without him, the other where he is alive and seeks to return to me. How do I balance these two possibilities?"

Tante Manya reached for the hoe beside her and pulled herself up from the bench. She shuffled along the row, slowly pulling dirt over the seeds and tamping it down with the flat side of the hoe.

"You cannot live two lives, girl. Embrace this day and walk forward in the light you have. God will show you the way if you submit yourself to Him."

"So many words, Tante Manya, so many ideals. I need solid facts to anchor myself."

"You already have them. You know the truth. Now you must live accordingly."

Luise looked up at the old woman and saw the love in her rheumy eyes, the faith shining forth from the wrinkled face. She heaved a huge sigh and smiled back at her.

"Tante Manya, if someday I gain even a portion of your wisdom, I will be therewith content."

"She is a wordy one, to be sure."

"I speak in all seriousness, Tante."

"As do I."

Tante Manya's mouth twitched and a giggle escaped Luise's lips. "And here I thought of myself as serene and quiet."

"Ha! If only you could hear yourself. The rest of us are hard-pressed to fit in a word here and there."

Luise's giggles turned to laughter while Tante Manya continued her sarcastic scolding.

"She laughed while we yearned for beans not planted, that's what they will say of you in years to come. If only she had applied herself to the planting we could enjoy bean soup, but alas, she spent her time struggling with the vastness of theological reasoning and we are left to starve."

Luise sank to the earth, weak with laughter, wiping her

eyes with her apron while Manya ambled back to the bench, her weathered face infused with life and light.

When Luise had collected herself, she said, "No more idle talk from me. Today I am planting beans for the future, Daniel or no Daniel."

"I'm sure he would approve."

"Do you know why Dubrowsky is so cruel?"

Josiah Marcowiscz felt Daniel's eyes on him from across the campfire.

"Because he's GPU. That's how they are trained."

"Yes, but not to the extent he has taken it. It seems he has no soul."

Josiah sipped his coffee and turned over possible answers in his head. "There are rumors, but I don't know the truth."

"Rumors are better than nothing."

"What makes you think he hates you more than anyone else?"

Daniel set his own cup on the ground and leaned forward. "Let me tell you. No one else in that hellhole suffered like I did. Every step I took, he watched me. Every wrong move I made, he beat me. The others he treated harshly, but me he singled out to grind beneath his boots. What did I do that was worse than any of them?"

"Well," Marcowiscz began, "from what I hear, Dubrowsky hates three things—Mennonites, *kulaks* and arrogance. You make full count."

Daniel blew out a breath and nodded. "I stood up to him and spoke my mind." His eyes pleaded for Josiah to understand. "He had just pushed my father to his death and I was angry. You would have been too. He had no right to—"

"That's where you're wrong, Martens," interrupted Josiah, his voice harsher than he meant it to be. "As a senior-major in the GPU, Dubrowsky has the right to do whatever he wants. You and I both know that. And before we reach civilization, you'd better let that fact sink into your thick head, or you'll have us both dead."

He sat back and muttered, "You must be aware of who your enemy is."

Daniel sat in silence for a while, and then said, "You still didn't tell me why he hates Mennonites."

Josiah rubbed a tired hand over his face. The air was cold and he just wanted to sleep. Maybe taking Martens along on this trek had been a mistake. He sighed.

"It's all hearsay, you realize. If people don't know the truth, they make it up."

He saw Daniel nod in the flickering firelight. "Tell me."

"From what I've heard, Dubrowsky began his service with the Bolsheviks in the Red Army that fought in the Mennonite colonies in South Russia. It is said that he was shot in the thigh by one of your *Selbstschutz* members. Crippled him. Kept him from rising as far as he wanted in the ranks of the GPU, and he's never forgotten the perpetrators.

"That's the story. He has hated them—you and your people—with a vengeance ever since and seeks revenge at every opportunity. Perhaps you are unfortunate enough to resemble the young man who shot him, add to that the fact that you come from a wealthy family. That's all he needs to fuel his hatred. Arrogance was the match that sparked the fire."

Luise carefully skimmed cream off the pail of milk she had brought in earlier. It was good to be home doing the things she loved doing, but she missed teaching at the school now that Schoolmaster Fast had returned.

"Hans, Nela, come help now."

When her young brother and sister appeared, Luise seated them by the butter churn. "Take turns until the butter is ready."

They began to grumble, and Luise stopped them with a look. "Do you like to eat butter on your bread, on your potatoes?"

At their nods, she said, "Then you must churn. You can't make butter by frowning at the milk."

Nela giggled and started churning.

Luise poured some of the skimmed milk into a pot, and heated it on the stove. Before it boiled, she removed it from the heat and let it sit.

"Let's see how the butter is coming along," she said to the children. "Did you feel it separating yet?"

"I don't know how to tell," said Nela.

"The churning gets easier, silly," said Hans.

Luise checked, and then looked up when Anna entered the kitchen. She seemed better this morning. Perhaps the spring air had revived her once more.

"The children need to go to school now, Luise, or they'll be late. Off you go. Give Mama a kiss."

When they had gone, Anna lowered herself into a chair by the table and watched Luise.

"I'll rinse the butter while you clean the churn."

Luise glanced at her stepmother. "Thank you. Are you feeling better today?"

"In body. I do not like the new man they've sent here from Moscow."

Anna poured off the buttermilk and began to knead the butter in a bowl of cold water, pressing out the remaining buttermilk until the water ran clear.

"You mean Ivan Mironenko?" asked Luise, greasy hands poised above the churn. "Has something happened to frighten you?"

"He beat Aaron Peters; you saw him. He's like that Dubrowsky from Alexandrovka who took Daniel away."

Anna pushed the butter into small wooden forms and poured the buttermilk into a jar to keep until it could be used to make bread. "They're closing in again."

Luise shivered as she washed her hands and set the butter churn back in its corner. Old, familiar fears resurfaced. She stirred several spoonsful of thick sour cream into the warm milk waiting on the back of the stove, then set the pot in the warming oven above. "There. We should have clabbered milk by tomorrow."

Luise felt Anna's eyes on her. "Why did they send another man? Are we so difficult that Rashidov can't handle us? Are we such enemies of Mother Russia?"

"I fear Russia is no more. We are now a Soviet republic, whatever that means."

"They say it will only get worse."

Luise pursed her lips and stilled her racing imagination. "Mother, you tell me 'they say' this and 'they say' that. Who do you mean by 'they?' "

Anna wiped her hands on a rag and tilted her head at Luise. "The Communists, of course. Stalin's men. They've followed us here, as I feared they would. Now we wait to see what they do."

Anna's words bothered Luise. Fear seeped in through the cracks in her faith and contaminated the tentative peace that had finally begun to settle on her. Just when she had shut out her fears, the Soviet had stuck a boot in the door again.

⁂

"You think Luise waits for you in Alexandrovka?"

Daniel considered Josiah's question as he knelt to wash himself in the stream near Tomsk. "I don't know but I must find out for sure. I hope she has gone with her family, but she can be stubborn at times."

Josiah grinned. "You two make a good match then."

"We were married, you know," said Daniel, without an answering smile. "The day before my father died, before they arrested me."

The horse trader had the grace to remain silent, but his eyes gave away his pity.

Daniel changed the subject, shaking the water from his hands and closing his pack. "Where will you go from here? A man can only be a horse trader if he has horses to trade, eh?"

"You are correct. I go to Tomsk for horses, and then to the bazaars in Omsk and Novosibirsk to trade. The people there pride themselves in owning good Don horses."

"What will they give you in exchange?"

"Altai, like these two."

"Hairy little beasts."

"They may be small and long-haired, but they will outlast your Dons when it's cold. They slow their breathing, you know."

"My Don has become the Don of my enemy."

"What?"

"Dubrowsky not only took my father's life and livelihood, and my future, but he rode out on Prince."

Josiah winced. "That cuts deep. Prince was the best horse I ever sold to your father. I would know that one anywhere. A long tail like a parade horse and the head of an aristocrat."

"Well, he's gone now like everything else I once called mine, so there's no use talking about it."

The trader stared at him. At last he stood and stretched out his hand to Daniel.

"I take my leave now. Meet me in Omsk if you can, or look for me in Novosibirsk. From there I go east and we could again travel together for a time. Take care for yourself and I hope you find your girl—er, your wife."

Daniel ignored the hand and embraced Marcowiscz. "I owe you for restoring my purpose to me, and for getting me on my way. I hope our paths cross soon again."

Marcowiscz secured his pack to one of the horses and started toward Tomsk. A short distance away he stopped, turned and stared back at Daniel.

"Remember, Martens, keep your thoughts to yourself

and trust no one—not even me." A grin replaced the sternness on his tanned face and he waved as left.

Chapter Twenty-five

After Marcowiscz rode away to the west, Daniel headed south, staying between the Ob River and the road until he arrived at Novosibirsk. Seeing this city again brought back the ugly memories all too vividly. Images of his capture and torture assaulted him until he wished he could blot them out. He had no wish to meet anyone connected with the prison camp or their stopping places in the city, but he was determined to return to Alexandrovka. He had to make sure Luise had not stayed to wait for him.

It's been two years since you left. Do you really expect her to be waiting in the village? Surely Abram would not have allowed her to stay. But even as the voices warred in his mind, he knew he would never be content without knowing for sure. Still dressed in his skins and leathers, his frame much leaner than it had been, a full beard covering much of his face, he hoped no one would recognize him; no one but Luise.

But Marcowiscz had known him, had recognized him almost immediately. How many others would do the same?

His fear tempered by determination and hope, Daniel set his feet southward from Novosibirsk. He could not afford to meet Leonid Dubrowsky, or Victor Magadan, or any of the authorities. That would be a death sentence.

He continued to follow the Ob as it curved southwest, and when it changed direction, he struck out across country toward the Slavgorod Colony and home. Home? He had no home. Everything he had loved had been taken away by the Soviet. He was nothing but a number in their exhaustive records in Moscow, but hopefully that number had been relegated to the files of the deceased. If they believed him dead, they would not be looking for him. Let it remain so.

As he walked, Daniel considered selling a pair of mukluks and purchasing a train ticket from Novosibirsk down to Barnaul and across to Kulunda, then back up to Slavgorod, but he was used to walking. Riding the train would feel lazy, besides, there were too many people in close proximity, especially in that area. If he had to go east later, he would take the Trans-Siberian, but for now he would walk.

The days lengthened and warmed as he moved southwest, and soon the gentle hills beckoned, and in spite of himself, he felt a sense of belonging. Pockets of snow still remained on the north faces of hills and mountains, melting slowly as they became exposed to the strong rays of the late spring sun, but the river was still ice-bound in places. He stopped to fish whenever the need arose and ate well off the land. The nights were still cool, but in his furs he stayed comfortable enough.

When Daniel saw his reflection in the crystalline surface of lakes he passed or camped beside, he saw a man whose hair had grown long and curled over his collar. His moustache still made him proud, but he was not sure how he felt about the massive beard. Ostic had teased him about it, poking fun and laughing. But for now it proved a helpful disguise, and it covered most of the scars left by Dubrowsky's whip.

Daniel let feelings of nostalgia sweep over him as he trekked familiar fields. He borrowed an old horse at Znamenka—Marcowiscz had said to leave his name if he should ever need a horse in the area—and plodded into the colony, past Reichenfeld and Olgafeld, and then across to Alexandrovka.

As Daniel reached the top of the low hill overlooking Alexandrovka, he stopped to stare at the village that had been his home. Along its straight main street the houses faced each other primly, as they always had, backed by neat yards and gardens, opening onto the fields.

There was an openness about the place, something he hadn't realized he'd missed in the northern forests. A person could breathe here. Scattered poplar and birch trees waved welcome in the breeze, waiting for him to make his usual trek past the school and the church, to the end of the street where his father's house stood proudly.

But he could not go there. They would certainly see him.

He stood in the shade of an old poplar and contemplated his next step. He dared not go to his father's house in case it was watched. Had his family also gone east?

Then the thought came to him. Wielers. He would go to Phillip Wieler's place and they would give him the information he needed.

He turned his horse along the backside of the village, coming up behind the Wieler home, and tethered his animal securely in a stand of stout poplars.

Making his way quietly through the yard by way of the lilac hedges, he stopped at the back door and knocked.

"Suse! Go see who is at the door."

A young girl cracked open the door and stared at him, then shut it again. He heard clipped conversation, denials, questions and answers, then saw the curtain move in the kitchen window. The door opened again and Frau Wieler stood there.

"What do you want?" she said in Russian.

He answered in German. "Frau Wieler? I am Daniel."

As she stared at him, he saw recognition creep into her eyes. "*Ach Lied!* Where do you come from? Come in, come in." One hand snatched at him, the other covered her mouth.

Daniel slipped inside with a quick glance behind him and pulled his cap from his head. "Frau Wieler, thank you for letting me in. I've come a long distance to find out what happened to my family and Luise."

The woman flitted here and there fixing food for Daniel, chattering as if her tongue were hinged in the middle.

"Sit down first and eat, then we will talk. Oh you poor man, what all you have had to suffer." She wiped tears from her cheeks and kept talking. "What did they do to you? Where did you get those scars on your face? And your family gone too. What will you do?..."

Remembering how she was, Daniel dipped the roasted zwieback in his coffee and let her talk herself out. Eventually the well would run dry and he would have a chance to speak. He had spent many an evening here with Phillip's family, just as Phillip had done at his house, and he knew trying to interrupt Frau Wieler would be like trying to divert the course of a river.

"Where did you come from? We thought you were dead! They told us you were dead. Phillip said no one could survive or escape the north, and that official, that Dubrowsky, he said you were dead... But you look healthy, except for the scars and I...how did you do it?" Suddenly a thought hit her and she glanced nervously out the window. "Are they seeking you? Have you escaped?"

He shook his head and held up a hand to stop the flow of words. "No, no, Frau Wieler. They think I'm dead. No one will be looking, although I do not wish anyone to see me here. No need to raise suspicion. Frau Wieler, I need to know: where is Luise? Did she go east with her family?"

"Jah, jah, of course. Abram would not leave her behind. It was awful watching her those days, her face a mask of grief. How she wept when they left, making her friend Valentina promise to write if she heard anything about you. But no one heard anything, not even Phillip, not until the official came back from up north. Phillip said—"

Daniel felt relief that Luise had gone with her family, yet his secret wish had been to find her here. But her safety was more important. "Where is Phillip? Is he still here?"

"Phillip? You don't know? Of course you don't know;

you've been gone. Phillip stayed behind when your family went, but he and Jasch Fast left a few months after. The authorities, they questioned them since they had been friends with you and so they got scared and left. They didn't want to be arrested too. They almost died on the way, you know. My sister-in-law—that's Maria Friesen, Johann's wife—she wrote to us, so glad she was to tell us our Phillip got there alive. He was so thin and weak when they finally arrived in Shumanovka, but now he is better and he has apparently been spending time with..." She put her hand over her mouth and her eyes widened.

"What were you saying?"

Still she stared at him. "Nothing. She wrote a lot of things." Frau Wieler busied herself in the kitchen, heating more water for coffee, her face hidden from him.

Daniel stood and walked toward her. "There is something you aren't telling me. What is it?"

Wringing her hands, she faced him, but her eyes flitted here and there. "Well, you know Phillip told us you could not survive the ordeal and even if you did, you would never return from the north. So we all came to accept the fact that you were most likely dead, and then Senior-Major Dubrowsky returned and confirmed our suspicions."

She perched on the corner of a chair like a bird ready for flight, picking at a seam on her apron. "Phillip has, um...he has been courting your Luise. Not that she accepted him, but he likes her, you know, and since he was thinking you wouldn't be coming back, he thought Luise needed someone to look after her and he probably was thinking of you and..."

She stopped speaking and Daniel stopped breathing.

"Courting my Luise? She's a married woman. Phillip is my best friend. How could he be courting her?"

"Well, maybe courting is too strong a word. He has been spending time with her, but," she looked up at him hopefully, "apparently Luise has not been receptive of him.

She always was strong-willed, that one, and…"

Her words droned on as Daniel's heart pounded in his ears. He paced the floor like one of Marcowiscz' untrained horses. His Luise spending time with Phillip? He had grown up with Phillip, had always thought of him as a brother. Their pranks and escapades could fill a book. But Phillip had only ever been friendly toward Luise, or maybe Daniel had missed the signs.

He sank into a chair and rested his head in his hands. "My Luise?"

"Oh, Daniel, I'm sure she loves you still. She just doesn't know you are alive. How is she to survive alone in that far off place?"

He looked up. "She has her family. And Phillip. Why should she wait any longer? I've been gone more than two years and word is I am dead." He felt the dull thud of his heart beating, but the emotion had seeped out. Thud, thud, thud.

"Daniel, shush. She has not forgotten you, or she would not be spurning Phillip. So go to her before it's too late. I will write a letter to Maria today, but you know how unreliable the mail is these days, and everything is monitored. We have to be so careful. But I will do what I can, and when they receive the letter, all will be made right again, you'll see."

Thoughts tumbled about in Daniel's mind. Perhaps there was a chance. Surely Luise would sense that he was still alive. Surely she would not accept Phillip.

"I must go," he said. "I must get there as soon as possible, before..." He could not finish the sentence, the thought. The unthinkable could not happen.

Frau Wieler put a restraining hand on his arm. "Stay the night with us," she said. "It is too late to go far tonight and the officials are always watching. They know everything we do and say and where we go."

"Then it is expedient that I go under cover of darkness. They don't know I'm alive, so I have an advantage. They're not expecting me and I certainly don't want to put you under suspicion."

"Expecting or not, they are a crafty lot."

"Why did you not move east with the rest?" Daniel wanted to know.

"Why indeed! My man doesn't think they will be safe long, even on the Amur. He says we are just as well off here where we know the enemy."

"And you? What do you think?"

She seemed surprised at his question. "Well, I think the same as my husband, of course. I agree with him. But I do wonder sometimes if we should have gone. Nah jah, it has been decided, and so we will adjust, eh? We have a sturdy house and my husband, he has work always, and so we eat, so far. But it frightens me sometimes, these secrets and threats."

They stood silently watching each other, not sure of words. Then, simultaneously, they spoke.

"I must go."

"I must send food along with you."

With a smile she pushed him into the parlor. "You lie down in a soft place for a few minutes while I gather some things for you to take with you."

Against his better judgment, Daniel sank onto the divan, careful not to rub dirt on the rug at his feet. He relaxed into the softness and inhaled the once familiar scent of cleanliness. A snore woke him and he realized it was his own. Leaping to his feet, he entered the kitchen to find Frau Wieler busy at her stove, a large pillowcase stuffed and ready on the table.

"Frau Wieler, how long have I slept?" He glanced out the window and saw faint tinges of orange and pink staining the blue of the western sky.

She turned in surprise. "Only an hour or so. I thought you needed a rest. Supper will be ready soon if you stay." She seemed to be trying to make atonement for being the purveyor of bad news.

He smiled and thanked her. "I really must be going. You have been thoughtful and I will always appreciate it."

"I have written the letter," she said, pointing to an envelope on the table. "I didn't mention you by name but they'll know who I mean."

"Thank you. I would ask that you also pray it would arrive in a timely manner. It is a matter of life and death for me."

"Jah, I imagine it is. Well, if I cannot persuade you to stay, then be off and may God watch over you."

Instinctively, she pulled him down into a firm embrace and then, red-faced, sent him on his way. "You have always been like a brother to my Phillip."

Daniel checked around before stepping outside, then headed to the thicket where he had left the horse tethered. It was still there, and he felt relief settle in as he mounted and turned the animal back in the direction of Znamenka.

His eyes took in the expanse of the village, the familiar lay of the land in the fading light, the ordered dwellings, the clean main street where he had often walked with Luise, the thickets of poplar and birch crowding the back yards. He would miss this place.

He rode back toward Znamenka as the sun eased behind the horizon and the stars winked on in the darkening sky. He would leave the horse there, sleep somewhere nearby for the night, perhaps find a good breakfast in the morning and head east to the Amur…and Luise. It was a good plan.

It was then that he heard the sound, as subtle as an air current.

❧

Dearest Daniel,

I'm having another sleepless night. In the darkness I imagine that somewhere you are sleeping peacefully, yet by morning's light I know that is unlikely. I miss you.

Peace keeps its distance from us here in Shumanovka also. The authorities have ordained that the villages of Kleefeld, Freidensfeld and New York will join our village to form a collective farm, the Shumanovka Kolkozy. This decision is not to our advantage, but one consolation is that Jakob Siemens was chosen as the leader. Perhaps he will be able to help the farmers fulfill their responsibilities to the government without us losing our limited freedoms here.

The Soviet government has seen fit to dispatch another official to Shumanovka, apparently to help Yevgeny Rashidov, or to serve as the dark side of an official twosome. His name is Ivan Petrovich Mironenko, but I call him Ivan the Terrible.

I have received no news from our former home. Valentina wrote once and that was the end of it. I miss her, but have befriended Frieda Klassen. She and I walk and talk together in the evenings when the weather is agreeable, or on Sunday afternoons. It is good to have a friend to talk to, even if she is not Valentina. I hope you are also able to share your thoughts with someone.

Anna seems much improved with the arrival of spring. She helps in the kitchen and even in the garden sometimes

I still teach at the school from time to time, whenever Mr. Fast is needed in the fields or at the volost office.

I miss you every moment of every day. May God care for you, whether you are still on this earth or in heaven's glory.

I love you always,

Your Luise

Daniel heard a soft whistle in the trees to his right. Even before he decided whether or not he had heard something, he instinctively slid from his horse, keeping it between him and the direction from which the sound had come. He couldn't let anyone know he had been in Alexandrovka, especially not the Soviet's spies.

He stood perfectly still, his hand on the horse's nose, and waited, trying to see through the darkness, to differentiate between trunks of trees and moving bodies. His ears listened past the croak of bullfrogs and the subdued song of nightbirds. Nothing.

Then, almost next to him, a small figure appeared.

"Do not fear, Martens," it whispered. "Bruyevich at the livery sent me to get the horse. He said not to come; there are those who wish to harm you. They saw you in the village."

Daniel forced his heart back into his chest and tried to even out his breathing. "You are very good. I did not see you."

"But you heard me. I must practice more."

Daniel heard a smile and answered in kind, then remembered the gravity of his situation. "Who waits for me and why?"

"GPU. They don't know who you are, just that you acted furtively, they said. Bruyevich says he wouldn't turn his mother-in-law over to that lot."

Daniel thanked the boy and untied his sack of provisions from the saddle of the horse. He worried about the Wielers. Would they suffer because of him?

"Thank Bruyevich for me when the men have gone."

"I will. He says don't go east. Wait a while."

Don't go east. Daniel felt his plans dissipate with the last light. How was he to reach Luise without going east? He knew Bruyevich was right; the GPU would expect him to go east. Well then, he would take up Marcowiscz' offer to join him. He would meet the Irtysh River, and follow it up to Omsk.

He reached into his pack for some roasted zwieback for the boy, thanked him once more, and backtracked around the edge of the Slavgorod Colony. He would rest along the way, but first he must put some distance between himself and the GPU. It was already end of April, this year of 1929. He prayed that his Luise would wait.

Perhaps he should refrain from calling her *his* Luise, but no! She was his wife. They had promised to remain faithful to each other as long as they both would live. Yes, Daniel, but she now thinks you are dead. That releases her from the contract, at least in her own mind. But what did Phillip think he was doing? How could his friend press his present advantage? It would be a cold day in hell before he forgave Phillip, if he ever did. He sighed, the weight of unforgiveness heavy upon him.

Daniel lay down on dry leaves in a grove of aspen beside a stream and tried to rest, but his mind would not obey. Morning finally freed him from his restlessness and he set out again, walking steadily westward to the river and then northwest to Omsk. He camped out at night, building dreams of hope, only to have them crash again with morning light.

The bundle Frau Wieler had given him had been a welcome change: roasted zwieback, cheese, smoked sausage and a few wintered carrots, but by the time he reached Omsk, he had fallen back into the routine of fish or rabbit cooked over a small fire. It was enough to sustain his body, but his soul was starving.

Josiah Marcowiscz knew horseflesh, and if the horse he now saw at the rail in front of the pub was not Prince, it was time he gave up his vocation.

Josiah looked up and down the busy street, searching for the man who had stolen this fine animal, but he didn't see him. Must be inside having a drink. Josiah moved closer and stroked the horse's neck. Under the hair, he felt welts that had not been there when he had sold the animal to Peter Martens, and he did not believe either of the Martens men would have whipped such a fine horse.

"Well, well, my friend. How did you get to this place? Your present master treats you like he treats two-legged animals, eh Prince?" Prince shook his mane and nickered, as if he remembered this voice.

An idea came to Josiah in that instant. "Perhaps I can return you to your rightful owner. He would certainly treat you better."

Prince jerked his head back, his eyes widening, and Josiah whirled to face Senior-Major Leonid Dubrowsky.

"What do you think you're—well, if it isn't the horse trader." Dubrowsky passed a hand over his face, and the menacing look slipped away as if he had swept it off into his pocket. He leaned on the rail. "You like my horse." It was a statement rather than a question.

Josiah felt disquiet creep over him in the presence of this man. He had dealt with him several times before, but the transactions had always been tense.

"A fine horse, to be sure. Have you had him long?"

Dubrowsky's eyes narrowed and Josiah felt his skin prickle.

"What business is that of yours?"

Josiah squared his shoulders. He was taller than Dubrowsky, and broader in the shoulder, but the man still seemed to diminish him with his presence.

"I'm always looking for good horses. Would you consider selling him?"

Dubrowsky's cold laugh chilled Josiah. "Absolutely not. He holds a certain meaning for me."

"Too bad. I purchased a number of excellent mounts of superb quality in Tomsk that would suit you well. Younger horses with more stamina than this fellow, fine as he is."

"He's not old. He suits me fine. Why do you want him, eh?" Dubrowsky stared at Josiah and the trader fought the urge to look away. "Eh? You know this horse? Come," said the GPU Senior-Major with a command in his voice, "we will drink together."

Josiah struggled to maintain clarity of mind as Dubrowsky pushed glasses of vodka at him, but the drink took him in as it had so often before. It gradually loosened his tongue. "I sold this horse to someone a few years ago. Best horse I ever handled."

"To whom did you sell him?"

"I…he…no, I think maybe it was another horse. I am mistaken."

"I think you know. You even know the horse's name. But Martens is dead, right?"

Josiah hesitated for a second. "I…I don't know, is he?" He rose and held onto the table to steady himself.

"You tell me." Dubrowsky's voice was cold and his hand reached out to grip Josiah's arm. "When did you last see him?"

Josiah tried to shake off Dubrowsky's hold, but he fell backward, tripped over his chair, and fell with a thud to the dirt floor. Dubrowsky knelt beside him and held him to the ground with a hand around his throat. "You've seen him."

Josiah's eyes widened and he shook his head wildly, but he knew Dubrowsky had heard his words to Prince, and read the truth on his drunken face. He groaned as Dubrowsky let go of his throat.

"I will be watching you."

It would be a long night, hopefully not his last in this life.

Chapter Twenty-six

Omsk was the widest city Daniel had ever seen, sprawled along the banks of the Irtysh River on a vast, flat plain. Clouds scudded across an open sky, casting shifting shadows like warnings across Daniel's path. Passenger and freight boats plied the waters of the Irtysh and Ob Rivers from as far as the mining towns of the Kazakhs in the south to the lumber camps of the north.

On that first day, Daniel kept to the outskirts of the city. He wondered where he might find Josiah Marcowiscz, or if his friend had long since finished his business here and moved on. Daniel itched to get on the road eastward, but valued the advice of Bruyevich in Znamenka.

As Daniel wandered the city streets, he began to formulate a plan in his mind. Since both branches of the Trans-Siberian Railroad ran through Omsk, the train seemed the most sensible means of travel. If he walked, as he had done so far, it would take him months to reach the Amur. He did not have months. He needed to be there now.

He walked along Lenin Street, past the Cathedral of St. Nikolas, butter yellow in the afternoon sun. His wanderings led him to the bazaars, and from there to the temporary corrals where traders bought and sold horses. Omsk, being the administrative centre of the Siberian Cossacks, would boast many horses. Perhaps Marcowiscz would still be here.

The air smelled of manure and the sweat of men and horses, and dust drifted across the assembled crowd. Daniel kept to the periphery, admiring the fine horseflesh and the skill of the trainers. He and his father used to have fine horses like that, until the Reds had found better use for them. He'd always loved a good horse, one you could depend upon and communicate with, and he'd had plenty although none equaled Prince. Now he walked wherever he needed to go, owning nothing but the few things in his pack.

"Take it or leave it!"

The voice pulled Daniel from his musings. He knew that voice, had heard it not long ago. He listened intently to locate the speaker.

"That horse is too good for you. You would spoil him."

Daniel moved to the right, under the shade of a canopy, and saw him—Josiah Marcowiscz. In this strange and colorful city where he had so far felt alone, he had found a friend.

He waited until Marcowiscz had completed his business deal. When the horse trader backed away from the crowd to count his money, Daniel sneaked up behind him.

"That horse was too good for him, you know."

Marcowiscz whirled around, fire in his eyes and the money magically out of sight. Incredulity and something like dread passed over his face as he stared at Daniel.

"Josiah Marcowiscz, I can't remember if I've ever seen you speechless." Daniel squinted at him against the setting sun. "You look terrible. What happened?"

"Nothing happened," he answered. "I've been busy."

Daniel lifted both hands in a truce. "You suggested I meet you here. Things were not favorable in Alexandrovka so I came here, but you don't look very glad to see me."

Josiah's eyes flitted across the crowd. He put an arm around Daniel's shoulders and ushered him swiftly through the crush of people. "You surprised me. I thought you might have gone east already. Might be a good idea, you know. You could catch the Trans-Siberian tonight and be in Novosibirsk by morning. Let's find us a nice, quiet place to share a glass of vodka—or tea. You haven't cleaned yourself up much yet, have you Martens?"

Daniel snorted. "I wouldn't talk, Josiah." Then he

stalled. "I'd like to see your new string of horses before we go for a drink."

"Later, my friend." Josiah slapped Daniel on the back and pushed him into a small, dimly lit pub where vodka—and tea—flowed freely. Daniel felt very ill at ease, especially with Josiah watching the door the whole while. What trouble had he got himself into? As a rule, Marcowiscz was self-assured and in control of his circumstances.

That night, Josiah pointed Daniel to a dark corner of the stable. "I will sleep near the door to protect my animals," he said.

Daniel felt bewildered, but soon the unfamiliar affects of the vodka lulled him into a sound sleep. He awoke next morning with the sun slanting into his eyes and winced. He rose with a groan, holding his head to keep it from exploding, then made his way to the front of the stall. Marcowiscz was gone. As were his belongings. And all his horses.

❧

Luise stopped mid-sentence when Gerhardt Klassen pushed through the schoolhouse door without knocking. His eyes hard, he marched up the center aisle and slapped a paper onto her desk.

Why would Gerhardt come to the schoolhouse? He hated being there and was supposed to be helping the men in the fields, something he much preferred to sitting under Luise's teaching. Meanwhile, Gerhardt stood waiting for her to read the message.

"Is this from you personally?" she asked.

"Of course not. I have no idea what it says. I was told by your father at the village office to deliver it and to wait for instructions."

Luise unfolded the paper and turned away from the children to read it. One hand flew to her mouth and the other reached to the desk to steady her. Heart pounding, she masked her fear as she faced the students.

"This is such a beautiful day, children. I believe we should take a walk." She forced a wide smile. "Put your books away and fetch your jacket if you brought one. Let's go out the back door for a change."

The younger children's eyes shone with excitement, but a few of the older students stared at Luise, tension obvious on their faces. Gerhardt's frown deepened. She gave him a barely perceptible shake of her head and continued to smile.

"Come, come. I hear the birds enjoying the sunshine. Let's share it with them. Gerhardt, would you please lead us on the road to the pasture? The rest of you, pair up with younger children, and I will come last. Let's go."

The younger ones took the hands of older students, ready to file out. When Gerhardt passed Luise, she whispered, "Walk quickly and stay in the shelter of the trees. There's trouble coming."

He nodded, eyes puzzled but not belligerent, and led the group like a Pied Piper without a song. Luise ushered the group out the back door, and glanced again at the slip of paper.

Trouble on the way. Protect children.

She stuffed the scrap of paper into her pocket, and followed the pupils, casting a backward glance toward the front door. Thank goodness Papa worked at the village office.

What purpose did the Soviet officials have in frightening children? She attributed the planned disturbance to the new official, Ivan Mironenko, but it never happened when Schoolmaster Fast was here. Why did they pick the times when Luise taught? She had strong suspicions about Fast.

From his lookout behind the Omsk train station, Josiah Marcowiscz nodded in satisfaction as Daniel Martens climbed aboard the Trans-Siberian Railway car heading east to Novosibirsk. He hoped the young man would forgive him when he realized the truth. When the train had chuffed its way out of the station, Josiah returned to his horses and strung them together for his own departure.

He led them past the pub frequented by Soviet officials. He would go west. Now he had only to convince Dubrowsky to follow him. He didn't know what else to do.

Trust no one, Marcowiscz had said. Not even me. Daniel had thought he was joking. Why had Marcowiscz offered him help and companionship, and then disappeared? Was he himself being watched? The GPU knew everything. Perhaps they also had Marcowiscz in their sights.

Daniel watched the world speed by from the window of the train car. At Novosibirsk, he got off the train to purchase the ticket he would need for the rest of the journey. The station was crowded and he had to push through a throng of people to find a quiet place to unpack the mukluks he planned to trade for his fare.

As he rummaged in his knapsack, he pulled out a small bag that had not been there before. Shielding his pack from the eyes of the other travelers, he opened the bag and stared at the rubles within. Stuck in with the money was a crumpled paper. Daniel flattened it and read the words written in obviously hasty script,

"Will do what I can. Godspeed to the sunrise."

The realization hit him like a punch to the gut. Marcowiscz was playing the decoy, urging Daniel to proceed east with all haste. He knew I'd never let him sacrifice himself for me, so he didn't tell me. Humbled and shocked, Daniel purchased another train ticket, saving enough to buy food along the way. He wouldn't be able to run off into the bush after a rabbit, and the trip to Blagoveshchensk would take a couple of weeks at the very least.

He didn't like to be in the midst of such a crowd. He

had grown used to his own company and still feared meeting anyone who might recognize him. He kept his face averted as much as possible, although his full beard and moustache hid most of the scars, and his cap helped to cover part of his face.

Except his eyes. Ice blue, Luise had always told him, disguising the warmth in his spirit. He smiled to himself as he remembered Luise's loving gaze.

When Daniel glanced at his reflection in the mirror of the lavatory in Novosibirsk Station, he did not recognize himself. He wondered if he was as changed on the inside as he was on the outside. Memories of his past came to him as from a hundred years ago, except for the memory of Luise. He felt her touch, heard her voice, saw her face.

Having led the children to the edge of the village where the cattle grazed during the day, Gerhardt approached Luise.

"Frau Martens, what's the problem?"

"I'll tell you in a moment, Gerhardt."

She called a few of the older girls to her and instructed them to organize some circle games to amuse the children. Then she turned back to Gerhardt, her eyes still on the group.

"Apparently there was a disturbance planned for us today. I didn't want the children to be frightened. I think we are safe here."

Gerhardt's forehead creased and the edges of his pursed lips turned white. "What are they trying to prove, intimidating the children?"

Luise turned to him then. "I don't know, Gerhardt, but we escaped this time. We'll stay out here for a while and then I'll walk the younger ones home."

"I'll make sure they all get home before I go back to work."

"Thank you, Gerhardt. I don't know what I'd have done

without you today."

Something sparked in his eyes and Luise saw his shoulders straighten.

"I hope that your husband comes back, Frau Martens."

As Josiah Marcowiscz led his four newly purchased Don horses onto the road to Kurgan, he looked back over his shoulder and wondered when he would spot his tracker. He had no doubt the GPU would have him in their sights. If he could draw them northwest for a spell, he could buy Daniel that much more time to speed eastward on the steel rails.

Josiah didn't have long to wait. By the time he reached the business district of Kurgan, he had spotted two riders behind him. He stopped at the livery stables and paid to have his string of horses fed, then he walked to the local pub to wait for the inevitable confrontation.

After ordering supper and a drink, he turned to find the senior-major himself sitting at a table at the back of the room.

"You left without saying goodbye, Marcowiscz. You said you wanted to buy my horse."

Josiah started to sweat, but he was committed now. "I sold him to Peter Martens several years ago. To the best of my knowledge, he never sold that horse to anyone else."

"He must have changed hands, my friend, because I've been using him for more than two years." Dubrowsky smiled, but his eyes, even in the dimness of the pub, glittered coldly.

Josiah smiled back in kind. "I didn't say he hadn't changed hands, I said he hadn't been sold."

Dubrowsky leaned forward and narrowed his eyes. "What is your angle, Marcowiscz?"

Josiah sat back and lit a cigarette. He blew the smoke into Dubrowsky's face and watched the man.

Dubrowsky laughed. "Peter Martens is dead. So is his son. Isn't he, Marcowiscz?"

"You don't know? According to word in Alexandrovka, he was executed. That would make him very dead."

"So one would think. Then why are you concerned for his horse?"

"Maybe I just want to see him returned to people who value him."

Dubrowsky made a motion with his hand and another officer appeared from the shadows. "Marcowiscz, where is Daniel Martens?"

Josiah avoided Dubrowsky's eyes. "You said yourself he was dead."

Dubrowsky grabbed Josiah by the collar and pulled him to his feet. "Then why are you leading me on this crooked course?"

Abruptly, Dubrowsky snarled and shoved Josiah against the wall, where he fell heavily to the floor. "Finish him," he instructed the other official, and marched out of the pub.

Josiah didn't wait to see which way Dubrowsky went. He scrambled beneath tables and chairs, and rolled out a back door with the second official swearing close behind him. Josiah didn't know if he could escape, but he hoped his ruse had been worthwhile for Daniel.

By the time the Trans-Siberian reached Irkutsk several days later, Daniel was thoroughly tired of sitting. His mind revolved in rhythm with the wheels of the train. What if Luise didn't recognize him? What if her ardor had cooled? Perhaps Frau Wieler's letter would not reach Shumanovka and Phillip would persuade her that her husband was indeed dead.

With a twenty-four hour wait while the train was re-fueled and serviced, Daniel toured the part of the city nearest the station. Vendors' stalls lined the street, offering everything from stew cooked over open fires to freshly roasted *shashlik* on skewers, from Orthodox crosses to hand-carved totems of the Buryat people, from Chinese silks and spices to performers strumming the *balalaika* for spare coins.

Daniel marveled at the diversity of business endeavors as he wandered back toward the train station, sipping a cup of hot coffee. This latest adventure was a completely foreign experience. He had rarely been away from the Slavgorod Colony until his arrest and exile. Aside from several business trips to Novosibirsk, he had never stepped foot into a large city until Omsk. And now Irkutsk.

After wandering for some time, Daniel returned to his seat on the train and sank into its comfort. He would enjoy the breathtaking beauty of the Baikal region for now and leave his worries for another time. At the rate the kilometers flew by, this journey should end soon. Daniel let his head fall back against the seat as the Trans-Siberian set out for Ulan Ude. It felt good to relax.

❧

"Mama, we had a walk and a picnic today," said Nela the moment she entered the house.

"A picnic?" Anna's eyes found Luise's, and she leaned on a chair to support herself. "The children do not go to school for picnics, Luise. They are supposed to be learning."

Luise pushed down a sharp explanation. "It was such a beautiful day today, Mother."

"Yes," said Hans, "and we didn't want to get in trouble with the fishuls."

Luise and Anna both turned to stare at him.

"What do you mean, Hans?" asked Anna.

He glanced up at Luise, then pressed his lips together. "I have to go help Papa in the shop." And he ran out the door.

"Why don't you go gather the eggs, Nela?" suggested Luise. "We'll need some for supper."

When her sister had gone, Luise faced Anna. "Mother, the officials threatened to come to the school and disrupt our classes. Papa sent a warning and I decided to take the children away so they wouldn't be upset."

Anna just looked at her. Then she sat heavily on the chair and held her head. "What is to become of us here? It is all happening again."

Luise sat down beside her stepmother and placed her arm around her bony shoulders. "I don't know, Mother, but we must not lose hope. God knows what is happening here."

Anna's eyes as she looked at Luise were a child's eyes, full of fear and uncertainty. Luise's hand closed over Anna's. It was the only comfort she could give.

Daniel had just returned to his seat after a brief stop at Ulan Ude. The next stop would be Chita, ever closer to his destination. As he sat watching passengers board the train, he noticed a locomotive of a man moving toward him down the aisle. Daniel hoped he would pass him by, but the large man sat heavily beside him and blocked his way by the sheer size of his bulk. A shock of suspicion coursed through Daniel's brain.

The man wore a city suit and reached over to shake his hand. "How do you do? Samuel Govorukha. Where are you headed?"

Daniel shook the man's hand.

"Hello."

Govorukha waited for more, but as it was not forthcoming, he began to talk about himself, crowding Daniel into the window seat. "I have business in most of the cities where we stop: Krasnoyarsk, Ulan Ude, Chita and Khabarovsk. I will go down to Vladivostok as well, and then make my way back to my home in Birobidzhan."

Ah, the Jewish Region. Yes, Samuel was a Jewish businessman. There were also many Jews involved in the GPU. Daniel tried to suppress his suspicions.

Govorukha continued to ply Daniel with questions, trying to draw him into conversation, asking about his family, his work, his experience, even calling him Comrade and asking after his opinions of the Soviet system. Daniel offered vague responses, remembering Marcowiscz' warning near Tomsk.

On the long journey to his place of exile, Daniel had learned much from his fellow prisoners about how Moscow kept information on Soviet citizens, how they had eyes everywhere, how anyone opposing the regime either disappeared or was killed. He decided to consider this man the enemy for the sake of his safety. His goal was to reach Luise before she gave up on him, and he would do whatever it took to stay free to pursue that goal.

"How long will it take for you to reach Vladivostok?" Daniel asked, as a matter of changing the subject from himself to something safer.

"From here? A couple of days, depending on how often the train stops and how long my business takes in each place. It is surely a long trip across this vast country, my friend."

So, if it took two days to arrive in Vladivostok, then it would take only a very long day to get to Never, the last stop before Blagoveshchensk. Luise, I'm coming. The steel wheels took up the chant: I'm coming, I'm coming, I'm coming, and Daniel turned to the window and let the steady rhythm lull him to sleep…

In his dream Daniel saw Luise standing at the edge of the village of Shumanovka, waiting for him, then running to him as she had when he had returned from cutting lumber in the spring of '27. She leapt into his arms and he spun her around and around and they kissed passionately. He felt her hands on him, touching him to make sure he was real, that he had returned to her. She reached into his jacket pocket and…

Daniel awoke with a jerk to see his seatmate Samuel avert his face and fold his hands across his lap self-consciously.

"You were trying to rob me!"

Daniel's words came out louder than he had anticipated, and heads turned all over the coach.

"I was not." Samuel whispered as if to shush him.

Daniel didn't care for Samuel's sake. The snake had smiled his oily smile and spoken of personal things that were probably as much made up as what Daniel had answered him. But now everyone stared. The conductor made his way back to Daniel's seat and stared too.

"You have a problem?"

Daniel hesitated. He could feel the tension in Samuel beside him as he awaited his words and no doubt worked out an appropriate response. And whom would the conductor believe, a man of business or a leather clad tramp with hair covering his face?

"No, I'm sorry. I must have been talking in my sleep."

The conductor shook his head at Daniel, taking in his appearance with a sweep of his eyes. When he had gone, Daniel lowered his head and spoke in a low voice.

"What were you looking for, Samuel Govorukha? Is information gathering your primary business?"

Samuel began to talk about hunger and money and family and coercion. Daniel silenced him with a look.

"Do not think me an idiot, Govorukha. You were picking my pocket. What are you looking for?"

"It's not as it seems," returned Samuel. "I was merely interested in who you are and where you are going. You must admit you do not resemble most of the other passengers on this train."

"And so I am to be robbed? Is that the rationale of the Soviet? Whoever does not match the status quo, whatever the government deems that to be, must be singled out and questioned? Is there no freedom left in Russia?"

The oily smile returned to Samuel's face. "It is people like you who become problems, people resistant to change. This is the Union of Soviet Socialist Republics now, not

Russia. It may save you trouble later on if you remember that bit of information."

"So it does not matter what your methods are, as long as you achieve your goal? Is that what we are to accept?"

Samuel pulled a gold watch from his vest pocket and checked the time as the rhythm of the train slowed. "I get off at Chita. It has been a distinct pleasure." He stood and pushed his way out of the coach as the train slowed. As it pulled into Never Station, Daniel contemplated getting off. His suspicions had become stronger with every kilometer, but the train carried him so much faster than his feet, and he hated to let go of this advantage.

He had already stood to leave, but changed his mind and slumped back into his seat as the train chugged ahead. Know your enemy.

What to do? As long as he stayed on the train, he would be ahead of whoever Dubrowsky might send after him, should he find out Daniel was still alive. Unless...unless a pursuer switched to the Amur rail line and came out ahead of him.

In a sudden panic, Daniel grabbed his pack and lunged out of his seat and into the aisle. He lurched to the end of his car and stepped outside onto the small platform that connected it to the next car. For several minutes he watched the mixed forest of the Amur region fly by, and then, when the train had slowed for a particularly steep incline, Daniel tossed his pack and jumped.

Chapter Twenty-seven

After the family had finished supper that evening, Abram answered a knock on the door and invited Phillip Wieler into the house. The young man's presence surprised Luise. She had supposed her sincere words to him about her lack of interest had finally hit home, but here he was again, his eyes fixed on her.

Phillip sat and visited as long as politeness dictated, and then asked Luise if she would like to walk since the evening was mild. She could not think of a reasonable excuse, so she agreed, all the while muttering to herself.

"What was that?" asked Phillip as she preceded him out the door.

She clamped her lips together. She would be courteous, but she simply could not encourage him at all. Her thoughts had been full of Daniel lately, the pain as fresh as it had been when he was arrested and exiled.

"I came as soon as I heard," Phillip was saying.

Luise turned to him, perplexed. "As soon as you heard what?"

"Why, that you and your students were threatened."

Luise grimaced. "We were not threatened. I was informed that there was to be a staged disturbance. The children, at least the younger ones, are unaware that anything was amiss."

"Call it what you will, I was worried for you when I heard. You shouldn't be in the schoolhouse alone."

"Phillip, I wasn't alone. All the children were there and Gerhardt helped me. I have a responsibility for them and so I protected them."

"And did an excellent job of it, I'd say. I just wish I could have been there to protect you. As a woman, you are vulnerable."

His words bothered Luise, but she didn't want to let on, or he would feel more urgency to protect her, and she did not want him hovering.

"I'll be fine, Phillip, but thank you for your concern. How have you been lately? Do you enjoy working for Siemens on the collective?"

"For Siemens, yes; for the collective, not so much. In a kolhkoz you just do what they tell you. Except that Siemens keeps us working as if this collective farm was our own."

"Is that a bad thing?"

"No, but when you think about it too long, it seems futile."

After Phillip had seen her home again, Luise continued to think about her situation. Were these memories of Daniel a final healing, a nudge to let his memory rest, to let Phillip into her heart? She pushed the thought away, but it persisted.

"Oh Lord, what shall I do?" Her prayer seemed to bounce off the ceiling of her bedroom. She lay awake a long time into the night, thoughts of Daniel and Phillip quietly scuffling in her head. She did not feel for Phillip anything near the love she had always had for Daniel, but perhaps that kind of love only came once in a lifetime. And perhaps that time had come and gone. How was she to know?

Daniel regained consciousness slowly. He lay in deep grass in the shade of a tamarack tree and stared at the darkening sky. How long had he lain here? He remembered jumping and rolling into a ball. Pain pierced his side, and the leg that had been previously broken felt stiff and sore. He hoped he hadn't dislocated his neck again, but when he tentatively moved his arms and legs, everything worked.

Relieved that he was not hurt, he scoured the area for

his pack. He had thrown it a moment before he jumped, but how much distance had passed from one action to the other? He wanted his pack—the matches, the two last pairs of boots and the deer jerky he had purchased from a vendor in Chita. After an hour-long search, he found the pack in a low spot some distance back from where he had landed. He gratefully fingered the matches and looked for a place to start a fire. He would trek farther into the trees and see if he could find a small clearing. Night would soon be upon him and he didn't know the terrain.

When Daniel awoke later, energized by sleep and food and eager to move on, an invisible hand had begun to brush the eastern sky with pink and purple and orange. He had jumped off the train as close to Blagoveshchensk as he could. He guessed he had roughly one hundred kilometers to travel. Depending on how the land lay ahead of him, he thought he could make it in three days. From there to the village of Shumanovka wouldn't be far at all. Perhaps he could even catch a ride from someone going out to the colonies. He was sure the men had business in Blagoveshchensk from time to time. Today he would meet the Amur River and follow it.

The sight of the Amur in all its vastness robbed him of breath. That night he camped in a low spot surrounded by scrub brush. There were scarcely any trees in the floodlands, and when he awoke and stood up to survey his surroundings, the sun glinted off a vast expanse of sparkling blue. It was a wide river, the Amur. He enjoyed the view while he ate his breakfast of deer jerky, and then packed up his kit.

As he sat observing the river, a thought struck him. If Samuel Govorukha was an agent of the GPU, he would have reported his meeting with Daniel. He might have been sent to locate him. Considering the extra time spent in Irkutsk, and now this stretch of foot travel, a pursuer would have time to catch up with him. Or get ahead again. What if

Govorukha or some other official met him in Blagoveshchensk? They could easily guess his destination. He must avoid the city.

He stared at the river in deep thought, and then smiled. He would float past Blagoveshchensk and on to the colonies. If anyone waited for him in the city, he would pass them by.

Daniel neared the edge of the river and searched for signs of life. There must be boats available. He walked north on the shoreline until he came upon a small settlement of *Nanai*. Between their trade-related understanding of Russian and Daniel's hand-signals, they managed an exchange—two pairs of bearhide boots for the use of a small skiff, complete with a young man to row it upriver and return with it later.

The Nanai insisted he stay in their camp that day and leave the next morning, and although he wished to get underway as soon as possible, he felt it proper to accept their hospitality.

The feel of the Nanai camp reminded him of the Khanty settlement, but these people wore salmon-skin clothing and beaded bracelets. He noticed the talisman worn by the leader of the group, probably a shaman, and tattoos on the arms of the women. He wondered about the tattoos. Perhaps they were also a form of talisman, an ever-present protection against evil.

The people spread out under the stars to sleep. These were truly a nomadic people with nothing to keep them in one place except the river, and their river was one of the longest in the world.

As he lay awaiting sleep, Daniel wondered what it would be like to settle down again to ordinary life in the village. He'd been on the move for so long. But with Luise at his side...he smiled. He drifted into slumber, then started awake again. What if Luise accepted Phillip Wieler's proposal before he reached her?

Lantu settled onto the rough bench in the middle of the

boat, facing Daniel, picked up the oars and slipped them into the locks. Another Nanai untied the bowline and threw it to Lantu, who coiled the line and set it behind him on the floor of the skiff.

Daniel felt free as Lantu pulled the rowboat into the river and turned it to glide with the current on its way north to the Sea of Okhotsk. Daniel watched the land pass beside them. He appreciated the speed with which he neared his destination. His excitement made it difficult for him to sit still.

How long would it take until he stood before Luise, lost himself in her eyes, took her into his arms? Not long, sang the oars, not long. He looked with interest at the land to his right. China. Who would have thought his travels would take him within mere kilometers of that ancient land with its intriguing history? Perhaps one day he would see China for himself.

As Lantu pulled them along the river, Daniel let his thoughts ripple past like the water beside him. Days and weeks and years passed beneath the boat, some sweet, some bitter, all blending together to form the river that was his life's journey. He wanted very much to dock soon and stay moored in a quiet inlet for a while. Shumanovka could not come too soon.

Daniel and Lantu camped along the river the first night, and then came within sight of Blagoveshchensk the next day when the sun was at its zenith. He had made it plain to Lantu that he wanted to slip past the city and stop on the other side, but as they neared Blagoveshchensk, Lantu started to guide the boat into the docks.

Daniel signed to the young man to continue on past the city, but Lantu acted as if he did not understand and kept rowing.

"What are you doing?" yelled Daniel, frustrated with his lack of control in the situation, but still the young man kept drawing them into shore. Daniel leaned over to grab the oar, but Lantu let it fall in its pivot and pulled a pistol from the folds of his jacket.

Confusion and shock rippled through Daniel's body. Was he being robbed? Why had Lantu not robbed him during the night if that was his plan? He had already been paid for his services. What more—suddenly Daniel understood. He had been betrayed. He was at the mercy of this young man in a small craft on the Amur River, and he knew whom he would see when they docked.

⁂

That evening when Abram returned from the volost office for supper, his eyes reflected sorrow, but he did not speak of it.

When Luise had finished clearing away the supper, she announced her intention to sit outside on the bench to absorb the last of the autumn weather before winter swept it away. As she had hoped, Abram joined her.

They sat together, enjoying the weather, but Abram still did not speak. Finally, Luise confronted his silence.

"Tell me what makes you sad, Papa."

"You read my mind, Lise. I can't hide anything from you."

"You're not trying very hard."

He was quiet for so long she wondered if he had forgotten about her, but then he spoke, picking up her hand in his.

"In my work at the village office I have access to all the records. The officials have detailed information on all of us and our families. For some reason they don't seem to mind if I see them. They have dossiers on you and Daniel as well."

He hesitated and Luise's eyes riveted to her father's face, even though the twilight hid his expression.

"Papa?"

"They list him as deceased, Lise. The records here match those in Alexandrovka. They say he is dead."

She tried to pull her hand away but he held it fast.

"We can no longer deny the truth."

Luise's mouth puckered and her eyes burned as she fought her raging emotions. "I don't believe it. They don't know."

She pulled her hand away and covered her face, trying to hold back the tears, but grief won out. "They have taken so much already," she sobbed. "Must they take my hope also?"

"Lise." His endearment made her stop and turn back to him. "I know what it's like to lose your heart's desire. No one expects you to forget. Tend your grief, but don't let it consume you."

She closed her eyes and nodded. "Don't ask me why my belief flies in the face of reason." She wiped her eyes. "I do know that I cannot accept another. Do you understand?"

Abram nodded, his eyes on the ground at his feet. "Yes. I understand."

Daniel wondered if he could escape. Should he jump ship now? It was too far to the shore and he wasn't a great swimmer. Besides, a bullet would pick him off instantly, he had no doubt.

Daniel stared at the gun in Lantu's hands. The Nanai couldn't aim the gun and steer the boat at the same time. His actions swift, Daniel leaned over the side so Lantu had to adjust his balance. The Nanai dropped the gun, but at the same moment swung his other oar around toward Daniel, catching him on the side of the head. Daniel groaned and hung onto the side of the boat, trying to grab the oar. The struggle took all his effort, but Lantu had the advantage and the weapon, and a second hit on the head knocked him senseless.

"They've taken Friesens' farm machinery and forced them out of their home." Abram delivered the news one evening soon after he had told Luise of Daniel's record of death.

"What did they do to deserve that?" Luise crossed her arms to still their shaking.

Abram's face was angry in the lantern light, but he kept his voice calm. "They are too wealthy. They work hard but don't grow rich because any surplus is taken by the Soviet. It's Daniel's story all over again in another place."

Luise stood rooted to the floor beside the stove, her hand poised over the pot of simmering stew, its homey smell mocking the sourness of her fear. "And when will they come here to remove us from our home?"

"Luise, don't fret," said Tante Manya. "It's fortunate your father works in the volost office. We are living as an extended family in one dwelling. We own no equipment besides your father's woodworking tools he brought with him from Slavgorod. We do not look like typical kulaks."

"Small comfort," retorted Luise. "The GPU guards are so heartless that the truth and individual circumstances don't matter. They seem bent on making life miserable for as many people as possible."

"They do as they are told," said Abram. "It all comes down from the central government in Moscow, part of the implementation of Stalin's Five-Year Plan."

"Do you defend men like Mironenko?"

"Of course not, Luise. Ivan has shown his true colors many times, but Yevgeny must work within the system too, or he could suffer the same fate as the rest of the citizens. Think of Vasili Bakunin. Although he is a good man, he also must work within the confines of the Soviet regime. No one is safe here. There are spies everywhere, even among our own people."

Luise shuddered. "Spies. Arrests. Exile. Betrayals. Is this to be our lot for the rest of our lives?"

Abram stood before Luise, his forehead creased into a frown. He spoke with controlled quiet. "Luise, we must be patient. We are not without a plan."

"Pray tell, what is it then?"

He grimaced and she knew she had angered him, but this was her future they spoke of too, not just that of the farmers of the Shumanovka collective.

"We have elected Jakob Siemens as the leader of our collective. The officials respect him. We must earn and keep their trust if we are ever to—"

"To what? Papa, what are you talking about?"

He sat in the chair next to hers, leaned forward and kept his voice low.

"Several families have already gone to China on their own, as you know. The Wielers, Friesens and Funks left last year before Christmas. This March twenty-four families went across the Amur."

"But there are also some who have tried and have had to turn back and pretend they had never gone."

"And some have been shot as they fled." Tante Manya's mouth caved together as she spoke, her eyes on the table.

"It's a tricky business, this illegal emigration," said Abram.

"I don't suppose there is a legal way to work it out."

Abram rubbed a hand over his face. "Negotiations have proven ineffective, other than causing the authorities to observe us more closely. The government is simply not letting anyone leave the borders of the republic."

"Frieda says some people are talking about going to Moscow, that there's a chance they will be able to leave from there."

"Luise, that is the ultimate risk. If they are refused, which is likely at this stage, they have nothing to come back to, no home, no job, no money, and a record of flight."

"You don't think they'll be successful?"

Her father shrugged. "It's highly unlikely. In the meantime, Jakob Siemens is a wise and patient man, and I would trust him with my life."

"It seems we are all to trust him with our lives, whether or not we wish to."

"You must trust me, Lise."

"So we must curry favor with our captors?"

"In a manner of speaking."

"Good work."

Daniel knew the voice. He even understood the words, spoken in Russian. Daniel blinked and cautiously opened his eyes. He lay in a corner of a large warehouse, the water of the Amur sloshing below him. He could see Lantu, could hear him responding to Dubrowsky in Russian.

What an idiot I've been. All along we could have conversed, but he pretended not to understand. This has been a set-up since I rented the boat

But how had Dubrowsky known where he would be? Had he really been tracked all the way from Ulan Ude? Had Dubrowsky found Josiah in Omsk? He prayed his old friend had not been tortured or killed. He could not let his sacrifice be for naught.

Daniel looked around him and tried to move, but his hands and feet were bound. He might possibly have untied his bonds, but any sound would give him away and he would have no further chance. To delay the meeting with Dubrowsky was uppermost in his mind. There must be a way of escape. He begged God for guidance, for ideas, realizing that in this impossible situation, his faith still remained a part of him.

He wondered why Dubrowsky had not shot him immediately, to make sure that this time he was truly dead, but then he thought the man probably wanted to gloat. Well, they would deal with that when the time came. Daniel decided he would not give Dubrowsky the pleasure of seeing his fear.

"You were given the amount we agreed upon. You have done your duty, now go."

"You have not been fair. This is only half the money. I want it all."

"Everyone is greedy these days. Don't you know we are all equal now? We must be satisfied with what we have, boy."

Lantu's fists came up and he said, "I demand money as agreed."

Daniel tensed, knowing the hardness of Dubrowsky's heart. He heard Dubrowsky curse. A shot answered Lantu's arrogance and Daniel watched wide-eyed as the boy fell to the floor and lay as still as death.

Bile rose in Daniel's throat. What chance did he have? Please, Lord, help me. I cannot do anything for myself. His prayers wafted away on the evening breeze as Dubrowsky's boot kicked Lantu aside and he came into Daniel's view.

"So. Here we are again, you murderer." Dubrowsky's hand went to his neck to finger a thick, purple scar. "I do not know how you survived; the two fools who were supposed to finish you off apparently thought you already dead, but this time there will be no doubt."

Dubrowsky pulled a knife from his belt and carefully ran his fingers along its edge. "Ah," he said, putting bleeding fingers to his mouth.

He advanced with a devilish smile, but Daniel felt a strange calm steal over him. He felt surrounded by a strange peace, and remembered the story in the Old Testament about Elisha showing his servant the unseen army of the Lord protecting them on the mountain.

"God is my refuge. I will not fear what man can do to me."

Dubrowsky let out a heinous laugh. "You had better pray. You are a dead man."

"You can do nothing to me that God has not allowed," said Daniel.

"Arrogant talk when I have the knife. Let us see how your God intervenes."

༺༻

Ropes bound Luise, and she thrashed to free herself. Then she froze at the subdued buzz of voices nearby, harsh, threathening voices. Luise sat up in bed, damp with sweat. Nela's whimpers roused her from her fright and, out of habit, she soothed her sister back to sleep, straightening the blanket.

The voices from her restless dreams continued, and Luise realized they came from her parents' bedroom. She slipped from her bed and tiptoed into the kitchen, then stood to listen. Abruptly, the door opened and her father entered the kitchen. He jumped when he saw her standing there and put a hand to his chest.

"Is something the matter, Papa?"

"Anna is hallucinating." His eyes settled on hers and he seemed about to say more, but then he turned to the kitchen. "I thought perhaps a cup of water might settle her down."

Luise frowned. "I'll talk to her."

Her father turned back, again ready to speak, then shrugged and moved to get the water from the pail on the counter.

"Mother?" As Luise moved quietly into her parents' dark bedroom, she could just make out Anna's form sitting up in bed, muttering to herself, coughing as usual.

"Mother, what's troubling you?"

"What? Oh, Luise. The dream. I've had a dreadful dream. I hate to tell you of it."

Luise shuddered, her own dreams floating in her subconscious. She settled on the side of the bed. "Tell me. It may help to talk about it."

"Luise, we must pray. Your Daniel is in deep distress." And she commenced to do so in jerky syllables, as her body rocked back and forth.

Luise felt her father's presence beside her. He knelt down beside the bed and tried to quiet Anna. "Please, my dear. You must sleep now. Daniel is in the Father's care."

No matter how often she heard those sentiments, Luise could not accept them. In all probability, Daniel now walked the streets of gold beside a crystal sea, yet Anna, with her sixth sense of knowing, proclaimed him in need of prayer. Luise shivered in the cool of the night. She too had dreamed of Daniel this night. Snippets of his troubles played out in her mind, robbing her of a peaceful sleep. Were these dreams real? Were they connected?

"Now Anna," said Abram. "You must quiet and sleep. Please."

Her head turned toward him in the gloom. "Do you not care for the well-being of your son-in-law? I'm surprised at you."

"Papa, I too have dreamed of Daniel in trouble this night. Let's pray together," and Luise knelt on the floor beside her father. When they had prayed for protection for Daniel, Anna drank the water Abram had brought her, then lay down and heaved a sigh. Within moments, she was asleep. Luise stared at Abram, the faint glimmer of the moon reflected in his eyes.

"I'm sorry to upset you, Lise," he whispered. "She doesn't know what she's saying."

Without further words, they stood and Luise returned to her bed, her thoughts confused and troubled. She lay awake for hours, praying and pleading, wondering if her father also watched the night. And then, releasing her heart's desires to the Father who watched all things, she slept.

A slight movement from behind Dubrowsky caught Daniel's attention, but he kept his eyes focused on his enemy. Lantu lifted his head and shook it, as if to clear his thinking. He looked in Daniel's direction and seemed to assess the situation.

Dubrowsky marched back and forth, his boots carving an arrogant rhythm on the floorboards, and smacked the knife on the palm of his hand. His face looked dark red, even in the muted light of the warehouse, and his eyes had become the eyes of a demon.

Daniel cast a furtive glance toward Lantu and saw that he had moved closer. The Nanai winked at him, an unexpected allegiance.

"I am going to let you beg," said Dubrowsky. "You will, you know, because I have something you want, in fact, you would probably give your life for it. I am sure you will beg for mercy because of it."

"I have nothing. I am no one. What could you possibly have that would interest me?"

Lantu inched nearer.

"Well, dog, it is not as much what as whom."

Daniel struggled to keep the fear and shock from registering on his face as it pierced his heart.

Dubrowsky smiled. "Ah. You understand me. Yes…I know all about Luise. You were married to her, as I remember. Too bad you will never see her again."

In spite of his fear, Daniel answered calmly. "If I am never to see her again, as you say, then why would I beg you for anything?"

"You may not care for your own life, but I believe you care for hers. I have sent emissaries before; this time I will go myself."

Daniel wracked his brain for a way to stall for time. He could not allow Dubrowsky to hurt Luise, and he had no doubt the man would. He had to be demented beyond reason to track him across thousands of miles. And what did he mean by an emissary? Had he already hurt Luise?

"Oh, come now, Martens. How much is it worth to you to keep your woman safe?"

Just as this was time for a miracle, it was also time for risk. If he lost his life, Luise might also lose hers, or worse.

"If you kill me, you will lose your leverage."

Dubrowsky narrowed his eyes and smiled. "Oh, I will

kill you, eventually, but first you will see everyone you love suffer—Luise, her father, her stepbrother and sister, and her old aunt. I wonder which she would grieve for the most."

In spite of Daniel's determination not to show his panic, the fact that Dubrowsky knew these things chilled his heart.

Dubrowsky continued. "Did you know your father-in-law built himself a fine new house? It would be a shame if it should go up in flames. I would hope no one would be trapped within."

All pretence aside, Daniel said, "You can threaten and blackmail me all you want, but if you are going to kill me anyway, why would I lower myself to begging. You have no heart so it would make no difference that I was not the one who maimed you."

With a snarl, the man kicked at Daniel's face, and at the same moment, Lantu reached out and grabbed his other foot, pulling him down. The knife skittered across the floor. Dubrowsky fell hard, landing with a thud almost on top of Daniel. While the GPU official struggled for breath, Lantu, blood seeping from his chest wound, dragged himself nearer and pulled Dubrowsky's gun from his belt.

His breath coming in gasps, he held the gun to the man's temple. He looked at Daniel. "I will be dead soon," he rasped in Russian, "and so will he. But you must live." He stopped to breathe and the sound rattled in his airways. He nodded in the direction of the knife.

"Get yourself free."

Daniel wriggled to where the knife lay and grasped it between his tied hands. He sawed at the rope until his feet were freed from their bonds and then went to work on his hands. It was tricky but he was desperate, and his blood flowed strong. Meanwhile Dubrowsky lay sweating and swearing, the gun pressing into his temple. Daniel saw Lantu's hand tremble.

One last thread remained and Daniel snapped it, freeing his hands. He knew it would not be long before Lantu lost his strength, and it could be any moment that Dubrowsky would attempt to overpower him.

Daniel stepped on Dubrowsky's arm. "Do not reach for your other weapon."

"Kill him." Lantu blinked fiercely and the gun trembled in his hand.

Daniel slipped the second gun from Dubrowsky's boot and trained it on him, but he could not pull the trigger. In his mind, he saw the fishing line stretched taut between his hands and remembered the remorse he had felt after his attempt to murder this man. He had no right to end a life. Only God could judge. He knew that now.

Dubrowsky stared at him, a knowing settling in his eyes, on his face. Daniel saw him tense and prepared to fend him off, but a sharp report startled them both and Dubrowsky's entire body spasmed. Daniel cried out as he leaped backward and cast his gun from him. It bounced against the wall of the warehouse, slid along the floorboards and splashed to the river beneath. Heart banging at the walls of his chest, Daniel stared at Lantu. The young man's fingers relaxed on his gun and he fell to the side, coughing up blood. His eyes rolled back into his head. Then he jerked and lay still.

A wave of nausea hit Daniel as he stared at Dubrowsky, blood flowing from a wound near his ear. You are my witness, Lord, I did not do this thing.

He dragged Lantu out a back exit where he surmised the boat must be, and pulled the body into the boat with him. He eased the craft out of the dock and pulled for the middle of the river. Once there, he pushed Lantu's body over the side and let it slip beneath the dark water. There was no way he could let his family know what had transpired, and he did not wish the young man to be found in the warehouse. His people would prefer he return to the earth and water than be left alone at the mercy of men.

Stars winked at Daniel as he pulled with the current,

distancing himself from Blagoveshchensk and the man who had so long sought his life. He knew he should feel relief, yet it evaded him, and he felt as if the man's blood stained his hands.

Fatigue claimed him as he drifted upriver toward Konstantinovka

ജ

A short way out of Blagoveshchensk, Daniel glimpsed a Chinese town east across the wide and gentle Amur, then two smaller rivers that branched to the west. He was so close now he could feel the heartbeat of the Mennonite villages in their respective colonies of Shumanovka, Usman and Savitaya. To think he had almost lost his battle so close to the end of his journey. If only he could rid himself of the image of Dubrowsky's blood-spattered face and damaged ear in the dockside warehouse.

The village of Konstantinovka loomed ahead just past the outlet of another Amur tributary and at the top of a brief northerly bend of the river. He would leave the boat there and continue on foot.

As Daniel disembarked at Konstantinovka, several guards approached, guns at the ready.

"Where are you going?"

"I go to Shumanovka."

"What is your name?"

Daniel hesitated to give that information, wondering how many men Dubrowsky had commandeered into this search. He wished neither to lie nor to invite any unnecessary trouble. He just wanted to find Luise.

"My name is Daniel Martens, son of Greidl Martens of Shumanovka Colony, the village of New York."

The guards stared at him, but he refused to be intimidated. He stood tall and easy, glancing around him at the drying marsh grasses along the riverbank, looking far in the distance at thin stands of poplar and birch. The guards indicated that he should accompany them to the guardhouse, almost invisible in a thicket of water poplars.

The official at the guardhouse checked his records, glancing up at Daniel now and then as he read. His scowl deepened with each glance.

Finally, slapping the book closed, he barked an order to his aide. "Lock him in the back room."

Daniels heart dropped into his boots as he was led away to a tiny, bare room very like the one in the volost office in Alexandrovka. So near. He had almost made it. Perhaps they would allow him to write a letter to Luise. He would explain everything and free her to marry Phillip if she had not already done so. He did not doubt he would again be exiled.

Just when he thought his heart would die within him, he heard a new voice in the outer office.

"What was the name?" asked the new man.

"Daniel Martens."

"Going where?"

"Shumanovka, he says."

"I will speak to him."

"Why?"

"Do not question me!"

Daniel stood warily as keys jangled in the lock and the door flew open. A tall young man stepped inside, his expression fierce as a summer storm, and closed the door behind him.

"Daniel Martens?"

Daniel nodded.

"What is the name of your wife?"

Daniel swallowed the lump in his throat. Apparently, Dubrowsky had set everything in motion, even though he was out of the action. He sighed. What matter? They knew anyway.

"Luise," he whispered.

The official regarded him in silence, then said, "Wait here."

Daniel heard continued conversation beyond the

wooden door and held his breath. The young official—Bakunin, the other two called him—seemed to have authority over the others. Daniel leaned toward the door to listen.

"There is no—oh, here. There is a Greidl Martens and a Johannes in New York. But he said his name was Daniel."

Bakunin said, "Sometimes they go by other names. Call him in here."

Daniel stood silent while the guards checked their records once more.

One of the guards turned to him, with a glance cast at Bakunin. "Very well, you are free to go home…Johannes. It is a bit of a walk yet."

Bakunin stepped up. "I will accompany him part way to the village, make sure he goes where he says he is going."

Daniel nodded and walked away, struggling to keep his nerves from giving him away, wanting above all to run but knowing he must not. Bakunin marched by his side, climbing the steep embankment to the plain of the Amur River.

Johannes, indeed. Am I a liar, or simply as crafty as a serpent? Daniel didn't know, but he was not about to create another delay at this stage of his journey. He would take this as an opportunity handed to him.

"This way," instructed Bakunin, turning into the nearest village.

Surely, this was not yet Shumanovka. Tensing, Daniel prepared to run. Before he could escape, Bakunin spoke.

"Do not fear me overmuch, Martens. I am Commissar Vasili Bakunin of the GPU. Luise Martens from the village of Shumanovka stayed with my wife and me for a month last year, brought my wife back to health, healed my family. I will see that you are allowed home."

The shock of his statement assaulted Daniel. "She did? You would do that for a stranger?"

Vasili shrugged. "I would do that for Luise." He cast a

sidelong glance at Daniel. "We will stop by my house before you go to meet her. If she sees you like this, she may well change her mind."

A momentary twitch of the corners of his mouth upward disarmed Daniel, and he followed the official to his small but neat izba. He could hardly believe how this day had taken shape. Divine intervention now seemed the only explanation, and in his heart he was thankful.

Daniel allowed Bakunin and his excited wife to help him clean up; they said nothing about the scars, but shared several long looks. He felt like a new man, almost like the man who had left Alexandrovka more than two years before.

"Now go home," said Bakunin's wife, Tatiana, pushing him out the door. "Run if you have the strength. Evening approaches and Luise will be waiting."

As he stared into her face, she nodded and grinned, clasping and unclasping her hands.

"Let's sing *Ich Werde Ihn Immer Lieben,*" suggested Martha, her eyes on Phillip. Luise watched him move away from Martha and come near to where she sat playing her violin. *I will always love Him, He's done so much for me…* The words of the song touched Luise's heart on two levels.

"The house is stuffy with all these people in here," Phillip said to her. "Would you like to step outside for a breath of fresh air?"

Luise lifted her eyes to his as she finished the song, smiled and placed her violin in its case. Martha pushed past them, glared at Luise, and marched out the door. Phillip didn't seem to notice, but Luise felt waves of anger floating in Martha's wake. She decided it was not her problem and followed Phillip.

He led the way down the steps onto the front walk and opened the gate, waiting for Luise to pass through first. They walked along the road heading south. Their shoulders brushed and Luise felt him reach for her hand. She had never held anyone's hand except Daniel's. Well, not counting Nela and Hans. In a way it felt good and right, like she belonged to someone again, but she struggled against uncertainty. What if? What if Daniel still lived? Even if he were dead, as everyone assumed, would Phillip ever be able to meet her expectations, since they were based on her relationship with Daniel? Ever since she was a child, she had known Daniel as her other half.

They walked silently for a time, then Phillip's grip on her hand tightened and he asked, "Have you changed your mind about me, Luise? Could you give me a chance?"

She tried to pull her hand from his, but he held on firmly. The crickets echoed Phillip's questions, the stars above seemed to await her answer.

"I don't know."

"What don't you know?"

Her hand felt clammy in his, even though the evening air had a chill to it. "I don't know what I feel. If I'd never met Daniel, there is a good chance I would be attracted to you."

"But no one will ever match him in your eyes, is that it?"

"Phillip, you are a fine man and I appreciate your patience with me, but I am married to Daniel. Married. We exchanged vows that I committed to keep for as long as I live. They still stand in my mind and in my soul."

"I think the phrase is 'as long as we both shall live.' How long will they stand? Until you're old and gray and lonely? Is that what you think Daniel would have wanted?"

"But what can I do?" They had come to a stop under the stars. "I cannot feel peace about encouraging you in this relationship. Neither can I expect you to wait forever while my heart decides and heals."

Phillip held her hands in his and studied her. "If I knew that your heart would eventually decide in my favor, I would wait for it to heal, even if that meant years."

Try as she might, she felt nothing more than pity for him. "I don't know what to tell you. I don't want to make you wait years. There are others who would gladly—"

"What others?"

"Well, you know Martha does her best to gain your attention."

"Martha? Martha Lepp? You must be joking."

"No, Phillip, I'm not. In fact, she hates me because I stand between you."

He laughed. "She had better look elsewhere. But I don't want to talk about Martha. I want to talk about you, about us."

The sounds of the night creatures heightened as evening fell: owls, mourning doves, crickets, mosquitoes, and the sounds of laughter and song from the house they had left.

Luise watched Phillip's eyes shine in the moonlight and then felt him leaning toward her. At the last moment, she bowed her head and shook it.

"I can't."

He dropped her hands and held her shoulders. "Look at me, Luise. I love you. I probably always have but I never dreamed of interfering with Daniel's claim on you. I will try my best to abide by your wishes from now on. I hold you to nothing, but if ever there comes a time when you think you can open your heart to me, it is yours."

"Oh Phillip, I'm so sorry." Her tears fell and she rested her head on his chest while he held her. She felt his shuddering sigh come from the depths of his being.

Daniel's feet found their own way toward the village, while his head buzzed with scenarios. He would find Luise as he often had in Alexandrovka, bent over the washing bowl after supper, a few strands of hair falling loose about her flushed face, her dark eyes lifting, wide and welcoming at his entrance.

No, the supper hour would be long over by the time he

arrived. Perhaps she would be walking along the road and she would recognize his walk and come running to meet him, leaping into his arms.

He grimaced. The picture in his mind was lovely, but he really hoped she did not wander alone at night, considering the guards he had met at the river station.

If she were asleep, how would he know where to find her? He could not possibly wait until morning, could he?

"Get hold of yourself, Martens," he chided under his breath. "You've waited this long, one more night would not kill you." But in his heart he knew he would wake the dead to find his wife as soon as he arrived. He didn't care whom he inconvenienced in order to do so.

And then tomorrow, perhaps in the afternoon, he and Luise would go to New York to see his family, and they would be overjoyed to see their son and brother alive.

His mind wandered as he jogged across the wild rye grass and onto the dirt road leading to Shumanovka. Would Luise really be there to meet him? Would she be overjoyed or appalled? He pushed aside the negative thoughts and let his imagination travel to good memories of his life with Luise.

In spite of the darkening day and the distance still to be traveled, Daniel began to whistle, something he had not done since he had been arrested more than two years past. As he walked, he whistled hymns from his memory and the folksongs of his childhood. The kilometers passed quickly beneath his bear hide boots and his pace quickened as he saw the twinkling lights of lanterns in distant windows.

"Soon, Luise. I will be there soon. I'm coming home."

The sounds of voices and singing reached Daniel's ears before he saw the figures in the distance, taking their leave of a house at the outskirts of the village. It was then he noticed the couple silhouetted in the moonlight, in close embrace.

He grinned, thinking of how he would hold Luise when

he found her. His steps light, he advanced on the couple, feeling no hesitation at interrupting their tryst.

As he spoke, they turned to him as one.

Chapter Twenty-eight

"Sorry to interrupt this touching scene," said a voice from the darkness. "I'm looking for—"

"Daniel?" Luise started. Even the creatures of the night seemed to still as recognition hit her.

"Luise?"

His voice when he said her name sounded like someone falling down a bottomless pit.

She stood frozen to the spot, her mouth open in shock, her heart beating wildly against her chest.

"Daniel? Can it be? My Daniel?" She moved like one in a dream, her arms rising toward him, her eyes dry in shock. Even though she had been unable to believe he had died, she now could not believe he stood alive before her in the moonlight.

"Yes, Luise. I have come home to my wife. Too bad I came too late. I did not think you would forget me so soon." He took a step back from her.

She shook her head. "No, you are not too late."

He snorted. "Well done, Phillip. You are a fast mover, if not a loyal friend."

Daniel slapped a mosquito on his arm in lieu of punching Phillip in his deceitful face. Latent anger welled up in his chest. His hands balled into fists. How dare Phillip steal his girl—his wife? All through the long, anguished months, Daniel's dreams of Luise had kept him going. She was his beacon. Without her, what was life worth? He started walking toward the village.

He heard Phillip call his name but kept walking. The

shock of seeing his best friend caressing his wife was not what he had expected. Of all the scenarios he had run through in his mind, none of them matched this painful reality. He couldn't draw enough air into his lungs. Then Phillip called his name again and grabbed him by the arm.

Daniel shook off Phillip's hand and glared at his childhood friend in the moonlight. "Have you not had enough victory tonight?"

Phillip didn't even have the grace to look penitent. "If you would shut your mouth and listen, we could all begin again."

"There is no more beginning," Daniel answered, his voice low. "All between Luise and me is lost. When trust is gone, there is nothing more."

"Shame on you."

"Shame on me? I'll show you who should be ashamed." Daniel pushed up his sleeves and set his feet in a fighter's stance. Even though he knew he had a stronger arm, he wouldn't have cared if Phillip killed him right there. He had no future without Luise.

"Put your fists back in your pockets, Daniel. I'm not going to fight you, unless you don't let me tell you the truth."

Daniel narrowed his eyes and clenched his fists, even as he heard Luise running up to them.

"Please, Daniel, listen to Phillip. You need to hear him. And if not, then allow me to explain."

"I don't care for explanations. It is quite obvious what has happened in my absence." What kind of fool did she take him for?

"Oh, don't be pig-headed, Daniel. You always talk before you listen."

Daniel cocked his head at her. "Such loving words after our lengthy separation."

"I long to tell you what's on my heart, but first you must listen to Phillip."

Daniel ran his hands through his hair and turned away from both of them. The pain in his chest hurt worse than any physical pain he had experienced during his exile and subsequent journey eastward, outweighing even Dubrowsky's brutality. Putting his hands on his hips but unwilling to face them, he said, "Speak your piece."

"Thank you," said Phillip. "Daniel, you must believe I am completely in shock at your return. My mother sent a letter months ago saying you were listed in the village records as deceased. The official returned from up north himself to confirm the details."

"Dubrowsky?" He turned half around.

"Yes. He made it clear you were dead. I would never have dreamed of pursuing Luise if I thought there was any chance you were still alive. You must believe me."

"But your mother also sent you a letter saying I was alive. She wrote it while I was in her house this spring. Even if I do believe you, what difference does it make? Luise apparently doesn't mind your attentions."

"Oh shut up, Daniel," he continued. "First of all, I received no letter from my mother saying you were alive. And in spite of what you may have seen and assumed, Luise has just finished telling me, for the tenth time if not more, that her heart belongs to you, to her husband. She told me that even if you were dead, her heart wasn't hers to give to anyone else because it still belonged to you."

Daniel turned to look at Luise. "You said that?"

She nodded, moving nearer.

"Did you mean it?"

"As much as I ever did and more."

"You weren't involved with Phillip?"

"We are friends, but there was never any more than that on my part. I took my vows and I meant to keep them. I love you, Daniel, and right now I need you to hold me."

He stood staring at her, his arms hanging limply at his sides, doubt and wonder mixing in his mind. She moved closer. His arms rose to catch her and he groaned as he pulled her to him.

"Oh Daniel, I have dreamed of this for so long. Everyone told me you were dead, but I couldn't believe it. I wouldn't believe it."

"Luise." He said her name over and over into her hair, into her neck, kissing her again and again, then stopping to pull away and just gaze at her in the moonlight. She reached up and wiped away his tears.

They looked around for Phillip and saw his silhouette disappearing down the road. Sighing, they decided to deal with him later. For the present, they could think of nothing except each other.

"Are you cold, Luise?" Daniel held her close as they walked slowly toward the village.

"No," she said, turning her face up to him for another kiss. "I'm in shock. I can't stop shaking."

He held her closer and stopped walking. "I don't want to share you with anyone yet. I have waited so long and everyone will be full of questions. They will know if Phillip has anything to do with it."

Luise smiled. "Somehow, I don't think he'll say anything. He feels very badly for everything."

Daniel stared into her eyes. "Did you have a lot to do with each other? He said he has asked you ten times or more."

"No, love." She shook her head and leaned against him as they stood still again under the bright night sky. "Just this evening I asked Tante Manya if I had been too hard on him, if I was wrong in putting him off."

"And what did the wise woman say?"

"She gave me a wise answer, that she could not tell me how to live my life, that I could not live my life as she had lived hers, and that I must face my dilemma and go forward, one way or the other."

"She has not forgotten me either, has she?" He thought

of her wizened face and smiled.

"Oh no. But I wouldn't bet on a warm welcome from Mother."

"Nothing has changed there, eh? Too bad. Is she better?"

"No, Daniel. She coughs almost constantly and she is as thin as a water poplar. I don't know how much longer she can survive."

"Come, let's sit in this grove of trees," he said.

As they settled themselves, he asked, "Is there anything that can be done for her?"

"I don't think so. We have had the doctor look at her and the old healer woman from Gnadenfeld also—she won't let the midwife, Frau Klein, near her. The herbs seemed to ease her cough for a while, but now she is just as bad as she was before."

Daniel played with her hair as they sat, basking in the feel of her, the smell of her skin. He whispered something into her hair.

"I'm sorry; what did you say?"

Daniel felt her tremble in his arms at his husky chuckle, and then she melted into his embrace. No words were necessary to convey their passion for each other, the long-denied ecstasy of knowing each other completely.

Daniel jerked awake to find Luise in his arms. "Oh, my Luise," he whispered, and leaned to kiss her brow.

She stirred and smiled up at him. "Is this heaven or is it a dream?"

He touched the tip of her nose with another kiss. "Neither, my love. This is the way it will be from now on. 'There go Mr. and Mrs. Daniel Martens,' people will say. 'They can't keep their hands off each other.' "

Luise giggled. "We shall have to practice propriety."

"Propriety be hanged. I will kiss you in the middle of the street if I wish."

"Please, Mr. Martens, you must restrain yourself. I'm not that kind of woman."

He pinned her to the ground. "Your most recent conduct does not confirm that, my dear."

He kissed her neck and she giggled again, fighting him. Both of them started at the closing of a door, and a voice calling into the night.

Daniel released her and Luise jumped to her feet and straightened her dress. "Papa will be so worried. I should have been home hours ago and he was probably asking at Wieler's to find out where I had gone. We must go back."

Daniel reached out to smooth her messed up hair and then took her arm. He did not want this dream world to end. He wanted to keep Luise to himself, away from the world, away from all the trials and sorrows that fill each life, but he could not conceive of a way to do that.

"Let us go then, back to the world of men."

"Luise! Are you out here?" The voice came through the darkness.

"Papa, I'm here. Don't worry, we're coming."

"What on earth?" The voice became louder and they saw a figure running towards them.

"Phillip, what are you thinking, keeping this young woman—"

Abram seemed to realize it was not Phillip who held Luise's arm. All at once he shouted and embraced Daniel with such exuberance he almost knocked him to the ground. Gasping and exclaiming, Abram pumped Daniel's hand, then looked toward Luise and shook his head.

"Dear girl, I never would have believed it. When—? How—?" He swiped at his eyes with his knuckles.

They laughed and cried at his loss of words.

"Have you just come, Daniel, or have you had time to talk?"

Daniel couldn't hold back his grin. "We've had a little time to talk, sir."

Abram glanced from Daniel to Luise, and cleared his throat. "Yes. Well. Good then." He turned toward the village and motioned them to join him. Daniel's grin widened and he felt Luise poke him in the ribs. She leaned into his shoulder as they walked, and he felt as if he could face anything the world threw at him now that she was at his side.

Luise awoke to the sun on her face. She threw aside the covers to rise, but a hand held her fast. Remembering, she smiled and lay back against Daniel.

She had dried his tears in the night when she had told him of Baby Sarah. He had dried hers when he referred, albeit circumspectly, to his ordeal. But the joy of being together overcame the sorrows past.

"What's your hurry, my lady?"

"I feel like a sluggard," she whispered. "I don't know if I've ever slept this late."

"Well, you've had a rough night, my dear."

"You embarrass me."

"Get used to it, Mrs. Martens."

A muffled rap at the door stopped their whispered dialogue, and Hans' voice called, "Luise, I want to see Daniel. Papa said I must ask before I come in."

"Just you wait, little brother. Daniel will come out to see you."

Daniel pulled the covers tighter around himself while Luise tugged at them.

"Careful, Luise, we're going to…"

With a thud, Daniel slipped off the bed and landed on the floor.

Luise buried her head in her pillow to muffle her laughter while Daniel glared at her over the edge of the bed. Forcing a frown, he pulled on his clothes and moved toward the door.

"We will finish this later, wife."

He left the room and Luise scooted out of bed and dressed, then remade the bed and straightened up the room. She heard her family laughing and talking—and her stepmother coughing—and hurried to join them. When she emerged from the bedroom, tucking the last pin into the hair bundled at the nape of her neck, she felt her face heat. They stared at her as if she had grown two heads. Nela sat coyly on Daniel's lap and Hans' chair nudged up to his brother-in-law's.

Luise cleared her throat and said a good morning before taking a chair as near to Daniel as possible. She needed to feel him close by.

"Almost afternoon already, Luise. Shame on you."

This morning even Anna's rudeness could not keep her smile away. She felt as if it would split her face.

"My husband has come home, Mother. Aren't you glad for me?"

"It certainly took him long enough, but I knew he would come eventually."

Luise saw Daniel's surprise. "You knew I would come?" he asked Anna. "How did you know?"

"You young people are all the same." She stopped to cough, her entire body shuddering from the effort. "You have no respect for things you do not understand. I know things."

Luise put a hand on Daniel's arm. "Mother sometimes has this sixth sense, an intuition."

"It is not intuition, girl. God tells me things."

"It's true, Daniel," Luise continued. "Mother knew all along that I would be traveling here with my family. That's why she kept telling me to pack and be ready to go."

"You didn't want to listen then either. You never want to listen. And now that fine young man Phillip will not come near anymore. He would have looked after you."

Tension charged the air until Hans piped up, "I like Phillip too, but Daniel belongs to us."

"Well said, young man," said Abram. "Daniel is family."

"I love you, Daniel." Nela's sweet words hit their mark and tears touched the eyes of everyone around the table. Tante Manya caught Luise's eye and smiled so wide her gums showed. She lifted a hand to cover her mouth and wiped at the tears finding their way through the wrinkles of her lovely face.

"Joy cometh in the morning," she said.

"Joy came last night," corrected Luise. "And it's here to stay."

She caught a glimmer of caution in Tante Manya's eyes, but her joy was too full to worry about it. This was a day for celebration.

As Daniel told of his incarceration and escape, Luise saw something flicker in his eyes, something that resembled fear. Her heart squeezed. The old Daniel had never been afraid of anything. Nor had she ever seen him as angry as he had been at Phillip, a quiet, dangerous anger.

"Did you have any friends in all this time?" asked Abram.

"Klaas Enns from Ebenfeld and the Khanty couple, and Josiah, of course. But you know how the Soviets are, they have to know everything about everybody, and their spies are everywhere. I avoided people as much as possible."

"Doesn't the Soviet already know enough?" asked Tante Manya.

Abram toyed with a teaspoon, turning it end for end in his hands and watching it as if to avoid eye contact. "Working in the village office," his voice lowered, "one realizes just how much we are all watched and how much is noted."

It's happening again. Luise knew this just as she knew she was not safe to walk alone after dark anymore, as long as Ivan the Terrible worked in the village, and it made her angry that reality reached out again to threaten her…them.

"What do they hope to gain with this knowledge? What possible harm can we do to them? I wish they would just leave us alone."

When the children had run off to school, Daniel turned his chair around and sat astride it, his arms resting on its back.

"What of this Ivan who causes such fear? Is he still here in this village?"

"Yes, but he hasn't showed up at the school for a long time." Luise saw the worry in Daniel's eyes and didn't want to cause him more concern.

"Has he threatened you in any other way?" Yes, the worry, the fear, was there.

"He has threatened, but nothing more. I'm sure it's just a fear tactic." She put a hand on Daniel's arm.

"These things happen, son," said Abram. "We must trust that God looks out for us, and use our common sense to stay out of trouble's path. This is Soviet Russia. We are still much more fortunate than some."

"I can deal with violence directed toward me," said Daniel, rubbing a hand over his forehead, "but I cannot abide it when it touches my family."

"They know that."

Tante Manya shook her head and mumbled something about the way of the wicked.

It saddened Luise, this fear that invaded their private lives. It felt as if a huge iron fist was raised against them, ready to smash them whenever it chose, and they could do nothing to withstand or delay it. The hand of repression they had felt in Alexandrovka had followed them to the eastern reaches of the republic.

While Daniel's eyes sparked with pain and doubt, Abram's conveyed a sense of strength. He held a secret within him, and Luise wished he would share it.

"What are you thinking, Papa? What do you know that we do not?"

"There are ways for us to avoid conflict."

"Is it something you learned at the village office, sir?" Daniel leaned forward, his expression expectant.

"In a manner of speaking, yes, but possibly not as specific as you might expect." He looked at each of them in turn before continuing, as if gauging their willingness to consider his suggestion.

"Cooperation."

He seemed to wait for their responses, but no one replied.

"Listen, all of you." He tapped the end of the teaspoon on the table as he spoke. "There is a level of cooperation that will allow us to live in relative peace and safety, while still holding to our beliefs, our way of life."

Daniel gripped the back of his chair with white knuckles. "With all due respect, sir, how can we, in good conscience, cooperate with an ungodly and repressive government? How can we maintain our values and our integrity?"

Luise saw fire in her father's eyes and waited for him to explain.

"I do not suggest we forfeit our values, Daniel, but that we learn how to co-exist."

Abram glanced around the table and Luise felt herself somehow excluded from further discussion. The exclusion irritated her. She knew there were things her father could not divulge to anyone. If there was something he could not reveal, she would respect that, but she had as much right as Daniel to hear her father's opinions. The idea that men could know what women could not grated on her sense of personal worth. She pressed her lips together in a hard line as her father spoke again.

"Daniel," he said, "I would like to invite you to come with me to Jakob Siemens' house this evening. We gather regularly to discuss the business of the collective. I'm sure Jakob would welcome your inclusion."

Daniel glanced at Luise, and she shrugged one shoulder in resignation.

"I would be glad to accompany you," he told Abram.

As much as Luise wanted to be a supportive wife, she would have loved to sit in on the meetings at Siemens' place, but as a woman, she knew that would never be. She would speak to Daniel about it later.

Chapter Twenty-nine

Daniel's heart warmed as he remembered his mother's tears that afternoon at seeing her son alive and well. His siblings had grown, his family seemed content, and he could give them joy just by being alive. But it was not long before his mind returned to Abram's comments of the morning. As much as he disliked leaving Luise behind, he looked forward to what Jakob Siemens had to say at the meeting.

Strange how the things we wish most to avoid tend to follow us. So thought Daniel when he stepped into Jakob Siemens' house to see Phillip Wieler sitting at the kitchen table with several other men. He narrowed his eyes at Phillip and proceeded to ignore him.

"What is it that brings out the anger of the government against us?" questioned Daniel when the meeting commenced. "I see here the beginnings of a prosperous and thriving community of villages that could grow food not only for ourselves but for our neighbors as well. Why do they want to stamp that out?"

"Because they're crazy."

Young Franz Goerzen pointed his finger at his head and drew circles in the air. Daniel ignored him. He wanted answers, not silliness.

Jakob Siemens, at whose kitchen table the men sat, smiled slightly as he rubbed his hand over the surface of the table. "If they are crazy, we need to know what makes them so. After all, they are men, just as we are."

"Some of them, maybe," said Goerzen.

Siemens spoke again, looking from beneath heavy brows at Franz Goerzen, then around the table at Abram,

Daniel, and several other men who had gathered in the Siemens house to discuss, ostensibly, the workings of the kolkhozy.

"The officials do as they are told; they are as much under the thumb of the government as we are. Their mandate is to keep the common people poor, helpless and dependent. They clamped down on us in Slavgorod because we prospered. They had to shake us around, mix us up, and frighten us." He glanced meaningfully at Daniel, who frowned at the memory of the anger that had killed his father, at a similar anger that had taken up residence in him these last two years.

"As Daniel has already suggested, our little settlements have begun to prosper here. In as little as two years we have turned this previously unproductive land into a bountiful breadbasket. They have noticed this success."

"So they attempt to control our prosperity." Daniel grasped Siemens' reasoning. "They only wish us to succeed so they can prosper."

Jakob Siemens ran a hand over his dark moustache and beardless chin. He was not a handsome man, but his quick eyes and calm manner conveyed integrity, and Daniel trusted him. Siemens was not a man to be pushed, but one who would put much thought into his actions. Daniel understood why Abram had brought him here this evening. He needed to hear and consider what was happening in the Mennonite settlements here in the Amur Region. It seemed their lives were again becoming unsettled.

"My father-in-law mentioned the word 'cooperation' when we spoke of how to deal with the Soviet threat to our way of life. How do you see this?"

Siemens seemed to appraise Daniel as he listened to his question, then considered his answer thoroughly before voicing it. Franz Goerzen apparently thought the answer was not forthcoming, and stood to get more coffee from the pot on the stove.

"Cooperation. That is one way of explaining it. We can rebel and react and refuse to do as they say, which, if you will forgive me for referring to what happened to your father, is what some have done, to no avail and to their detriment. And so one more of our best is silenced and we feel the loss keenly. In my humble opinion, that response is ineffective and dangerous."

Daniel stared at the man as he listened, drawn in by his calm reason. He could listen to a man like this. But he wanted more specifics.

"How can we willingly give up our food and our seed when we need them in order to survive? How are we to cooperate when they threaten our families? I have deduced—he looked at Abram before he continued—that Commissar Ivan Mironenko was sent here some time ago, specifically by Senior-Major Dubrowsky, to intimidate Luise."

"He what?" Daniel saw shock in Abram's face, but the words came from Phillip.

"I believe it's true, but we can speak of that later."

"We have to draw the line someplace," said Isaak Kruger. "Soon we end up like our relatives who stayed in South Russia, starving, sick and in the middle of war. The Reds will ruin our land and our lives in the process."

"Yes, Isaak," said Abram, "but as long as we live here, it would be pertinent to at least put an effort into getting along with them. Perhaps we can even get on their good side."

"They have no good side," interrupted Franz, as he poured coffee all around. "They are bad through and through, the whole lot of them."

"Ah, Mr. Goerzen, that is a misconception. There are few men who are completely bad. It will benefit us to remember that."

"How can you say that after what Daniel revealed about Ivan Mironenko? They are our enemies." He replaced the coffee pot on the stove and sat down.

"And how does Christ ask us to respond to our enemies?"

Abram's chastisement did not sit well with Franz. He erupted from his chair and pointed a finger at him. "How dare you belittle what happened to my family. The GPU took my father and killed my sister. I am left to look after my sorrowing mother and little brothers. I hate them, the whole lot of them, and I will not cooperate in any way."

His ire vented, Franz sat trembling beside Daniel, who felt a twinge of guilt for his assumptions about the young man. They had all suffered, or they would not have left a comfortable home to travel to this remote land across the river from China.

No one spoke for a time, each lost in his thoughts or unsure of how to respond to Franz' anger. Then Daniel felt Jakob Siemens' eyes again as he let his gaze rest on each man in turn.

"Listen, friends, we do not minimize anyone's trials and tribulations by what we discuss this evening. We have all lost loved ones or livelihood—or both. We have become a people without a home as we travel from one part of the world to another. That has been the story of our existence since Menno Simons. It is nothing new to our people.

"The other thing that has not changed is that we are a people of peace. We do not unsheathe the sword in order to have our way; we do not attempt to bring down disaster upon our enemies."

Daniel still felt Dubrowsky's gun in his hand. He had almost pulled the trigger.

"We are to love our enemies," agreed Isaak Kruger.

"Whom have you lost?" Franz glared at Kruger with pain in his eyes. "You have your family all around you."

Kruger hesitated, staring at his gnarled hands, then raised his eyes to Franz. "I watched Machno hack my parents to pieces and rape my sister. I only escaped because the brigands were too drunk to catch me. Do you think that picture will ever leave my mind? It is engraved as if in blood every time I close my eyes. As Siemens says, we have all lost. But the command still stands: love your enemies. It is easy to love our friends, but we do not live for ease. We live to obey Christ."

Franz' chin quivered with his struggle to maintain control. He tried to speak once but stopped before his emotions destroyed him. Shaking his head, he got up and went to stand at the window. Daniel knew how these experiences could affect one's faith in God. What Kruger had said crackled hot in Daniel's mind like the wood in the stove behind him.

"I believe we all want the same thing," Siemens broke the silence. "We wish to live in peace and safety. This may not be possible here, but perhaps someday it will be. For the time being, we must be united in our attempt to give the officials nothing with which to accuse us."

"As pure as doves and as crafty as serpents."

Abram's words hit home with Daniel, as he realized his father-in-law dealt personally with Ivan Mironenko and Yevgeny Rashidov daily, and often with their superiors as well. Abram Letkemann and Jakob Siemens would be the ones to show the way for the rest of them.

After speaking of some day-to-day issues of the farm, the group dispersed with few words, but Daniel shook Siemens' hand and thanked him for his insight. "I agree with your assessment of our situation, sir, and I will consider what we have spoken about tonight."

A rare smile lit Jakob Siemens' face as he shook Daniel's hand.

As Daniel turned to go, he heard Phillip call his name. "I'll walk partway home with you," he said.

Daniel declined to answer, just turned and walked out with Phillip by his side.

"I'll meet you at home then," said Abram.

"Daniel," Phillip said, "I know you have not forgiven

me for what you think happened between me and Luise, but with the state of affairs here, we need to be able to work together."

Daniel merely cast him a dark look, lost to the night around them. He heard Phillip sigh and felt a touch of pity, but not enough to speak.

Phillip continued. "I cannot apologize for my feelings for Luise, but I can certainly assure you she did not respond to them. If I had at any time thought you might be alive, I would never have stepped into her life. As it was, I truly felt the need to protect her in your stead."

"You expect thanks?"

"No!" Phillip's voice was loud in the night and he repeated himself in a whisper. "No. I want only for us to bury our resentments and be able to work together in harmony. Is that not possible?"

Daniel remained quiet as the snow crunched underfoot. "I don't know," he said, finally.

"Daniel, we were once such friends. Like David and Jonathon, we were. Nothing could come between us."

"Seems we were wrong."

"You are as hard-headed as you always were."

"And you as tactless."

The rebuttals came fast and furious now from both men.

"Stubborn as the proverbial mule."

"What's proverbial about a mule?"

Daniel heard a smile in Phillip's response. "Dense as the day is long."

"Days are not dense. Forests are dense," Daniel fired back, a chuckle in his voice.

"Can't see the forest for the trees." Phillip was laughing now, trying to keep his voice from echoing across the village.

"If it weren't so blamed cold, I'd have it out with you right here in the street."

Phillip threw a playful punch. "Time someone knocked

some sense into you."

"You wouldn't qualify." Daniel punched him back.

They scuffled as they walked until both were tired and laughing, then continued on when Daniel put his arm around Phillip's shoulders. "Life it too short for grudges. I always trusted you before and I shall trust you now. Let's talk no more of it.

"Did I tell you the horse trader, Marcowiscz, saved my life?"

Phillip stopped short. "I never thought to mention this: My mother wrote a letter, said she had seen the horse trader in Alexandrovka."

Daniel grabbed Phillip by the arm. "Marcowiscz? He was in Alexandrovka?" Could it be that he had escaped?

"He was in a hurry to move on, said he was going far away from there."

"Thank heaven! I thought they'd killed him because of me."

"What a terrible thing!"

Luise thought of Franz Goerzen's tale of terror and loss as she stared into the darkness of night, lying close beside Daniel in their bedroom in her father's house. "Is there something we can do for the Goerzen family to make it easier for Franz?"

She knew Daniel was not asleep and waited for his answer.

"I'm sure there's something, Luise, but I don't know what it might be. This is not necessarily a physical need. People react in different ways to such unspeakable experiences; it's not always easy to see what they really need."

"Perhaps I will pay a visit to Franz' mother. Sometimes a listening ear is better than nothing."

Daniel cradled her against his side and kissed her hair. "You are an angel, my dear Luise. This is how I dreamed of you all the long years of endless nights while we were apart."

She snuggled closer, rejoicing that the Lord God had seen fit to answer her prayer by sending Daniel back to her whole. Well, almost whole. She knew he kept some things hidden away, things that had happened to him during his exile, things he would not or could not share with her. She had witnessed his fear and his anger, but she hoped and prayed that patience would win the day. Besides, she had secrets of her own, the truth of her fears of Ivan Mironenko.

She and Daniel had known each other most of their lives, but living together revealed things they had not known about each other. She would do her best to meet his needs, as the Lord gave her strength.

Luise talked with Tante Manya about it the next day.

"Tante Manya, when you were first married, did you ever feel disappointed in yourself for not knowing more about your husband?"

Tante Manya leveled a gaze at her. "Heavens above, what questions you ask."

But Luise would not be put off. She had no mother to ask, and her stepmother had neither health of body or mind to satisfy her questions.

"Well, Daniel and I know each other's families, each other's likes and dislikes, each other's hopes and dreams. And then something comes up that surprises me about him and I think I should have seen it sooner. Do you know what I mean?"

"I know what you mean, but you have a habit of piling guilt upon yourself that you have no business carrying."

"But is it not the job of the wife to read her husband's needs before he has to express them?"

"Is that what you have observed? Lise, child, you are not a slave; you are a partner. You and Daniel have committed to walk together on life's path, each exercising your own gifts. You will probably have more sensitivity, being a woman, but you are not a seer. You must earn your husband's trust so he is willing and eager to tell you his mind. Then you can help him deal with his feelings, because you are probably better at that than he."

"So I should not be hurt or alarmed if he does not always share his heart with me?"

"Do you share everything with him?" She looked pointedly at Luise. "As you live together, you will begin to know each other's minds, but there will always be areas that lie beyond your understanding of each other, and you must not fight that. Allow Daniel to be Daniel. And you must be you. And," the old woman's eyes twinkled, "enjoy the journey."

"Thank you, Tante Manya. You are a wise woman indeed, which is something I've always known but see more fully as the days go by."

"Flattery gets you nowhere."

"It's not flattery; it's the truth, spoken in love."

"My head is beginning to swell at such praise."

Luise leaned over and placed a kiss on the old woman's forehead. "Then I must make you a bigger kerchief."

Tante Manya chuckled and Luise smiled, hiding the questions in her mind as to just what secrets Daniel carried that he was still unable to tell her. He and Abram spent many hours together in the woodshop, and attended meetings at Jakob Siemens' home, and yet he had little to say to her about it. Instead he busied himself as a farm laborer and told her about that. She sensed there was a sinister thread beneath the warp and weave of their daily lives, and she wondered how knotted and ugly the underside of the fabric looked. What upheaval loomed in their future, and furthermore, what could she do to prepare for it?

Chapter Thirty

Luise hurried along the street with Hans and Nela on either side of her, wrapped warmly against the November cold, and stopped at the schoolhouse.

"I'll see you after school," she said. "Please come straight home."

"We will, Luise," said Nela, but Hans looked away, either hesitant to make such a confining promise or already distracted by his friends.

"I'll make sure he comes home," Nela assured her.

Luise missed teaching the children, but she was relieved to have time for other things, including her present mission.

She stopped at the small cottage surrounded by dried vines that had shaded the entire verandah in the heat of summer, thankful that Daniel had been progressing toward wholeness. Passing through the arbor, she knocked on the front door and waited.

"Come," a voice called from within, and she pushed open the door to the scent of onions and garlic. She had never visited Frau Klein at her home, and the experience made her nervous. But she wanted to know for sure, and apparently this woman had ways and means of knowing.

The little house held more than Abram's large one, although it couldn't have been half the size. Tables and chairs occupied every available space along the walls, the floor was a scattering of colorful hooked rugs, and every surface had been commandeered to hold piles of papers or books, or jars with indeterminate contents. Several cats either watched or ignored Luise from their perches, looking regally pleased with themselves. She felt a sneeze coming on, but talked herself out of that or she would be sneezing the entire time. Cat hair floated through the air at every movement.

A shuffling in the next room brought Luise to attention, and then the stout, bespectacled woman appeared in the doorway to the parlor. Her eyes were magnified behind the round spectacles, and her smile stretched from ear to ear at the sight of her visitor. She wore no kerchief, as was customary among older Mennonite women, and her gray hair wisped around her head in all directions, unmindful of the pins that had been stuck in at random.

Luise offered Frau Klein a tentative smile.

"Do not be put off by the way things seem, my dear little mama. Sit down, sit down. Have you been to see Tatiana? How is she? And her family?"

"Sh...she's very well, as is her child." The woman's salutation made Luise stall her retreat. Perhaps she did know something. Frau Klein shooed a cat from the divan and pushed some books over to make room for Luise.

"Sit, sit. I will make some tea. You like tea? Of course you like tea. If you don't, you should; it's good for you. Sit."

Luise sat, receiving a distinct scowl from the cat that had been relocated in her favor. She glanced to the window, but it and all its mates were so dirty she could see nothing through them.

"Here we go."

Luise balanced the tea on her lap and sipped it, avoiding the cat hair on the side. Her breakfast shifted higher and she forced her mind to other things.

"Feeling a bit squeamish, my dear? Not to worry. It won't last long, at least not more than nine months." The little woman's cackle filled the cottage and the cats meandered nearer to rub on her legs. "But then you know about the first part, don't you? Tsk, tsk, what a shame."

She reached down to stroke one of the cats, then handed Luise a piece of plum cake.

"Oh, no thank you. I've only just finished breakfast."

"Always room for a little *plume plautz,* no? Oh well, maybe not this morning. But you'd like some, wouldn't you, Empress?" She pinched off a piece for the large calico and let the animal lick her fingers.

Again, Luise's stomach planned revolt. She must clear her mind or she would lose her breakfast.

"I'm sorry to bother you, Frau Klein, but I wanted to know if you could confirm…my situation."

"Ha, ha. Your situation. So delicately put. You are in the family way and I have only to look into your eyes to see it. I can examine you if you wish, but I already know, as do you."

Luise's face warmed with embarrassment. "Perhaps I did, but I wanted to know for sure before I told my husband. I cannot discuss it with my stepmother. My own mother is dead and my stepmother is…well, her mind is affected."

"Yes, I know."

"It became noticeable after she bore her second child." Luise screwed up her courage and asked her questions. "Which brings me to asking why that should have happened and how it can be avoided."

The little woman pushed out of her soft chair and wobbled into the kitchen for more tea.

"I am a wise woman for my size," she laughed, "but I do not know everything, hard as that is to believe. Sometimes these things happen, maybe because of age, or her bad feelings toward another or just stored-up bitterness, or something completely without reason, but I think you are safe, my dear.

Relief flooded over Luise at the little woman's words, and she couldn't help herself for asking further. "Have you always lived alone? Do you have a family?"

The magnified eyes locked onto hers and Luise regretted her prying questions. "Braver than I thought you were, little mama." She bent to stroke a cat on the table, then looked back at Luise.

"Back in the south is where I began my life. During the troubled times I had a child, a son. It's not a secret, just something that happened in those days with soldiers about. So it goes. My son was the apple of my eye, but others didn't understand him. He was sickly and small. But I loved him every hour of his short life. We lived together, just us two, in a little hovel on the outskirts of our village, and no one bothered us."

She stared at Luise for a long moment before she spoke. "I have been alone, and I have been afraid. I have loved and I have lost. I have carried on through dark days and light, so I can tell you to continue also. But I don't need to say that to you because you are loved. I can see that as plain as if it were written on your forehead. You carry the blessing of love. Tend it well and it will give you joy. Stand up now."

"Pardon me?"

"I said, stand up. Take off your coat. My goodness, I should have taken your coat before, excuse my poor hospitality, I'm not used to visitors. Turn around."

Luise obeyed, anxious to placate the woman and leave this cottage.

"It will be a son. Yes, now sit down again. You look a little green. Drink the tea; it will settle you. Yes, you and your man will have a son."

Luise gawked at her, forgetting her manners entirely. "But how do you know this? How can you tell?"

" 'Tis a gift, child. One does not question a gift." She nodded to herself. "I always know."

"Well, I must go." Luise stood and pulled her coat on again, stepping around cats and books. She needed fresh air more than anything right now, but the tea had settled her stomach.

"Here's a little to take with you, my dear," said Frau Klein, handing her a packet of tea leaves. "Come for more if you like. I don't mind a fair trade of goods now and then."

"I'm sorry, I have nothing but a few rubles for your time and opinion." Luise held the coins in her open hand.

"Oh, don't worry about payment," she said, taking the rubles and stuffing them into the pocket of her apron. "We do what we can for each other in these difficult days, eh?"

"Thank you for your time, Frau Klein. We shall see if you were right in your prediction."

The woman smiled widely. "I am always right."

Luise breathed deeply of the crisp air as she left the house, checking the street. She walked home in a cloud of exhilaration and fear. Little Mama indeed. What would Daniel say? He seemed so consumed by his past and the political changes taking place in the villages that he hadn't even considered the possibility of fatherhood. Well, he would have to begin considering it now. Luise bit her bottom lip to contain her smile.

❧

Daniel explained his news to Luise, but she didn't seem interested. It frustrated him that she maintained a distance from what was going on all around them. Change was inevitable; they must face it.

He wondered if his angry outbursts had frightened her into denying the things that faced them all. Guilt and regret pressed on him. His prayers to return to Luise had been answered by a God he had pushed to the periphery of his life. He had been shown mercy, but he did not deserve it. He supposed that was the meaning of mercy. Still, he missed the carefree days of young love before the realities of desperate times had crushed him. He needed Luise to listen to him, to understand his perspective on the way they were responding to the Soviet system.

"Luise, this is important business and I need you to care about it."

The hurt that flickered through her dark eyes made him wish he had spoken more gently, but this was important.

"You don't seem interested in what I'm telling you, but

this effort at cooperation will affect all of us, you know. It might be better if you tried to understand."

She blinked rapidly and shifted her gaze away from him, her hands at her stomach. What was wrong with her? She didn't usually act this way.

"Luise, look at me, please. Are you ill? Did something happen?"

She bit her bottom lip, something else she hadn't used to do, her gaze wavering from his.

"Well, there is something…"

Daniel felt a chill slide down his spine.

"What is it? Tell me."

Something else flickered in her eyes, something he couldn't read. He grabbed her shoulders while she searched for the right words.

"Daniel, I am not ill, well, not really. Sometimes I feel a bit weary and queasy, but for the most part I am well."

He held her upper arms and forced her to look at him, while inside he felt something begin to die. She must have seen the trauma going on in his mind, because she reached up to touch his face and smiled at him, the smile that had always locked his heart to hers.

"Oh Daniel, don't be afraid. I'm not ill. I am expecting a baby. Our baby. You're going to be a papa, Daniel. And I'll be—I suppose I already am—a mama. That's what has been consuming my thoughts and attentions lately."

He stared at her, his mind blank. He had not expected such news. There was no excuse of course; he knew the facts of life. But it had been a very long time since he had thought of himself becoming a father. This was a surprise indeed.

He realized Luise waited for his response, her eyes showing doubt and concern.

"I…I…" He shook his head, stuttered some more, and sat down on the bed, pulling her down onto his lap. "I didn't expect this."

"Well, Daniel, it is a natural consequence of our

actions." She colored at her own words. "But is it not wonderful?"

"Yes. Yes, it is. The more I think of it, the more wonderful I know it is. I'm sorry for my awkward reply, it's just that I've been so busy with the collective farm process and trying to stay on the good side of that rat, Ivan and his sidekick, Yevgeny. I hadn't given a thought to us having a child."

"Well, Daniel Martens, you had better start thinking about it, because it will happen next summer."

"Really, that soon?"

"Apparently this one will take nine months."

"Yes, I know, but...you're laughing at me, Luise. That's not polite."

"No, but it is humorous, and we certainly could do with a little more humor around here."

Daniel stared into her eyes and then pulled her close. "I'm so sorry for all the pain I've caused you. Sometimes I think it would have been better for you if I'd never—"

She leaned back and covered his mouth with her hand. "Don't ever say that, Daniel. I promised to love you for as long as we both shall live, and I intend to do just that. I need you and I thank God every day for bringing you back to me, to us. God loves you dearly, Daniel. He has never stopped loving you."

Her words filled the empty spaces in his heart and he sealed her proclamation with a long, deep kiss. "Summer, you say? Is this a secret? Have you told Tante Manya?"

"I've not told anyone. I went to see Frau Klein this morning and she confirmed my suspicions, but I think Tante Manya knows."

"You went to see Frau Klein? Isn't she a bit strange? Did she hurt you?"

"She made me tea and looked at me and told me we were going to have a child, a son, in fact."

"A son? My son." He stared into space, not seeing

anything, letting his mind catch up with his heart. "I wonder if all fathers feel this way when they receive the news."

"Not all, I'm afraid, but I'm glad you do."

"Shall we tell them?" He nodded toward the kitchen.

"Let's wait a bit, make sure everything goes as it should. Maybe in a couple of weeks."

He smiled his agreement. "But now we had best appear for supper or they will wonder what is wrong. How do I keep this grin off my face?"

"I have no idea. I'm having the same trouble."

He took her hand and led her to the kitchen where the family was just sitting down for supper.

"Ah, the love birds have arrived," said Anna, as Abram helped her to her chair. It had been several days since she had felt well enough to join them at the table.

Daniel ignored her statement and joined in the conversation about school and his work at the village office and plummeting temperatures.

Then Anna said, "Well, Nela, you will have to help your sister in the garden next year. With a new baby, she will not be able to do all the work."

Abram's fork clattered to the table. "New baby? What are you talking about?" He looked to Luise for confirmation. Daniel also threw a glance at Luise.

"What are you talking about, Mother?"

"The baby. You are in the family way and summer is always busy."

Abram still stared at Luise. "Is this true, my daughter? Do we look forward to an addition to our family?"

Luise glanced at him, and Daniel said, "It's true, sir. Luise only just told me. We had hoped to wait a bit before telling everyone else, but somehow Mother knows."

"Of course I know. There are some things a woman knows and there are some things God tells me. This is one of them. Don't look at me so surprised. It's a fact."

"Tante Manya, did you know too? Was I the only one

who didn't guess?"

"Don't feel bad, Abram. Men don't notice these things easily, do they Daniel?"

Her withered-apple face collapsed into the beloved grin, and Daniel realized she read his mind. Or knew more about men than he thought she did. "You have me there, Tante Manya. I had not given it a thought."

"We always reap what we sow," she said, and Abram responded with "Nah, Tante, there are children present."

She laughed at him and Nela and Hans cheered when they heard they were soon to become aunt and uncle.

"Suzianna will be so jealous," said Nela. "Her sister just got married and she can't have a baby as soon as you, Luise. I can hardly wait to tell her."

Daniel took Luise's hand and whispered to her under the cover of laughter and excitement. "It looks as though the cat is out of the bag."

She smiled demurely at him and he lost himself in her eyes, feelings returning that had been hidden under layers of pain.

"Daniel! Please pass the potatoes." Hans elbowed him and he laughed with the rest of them.

Chapter Thirty-one

"Where is the bag of wheat we had stored in the cellar?" asked Luise when Daniel came in from the woodshop. "I want to make New Years cookies and I'm sure we haven't used it all yet."

Daniel's eyes flitted from her to Tante Manya and back. "It's under our bed."

"What? That's a strange place to keep wheat," said Luise. "Were you expecting someone to steal it?"

Luise understood the truth of her question as soon as it was spoken.

"So," said Tante Manya, "it's that bad again, is it?"

Abram entered the kitchen, interrupting Daniel's reply.

"You all look like you've discovered a nasty secret."

Luise turned to him. "Papa, when did times get so bad that we have to hide our wheat under our bed? Is it really as difficult as it was in Alexandrovka?"

He glanced at Daniel, then back at her. "At least as bad," he said. "Taxes have risen once again and everything that was harvested belongs to the kolkhozy."

"They want to starve us into submission, just like before. Fear and hunger."

"Nah, Tante Manya," said Abram, "do we need to be so severe in our forecast?"

"I've lived long enough to know how their minds work. They want us to be dependent on them in every way, to become mindless subjects in this game they are playing with our lives. They have no care for us, only for the success of the Soviet."

Luise had not been aware of Tante Manya's growing

fears.

"Don't everyone get upset about it," said Luise. "I'll just go to the bedroom and get some wheat." The ridiculousness of the situation struck her and she snickered. "The wheat's in the bedroom, shall we sleep in the cellar?"

Tante Manya scowled at her and Abram stared blankly. Daniel pushed his tongue into his cheek as Luise smirked at him. Long ago, she had vowed the Bolsheviks would not steal her soul, and she would need to buck up if she wanted to maintain that goal. One day at a time, one step at a time. They would survive whatever the good Lord willed for them.

Daniel had gone with Abram to help him with a house he was building in Gnadenfeld, and Luise had ventured out, that cold but sunny February day, desperate for fresh air and sunshine. Tante Manya had sent her on her way with a nod.

"Get outside these walls, once, Lise. I will care for Anna."

Luise basked in the kiss of the sun on her face, even though the cold nipped at her nose. Breathing deeply, she trudged through ankle deep snow on her way to the mercantile. She needed to be strong for the baby, and sitting in the house day after day did not make her so.

This walk to the store was like medicine. She didn't care if Martha Lepp worked today or not, she needed a change of scenery and perhaps a piece of fabric to sew a new dress for Nela. The little girl was quickly catching up to her brother in height, and Hans was not pleased with the development.

She pushed open the door of the mercantile and nearly ran into Martha. The other woman backed away as if she had received an electric shock, and stared at Luise with her brows drawn together.

The fresh air had so lightened Luise's frame of mind that she dismissed previous opinions of the girl and started fresh. "Well, Martha, I had thought I might run into you here, but not in such a physical sense."

Her smile was answered by a scowl. "What do you want?"

"Pardon me?" The girl's rudeness tested Luise's outward calm.

"I asked you what you want. You seem to always get what you want so the sooner you find it, the sooner you can leave."

This was beyond rudeness. It bordered on cruelty, and Luise had taken more than enough of it from this girl.

"Listen, Martha, we need to talk this through and—"

"I don't want to talk to you. I am paid to help you find what you want so—"

"So I can leave, I know. But I am not going to leave until we have come to some kind of understanding about what makes you bitter toward me." Luise unwound the scarf she had tied about her head and neck. "We can either talk here at the door where everyone who enters will hear, or we can go to the back of the store and speak privately."

Martha hesitated, then spun on her heel and headed toward the stockroom. Luise followed, determined to settle this misunderstanding once and for all. She hated to be at odds with people. Martha marched behind the counter and through a curtained doorway. She slipped through, letting the curtain fall in Luise's face. Turn the other cheek. She would have to keep those words clearly in mind during the next few minutes.

When Luise entered the small storage room, Martha turned to face her. The mixture of nervousness and loathing that came from the girl's eyes stunned Luise. Whatever it represented, she must stop it before it poisoned her and others.

"So talk."

"Martha, ever since last summer when I came in for dress material, you have given me a cold shoulder. I would even venture to say you have been indiscreetly rude. I need to know what it is that causes this reaction in you before I can do anything about it. So it's your turn. You talk."

"You're the one—"

"Oh for heaven's sake, Martha. Spit it out. What have I done to you that is so unforgivable?"

"As if you don't know!" She raised her voice so that Luise cringed, then lowered it again when they heard the bell over the door.

"Ever since you came," she hissed, "ever since Phillip came, you have been after him, even though you are a married woman. You behaved brazenly around him and tried to steal him from me, even though you didn't really care for him."

"Whatever are you talking about? The man followed me everywhere, trying to get my attention. I avoided him as much as possible without being rude, and I'm sorry if he just wasn't interested in you."

"He would have been interested if you had only kept away. You don't need two men, you know. You spoiled it all for me. Even when the letter came, I hated you because you led Phillip on. You—"

Luise's blood ran cold. She could feel her pulse throbbing at her throat, her hands turning clammy. Her voice was steely as she asked, "What did you say?"

Martha's face turned white and her eyes widened. "Nothing. I…I was angry that you led Phillip on when you didn't care for him."

"Martha, you mentioned a letter. What letter?"

The girl shrugged and turned away, but Luise grabbed her arm and turned her back. "What letter, Martha? It's time to tell the truth."

Luise could feel Martha tremble, could feel fear drift through her, but she would not give in now. She would know what this girl meant.

"It was just a letter."

"From whom?"

Martha looked away, her hands twisting in front of her. "Phillip's mother…in Alexandrovka."

"What did it say, Martha?"

"It said…it said that Daniel h-had come l-looking for you, and that he was v-very much alive."

An anger deeper than Luise had felt before surged through her, and she gripped Martha's arm so tightly the girl winced. Luise didn't care.

"When did the letter arrive and how do you know what it said? Was it addressed to you?"

Martha pursed her lips and shook her head. "It was for Phillip's aunt, from his mother. It…it came about a month before Daniel returned. I opened it because I wanted to know if there was anything in it about Phillip."

"And?"

"And…she said Daniel had been to see her and he was coming here." Martha's eyes flitted to Luise's face and away again.

Luise wrenched the girl's arm so she would look at her. "You knew for a month that Daniel was alive and you didn't tell me? You opened a letter meant for someone else and read it?"

The girl nodded again, a tear slipping down her cheek.

"Don't bother to weep, Martha. I have shed enough tears over the last years to make up for any sorry tears you might squeeze out for pity. How dare you? How dare you?"

"Ow. Luise, you're hurting my arm."

"I should hurt more than—"

She clamped her lips shut and breathed in deeply. "No, that would be stooping to your level. I cannot believe anyone would be so cruel as to withhold information on life and death for the sake of jealousy.

"Whatever came over you, Martha? Did you think that by hurting me, you would get Phillip to pay attention to you? I hate to be the purveyor of bad news, but it doesn't work that way. You have to act worthy of attention, positive attention, not backhanded conniving. I am very angry with you and have the right to get even, but I choose to forgive you. However, I do not trust you, and it will be a very long time before I will be able to look at you without disgust at what you've done."

Luise realized she might as well stop talking, for she had gone beyond Martha's comprehension. She guessed that the girl only felt remorse in that she had been found out, not by what she had done. Some people were just that shallow.

Using every bit of grace she possessed, she asked, "Do you still have the letter?"

Martha hesitated, but her eye wavered to a shelf beside her.

"Give it to me."

Martha eyed her, then reached into a box on the shelf, extracting an envelope that had been neatly steamed open.

"Were you planning to re-seal it and give it to Mrs. Wieler?"

The girl nodded. "I kept putting it off, thinking I might be able to use the letter sometime."

"And you most certainly did. Shame on you. You'd best think seriously about what you've done. If I report this, you will no longer be in a position to work here handling the mail."

"No, please." Martha's face registered alarm. "I need this job. It's the only way to make ends meet since Father died, and my family depends on it."

"So you are asking me to do a favor for you?"

Martha's eyes pleaded but she said not a word.

"Well, to show you there is decency in this world, I will not report it, at least not now. But should I ever hear of another infraction, be assured it will be your last."

"Thank you. Must...must I give the letter to Mrs. Wieler?"

"Whose letter is it?"

"Hers."

"Well, I think you're probably bright enough to figure out the answer."

Martha sighed and tucked the envelope into her apron pocket, but Luise was not quite done with her.

"Martha, I don't wish to live at odds with you. I'll not hold this over your head, but I want to be able to enter your establishment, and support your family, without enduring narrowed eyes and sharp words. Do we have an understanding?"

Martha nodded, her eyes on the floor.

Luise was not entirely satisfied with her response, but there was a limit to what you could expect from some people.

Without another word, she turned and left the store, all thought of buying anything forgotten. She trudged through the snow toward home, lost in thought, not even looking where she was going until she found her way blocked by a mounted rider.

"Well, look who came for a visit."

Surprised, Luise looked up to see Commissar Ivan Mironenko staring down at her. She hadn't realized she had taken the backstreet or that the sun was setting and people would be home for supper. She had inadvertently put herself in danger again, and no one knew where she was. She glanced about and Ivan answered her unspoken question.

"No, Yevgeny is not here to save you this time. It's just you and me."

Instinctively, Luise backed away, which was difficult in the deep snow on the edges of the alley. She knew there was no way she could outrun him, on foot in the snow, and he on a fine horse. She also realized that her screams might not be heard out here. If only she had made it a little farther to the next street. She thought of her baby. Would she lose their son as she had lost little Sarah, before she had even drawn one breath?

She took a gulp of cold air.

"I need to get home. They'll be expecting me for supper."

"I won't keep you long. You won't even be late if you cooperate."

Cooperation. That was the word Daniel and Papa had used with reference to the government officials. Papa thought it was the answer, as apparently did Jakob Siemens. Daniel was still undecided. As for Luise, she had just made up her mind. There would be no cooperation between her people and the Soviet officials when it involved a sacrifice of morals. Unfortunately, such musings did not help in her particular situation.

Ivan eased himself off his horse and moved toward her, speaking low as if to soothe a frightened animal. Luise felt her own animal instincts kick in. She would not surrender without a fight, without all of her energy. She prayed fervently for God to protect her unborn son. With every step Ivan advanced, she backed away, picking up her skirts so as not to trip over them. Her mind was as clear as the winter sky.

"Come, my little filly. I've waited long enough for you. Too bad that husband of yours had to show up; I could have had you all to myself. But, I don't mind sharing."

Repulsed, Luise swallowed her fear. "You exalt yourself. I am not interested in anything you have to offer."

"How do you know that unless you sample it. Come now, you're wasting my time."

I'll waste more than your time. But how would she stop him? He was stronger. I have the Lord on my side. Lord, please step in. I don't know what to do, but You can help me. Please.

Ivan stopped, his brow furrowing. "What are you doing? Who are you talking to?" He seemed more than a little unsettled as he watched her. "You need to be afraid of me. I have power over you."

"You have no power over me that is not allowed by God," Luise challenged him.

"Ha, we will see about that." He advanced upon her until her back was up against the fence and she could move no further. Taking her by the shoulders, he pulled her to him, but she thrust the heel of her hand up under his chin, jarring his teeth together. He yelped and slapped her face.

"How dare you, you little whelp."

Luise's pulse pounded in her ears and her cheek stung from the slap, but she blinked her eyes clear and fought his hold on her arms, her screams cutting through the cold. He threw her down to the snow and she put up her knee, catching him in the groin. Howling, he swore at her and she tensed for another slap, but the blow was never delivered.

Chapter Thirty-two

Ivan straightened, a stunned look in his eyes, then crumpled to the ground, still groaning from the kick she had delivered.

"Hurry, Lise! He's not out."

Luise looked up from the crumpled form beside her to find Hans standing not far away, his slingshot swinging from his hand. Leaping to her feet, with a terrified backward glance at Ivan twisting in the snow, she launched herself toward her brother, grabbed his free hand and ran with him toward home. Within sight of the house she began to gasp, unable to suck in enough air.

"Come on, Lise, we're almost home."

Hans' encouragement gave her the determination to keep running, but she did so without breath. He pulled her up the steps and into the house, where she bent over and gasped for air. Her airways began to clear and terrified sobs took the place of gasps. She still wailed when Abram and Daniel entered through the back door. Daniel was at her side immediately, lifting her, calming her, soothing her.

"Shh, Luise, it's all right. I'm here. What happened?"

She tried to speak but couldn't stop the sobbing wails.

Hans stepped up and said, "Tante Manya sent me to see if Lise was on her way home, that she had gone to the store. I went down the alley 'cuz it's the fastest way, and I saw Ivan, the mean one, and he yelled at her and threw her into the snow in the alley and she kicked him hard and he was mad and so..." He looked at his father, then continued, "I took out my slingshot and smacked him in the back of the head with a stone. I know I'm not s'posed to aim at people,

Papa, but I had to save Lise. I'm sorry I disobeyed you." He handed his slingshot to his father and hung his head.

Abram stood open-mouthed at the revelation and Daniel reached for Hans. "Thank you for looking after your sister for me."

Hans glanced at his father, who seemed to struggle with his words. "We will discuss this later. Until then I'll keep the weapon."

"Yes, sir."

"She will not be off alone like that again," said Daniel, "will you, Luise?"

Luise had calmed and sat next to Daniel on the divan when she felt the telltale tightening of her stomach muscles.

"No! Not again!"

Luise's cries pierced Daniel more deeply than the bullet that had nearly claimed his life. In a moment he was on his knees before her.

"Luise, what is it? What's the matter? Oh no! The baby?"

Her whimpers mixed with pleas to God, and Daniel didn't know what to do.

"Carry her to bed," said Tante Manya. "Abram will get the doctor or Frau Klein. We must pray."

Pray. Daniel didn't know how. He had pretty much ceased praying when God had discarded him in that lonely northern land. Daniel had returned the favor. How could he now plead with a God he had railed against and finally ignored?

On the other hand, how could he not plead with the God who alone could save his baby? *If this is my punishment, please find another way to administer it. I deserve it but Luise does not. Please spare this child for her sake.*

When Dr. Goetz arrived, he sent everyone from the room while he examined Luise. Daniel waited anxiously outside the door until the doctor emerged, shutting the door behind him.

"She is sleeping now. The pains have subsided temporarily. If they start again, come for me immediately." He nodded and pulled on his sheepskin coat for the chilly walk home. "Don't worry," he said. "Just pray."

Daniel quietly let himself into the bedroom, pulled a chair to the side of the bed and sat to wait for the outcome of this situation for which he blamed himself. He should never have let her go out alone. They had let down their guard. Apparently, Ivan had his orders.

He watched Luise's chest rise and fall, saw her face pucker in fear, heard her quiet cry. This is all my fault. I want to pray but I don't have the words. *The Spirit prays for us in groans that words cannot express.* He remembered the words of Scripture and understood them for the first time in his life.

"I gave up my Son for you," said a voice Daniel had not heard for months. *"I know how it feels."*

Daniel slipped from the chair and fell to his knees beside the bed. Sobs scorched up his throat and forced themselves from his mouth. He tried to hold them back because he didn't want to wake Luise, but they would not be quelled. Muffling his sobs in the blankets, he cried to the God who, as Luise said, had always loved him.

"Take my burden, Lord. Take the hate, the anger, the fear. Take me if You must, but please spare Luise and our baby. Please."

How long he knelt there with his heart spilling out he did not know, but he must have slept, because all at once he felt a hand on his head.

Although her body remained in the grip of sleep, Luise's mind awoke to the knowledge that Daniel needed her. She tried to speak his name but her voice and lips refused to obey. She struggled against the invisible bonds that held her body and suddenly she was fully awake. She turned her head and saw the silhouette of someone kneeling beside her bed.

"Daniel? What are you doing?"

His head came up and she saw tears glisten on his face in the moonlight that flowed through the window.

"Luise! How are you?"

She stopped to consider. "I seem to be fine. And you?"

He groaned. "I've been wrestling with God. For you, for our son…for myself."

"And have you given in?"

She saw his nod and heard his whispered, "Yes."

"Praise God!" Her own tears welled up and spilled down her cheeks as they embraced.

"Amen. Luise, I'm sorry I fell asleep."

"Don't apologize. Fighting against God is an exhausting experience. Daniel, will you lie beside me?"

"I'm not sure the doctor—"

"I need you."

Gently, he lay down beside her and she snuggled against him. It was then Luise felt a kick in her belly. Her eyes wide in the darkness, she took Daniel's hand and placed it there. The baby kicked again and they both chuckled through tears of gratitude.

"Feels like he's alive and well in there," whispered Daniel.

"Yes, I think so. I think he will be fine."

With a deep sigh of relief and contentment, Luise drifted into a dreamless sleep.

❧

In the early morning, Luise awoke, aware of her bruised arms and stomach muscles. Sleep fled from her and took with it the peace that had come in the night with Daniel's surrender to God. In its place, thoughts of Ivan the Terrible came to her mind. What made the man so cruel, so evil? Was the power he already possessed not enough? Why did he stalk her, looking for times when she would be alone and unprotected? She had never done anything to anger him, except reject his advances, and there was no alternative to that.

Daniel wrapped his arm around her in his sleep, and although she wished for the escape sleep would offer, it would not come. During the long months and years of Daniel's exile, Luise had hoped and prayed for Daniel's return so she would feel completed once again. Now she realized that Daniel was not the answer to her completeness. He could not protect her from her fears, no matter how hard he tried. This trust in God must be renewed over and over again. Even Tante Manya had trouble with fear sometimes, and she was nearly a saint.

Later that week, after another fitful sleep, Luise again awoke early, long before the winter sun had even thought to rise above the vague horizon. She slipped out from under Daniel's arm and pulled her robe around her before venturing into the kitchen. Standing at the window, she knew that, given daylight and fewer trees, she would see the *Lesser Khingan Mountains,* the Manchurian side of Russia's *Bureia Mountains.* Across the Amur River, the mountains of China signified freedom from the oppression of the Soviet regime. Perhaps…

There had to be another way. They couldn't keep moving every few years. Somewhere there had to be peace and safety. Rubbing her aching arms, she knew that place was not here, would never be here.

Anna had insisted that she and Manya hang a Scripture plaque beside the kitchen window. The words of the Psalmist echoed in Luise's soul as she stood looking eastward:

> *"I will lift up mine eyes unto the hills,*
> *from whence cometh my help.*
> *My help cometh from the LORD,*
> *which made heaven and earth."*
> *Psalm 121:1, 2*

Was the Lord trying to tell them something? Well over one hundred people had escaped across the Amur in 1929, family by family, group by group, convinced that the future was brighter on the other side. But what if it wasn't? Was it worth the risk? Perhaps it was the next step to freedom.

Luise struggled with her doubts, falling to her knees and leaning her elbows on the seat of a chair. Bowing her head, she released her worries to God once more, begging for direction and peace in the midst of this constantly escalating drama that was her life.

Daniel found Luise asleep with her head on a kitchen chair, as the moon shone cold slivers of silver on her satin hair. He had awakened feeling bereft, empty, and realized Luise was gone. Panicking, he had scrambled from bed, only to find her near and safe. Safe on the outside.

He lamented that he was not able to make her feel safe on the inside, but that was impossible when he felt no safety himself. He must do as Luise had done: unburden himself to the One whom he knew was in control. He had to remind himself once again that he had released his life to God, and even in his turmoil, the reminder calmed him.

The Soviet is not in control of me. Luise had told Daniel what she had said to Ivan, that he could do nothing to her that God had not allowed. He wanted to believe that, in fact, he did believe it, but in accepting it, new questions emerged. Why had God allowed him to be so abused? Why had God allowed baby Sarah to die?

Has it made me a better man? I am still afraid. Even if I do trust Him, I don't trust myself. I have learned that I am not trustworthy when faced with the ultimate challenge.

Luise stirred and he lifted her to her feet with soothing whispers. "Come, my love, come back to bed. It is warm there and I will comfort you. Come."

"Daniel. I'm sorry for waking you. I couldn't sleep."

She began to shake and he didn't want her to catch a chill. "It's all right. Just come to bed."

In the morning before rising, while the room was yet dark and they lay spoon-style, Daniel asked Luise when Ivan had come to Shumanovka.

"It was the summer of '27, just before I lost Sarah. Why?"

When he didn't answer, she turned over in his arms and stared at him in the dark. He felt her eyes even though he knew she could not read his face.

"Daniel?"

"There was a brief time that summer when Dubrowsky left the prison camp. His replacement seemed easy-going but I learned he had been given strict instructions to watch me, and to kill me if I attempted escape. Then Dubrowsky returned and Kubolov left."

"It coincides with the time Ivan came here. What do you think this mean, Daniel? Can there possibly be a connection? Did Dubrowsky send Ivan here to harm me, in order to spite you?"

He didn't answer, his thoughts on what Dubrowsky might have instigated to punish them for being Mennonite.

"There it is again—cooperation." Isaak Kruger thumped the table with his fist and coffee sloshed out of the cups onto the tabletop. "How can we cooperate when they want more than we can give?"

Jakob Siemens rose from the table and fetched a dishrag from the bowl on the counter. He sopped up the spilled coffee and rinsed the cloth with a bit of water from the drinking pail. As he hung the cloth back over the side of the bowl, he spoke.

"There are some things we can control and some we cannot. If we bide our time, we may be able to accomplish something, but if we panic and over-react, we may forfeit any opportunities we have."

"Opportunities for what?" Kruger wanted to know. "To become absorbed into the system? To become serfs to our overlords?"

"Listen!"

All heads pivoted toward Siemens, who rarely raised his voice.

"The GPU secretary rode through here the other day. Abram saw him, heard what he said. As a collective farm, I believe we should cooperate with the authorities."

"Is that what it means, a collective farm? That they collect all our goods and leave us to starve?" A few of the men chuckled at Elder Remple's words.

"It's the same as what they planned for Slavgorod, isn't it?" said Daniel. "My father was not allowed to own a tractor. He had to purchase it in league with at least four other farmers in order to qualify for ownership rights."

Kruger spoke again. "Our individual rights are being stolen and you want to go along with it? I don't understand, people."

"Only for a time, brother." Siemens' voice was low and even again. "We must plan for the future, even though we may have to sacrifice some things for the present."

"Explain it to me in farmer's terms, Jakob. I'm too old for games with words."

"This is how I see it. If we apply ourselves to serving the kolkhozy, make it our priority, we will eventually earn the trust of our superiors. They already have given me more room for decision-making. I believe we need to play along with this plan, for as long as need be."

Kruger started to speak, but Siemens held up his hand for silence. "If I read the situation correctly," his voice lowered so the men had to lean forward to hear him, "we will not be able to survive indefinitely in this country. Things are closing in on us." He paused while the men around the table grasped his inference. "But right now I see no point in panicking. If we remain calm and cooperate with the authorities, we may be able to make more solid plans to remove ourselves from this situation."

"You mean escape?" Franz Goerzen had been unusually quiet throughout the meeting.

"We will not speak the word at present, but you have my meaning. We will use patience to our advantage. But we must be agreed and stand united or everything will fall apart like a poorly built house in a windstorm. This is to be kept absolutely secret within this group. Is that understood?"

Nods met his gaze but more questions remained, many of which could not be satisfactorily answered. Daniel's mind spun with questions and possibilities as he and Abram left the meeting.

Chapter Thirty-three

As another year warmed and the time of her confinement drew to an end, Luise became more and more nervous. How could she care for a baby in this unsettled, dangerous time? How had her forebears done it?

"You are worrying about things that may never happen," said Tante Manya. "Stop torturing yourself about things you cannot control."

Luise, who had commandeered the rocking chair for the remainder of her time, sat with a cup of tea balanced on her extended abdomen. "I can't help myself, Tante Manya. Some nights I wake up in the middle of a dream and Ivan is there, trying to get at me. Daniel always stands in his way, and I wake up before any blows fall. But then I lie there thinking about it, and I don't want Daniel to risk himself for me. On the other hand, I would be terrified if he were not there for me. I don't know what I want."

"You want the same thing we all do: peace and freedom. That is a noble goal, but sometimes the journey to peace is long, and safety is not guaranteed for us here. This is not heaven, Lise."

"I wish it were. We would be done with all this."

"And Ivan and Yevgeny and all the others would have no one to show them life as it should be lived."

Luise's frown deepened. She knew she should care for these people. Love your enemies, Jesus said. But try as she might, she couldn't muster up any compassion for them.

Tante Manya continued. "Everyone has a past, a heart full of hurt. We have no idea what Ivan has witnessed or experienced in his life. He does whatever he finds to do that eases the inner suffering that nags at him day and night."

Tante Manya's words bothered Luise. How did the woman find that kind of compassion?

"Are you not afraid of him, Tante?"

The old woman shrugged. "I have been, but God has been speaking to me. I suppose I would feel fear if he confronted me, as he did you, but mostly I feel pity for him. We at least have hope. He has nothing. He does not know that anyone cares for him. He does not know that one man loved him enough to die in his place."

Tante Manya's words dug into the selfish places of Luise's heart and haunted her in the days following. Papa must have a degree of pity for Ivan too, or he could not bear to work day by day with a man who had accosted his daughter. Yes, Papa was going along with Jakob Siemens' plan, to cooperate as much as possible with the enemy. Win their trust. Do nothing to put them on guard. But could it be done? Would it make the difference? Could she, Luise, make a difference in this time and place?

She pushed herself laboriously from her chair and waddled outside to sit in the shade of the birch trees and smell the sweet breeze of spring, to watch the clouds drift across the sky, to focus on God and think the deep thoughts that Tante Manya had brought to mind. Indeed, what could she do to make one person's life more bearable? In her present condition, there was not much more she could do but pray. Then she chastened herself for thinking of it as the least thing. She would pray. Daily.

Daniel had been brought into the collective meetings, along with every other able-bodied man, with the exception of Schoolmaster Fast and one of the other farmers who lived on the outskirts of the village. Apparently, even the patience and far-sightedness of Jakob Siemens seemed not to stretch to the extent of working with those men. To the chagrin of the children, Nela and Hans among them, Fast would be allowed to remain at his desk in the schoolhouse at

Shumanovka. Luise had neither the will nor the ability at present to fill his shoes. He would finish out his year of teaching until the children took a well-deserved break during the summer. The older boys had already turned their backs on the schoolhouse in favor of working alongside their fathers and uncles in the fields.

৺

"We have become a model for the collective farm plan." Abram had brought the news home from his work at the village office, which had now expanded to include all the paperwork necessary for the Shumanovka Kolkhozy. He would know the details of the workings of the collective and would therefore be a great asset to Siemens' leadership and planning. Siemens proved to be a leader worthy of the trust the men placed in him. The seeding of the crops—wheat, rye and sunflowers—went so smoothly and efficiently that the GPU officials were amazed.

"The GPU secretary is so pleased by the cooperation of the Shumanovka farmers that he has promoted Jakob Siemens to more responsibility," Daniel told Luise when they were alone. "It will most likely demand all his time from now on."

"So things are humming along as they should, then."

"You could say that, but the relationship of our people and our Soviet bosses is still as insecure as a weed seed in the wind. We are dealing with people here, not facts in black and white, and these people do not have our best interests in mind. We must show them a strong work ethic and be willing to follow their commands."

Luise broke eye contact. "Have you discussed, in any of your frequent cloistered meetings, the boundaries of your cooperation, as it affects your family and your future?"

He seemed affronted by her challenge. "Of course we have. We have our beliefs, our consciences to live with. We will not step over that line."

"It is difficult to believe that several hundred people are

all agreed on where that line will be drawn."

"Well," he pulled at his ear, a sure sign of discomfort she had observed, "there are differences of opinion regarding some matters, but for the most part, Luise, we are agreed on how far we will bend to their demands."

She sighed, not wanting to be difficult. "Is Ivan still in the Shumanovka office?"

"Of course. Your father would have told us, I'm sure, if he had been transferred."

"My father avoids any mention of Ivan because he knows it frightens me, but I want to know if there are any changes there."

Daniel smoothed her hair and lifted her chin. "Please don't waste precious hours and days worrying about him. He is not worth the bother. We pray, we take care not to put you in vulnerable situations, and your father and I do out best to watch over you."

"I know, and I appreciate it. It just seems to me that if it happened a third time, well, he might succeed." Her hands gently rubbed her belly and she felt the answering kick. Smiling, she motioned Daniel over.

"Here, feel it. Our son is a strong one."

Daniel seemed entranced by the movement of his unborn son. Then he grinned. "Wouldn't it be a surprise if he turned out to be she? She seems to have the determination and feistiness of her mother."

"Oh you! Go back to work."

He kissed the end of her nose and left the house, his smile still in place. Apparently, he really wouldn't mind if it were a girl. If only they could enjoy this time instead of living with the overwhelming worry of what the future might hold. She tried to put her fears aside, but they hovered like flies on spoiled food.

With the summer sun and the busyness of gardening and the slowness of her movements, Luise found her cares and worries easing. She was too busy to think about much more than keeping up with the weeds in the garden, sewing diapers and baby layette, and keeping Hans and Nela out of their mother's way since they did not have school to occupy their time.

Daniel had returned from the fields at dusk the previous night, eaten a hasty supper, and then left with a quick kiss and a thank you for the meal, not to return until Luise had retired to bed. She knew he needed to keep up with the business of the farm, but she didn't like him gone so often.

Her father had left also, but at a later time, and he had set out in a different direction. To one watching from the shadows, it all seemed rather clandestine. What were the men up to that required secrecy? How many meetings were needed to plan the work of the collective? All they had to do was follow the commands they were given and allow Jakob Siemens to organize them. Luise did not complain, but she certainly wondered.

During the pleasant evenings, Luise sat in company with Tante Manya, sewing the baby clothes while Anna watched and sometimes helped from her cot on one side of the room. Anna seemed to have improved slightly with the coming of summer, as if the warmth dispelled some of the congestion in her lungs. Even her temperament had shown improvement, for which Luise was doubly grateful.

During these evenings, the three women shared advice and experiences and stories of childbirth, although Luise would have preferred not to know some things. She felt apprehensive as her delivery drew near, hoping the midwife could be summoned in time.

Luise had felt strange since the day before the baby came. It was as if she could not harness her energy. She had to use it. When Tante Manya had seen her industriously weeding the garden, she had shuffled outside.

"Nah, Lise, what is with you? You want the baby to

come before its time?"

Luise stopped, pushing her damp hair behind her ears, wiping the perspiration from her face.

"He can come anytime he wants, Tante Manya. I'm ready."

Her aunt shook her head and beckoned to her. "You come sit down and I will get Hans to fetch you some buttermilk from the cooling hole in the back yard. Daniel and Abram can help with this when they return home for supper."

Bunching her lips, Luise put her hands on her hips. "I wanted to have it done, just in case."

"Not all in one day, child," she answered, taking Luise's arm and leading her inside to the rocking chair, "and I do not think it will be well received." She looked meaningfully at Luise, who surrendered with a puff of breath.

"Very well. I just needed to do something."

"Seems to me you have enough to do already, and you need to be saving this energy for the baby's coming. It won't be long."

Tante Manya poured them each a glass of buttermilk and sat on the soft chair to visit.

"Do you ever feel cheated that you were not blessed with children, Tante?"

The old woman sipped her cooling drink and shook her head. "I have learned long ago that the key to a happy life is to accept what you have and not cry about what you do not have. Otherwise you miss something else. Life's best times sometimes happen as we are busy worrying about other things. Take time to notice them and you will be blessed."

Luise smiled at her great-aunt. "You have been one of the greatest blessings in my life." She did not complete her sentence—more like a mother than anyone else—in the presence of her stepmother, but she was sure Tante Manya understood her unspoken words. She leaned over and patted Luise's hand.

"We will all be here for you when your time comes. I have been praying that the Lord would grant you a safe delivery."

"Thank you, Tante. Right now I am so tired of feeling like a locomotive that I am anxious for the procedure to begin."

She wondered at Tante Manya's wordless nod. Perhaps she should be concerned.

It was later that night, after Daniel and Abram had come home and all had gone to bed, that Luise felt the tightening across her abdomen, as if a large band had been tied there. Breathing deeply to relax, she eventually drifted off, only to be awakened a short time later with another squeezing of her body.

Oh Lord, she prayed, help me through this. I cannot turn back now. I must see this through. She slept then, until morning, and thought perhaps it had been a false alarm, but that thought was dispelled as the morning wore on and she could not longer hide or ignore her labor pains.

"Ah, it begins," said Anna from her cot. "Breathe deeply, girl. It will not be too difficult, not like mine with Nela."

When her labor began in earnest, it was too late to worry about anything but maintaining a degree of calm. She looked around her at Anna, Tante Manya and Frau Klein, and told herself that every woman here, in fact every person in the village and in the entire world, had been born. Each one had a mother who had given birth. If they could do it, so could she. Taking a deep breath, she blew it out and held to the midwife's arm as they walked slowly around the house, stopping when the pain became unbearable.

Hans and Nela had been sent to play at Friesens', a welcome reprieve from their regular chores. To be allowed to accompany the neighbor's children to the creek to fish and swim was a great deal better.

Daniel and Abram had also been banished from the

house, not to show their faces until they were summoned. This was the one thing Luise did not understand, that her husband, father of the child entering the world, should be banned from witnessing the event. If they lived alone somewhere in the far north, he would be her midwife. They would get through this together. But that was not how it was done. The men waited while the women suffered the curse of Eve.

But the time for meditating was past. Now was the time for determination and hard work.

The appearance of the little Martens child into the world that June day of 1930 was a joyous one. As usual, Anna had made an accurate prediction; the labor had not been as difficult as some had endured. By twilight, as the mosquitoes emerged from their hiding places and the flies settled down to wait out the night, Luise was delivered of a beautiful, perfect little son. He balled up his fists and wailed, at which all the women in attendance rejoiced.

Tante Manya's eyes shone as she presented the cleaned, wrapped baby to his mother. Luise was glad she could share this moment with her precious Tante. But as she examined her baby, she forgot everything else but her love for him.

"He's so perfect. Look, he has all his fingers and toes. See him turn his head to my voice? He's looking at me."

Anna had wearily stretched out on her cot, having done more than she had in a long time, and Frau Klein busily cleaned up all traces of the birth and pulled the curtains so Luise could rest. Tante Manya stepped out to summon Daniel, and Luise could hardly wait to present him with his son. She yawned widely and snuggled her son to her side.

When Daniel's eyes adjusted to the dimness of the bedroom where Luise lay sleeping, his eyes darted from her face to the tiny form beside her. It was so small. Was something wrong with it? Had it come too soon? No, Luise had been ready for it.

He crept closer, unwilling to wake Luise after her ordeal, but unable to wait for her to awaken before looking at his precious child. It lay so still.

Tentatively, he reached out to the blanket that swaddled the baby and pulled it back. The face that met his eyes was pink and alive, eyes flitting behind closed lids, tiny mouth pursing. As he pulled the blanket further, two tiny arms flailed and lifted above a head covered in dark fuzz. Daniel watched the baby's face pucker and redden, and stepped back as it gave forth a wail that woke Luise and stunned Daniel.

Eyes darting again to his wife, he apologized. "I didn't mean to wake you, but I had to see…is it a boy?"

Luise's smile widened at the sight of him. "It is a boy and he's anxious to meet his papa."

She re-wrapped the baby, then lifted him in Daniel's direction. He remembered when his brother and sisters had been born, but this was different. He reached out, took the child in his arms and held him to his chest. Then it happened. A sense of wholeness he had seldom experienced crept in through his eyes and hands, seeping through into his emotions. This child whom he had just met was his son. He would love and protect him as long as he had life and strength, would indeed give his life for him.

In amazement, he pulled his devoted gaze away from the baby and let it slide to Luise's eyes, and he knew she understood. He sat carefully beside her on the bed, the baby still close to his chest, all its cries quieted in comfort, and felt a tear slide down his cheek.

Luise reached up and caught it, then brushed her own tears away. "Is this not a miracle, my love? God has given us a son today."

"What shall we name him?"

"He should be Daniel, after you, of course."

"Do you think so? He could also be Abram, you know, or Peter."

"Yes, but I would like him to be Daniel, after you."

"How about shortening it to Danny?"

"All right," said Daniel. "Danny it is."

He lowered the baby to the bed so Luise could also see his face and said, "Dear little man, you are Danny. Today you have been born into our home and forever you have carved a place in our hearts. May God grant you a good and a long life, may you be a man of strength and confidence and joy. May you do what is right, may you love mercy, and may you walk humbly with your God."

Daniel and Luise joined hands as Daniel prayed a prayer of dedication over their son, and at their amens, he awoke and demanded to be fed. Again, Daniel was overwhelmed with love and thankfulness as he watched the bonding of his wife and son. It saddened him to think of the little girl they had lost, that Luise had known inside herself, that he had never been able to see or touch or hold, but he refused to allow Luise to see his sadness. He would deal with that privately. She needed to rest and heal from her labor.

"So Frau Klein was right in her prediction," said Luise, looking up from her nursing.

Daniel's brow wrinkled. "She had a fifty-fifty chance of being correct. Those are good odds."

She smiled at him. "Frau Klein is a special little woman. Stay on her good side, we may need her again."

Children sometimes bring out the worst in people, but little Danny brought out the best in Anna. She reached for him with joy on her face and held him to her narrow chest.

"You are a sweet boy," she crooned. "Yes, little man, you will be your father's right hand man and the pride of your mother."

Luise's skin prickled as she listened to the prophecy of her stepmother, spoken in that voice of knowing. What did her words mean? Was she, Luise, reading too much into them? She wanted to believe Anna spoke from the spirit of knowledge that touched her from time to time, that this little boy would grow up strong and true—and safe. She wondered if all mothers worried so about their children.

That evening, the entire family gathered around the parlor as Abram read from the Bible and discussed the words of Micah 6:8 that Daniel had referred to earlier in his blessing to his son. At the moment, Nela, looking proud and pleased, held little Danny on her lap on the cot next to her mother. Hans waited impatiently for his turn and Tante Manya, for the first time in many years, hovered. To Luise's eyes, it looked as if the baby had also claimed a fair-sized corner of the old woman's heart.

Blessedness flowed over Luise as she let her eyes move from person to person in the room, all the people she cared for the most, together in relative peace and security. Even though she knew it could not last, she would cherish this moment. There would be no lack of help in raising this little boy.

Through a joy-filled autumn, Luise and her family lived as normal a life as they had yet been able to do. Each day was viewed as a treasure, but there were always the niggling reminders of their tentative safety. When Abram returned home from his job at the village office with worry in his eyes, the rest of the family reacted with questions and fears. Worry clouded every joy.

The men of Shumanovka Collective continued their clandestine meetings from time to time until harvest arrived with long hours spent in the fields and not enough energy left at day's end to even worry. Jakob Siemens kept the men organized and working efficiently, and to the satisfaction of the farmers, the GPU Secretary named them a model collective. Luise wondered what it meant.

It was Yevgeny Rashidov who delivered the announcement on Harvest Day, another of Jakob Siemens' ideas.

"You have done very well in your efforts for the Soviet. The Shumanovka Kolkhozy is a model for others to follow, a model of efficiency, of cooperation, of success. It bodes well not only for you as individuals, but as a collective and an extension of the Soviet. It also makes our work easier," he said with a grin. "We applaud you."

He began the applause, and Ivan Mironenko was forced to join in. Ivan, with his grudges and depravity, was not as quick to confirm the positive report brought by Yevgeny, but neither could he deny it. He had not bothered Luise or her family since he had been hit in the head by a stone from Hans' slingshot, and Luise hoped against hope that he never figured out what had hit him. She knew that if he ever found out, there would be hell to pay. He would pursue them to the ends of the earth.

The people of the village and those who had attended the picnic from the other villages that were part of the collective, clapped along with the officials, but all of them wore what Luise called "the look of caution." No one wanted to be noticed. Everyone preferred anonymity. Being an unknown pawn on the chessboard had proven safer than doing anything, good or bad, that brought notice. The only one who managed to handle a higher profile with humble confidence was Jakob Siemens, and Luise envied him his poise.

She wondered how long they could keep up motivation to work hard for the Soviet when all the while they were diametrically opposed to the regime with which they cooperated. However, she kept her mouth closed on the subject. Sometimes, in the privacy of their bedroom or on a moonlit walk beneath the stars once little Danny had been fed and put to bed in his cradle in their bedroom, with Tante Manya hovering and Anna watching, Daniel offered encouragement to her to keep faith in God, that He knew their plight.

The news that arrived in October bothered Luise more than she had expected. Abram told them after Hans and Nela had gone to bed.

"A number of our people have received exit visas through Moscow and have emigrated."

"What in the world!" was Tante Manya's response.

Daniel wanted to know how they had managed it. Luise could see the wheels turning in his mind.

Abram seemed to read his thoughts as well. "Some still have been holding out hope that they can follow their families to Canada and the United States, but those countries, at least Canada, have become more determined to keep out what they call 'useless immigrants.' "

Daniel held Abram's eye. "What are their chances of getting out?"

Luise knew he thought of their little family of three. Perhaps they could manage to slip out with the rest. They were all strong and healthy. But Abram did not hold out much hope.

"Think long and hard about this, Daniel. There are some going to Moscow from here even, hoping still to get exit visas, but if they are unsuccessful, what happens then? I fear for them."

"Who is going from here?"

"Apparently Peter Mandtlers and Heinrich Loewens, you know, the minister. I'm not sure of any others."

"Do they have any contact with the authorities? Any promises?"

"None. That is why I advise you to exercise caution. There may be other ways."

He said no more, and Luise wondered what he meant. She desperately wanted freedom from the bands of oppression that gradually tightened around them like labor pains. She dreamed of it many a night, in fact, but from where would deliverance come? Was their freedom from Soviet servitude to come from a long trek westward across the vast Siberian plains and forests, to Moscow, in hopes of getting exit visas? Or were they to keep their eyes on the distant *Xiao Higgang,* the blue mountains of China? Or were they destined to remain on this soil, working for a meager living, expending their energies and forfeiting their religious and ethnic freedom until such a time as they were swallowed up by the system? That thought made Luise shudder.

Already they were not permitted to have churches in the villages. It was acceptable to gather in small groups in homes, but there was to be absolutely no proselytizing of any kind, either among their own people or among their Russian neighbors. No religious instruction was to take place in the schools—Luise doubted that Schoolmaster Fast found this a problem—and German, of course, was completely outlawed. They still spoke it in their homes and businesses, but Russian had quickly become the language of commerce and daily life, by reason of necessity and survival.

Even though things remained fairly calm on the surface, especially since the collective had been formed and Siemens and his men were behaving according to expectations, there were still instances that made the blood of the villagers run cold.

Only a month ago, one of the men from Kleefeld had gone missing after an altercation with an official about his part-time preaching. His wife and family had no idea what had become of him. Luise felt for the wife, understood what it was like to mourn for someone without closure. And then she thanked God again that He had seen fit to restore Daniel to her. As she looked into the eyes of her baby, she prayed, pleaded with the Lord to allow them to stay together for years to come, according to Anna's predictions, but she knew all was in God's hands and He did not promise an easy road.

From where does my help come, O Lord, she prayed within the silence of her soul. And Scripture she had hidden in her heart long ago answered, "Thy help cometh from the Lord who made the mountains... Be still and know that I am God."

Chapter Thirty-four

The men of the Shumanovka Collective had a plan. Luise read it in Daniel's eyes as he and Abram returned from another meeting at Siemens' place. She noted it on Abram's face when he came home from his work at the collective office on those autumn days when the birch leaves dropped to the ground in painted piles and the blue of the sky gave way to snow gray. She sensed something was afoot, but neither man offered any details.

"Be patient and have faith," were the words given her to chew on, to contemplate and digest. Daniel said it would be better if she knew nothing, but she would have preferred to be the judge of that. She hoped it was a portent of something good, but what good could come to them in this place at this time?

The plan, when she first heard of it, was not the comfort for which she had hoped. In fact, it caused her great consternation.

"What do you mean, you are leaving for the winter?"

Daniel walked beside her with his hands in his pockets, looking fit to burst. "Luise, you must—"

"My dear Daniel, with all due respect for you as my husband, I am quite fed up with the kind of assurances we might make to Nela or Hans. I am a grown woman, your wife, if I may remind you, and my life is as much in the balance as is yours. I no longer wish to be placated with a pat on the head. I want to know what's going on and why on earth you would choose to leave us here without our men. Are you forgetting about Ivan the Terrible?"

She stopped for breath and Daniel silenced her with an

uncharacteristic, "Hold your tongue for one moment, Luise."

His reprimand so surprised her she was left speechless.

"As I tried to say before you rudely interrupted me—yes, you did—you must trust me. It is all for the best."

"That's what you've been saying for the last weeks. How could your leaving—again—be for the best?"

He grimaced and hesitated, obviously choosing his words carefully. "All I can say is that the men of the villages of Shumanovka and New York have decided to offer our services to the Soviet, on behalf of the collective, to go north for lumber this winter. I can say no more now."

"And why is this so important to all the men?"

"It's a matter of earning the trust of the officials."

Luise slipped her hand through his arm and sighed. "Oh, Daniel. I don't understand, but I'll try to be patient. You are married to a woman who can't abide being kept from knowing things. What can you tell me?"

Daniel's other hand came out of his pocket and covered her hand.

"I can promise you will not be left defenseless against Ivan and Yevgeny."

"I'm not worried about Yevgeny, in fact, if not for him, I would have come to harm much sooner than I did. It's only Ivan. How can you promise our safety if you're gone for several months?"

She remembered with growing sadness the months prior to their marriage when Daniel had been forced to accompany the men to the forests to cut lumber, and how she had missed him. Then she was young and eager. Now she felt older and heavier with the responsibility of a child and the rest of her family.

"Will Papa go too?"

She noted a slight hesitation in Daniel's answer. "Abram will not be forced to leave you. With his job at the collective office, he would not be allowed to go, I'm sure. So rest your mind on that account."

"I wish you had an excuse to remain behind as well."

He patted her hand and looked away into the distance. "Let it rest for now, Luise." His words infuriated her, but she could not coax more from him.

That evening as Daniel assisted Abram in his shop attached to the house, he spoke of his conversation with his wife."What am I to say to her? She knows something is afoot and I know she would be trustworthy, but I can't betray my promise to the group, nor can I put her in danger of carrying knowledge that might prove dangerous."

Abram sanded the wood with long, smooth strokes. "You've answered your own question," he said between strokes. "She hates to be left without explanation." Stroke. "She makes you feel you are being extremely unfair." Stroke.

He looked up at Daniel. "You've made the right decision."

He bent over and blew the sawdust off the fine piece of wood. "It won't be long before we will have to tell the women something."

Daniel raised an eyebrow at his father-in-law. "What will we tell them?"

"We'll know when the time comes."

Daniel had a hard time carrying on with the familiar duties of working on the collective, threshing and cleaning and storing the harvested grain, working with the animals, helping Abram with building here and there—without spilling his excitement and fear over to Luise. He felt the distance between them because of his silence, but it was not his choice to alter decisions made by the group. Siemens had been adamant. Goerzen and Kruger and the others had agreed to keep the details between themselves.

Abram took responsibility to tell his family what he thought they needed to know.

"Anna, Tante Manya, children; the men of Shumanovka

and New York have offered the officials in charge of the Shumanovka Collective that they will travel north to the forests and cut and haul wood for the collective this winter, and the plan has been accepted. They plan to leave mid-December and will return when they have collected sufficient wood for our villages."

A somber silence reigned as Nela and Hans watched the adults try to maintain their composure. Luise stood to rock little Danny in her arms, hiding her face in his blankets.

"I've requisitioned the Soviet for wagons, horses and supplies for the endeavor, and these should be arriving any day."

"We must celebrate Christmas early then," said Tante Manya. She stared across the table at Daniel, but instead of casting accusatory looks, her eyes seemed alive with secrets of her own. She smiled at him and carried on with her meal, and he knew that whatever she guessed would remain with her. He dared not meet her eyes again. If Luise should guess something unspoken had come between him and Tante Manya, and that she, Luise, had been excluded, she would breathe fire.

Anna seemed unaware of the pronouncement, so concentrated was she on drawing her next breath.

"What will we do with Mother, Daniel?" whispered Luise when they had retired to their bedroom. "She's dying."

Her accusing tone pierced Daniel's heart, but he held his peace.

"Your father will be here. He'll take care of things."

She glanced at him, then the anger turned to tears and she sobbed into baby Daniel's blanket.

"We swore we would never again be separated. How can you speak so calmly of leaving for months?"

"Luise, don't worry. I promise it will work out."

"The only way it will work out is if you don't go."

He willed her to read the answer in his silence, in his

eyes. He didn't know if she did, but apparently she saw enough to quiet her. Soon he would explain.

By early December, the wagons and horses had been delivered, along with enough supplies to sustain dozens of men for many months, as long as they supplemented their diet with fish and wild game. Tensions moved beyond the Siemens kitchen to all the homes in the villages of Shumanovka and New York, creating no little problem for couples and families.

When Siemens gave the all clear to quietly tell the women the rest of the plan, Daniel breathed a sigh of relief.

❧

"Luise."

Daniel's whisper roused her from the comfort of slipping into sleep.

"What? I am very weary and I don't wish to wake the baby."

"All you need to do is listen. Hear me out and promise not to raise your voice."

All hope of sleep vanished in one cold instant as Luise raised herself on her elbow and stared at her husband in the semi-darkness.

"What on earth is coming now? More secrets you cannot tell me?"

"No more secrets. I'm free to tell you the full truth of the matter."

Cold clamminess descended upon Luise's shoulders and she pulled the blanket up around her neck as she lay down, awaiting Daniel's words.

"We're leaving."

"Yes, I know. Almost all the men are deserting us to cut lumber from the forests for the collective. I cannot be happy about that."

"No, Luise. We are all leaving."

She could not comprehend his meaning. Even intelligent questions evaded her. "What—please explain."

"Wagons, pulled by horses, stocked with supplies. We leave December fifteen for China. The entire villages of Shumanovka and New York."

In spite of the chill in the bedroom, Luise sat bolt upright, her mouth dry and her throat too tight for words. "China? I thought you were…I thought…"

"That's what the plan has been since the beginning, to wait until the authorities trusted us, then to requisition supplies from them for our escape."

Luise sputtered. "Why couldn't you tell me? How are we going to get everything packed, and how will we transport Mother, and Tante Manya is old and the weather is growing very cold already and—"

"Shhh. We can't let the children hear. All must remain calm and normal so we're not suspect. If the authorities should find out, we would forfeit our freedom and years of planning. There are spies among us who report everything they know to the authorities. We simply could not risk telling anyone sooner."

"But how will we be able to prepare in such a short time?"

"Luise." The tenor of his voice arrested her words. "What would you give for your freedom?"

She wished she could read his eyes, but the moonlight only granted her a silhouette of his head. Gradually, she understood.

"Everything except my family."

He nodded in the night. "That is what we will take. Our family. And enough food to see us through until we get to Harbin."

"Harbin?"

"That's where we're headed. We will cross the Amur at night—"

"How?" Her voice squeaked and she covered her mouth with her hands, then continued in a whisper. "There are guards with guns, even machine guns. What if they see us?"

He lay back and she rested her head on his shoulder, pulling the blankets up again to cover both of them against the cold that seeped like an evil thing through the walls of the house.

"We have a plan for the best place to cross. We know there are guns and guards. We are trusting God to give us wisdom and timing on December fifteen. That is the best we can do."

"All that planning, and so much risk."

"It's either that or we die a slow death here, starving or losing our identity and becoming statistics in the Soviet system. I ask you again: what is your freedom worth?"

She nodded into his shoulder. "Tell me the route."

"Across the Amur, then to Kani Fu—some of the others have gone there and the people offer food and shelter in exchange for rubles. Phillip and I have arranged for a Chinese guide to lead us across the river safely. Alexander, he calls himself. He is said to be reliable."

"You have been working with Phillip?"

"We must all work together. Phillip and I grew up almost as brothers. We can trust each other."

"Wonders never cease."

"This is life or death, Luise. Forgive and forget. From Kani-Fu we will make arrangements to carry on to Harbin, most likely by bus or train."

She felt his chest rise and fall deeply as spoke.

"There is much that must be left to the last moment. Even the packing of the wagons. It must appear that the men are heading out to the forests. We're building sides and backs on the wagons behind our stacks of straw."

"That's what you have been doing out there."

"Yes, to be able to pack in people and goods."

She shifted her body and stared up at the ceiling. "It will be very cold for our little Danny. How will we keep him warm?"

"We've requested many sheepskin coats and hats; some

can be redesigned for other uses. There are many blankets. Your own body heat is perhaps best, but you also must stay warm."

"How will we keep him quiet if he gets hungry?"

Daniel didn't answer and she knew there was no answer. They would go out of this land as the people of Israel had left Egypt: in the power and leading of the Lord God Almighty. This leaving would be secretive, but they would nonetheless be in the hands of God. Nothing and no one else could see them through this impossible journey.

Luise slept little that night, thinking of the journey, of the things she must leave behind, of how they would carry Anna and Tante Manya comfortably, of keeping little Danny warm, of what would happen should the guards along the river open fire. When she finally drifted off, it was to a sleep tainted by ice and gunshots and trouble.

❧

"When can we decorate our house for Christmas?" asked Nela. "I love to hang strings of popcorn and paper dolls and tree branches. Schoolmaster Fast won't allow us to talk about Christmas at all, but I want to talk about it at home."

Luise's hands stopped their work on the sheepskin bunting bag she was fashioning for her baby. All must remain calm and normal, Daniel had said.

"Why don't you make some garlands from paper now?" She put down her sheepskin. "I'll pop some corn and we can string it this evening as soon as supper is done."

Nela hopped up and down and danced into the kitchen. "Christmas will be so nice this year with our little baby Danny." She stopped to pat the head of the baby who kicked and squealed on Tante Manya's lap near the fire. "He'll be so happy to see all the pretty things we'll make."

"You're right," agreed Luise. "He needs to see his first Christmas with pretty things around." Who knows what we will see in China. This might be our last chance for quite some time to celebrate in our own home.

"I'll go tell Hans," said Nela, running to the woodshop.

Tante Manya had been quiet since news of the plan had been revealed, and Luise knew she worried about Anna too. Her stepmother had grown worse as the cold weather continued, often sleeping throughout the day, except for the times when rugged coughs shook her bony body. Her eyes had sunk into their sockets and her hair had thinned to a sparse covering of gray. She looked, to Luise, like a woman twice her age.

Abram spent his evenings by her side, reading aloud or silently, stroking her hand, kissing her cheek before he retired to his bed for the night. Luise had also found him there at night, sitting by her side as she rasped in her sleep, watching with sorrow as she slipped away from them.

How would they transport her to China? How would she withstand the trauma and the cold and the roughness of the ride?

"What worries you now, Lise?" Tante Manya jiggled baby Danny on her knees.

Luise watched them as she measured out popping corn. "She won't make it," she whispered.

Tante Manya shook her head. "No. Likely not even until December fifteen."

"But what will do we do if she's still with us?"

"You will leave her here with me, that's what."

Luise's hands stilled and she stared at her great-aunt with open mouth. "What?"

"I believe 'pardon me' is the proper phrase. She will remain with me for as long as she lives."

"What are you saying?" Luise's heart pounded.

Tante Manya's voice remained calm, but Luise detected a tremor in her cheek. "I have traveled from idyllic South Russia to Orenburg in the Urals, then to rugged Slavgorod Colony, and now here to Shumanovka. I will not move again; I am too old. If it weren't for your plight, I would have remained in Alexandrovka. It is winter and we have no home once we arrive in China. I would not survive it either. So stop worrying about Anna. I will be here to care for her as long as she lives and breathes."

"But…but Tante Manya, how would you manage? What would you eat? How would you get wood for the fire? How…how would I live without you?" Sobs rose in Luise's throat and choked out her words.

"Stop, child, before you break my old heart, eh?" Tante Manya held the baby to her chest and touched her wrinkled cheek to his smooth, new one. When she could summon her voice once again, she continued. "My days have been long and eventful, and the good Lord has granted me many pleasures and blessings, but my life is nearly over. The last phase shall be lived right here in this fine house my Abram has built. There is much wood in the shed. It will see us through. We will shut off the rooms we don't use and share the parlor and kitchen. That is all we require."

Luise stood in the middle of the kitchen, tears falling freely onto her apron. "But what if they hurt you? You know Ivan. And there may be others, when we are all gone, who prey upon the defenseless. What will you do once Mother is gone and you are alone?"

"The Reds have no use for a withered old woman like me. If they shoot me, so be it. I am not afraid."

"How can you be so calm? This is the end of the world."

Tante Manya's eyes pierced Luise's. "No, it is not. It is a new beginning for you, a new life in a new world. As for me, I will soon walk, free of aches and pains, on golden streets; eat fruit from the trees along the river of life; enter the crystal city through gates of solid pearl, see my Lord Jesus, the One who died that I might have eternal life. When once I am there, I will not look back to this short time of suffering. No, Lise, remember my love for you and then let me go to reap my reward." Her eyes shone with a light that eased into Luise's soul.

Little Danny began to squirm and Luise came to nurse him. Tante Manya took her place at the counter and poured oil into the pot. "This popcorn will taste wonderful."

"I'll make sure to leave a large sack full of roasted zwieback for you and Mother." Luise shook her head as the tears fell again. She couldn't believe what was happening, that her stepmother, as bitter and difficult as she was, lay near death in the next room, and that her beloved Tante Manya would not travel with them to the new country and freedom. She felt she might die of a broken heart, if it weren't for those who relied on her: little Danny, her husband, Nela and Hans. And Abram. He wouldn't leave his wife. She knew he wouldn't. She had not thought freedom would be so costly.

Chapter Thirty-five

Luise stood near Anna's cot.

"She struggles on," said Abram. "Her heart is strong, even though her spirit is failing." He held her hand.

"Do not speak of me as though I were already dead." The words whistled through Anna's lips and Abram leaned in to hear them.

"Forgive me, my dear. It's difficult to see you struggle."

"Going home. Luise."

"Luise? You wish to speak to Luise?"

She nodded almost imperceptibly and Luise handed baby Danny to his father and drew near. Anna pulled her hand from Abram's and reached weakly for Luise.

"Forgive me."

"Mother, there's nothing to forgive. I love you."

Anna seemed restless, turning her head from side to side. "Forgive me," she wheezed, her eyes fired with determination to convey her message. "Harsh toward you. Jealous of you and Abram." Her eyes fell closed and a tear escaped and rolled down into the pillow. Luise brushed the tired cheek with her hand and leaned over to kiss it.

"All is forgiven, Mother. Go freely into the next life. We will see you there soon."

A slight smile trembled on the woman's lips. "Not soon," she whispered. "You will travel far…love much…live long. I know this…"

Luise's pulse beat in her ears as she listened to Anna's predictions. They had proved true in the past and she hoped they would prove true in the future. She moved aside so Abram could resume his place at her side.

Anna locked eyes with her husband. "So kind…always…so good." Her eyes closed and the air felt heavy with anticipation, with dread, with the unknown crowding into the room.

Tante Manya moved near, Nela on one side of her and Hans on the other, their eyes wide with confusion, their hands clinging to those of their dear aunt. They sat down on the divan and Tante Manya lifted her voice in prayer.

"Father God, we sit in Thy presence as Anna takes leave of us and comes to Thee. Accept her in Jesus' name. Grant her peace, Lord, and take her gently to Thy side. Also grant us peace as we sit in Thy presence here. Remove from us all fear and dread, protect us from the evil one and bless us with joy even now. In Jesus' name and for His sake we pray, Amen."

A chorus of amens followed, and the very air of the room lifted and lightened. Luise felt it. he looked at Daniel and knew he felt it too. And Abram. Suddenly Anna's eyes flew open, she uttered a cry of joy, reached up her hands, and then collapsed onto the bed, a lifeless, shriveled shell.

Blessed silence reigned as the family allowed the peace of God to surround and fill their hearts.

"Is Mama dead?" Hans was the first to recover his voice.

Abram nodded his head, his eyes shedding their sorrow in tears as he folded his wife's hands over her chest.

"Mama?" Nela's cry stabbed at Luise's heart. She watched the girl run to her father and stare at her mother.

"You may touch her, little one. Kiss her. She's not far away and I think she knows us yet." Abram hugged his daughter and waited for her to reach out to her mother.

"She's so quiet now. Is she with Jesus? In heaven?"

Abram nodded again. Luise wanted to go to him, but knew she could not stem the tide of his grief. It would ebb and flow as he came to terms with the reality of Anna's absence. Luise could feel Anna's presence yet in the room, as if only a thin veil separated them, as if she could almost see through it.

They sat surrounding Anna's bed for the entire evening. At one point, Tante Manya went to the kitchen and set out some buns and butter. The children would be hungry, she said, even if the rest of them were not. A hallowed aura settled on the house and remained there until, spent and weary, they covered Anna and each went to see if sleep would come in their own beds.

Early the next morning, December fourteen, the women prepared Anna's body, and as the word spread down the streets and avenues of Shumanovka, people dropped by to offer condolences or to bring food or to offer an embrace. Luise felt the love of those around her as never before. Even Hertha shed more tears than words when she came to view Anna's body. They were united in their hopes and dreams and plans, these people of Shumanovka and New York.

They would hold a short memorial service in the afternoon and lay Anna to rest in a grave chiseled out of the frozen ground in the cemetery. Daniel and Phillip had set to work on that already, having lit a fire on the gravesite to draw out some of the frost. There was much to do, and the Lord had known they needed to see Anna off together. They would adjust. But how would they leave Tante Manya, who was still very much alive, and who would remain alone when they left? This occupied Luise's mind constantly, and she could find no peace for it.

❧

The morning of December fifteen, Daniel helped Abram pack his woodworking tools. The officials might not be surprised when Abram did not show up for work tomorrow since his wife had just passed away, but they would never expect him to run off. No one would expect two entire villages to escape at once. It was unheard of. Daniel shook his head at the foolhardiness of their plan. How could they ever accomplish this? A prayer settled his nerves for the moment and he continued to wrap his favorite tools in rags and position them carefully in a small box.

He preferred to stay out of Luise's path today. She would be anxious enough without having him wandering around the house with nothing to do but get in the way.

Luise threw the sack of roasted zwieback onto her bed beside the rolls of blankets and clothing. Hams and sausages, all prepared and packed, sat boxed on the floor. Sheepskin coats, hats, boots and mitts lay ready to pull on. An air of nervous excitement permeated the household and Luise had trouble controlling her thoughts.

Moving into the parlor, she untied one of the blanketed packages—her violin case—drew out her mother's instrument and tightened the bow. Looking at the cot where Anna had lain for so long, she realized her music would no longer bother the woman. She raised the violin to her chin and closed her eyes, allowing the bow to sing and sigh against the strings. She played softly, tears of release running down her face.

Tante Manya wandered into the parlor and sat in her rocking chair staring at the fire, listening to the music. Luise watched the old woman's shoulders heave as she rocked, and closed her eyes again. This is all too much, Lord. It can't happen. She put the violin and bow back in their case and went to kneel at Tante Manya's feet, tears streaming down her face.

The old woman put her hand on Luise's head and stroked her hair.

"The tears of an old woman. Pay them no heed."

"Tante Manya, I simply cannot leave you alone. Not now, not ever. Perhaps if Mother were still here, but not alone."

"Who said I would be alone?"

"Wh—pardon me?"

Tante Manya smiled and wiped her nose with her

handkerchief. "I do not intend to stay alone. Frau Klein is not willing or able to leave either."

"Frau Klein? Why did you not say something to me?"

"Because I did not know. We spoke yesterday after the burial and made our plans. Her house is smaller, she is younger and is able to cut the wood and keep the fire going. I'm able to help and we will keep each other company."

"But she is…her house…it is very dirty, Tante Manya. Have you seen it?"

"Ach, jah. I will help her clean it up until it shines. Mark my words, it will be a changed place."

Luise sat stunned on the floor, her hand encased in her aunt's wrinkled one. "You could knock me over with a feather," she said. "In a thousand years I would never have worked this out."

"That's because you were not meant to. It has been a matter of prayer for me, and God answered yesterday. Our God is a merciful God. He knows our hearts and our abilities, and so He placed Frau Klein and me together for the duration of our years."

Tante Manya chuckled. "We will get to see the reaction of the officials, of Ivan the Terrible and that poor young Yevgeny Rashidov. Perhaps once you're settled, we will be able to write to you of what happened.

"Now, no more tears. We have both shed enough for years, I think. Let us pack up your violin safely again and get some food ready for the family. Nela and Hans will need to eat anyway. They know something is afoot. Hans knows more than we give him credit for. Help me up, child."

"Luise."

Daniel motioned with his head toward the bedroom and she joined him there.

"What is it, Daniel?"

"Your father and I have an errand to take care of before tonight. We'll return shortly."

Luise's alarm showed in her eyes and he determined not to cause her any more anxiety than he already had. "Nothing to worry about. We need to make a visit to Schoolmaster Fast and a farmer on the outskirts of the village."

"Whatever for?"

"They are the spies among us. They've been reporting to Ivan all along whenever they think they have worthwhile information."

Luise slapped her thigh. "I knew he was evil through and through. What are you going to do with them?"

"May I tell you when I return? Then I'll know how it went."

"All right, but I don't know why you bother with the likes of them."

"Because they are people, our people. 'What does the Lord require of you but to act justly, to love mercy and to walk humbly with your God.' That's how Micah records it."

"You're a generous man, Daniel Martens. Much more so than I."

He smiled and kissed her cheek, hoping he would remember mercy when he saw Schoolmaster Fast and his accomplice.

Daniel and Abram were greeted briskly when Fast opened his door to their knock.

"What do you want?"

Fast's stern greeting made Daniel feel as if he were still in school and had been caught dipping someone's braid in his inkwell. He winced, then remembered the seriousness of his present task.

"We would like to speak with you, Abram and I," he said. "It is of the utmost secrecy and importance."

Something flickered in Fast's eyes and he stepped back to admit them into his spartan cottage down the street from the school where he had taught the past three years.

"Are you alone?" asked Abram, his eyes checking the

house.

"Yes. Jasch has gone to live with Wielers, so I live alone. There is no one else here."

The three men seated themselves around the kitchen table and Daniel looked to Abram to proceed.

"We are making an escape, Mr. Fast."

The schoolmaster's eyes widened and Daniel thought he saw excitement in them.

"Really? When? Is there any way I can help? Why was I not told sooner?"

"You were not told because everyone knows of your betrayal of us to Rashidov and Mironenko."

"My what?"

Daniel could not contain himself. "You are a dirty spy and we detest what you have done, but mercy and brotherhood demand that we give you another chance. So keep your mouth shut and listen."

Daniel looked to Abram and saw a nerve twitch in his jaw.

"Fast, we tell you this plan, as Daniel said, because of mercy, not that you deserve to know. We give you two choices: either you come with us—and we will keep you from spreading the word until we leave—or we tie up you and your accomplice, Farmer Froese, and let you explain it to the officials once we are safely away. What is your choice?"

Daniel watched Fast's face pale, his eyes blink rapidly as he processed this surprising scenario. He sputtered a bit, then said, "I…I will of course go with my brethren. I will not speak of it to anyone."

"No, you will not," replied Daniel. "Now, allow us to help you gather together some of your most prized treasures and we will proceed to another place until it is time to leave."

The absurdity of the situation hit Daniel's funnybone and he had to hide his amusement as Fast scurried about like a headless chicken, trying to decide what to take. Finally, he heaped up his belongings in the tiny porch, to be picked up later in one of the wagon-sleds, and preceded Abram and Daniel out of the house.

Daniel knew the state of Luise's nerves, so he had arranged for Fast to stay at the home of a widower with a grown son instead of at the Letkemann house.

"How did it go?" Luise's expression relayed her curiosity.

"We told Fast about our escape plan and invited him along."

"I modify my opinion of you: you are a generous man but also a crazy one. He's a spy, you told me so yourself. He does not deserve—"

"None of us deserves anything, Luise. We are all despicable sinners without the saving grace of Christ."

She shook her head and said nothing more.

That evening Daniel sat holding his small son in his arms, wondering what else he should do. He thought the ticking of the Kroeger clock would drive him mad. The pendulum swung back and forth as it had in Alexandrovka, incessantly marking the hours as if nothing had changed. In fact, everything had changed and today the lives of all those present, of all those in the villages of Shumanovka and New York, would be altered forever.

Tired of waiting, he stood suddenly, upsetting little Danny. Luise shushed the child, throwing Daniel an annoyed glance. The heaviness of the future weighed on him so he felt he could scarcely breathe.

"Nine o'clock. I'll go harness the horses."

Abram stood too. "I'll help you."

As they pulled on their sheepskin coats and hats, a knock at the door stilled them. Who could it be? Everyone should be busily harnessing their own horses or packing belongings onto the wagons. Perhaps Frau Klein had come to fetch Tante Manya. Daniel pulled open the door.

"Trouble," said a young boy. "We cannot go tonight."

"What?" Daniel couldn't believe the words. "What has happened that we cannot go? Who says this?"

"Siemens' order. Not tonight. I know nothing else." The boy stood stamping his feet and blowing into his hands. His nose, the only thing that could be seen of his face, was red with the cold. He stood a moment more and then ran off to the next house.

Daniel closed the door against the bitter cold and stared around at the rest of them. After a moment's thought, he said, "I'm going to Siemens' place to find out what has happened."

Without a word, Abram also pulled on his coat and mitts, and followed Daniel out the door.

Daniel pulled his hat down low over his face. There was no wind, but the air itself cut like a saber. He huddled into his coat and hurried down the alleys toward Siemens' place. Neither of them spoke. There was nothing more to say until they knew more.

The snow crackled and snapped under their boots, and Daniel wondered if his nose would freeze before they arrived. Once there, he saw several others wanting to know the details also. Siemens looked pained, and his wife as anxious as any of them.

"Please, quiet." Jakob Siemens motioned them inside, eight men stamping cold feet.

"There has been a complication." Siemens looked at a figure standing in the kitchen drinking hot coffee. "Mr. Mierau here has come from New York just a half hour ago. He says they are not ready to leave; they will need another week or so."

A murmur rose from the Shumanovka men and Siemens held up a hand for silence.

"We must sell our flour first," said Mierau. "We need the money for the journey."

"Why did you not deal with this sooner?" said Daniel.

"Besides, the Shumanovka Collective distributed flour and sunflower oil to every family with our flight in mind. You knew the date. We are ready to go and we must remain with our plans."

"You cannot go without us."

"We must. It's too dangerous to wait. We are ready."

"It is too late tonight," said one man.

Mierau lifted his chin and glared at the assembled men. "One week. If you do not wait, we will report you to the authorities."

"What?" Daniel burst out. "We are brothers. How could you even consider this?"

"Yes, we are brothers. You need to wait." He hesitated as if embarrassed to continue. "We will have guards watching you. We will report you if you leave."

More murmuring followed and Daniel felt the anger and disappointment like a living thing in the room. What could they do? The messenger seemed adamant, and they could not risk being reported. With sighs and mutters, the men of Shumanovka dispersed into the winter night, throwing looks of disgust at Mierau.

Daniel and Abram arrived home with the news: no escape this night. If there had been tension in the air before, it now increased exponentially.

"We may as well go to bed," said Abram. "There's nothing else we can do."

He led Hans and Nela to their beds and headed to his room. Meanwhile, Luise took baby Danny into her room and closed the door behind her. Daniel watched her go and turned to Tante Manya.

"Is it now my fault that we do not go? Am I shut out of my room because of the bad decisions of the people of New York?"

Tante Manya shook her head. "You are not shut out. She is tired and on edge."

"And I am not?"

The old woman smiled at him. "One more week with the family I love."

He grimaced and hung his head. "I'm sorry. I can't think about you staying behind. Perhaps you should—" but she was shaking her head.

"Do not speak of it again, son. The decision has been made."

Perhaps this whole plan was too ridiculous to work anyway. Perhaps this was the Lord's way of keeping them from being shot. Perhaps...there were so many questions swirling in his head he could not think clearly. Give me strength, he prayed. Let me trust in you. Let those in New York listen to reason. But who would speak reason to them?

He stood before Tante Manya with a sudden but clear decision. "I will go to New York. I will reason with them."

"It's so cold, Daniel. You will freeze."

"No, I'll wrap myself warmly. I must go. After all, my own family is there."

He glanced at the door of his room and then back at Tante Manya. "Tell her for me. I must go immediately. Perhaps we can still salvage our plans, try for tomorrow."

"You will tell Jakob Siemens?"

He shook his head. "I'll just go. I need to go."

Tante Manya's face pulled together in what Daniel had come to translate as disapproval, but she only nodded. "Very well. I will pray—and Daniel, stop at Frau Klein's for her horse. An Altai will manage the cold better than any other. She'll not mind."

Daniel nodded. He hesitated as he passed the door of his bedroom, but decided he could not deal with an argument this evening. He must ride as quickly as possible and make the men of New York understand the serious ramifications of further delay.

Chapter Thirty-six

Luise awoke feeling confused. Where was Daniel? The baby slept soundly beside her, since his crib was packed full of travel goods in their wagon-sled. Shivering, she remembered putting him to bed and crawling in herself, upset beyond words that the escape would be delayed, unfairly upset that Daniel could not make things right. She had needed to be alone, but now that she was, she longed for the presence of her husband beside her to calm her and speak reassurances. Where was he?

She pulled a robe about her and pushed her feet into her felt slippers before venturing out to the kitchen. On her way through the parlor, she saw Tante Manya kneeling before her chair, head in her hands, murmurs of prayers escaping her lips. What had happened? Was it Daniel? Why was Tante Manya alone?

Luise moved to put her arm around Tante Manya's shoulders, and the old woman started at the touch.

"Tante Manya, the floor is too cold for you to kneel here. Come, let me wrap you up. What has happened?"

She wrapped a heavy blanket about her aunt's shuddering shoulders and helped her onto the divan. Sitting beside her, she held her and asked again, "What has happened?"

The old woman's lips looked blue with cold and Luise's heart turned over at the sight.

"He asked me to tell you…didn't want to worry you…didn't want to wait to convince you."

"Convince me? Of what?"

"He rode to New York to try to reason with them there,

convince them to follow the original plan."

Luise sat back in alarm, her mouth dry, her eyes wide. "He'll freeze to death."

"No more than you all would have, going out this night."

The door of Abram's room opened and he peered out. When he saw the women, he joined them and they repeated their story.

Abram shook his head. "That man is as stubborn as his father was."

The truth of his remark made Luise sputter, but she could not argue. Daniel did not resemble his father in size or looks, but certainly in spirit. She desperately hoped and prayed that this latest leap to what seemed reasonable to him would not create greater problems or endanger him in any way.

"I'll make some tea so we don't all freeze to death," said Luise, as Abram bent to build up the fire.

After nursing Danny, Luise held him as she dozed in the rocking chair. She awoke later with a nasty pain in her neck from sleeping in such poor posture, and the events of the night returned to her in a rush. "Lord, protect my husband," she prayed as she lifted her wide-awake baby and jostled him on her knee. "Bring him back safely and soon."

Even as she prayed, she knew he would stay for as long as he felt it might take to make a difference. He was surely impulsive, but he was also determined.

A sharp rap on the door interrupted their quiet breakfast. Abram answered the summons and the same lad who had knocked the night before slipped into the room. His eyes glowed with excitement as he pulled his hat back and addressed Abram.

"Secret meeting right now at Siemens' place. You and Daniel are to come."

Abram reached for his wraps. "On my way."

"And Daniel?"

"He's not here. I will come alone."

The boy pulled his hat tight, earflaps snug, and ran outside. Abram followed without looking back.

Warmed by a roaring fire, Hans and Nela played games in the parlor while little Danny cooed and flailed near them. Tante Manya sat and took it all in. Luise wondered at the significance of this delay. Was there more to it than she had thought? Was it really God's way of stopping them from a serious mistake?

Her thoughts were interrupted by Abram's entrance, huffing at the cold. Luise threw a blanket over the baby until the door closed and the fire warmed the room again. She looked up at her father, trying to read his thoughts, but he seemed to be taking his time to hang up his things.

"Papa, what was that about?"

He turned then, his lips pursing, hands clenching. He rubbed them together as he squatted before the fire. Looking up at Luise through his brows, he said, "We are leaving tonight. Same plans as last night. We wait for the signal and pull out about ten o'clock."

"But what about the guards from New York?"

Abram shrugged his shoulders. "It's beastly cold out there, getting colder. The nights are so clear there is no cloud cover even. At least the moon is quite full; we should be able to see our way. They will never suspect us of being crazy enough to go in this weather."

"The enemy may also see us more clearly."

Abram leveled his gaze at her. "We go with God. He's in control."

Pulling her lips together, Luise nodded. "Yes, well I'll feel better once Daniel returns."

As the day dragged on, Luise was sure the clock had slowed. The seconds ticked by, the minutes gradually passed, but the hours seemed to stretch on endlessly. Perhaps the time moved slowly to allow for Daniel's return. As daylight fled with the early setting sun, Luise's worries began to solidify into one: what if Daniel did not come back in time? If he missed the escape, the officials would arrest him. He would be returning to walk into their hands. What should she do? Should she remain here with their son, while the others left? Tante Manya would be here. But what if she stayed and Daniel was arrested and taken away, and she was alone?

I have already gone through this particular testing, Lord. Do You not remember how I waited for Daniel when he was away cutting lumber, and then again for two and a half years while he was in exile? Must I go through it again? Please, Lord, give me some sign that he will be safe.

She wished then that her stepmother were here to offer one of her predictions. Then she remembered what Anna had said before she died, that they would live a long, good life together. She would hang onto that prophecy with all her heart and pray it came true.

As evening closed in around them, the household again prepared themselves for flight. All was in readiness. The horses had been harnessed, belongings stashed onto wagons, coats and blankets ready to wrap up in. Daniel's mother, sisters and brother had arrived in the early afternoon, ostensibly for a visit, their sled packed with the essentials for flight. And still Daniel had not returned. Luise knew all the family prayed fervently for his return. God is in control, she told herself repeatedly.

She scraped some of the thick ice off the window and looked out. She saw a man ride past on a horse. Daniel? Abram came up behind her and followed her gaze.

"Someone from New York, most likely," he said.

Luise let the curtain fall back into place. Fear sat like a stone in her stomach. She could not eat; she could scarcely breathe. She could certainly not sit still, so she continued to wander from one frosted window to another, wondering how they would escape under the watchful eyes of their "brethren." She checked the thermometer. The mercury huddled at the bottom, registering forty degrees below zero, Réaumur.

"A couple of young men have volunteered to go out to the road leading to Konstantinovka to make sure none of the GPU officials are approaching." Abram paced as he spoke.

Everyone jumped as they heard wagon runners slicing the snow. Had they missed the signal? Were the wagons pulling out without them? Perhaps it was Daniel. Luise raced to the door and opened it, but the sled continued on past. What was happening? Was it someone from New York? Were they going to report to the GPU?

"Shut the door, Luise, it's freezing in here."

Hans' voice cut through Luise's panic and she closed the door and leaned against it.

She watched the hands of the clock move close to midnight. "I cannot stand this tension a minute more. We were supposed to leave by ten." What had happened to the plan? Had Daniel come back and tried to persuade Siemens and the others to postpone the escape, just as New York had demanded?

"Well," Tante Manya's words interrupted the ticking of the Kroeger, "I would imagine the men from New York have given up for the night. No one in his right mind would attempt an escape on a night like this."

"Truer words were never spoken," said Luise. She glanced at the window again. Where was Daniel?

A series of shrill whistles split the silence and several dogs barked, the sound traveling through the village as if by megaphone. Abram leaped to the pile of coats and began passing them out. Numbly, Luise wrapped little Danny in his sheepskin bunting with the foldover hood she had created and nestled him in a bag inside her own coat, while Tante Manya helped Nela and Hans secure their wraps.

"Don't forget to cover your faces," she instructed. "You do not want to arrive in China without a nose. Everyone would laugh at you."

The children giggled nervously and Luise fought the pain welling up inside her. I won't think about it now. I must stay in this moment.

Abram took the children out to the wagon hidden behind the straw bales in the yard and Luise gave Tante Manya one last hug before she followed him.

"We will drop you at Frau Klein's on our way out."

Other families bustled across the street in the direction of the wagons to which they had been assigned. Their voices carried across the frozen air like sound across water in summer. Mothers shushed their children, fathers shushed their wives. Horses nickered and stamped. Wagons and sleds creaked as they settled under the weight of people and belongings.

The sleds pulled out into the main street, one after the other, lining up as they arrived from the homes and farms surrounding the village. Abram helped Tante Manya out at Frau Klein's and there was no time for tears. Nothing more than a swift, final embrace.

Somewhere, Luise knew, Schoolmaster Fast and his accomplice had been inserted among them. Sled upon sled, they moved like a parade, but Luise hoped and prayed that no one watched them who did not take part.

"There must be a hundred wagons," guessed Hans.

"Sixty," answered Abram. "Should be 217 people, if all are accounted for. No more talking now, son."

Two hundred sixteen people, thought Luise, her heart aching within her at the thought of setting off without Daniel—again. They were leaving the country, crossing a border, then possibly an ocean. She needed him by her side. Oh God, please.

One man, dressed in furs, walked ahead and motioned the sleds to follow. Luise looked to Abram. "Siemens?"

He shook his head. "Alexander. Our Chinese guide."

So, they were in the hands of a stranger, one who might

or might not get them to freedom. Abram had told her each family owed Alexander a horse upon arrival in Kani- Fu. She supposed that might be incentive enough to get them safely across. He would own many horses before the night was over, if all went according to plan.

Luise sat in the middle of the sled, surrounded by family, friends and neighbors, and cuddled baby Danny to her chest. They huddled under the shelter of a tarp the men had rigged as a protection against the elements. The cold air burned its way into Luise's lungs, searing her nostrils, and she fretted constantly about whether her little one had enough air. The sled bounced over a mound of snow and she readjusted the baby's blankets, her mind bouncing back and forth from his welfare to that of her absent husband. Her every breath became a prayer.

The sled runners slid through the snow along the road from Shumanovka toward the river. The wagons followed it for a time, then left the road in order to move farther from the villages. They could not afford to alert anyone to their escape.

Cold. So cold the snow under the sled runners snapped like breaking sticks and Luise's breath escaped in clouds that nearly froze solid before dissipating. The horses strained against the traces, heads down in their effort to break a trail through knee-deep snow.

A dog barked in Orlovka one kilometer ahead and all sixty sleds halted, horses stamping nervously. Luise knew of the Soviet guards stationed there with a machine gun to prevent citizens from fleeing. In recent months, the guard contingent had quadrupled at the river. Apparently, Alexander knew how to avoid them. Also, there was the fact that the men had originally been scheduled to leave for the northern forests about this time. But certainly they wouldn't have left at midnight on the coldest night of the year.

The sled train moved into deeper snow and she heard a crack like gunfire and a muffled command, "Whoa there,

Gypsy. Whoa." The entire caravan stopped. "Broken axle." The words passed from mouth to mouth, wagon to wagon. Every person shivered from a combination of cold and nerves. Would morning see them free or under arrest…or dead?

Luise's skin, beneath layers of wool and furs, crawled with fear and cold. Surely anything would be better than living within the squeeze of Bolshevism with spies around every corner and taxes that exceeded production and threat of arrest and imprisonment for living out their faith, but she had not counted on the degree of cold and fear. Daniel's question came back to her: how much would you give for your freedom?

They moved again, jerking along until the horses established a rhythm. Her silent chant as the sled bounced and slid over the frozen terrain distilled into one word: Daniel. Nela whimpered beside her, and Luise covered her with more blankets, considering again the madness of this plan. How could 217 people travel twenty kilometers and cross the wide Amur River on a night when the mercury sank so low that it barely registered? They were crazy to think it could be done, but once the plan had been set in motion, they could not turn back.

The caravan had moved past the villages and neared the river when pounding hoofbeats shattered the stillness of the night. Luise knew when the horse left the beaten track and imagined it plunging through the drifts. She hoped the mount of their pursuer would fall or trip or even break its leg so he could not reach them. She lost track of the horse and rider in the squeak and groan of sixty carriages.

Then she heard voices raised and leaned toward the back of the wagon to see what was happening. She heard questions and answers but not words. The rider caught up to her wagon and then she knew.

Chapter Thirty-seven

"Daniel!"

Her cry was shushed by many mothers and several male voices, but she didn't care. "Daniel, tell me it's you."

"Yes. Quiet now."

Her heart hammering in her chest, Luise whispered her thanks to God and spoke softly to the baby, huddled inside his cocoon of furs inside her own coat. She knew he would not cry; it would hurt his lungs too much to take in this cold air. And she must not; her tears would freeze on her cheeks.

The riverbank was steep. Too steep. A horse's scream split the frozen air, followed by more screams. More shouts. Bedlam. And a single gunshot.

"They've had to shoot a horse. Broken leg," came the explanation whispered from wagon to wagon. Luise wanted to jump out and run across the river to freedom, but instead she pulled her furs around her and shivered in the wagon beside the whimpering Nela.

"Don't fret, Nela," she whispered. "We're almost there. By morning we'll be safe in China."

She reached one arm around her little sister, who snuggled into her.

Quietly, very quietly, Luise sang, *"Nun ade, du mein lieb' Heimatland,"* for it was their beloved homeland to which they now bid farewell, even though the powers in Moscow had betrayed Mother Russia and her people. Others joined softly in the song.

"It won't work!" The words shot into the night like rifle fire.

"Too steep. We'll have to get out."

"All able-bodied people get out." The words passed

through the wagon train and everyone who could move obeyed. They were too cold to argue.

"We'll have to ease the sleds down so they don't tip over."

Luise, already stiff with cold, handed the baby to Greidl, climbed out of the sled, helped Nela down, and reclaimed her bundled baby. Hans jumped out and bounced around to keep warm and wear off his excitement. They stood aside in the bright moonlight, trying not to fall into the deep snow as the men gently coaxed the horses down the steep bank.

One wagon moved too fast, the horse spooked and the entire contents dumped over into the snow. Cries and wails lifted into the night as the wagon was righted and everyone pawed around in the snow to retrieve the contents that had scattered across the surface of the drifts.

Luise caught sight of Alexander, their guide, while the men had stopped to fix another broken sled, and she sensed his impatience as he strode back and forth, motioning with his hands and speaking in Russian.

One by one, the sleds reached the ice and people piled in again, rearranging their meager possessions around themselves, checking to make sure all the children were present. Luise felt the easing of the sled runners as they met the ice. The surface of the Amur was rough, and obstacles loomed up before them, turning into small mountains of river ice and thickets of trees, but the river gave them a faster surface than the mounds of snow.

Then the runners found purchase on solid ground again and the horses jolted up the much more manageable incline on the Chinese side of the river.

China. They were in China. How far yet? Had Nela asked her that or had she thought it herself? Luise strained to see out the front of the wagon and noticed lights in the distance.

"Not far now, my dear. Almost there."

When the sleds finally came to a halt on the street of a

village, some of the women wept openly, while others remained as quiet as death. Luise knew no one who had experienced this night would ever forget it. Each one would be forever changed. With the help of Daniel's sisters, she climbed out of the wagon and onto firm ground. She could not stop shaking and shivering and knew everyone felt the same. Daniel appeared beside her and ushered her into the building—a tavern of sorts. Abram led Nela and Hans in behind them.

"It stinks in here," whined Nela.

"Shh, we're free. We must be grateful for anything they offer us," Abram said.

As they sat down at tables and food was placed before them, they prayed God's blessing on the unfamiliar fare. The food was hot, they were hungry and the tea was bracing.

Nela whimpered again and scooted closer to Luise. Daniel smashed his hand on the bench where the girl had been sitting and smiled wanly at Luise over her head. Lice. Luise shuddered and held her baby closer.

A wail shattered the night as people continued to file into the tavern. A man tried to comfort a woman, who in turn held a young child to her breast. They laid the child on one of the tables and fully unwrapped it, but it did not move.

"No!" Luise's voice forced its way past her teeth.

The woman's wail rose and others joined in to comfort while she held the child and rocked it back and forth.

Daniel, who had gone to find out what had happened, returned to the table. "A little girl. Eighteen months. Died of asphyxiation."

Luise could no longer contain her emotions. A keening wail forced its way through her clenched teeth. She shook and shuddered and sobbed until the pent up grief and anxiety seeped out, then noticed Nela, who watched her with her broken soul looking out of wide eyes. Luise knew she must pull herself together.

She turned her back to the crowd and nursed her blessed baby, who promptly fell sound asleep. Warmth and food and he was content.

When they had eaten what they could and had drunk cup after cup of hot tea—poison tea Hans called it—the families found places to sleep and laid out extra blankets and furs on top of the long, flat stovepipes. Luise kept turning to even out the temperature on her body.

Unable to sleep, she stood to pace, and noticed how many others also had trouble sleeping. She searched through the bundles they had carried inside and located the one she wanted. Unwrapping the case, she unlatched it, lifted out her violin and tightened the bow. The instrument had warmed and she ached to play it.

She closed her eyes and imagined her mother playing this same instrument so many years ago in Orenburg. Her touch was shaky at first, but as she let herself go, the bow became one with her hand, with her spirit, and she drew music from the violin, music that floated across the room, across kilometers and years. Voices of her fellow travelers joined the voice of the violin. Freedom had cost much, but they still had hope. They still had their souls.

ACKNOWLEDGMENTS

Thanks to those who read my manuscript for consistency and accuracy, especially to Caroline Way for asking the difficult questions; to Melody Kube (missionary in Krasnoyarsk, Siberia) for her most helpful information on the countryside and its indigenous peoples; to Liana Dick for her educated opinion on medical symptoms; to Dee Robertson for explaining (repeatedly) the difference between oars and paddles, and where the sun would be at certain times of the year (et cetera); to Wayne for setting me straight on how male characters would likely think and respond; to *His Imprint Christian Writers* for their input over the years; to the folks at Helping Hands Press who first put this book into print; to my agent, Les Stobbe; and to other family members and friends who encouraged me in this endeavor.

There are several resources that deserve mention for their invaluable information: *The Mennonite Historical Atlas* by William Schroeder and Helmuth T. Huebert, *Events and People* by Helmuth T. Huebert, and the little volume *Escape Across the Amur River* by Abram Friesen and Abram J. Loewen, originally written in German in 1946. I merely arranged the facts into fiction.

For this second edition, thanks are due to many friends and writerly acquaintances who have walked this independent publishing path before me. Special thanks to Janet Sketchley for her patient suggestions, to Valerie Comer and others in the *Christian Indie Writers* Facebook group, to *Fred Koop Design* for the catching my vision for the cover, and to my husband who endured (endures) my struggles and triumphs.

But most of all, I'd like to thank my Lord Jesus for

giving me the capacity to complete this daunting project. Without Him I am helpless, but with Him, all things are possible. May you, the reader, be blessed by this story and by the One who inspired it.

ABOUT THE AUTHOR

Photo credit: Glenda Siemens

Janice was born and raised in southern Alberta, Canada into an ethnic Mennonite farm family. She has always loved stories of family heritage and the emigration of her people from Russia. Her aim is not only to share the faith journeys of her forebears, but also to showcase God's sovereignty in the midst of that milieu. Besides historical fiction, Janice writes contemporary novels and short stories, blogs, articles and book reviews.

Janice is the winner of the 2016 Janette Oke Award.

Check out Janice's blog/website: www.janicedick.com
and her Amazon Author Page:
https://www.amazon.com/author/janicedick.

In A Foreign Land

JANICE L. DICK

If you enjoyed *Other Side of the River,* you won't want to miss the second book in the *In Search of Freedom* series. Here's the first chapter of *In a Foreign Land.*

Coming Autumn of 2016 from *Tansy & Thistle Press*

Chapter One

The boy outside could not have been more than sixteen, but he talked like he owned the world. Dubrowsky growled and reached up to close the window, but the boy's next words, lifted by a breeze, stopped him.

"Our herd of horses is the best anywhere. Once we bring in the harvest, my father and I will pick out some to sell. We've had buyers from as far away as Peking."

Horses were not only a good trading commodity, but they offered considerable status. Senior-Major Leonid Dubrowsky had possessed a few fine ones in his day.

"Who is that boy?" he asked.

"What's that, sir?"

Leonid slammed the window closed and turned to bellow at a skinny young soldier working at a table on the far side of the dim room. "Are you deaf as well as stupid? Find out who that boy is and where he lives."

"Yes sir." The soldier scrambled out the door, leaving it open to swing in the breeze.

Leonid swiveled back to the window. Perhaps this foray into Chinese territory would prove profitable for him personally, as well as being politically beneficial for the Soviet army. He had thought of Lungdiang as a dead-end placement, but if he could nab a few good horses, it might make his tenure here more bearable.

The under-officer returned. "His friends call him Danny Martens. He lives…"

The name struck Dubrowsky like an electric shock. Could this boy—this young man— belong to Daniel and Luise Martens? He stopped to calculate. The group from Shumanovka had fled across the Amur River into China in 1930. It was now 1945. It fit his age. But surely the Martens family would have left for the Americas long ago with all the other Mennonites that had gathered in Harbin.

He stared out at Danny Martens and saw a combination of his old nemesis and his little Mennonite sparrow. This could be rewarding indeed. If he had believed in God, he would have called it providential.

"Where did you say he lives?"

"About an hour from here by horse, sir. Just across the creek from the Immigrantville settlement."

"Find out everything there is to know about him and his family and bring me the information as soon as you get it."

"Yes, sir."

Leonid heaved himself to his feet. "Get on with it, you idiot. You won't learn anything by standing there."

The soldier turned and ran from the room, his "Yes, sir" thrown over his shoulder. Leonid rubbed his hands together and limped to his makeshift desk, made from an old door laid across two empty pickle barrels in the front room of what used to be Liu's General Store. He pulled a wooden crate from beneath the desk and rifled through the papers inside, then with a grunt of satisfaction, pulled out a tattered dossier.

"You won't get away from me this time, Daniel

Martens," he murmured, fingering the thin purple scar that circled his neck.

❧

Insistent knocking woke Danny from a sound sleep. Beneath his second-storey room, he heard his parents stirring, whispering urgently. Then he heard the front door open and his father's voice.

"What has roused you from sleep so early, Helmuth?"

Relieved that it was just the neighbor from the other side of the elms, but still concerned about why he would come in the pitch dark of the early morning, Danny slid from his bed to place his ear on the heating grate above the kitchen.

"They've called a meeting," said Helmuth Giesinger, sounding breathless. "In Lungdiang. They—"

"Come in, come in," Papa interrupted. "Who called a meeting?"

"The Russians. The soldiers coming down from the Soviet Union. We're supposed to go in three days."

"Why should we go to Lungdiang? Do they want my horses? I'm not delivering them, probably won't ever see money from them anyway."

"It's not about horses, Martens. They want—they demand—all men who were over twenty when they fled from Russia to show up at the meeting."

"Why on earth?" Mama's voice shrilled through the grate.

Giesinger's response was so quiet Danny almost missed it. "Why do you think?"

Danny's mind churned with questions as he lay huddled on the floor of his bedroom. What now? This wasn't Russian territory, even though they'd apparently had their eye on it for years. He'd heard Papa talk about the civil war between the Chinese Nationalists and Mao Zedong's Red Chinese army, but up here in Manchuria, or Manchukuo as the Japanese had called it since they had assumed power in 1931, it hadn't affected their lives.

So where did the Soviet Russians get their power? He knew the answer even as he formed the question: the power was there for the taking. Since the end of the war there was no formal government in Manchuria. Papa said the Imperial Japanese government had been soundly defeated and ordered back to their islands.

Chairs scraped the kitchen floor and Danny realized he had missed the rest of the conversation. He pulled on his clothes and hurried down the steep stairs into the kitchen just as his father closed the door on Mr. Giesinger. His parents turned to him in surprise.

"What are you doing up, son?" asked his father. "Too early for chores. Wait till the sun comes up."

"I want to know what's going on."

Mama laid a hand on his shoulder. "Lower your voice. I don't want Ben or the girls up yet."

Papa sighed. "I didn't even think of calling you downstairs."

"Yes, but you can tell me now. What's it about, this meeting?"

Mama ladled a cup of water for him from the pail on the counter. She looked to her husband to speak but he hesitated, instead holding out his cup to be refilled.

"How much did you hear?"

"Just that some Russians are calling a meeting in Lungdiang and you are supposed to go. Do you have to? What if you ignore them? What can they do about it?" His voice had risen again and he tried to lower it.

Papa set down his cup with enough force to spill its contents onto the tablecloth. "What can they do? They can come get us, since they know exactly where we live. They can take us to the meeting by force. Or maybe they will just shoot us here. Save themselves the trouble."

"Daniel!" Mama's face was white.

Papa stared out the window, as if it were too difficult to

meet their eyes. "I'm sorry. It's just that I know these Russians." He spoke in almost a whisper, dread coloring the words. "They have found us. The meeting is merely a formality. We have no choice but to go find out what they have in mind for us."

He stood and moved toward Mama. "We have to face the truth, Luise. How many times have I been through this, how many times tried to reason with Russian officials? They don't operate out of reason. I have to go to the meeting. However, we will pray that God will intervene on our behalf."

She moved toward him, put her hands on his shoulders and looked directly into his eyes. "Oh, Daniel."

He wrapped his arms around her and spoke as if Danny were not in the room. "We have no choice but to be strong, my dear. This is not beyond God's knowledge or ability to preserve us. Remember His promise to give us strength for every situation. Let us pray together and put ourselves in His hands. "

Danny did not hear the words of Papa's prayer over his own pounding pulse and the words whirling in his mind: "maybe they will just shoot us here."

Danny Martens watched the colt cavort around its mother, tossing its dark mane in the wild west wind that blew in from Mongolia. He felt at home with these hardy and handsome Altai horses, just as his father did.

He could hear his Papa's words in his mind: a horse can smell a coming storm, just as it can sense fear in its handler or a wolf pack lurking in the trees. He looked around him, seeing nothing but endless prairie with the odd sprinkling of trees and shrubs, but he felt unease in the very air he breathed.

He hoisted himself aboard old Caesar to better view the herd. A fine lot to be sure. It made his blood warm to watch them. He wished Rachel had come with him today instead of staying back to help her mother with the laundry. He and Rachel Giesinger agreed on many things, but they differed on many more, and discussions were always lively.

He grinned in spite of his apprehension of the future. Nothing seemed to faze or frighten Rachel. All their lives, he and Rachel had lived here on the plains of the Songhua River basin, learned the ways of the wild wind, the wide water, the rustling grasses and the winnowing wings of geese. He couldn't imagine life anywhere else, didn't even care much what happened in the rest of the world.

He urged Caesar into the midst of the mares grazing the wild rye grass. They looked content. The stallion, however, stood on a slight rise, ears pointed sharply forward, front right hoof stamping. Must be a shift in the weather.

Maybe life wouldn't change that much here in northern China. Most of the world probably didn't even think about the people who lived here on their farms, the Chinese in their longhouses, the Russian expatriates in their *izbas* in Immigrantville, the Japanese military men and their families who still remained in villages like Lungdiang and Qiqihar and Mukden. And, of course, the Mennonite Martens and Lutheran Giesinger families who lived a stone's throw from each other just across the stream from Immigrantville.

It was time to bring in the harvest, time to get to work and forget the troubles of the rest of the world.

He was so lost in thought that by the time he noticed the cloud of dust in the distance, the riders had advanced close enough for him to see they were strangers. Danny's brow furrowed. The mares whinnied and ran to stand warily around the stallion. Something in the posture of the riders bothered him, a roughness, an arrogance. Not willing to leave the horses with these strange men, Danny nudged Caesar and rode to meet them.

The riders were foreign. Russian. Danny could tell by their clothing and hats before he heard their voices.

"Nice herd of horses," said a bearded man at the front

of the group. "You selling?"

Not to the likes of you, thought Danny, judging the man and his five companions. "I'd have to consult my father," he said instead. "We make the decisions together."

The man snorted. "Of course. We will come back tomorrow and by then you will have decided? You and your father?"

A snicker passed through the group. They turned their mounts sharply and thundered away, leaving Danny and Caesar in a cloud of choking dust.

Danny pulled Caesar back into a trot as he turned into his yard. The old horse was lathered around the saddle and where the reins touched his neck.

He leaped off Caesar's back and left him quivering beside the tie rail as he ran toward the house and burst through the door. Papa rose from his chair, his tall, solid frame and confident stance reassuring. Mama stood beside him like a willow in the shade of an oak, her dark eyes questioning.

"They're after our horses."

His father looked at him blankly. "Who's after our horses?"

"The Russians."

He saw his Papa's eyes narrow and heard Mama gasp. His impatience rose at his father's slowness to catch on. "The soldiers who are coming down from Russia. Some of them are interested in our horses."

"Isn't that a good thing?" asked Danny's sister, Manya, jangling the colorful bracelets her father had brought her from Harbin after his last visit there. "We raise horses to sell, don't we?"

Danny ignored her and focused on Papa. "I don't like the look of the men."

"So quickly it happens." Papa murmured the words, then cleared his throat and asked, "Did you talk to them?"

Danny took a deep breath to calm his racing heart. "They came in a rush, running their horses even though they were already lathered, wanting to know if our horses were for sale."

Glancing out the kitchen window, Papa said, "Seems they're not the only ones running lathered horses. Caesar isn't young anymore, son."

"I know. I'm sorry."

"Did they take them? Did the Russians take any horses?"

"Of course not. I said I'd have to talk to you first, and they said they'd come back tomorrow."

Mama collapsed into the cushioned chair and grasped its arms. "I knew it," she said. Her face had gone white, her lips pinched.

"Don't worry, Mama, we'll protect the horses." Danny hated to see her so distraught. He should have waited to speak with Papa alone.

"That's not what I—" Her gaze shifted to Papa's face.

Danny's eyes snapped back and forth from one parent to the other. They were talking without words again.

"What? What are you thinking?"

They looked at him, then at each other.

"Your mother will make supper now while the rest of you go out and finish the chores."

Danny fumed inside, but resisted the urge to argue. Past experience had taught him he would gain nothing.

Little Ben clung to Papa's leg.

"Come on, Benny," Manya encouraged, taking her brother's hand. "You can help me feed the kittens warm milk straight from the cow. Your sister's coming too, see?" She pointed out the window to where Sara had climbed nimbly aboard Caesar and headed him toward the barn, her hands stroking his neck. Danny felt bad for running the old horse, but he had been in a hurry to get away from the soldiers.

As Danny left the house, he heard Mama's hoarse whisper. "The Russians?" He remembered the story of his parents' crazy escape from Russia when he was just a baby.

"I was there too," he muttered to himself. "I deserve to know what's going on." But he knew he'd have to wait until they were ready to tell him. Unless…

He herded his siblings toward the barn and told them he'd meet them there shortly, then turned back to crouch beneath the open kitchen window in the shelter of a lilac bush.

"Daniel, what are we going to do?" Danny heard the fear in Mama's voice and the strength of it surprised him. "I thought we'd left Russia far behind."

Papa's response came in short bits, as it he were pacing the length of the kitchen. "We're not far from the Amur River, Luise. On the other side is Russia. There's no one to stop them."

"But the river is the border. Do borders mean nothing?"

"Not now." Papa's voice was close; he must be standing directly at the window where Danny crouched. "Now that the war's over, everything is in chaos until the Allies reset the borders. Right now it's a free-for-all."

"Are we in danger?" Mama's voice quaked.

Papa's answer took a while to come, and when it did, Danny sensed a false confidence in his tone.

"I doubt it. They probably just want horses. Maybe that's what the meeting is about. We'll sell them some, keep them happy and otherwise ignore them."

Danny heard his mother banging around at the stove. "Of course, you're right. We're not a threat. They don't care about us anymore."

Reviewing the conversation, Danny started to sneak away to the barn, but Mama's voice stopped him with its sheer terror.

"Daniel! Do you think it could be…him?"

"No!" The reply was sharp, followed almost

immediately by softer tones. "Don't worry, Luise. He couldn't have survived."

Danny's mind whirled with questions. Who were Papa and Mama so afraid of and why? And if the person had survived whatever they referred to, what interest did he have in the Martens family after fifteen years? His father preached at the neighborhood gatherings almost every Sunday, for heaven's sake. What kind of threat was that?

Danny continued to mull it over as he trudged to the barn to help with chores. When he entered the barn, Sara was wiping the saddle and bridle with an old rag while Manya and Ben milked the cow. Danny grabbed the pitchfork but stood lost in thought. What was so important that it had his normally calm parents worried? He was old enough to know the truth and he intended to have it.

❧

That evening after supper, while Mama put the children to bed, Danny seated himself on the corner of the parlor sofa closest to Papa's easy chair and tried to look as grown up as possible.

"Papa, what news did you and Mr. Giesinger hear when you were last in Harbin?" He felt a bit awkward since he usually had little interest in politics, but it seemed to be at the heart of the matter. Papa spoke without meeting his eyes.

"Change is coming, son. I hope we can weather it."

"Of course we will, Papa. What kind of change?"

His father regarded him for a long moment and Danny sat straighter. Papa sighed and rested his forearms on his knees, eyes on the floor.

"Now that the war over, I think the Russians are just flexing their territorial muscles, but we'll have to be watchful."

"Why? What do you think they will do?"

Papa glanced up at him, eyes dark with unspoken possibilities, but his face cleared instantly as he looked past

Danny toward the kitchen.

Danny turned to see Mama in the doorway.

"Come sit, my dear. We will soon be busy with harvest and have little enough time to relax."

Mama sat on the sofa next to Danny. Her smile seemed forced. Her eyes were wide as she looked at her husband, but she spoke of daily things as if nothing bothered her.

And then Danny knew that Papa was not only protecting the children, he was also protecting Mama from the whole truth. And Mama protected her children by pretending there was no threat. What could be so bad that his parents would hide these things from him and from each other? Maybe Mr. Giesinger had spoken more freely with his family. If so, Rachel would tell him. He'd ask her first thing tomorrow morning.

"Danny."

Rachel noted how he stood straighter and smiled when she said his name, his dark eyes on her face, on her hair as it blew freely in the breeze.

"How'd you sneak away from your mother? Doesn't she have endless work for you this time of year?"

She felt her smile fade. "She's all in a tizzy. I needed to get away for a bit." She turned to look out across the fields at the brilliant sunset. "What do you think it's all about?"

He shrugged. "Yesterday when I was out with the herd, a group of Russians came to ask about the horses."

"Yes, Carl told me. He was outside climbing trees instead of doing what Father had asked him to do, and he saw the men ride by. Scruffy bunch, according to him."

Danny broke a dead branch off one of the poplar trees and snapped it into smaller lengths, dropping them as they broke. "They were arrogant and demanding. I wouldn't trust them as far as I could see them."

"Do you think they'd steal horses?" Rachel watched him break off another branch.

"Wouldn't put it past them."

She laid a hand on Danny's sleeve. "Do you think we need to be afraid?"

At that moment Danny's face cleared and she knew he would try to ease her concern.

"No, I don't expect they are really dangerous. Just showing their teeth a bit, you know?"

"Don't play these games with me, Danny Martens." She moved to stand in front of him and met his eyes directly. "Is it the horses they want or is it us?"

"Why would they want us?"

"Danny, I've heard some things Father has said to Mother. He tries to protect her from the truth like you're trying to do for me now, but he's worried."

Danny grimaced and ran a hand through his shaggy hair. "From what I can figure, the Russians are not good at forgiving and forgetting."

"What does that mean?"

"It means our parents don't trust the Russians one bit, not even after fifteen years. But I'm sure there's something they're not telling us. They're awful worried." He looked about to say more, but stopped himself.

"I think you're right. Mother and I were at the market in Lungdiang last week and we heard some of our Russian neighbors from Immigrantville talking. They think it's only a matter of time until more Russian forces show up around here. Some of the army divisions that passed through Harbin are headed to the main military headquarters in Mukden.

"Some of them are also moving through here. Mother acted as if she hadn't heard the gossip, but as soon as we got home, she and Father had a long talk about it. Both sounded agitated, but they wouldn't tell us anything."

Danny frowned. "But why would the Soviets care that we're here? Surely they don't remember Papa or your father, or even the Russians settled in Immigrantville."

She snorted. "Or the two-hundred thousand White Russians settled in Harbin, many of whom are being sent back to Russia? Or the Russian settlement of Immigrantville that we can see from here, or the mostly-Russian city of Mukden—or Shenyang, or whatever they call it now? You're not the only one who eavesdropped, Danny." She tucked a strand of hair behind her ear and looked out at the fields again. "We'd best be listening if we want to find out anything. And praying that we'll be protected."

They walked back to the dirt path that connected their homes. "See you later," said Danny. "Let me know if you learn anything."

"Yes, you too."

She walked back to her yard through the dusky autumn evening, worry pulling at her mind like the wind pulled at her skirts and her hair.

CPSIA information can be obtained
at www.ICGtesting.com
Printed in the USA
LVOW13s1714270218
568057LV00013B/698/P

9 780995 031968